UNEA̶̶̶̶̶̶̶̶̶̶̶̶̶̶̶̶̶ PORTENTS

. . . . have inspired and terrified man since the dawn of history. Some supernatural phenomena have been explained away by science, others exposed as fakery or hysteria. What remains, however, is staggering evidence that an unseen world exists beyond the reach of nature as we know it.

In this extraordinary book, you'll find out all there is to know about the origins of the vampire myth, the secret rituals of the Black Mass, and the controversial sightings of legendary monsters and ghosts. From fairies, incantations and "white" magicians, to satanism, zombie and other manifestations of the living dead, this fascinating guide examines evidence of paranormal phenomena in search of the mysterious powers within man, as well as those outside him. . . .

THE
SUPERNATURAL

The
Supernatural

DOUGLAS HILL
and
PAT WILLIAMS

A SIGNET BOOK

NEW AMERICAN LIBRARY

NEW YORK
PUBLISHED IN CANADA BY
PENGUIN BOOKS CANADA LIMITED, MARKHAM, ONTARIO

TEXT CREDITS

Acknowledgment is made for permission to reprint
excerpts from the following works: Plenary
Session Paper at the 6th International Congress of
Psychotherapy—Practice and Theory: The
Present Situation by Dr. R. D. Laing; *Collected Ghost
Stories* by M. R. James, published by Edward
Arnold (Publishers) Ltd.; Leaflets published by Psychic
Press Ltd., 23 Great Queen Street, London, W.C.2;
Psychical Research Today by D. J. West, published by
Gerald Duckworth & Co. Ltd.; *The Dictionary of
Modern Spiritualism* by Norman Blunsdon, published by
Arco Publications; *Practical Mediumship* by
Muriel Hillier; *Treatise on Parapsychology* by René
Sudre, published by George Allen & Unwin Ltd.:
published in the U.S.A. as *Para-Psychology* by The
Citadel Press: in France by Editions Payot;
Adventures of the Mind by Arturo Castiglioni,
published by Sampson Low, Marston & Co., Ltd.;
Le Dictionnaire Pratique des Sciences Occultes
by Marianne Verneuil, collection La Lanterne d'Hermes;

**(The following page constitutes an extension
of this copyright page.)**

The Dawn of Magic by Jacques Bergier and Louis
Pauwels, published by Anthony Gibbs & Phillips Ltd.;
Ritual Magic by E. M. Butler, published by
Cambridge University Press; *Symbols of Transformation*
by Carl G. Jung, published by Routledge &
Kegan Paul Ltd.: reprinted in the U.S.A. by permission
of the Bollingen Foundation; *A Survey of the
Occult* by Julian Franklyn, published by Arthur Barker
Ltd.; *The Divine Horsemen* by Maya Deren,
published by Thames & Hudson, London; *Voodoo in
Haiti* by Alfred Métraux, first published in
Great Britain by André Deutsch Ltd. © 1959 Alfred
Métraux: © in France Editions Gallimard:
published in U.S.A. by Oxford University Press,
New York; *Dracula* by Bram Stoker, published
by Rider & Co.; *Thirty Years of Psychical Research* by
Charles Richet, published by William Collins,
Sons & Co. Ltd.

SIGNET, SIGNET CLASSIC, MENTOR, ONYX, PLUME, MERIDIAN
and NAL BOOKS are published *in the United States* by NAL PENGUIN INC.,
1633 Broadway, New York, New York 10019,
in Canada by Penguin Books Canada Limited,
2801 John Street, Markham, Ontario L3R 1B4

First Signet Printing, September, 1967

11 12 13 14 15 16 17 18 19

PRINTED IN THE UNITED STATES OF AMERICA

True science will not deny the existence of things because they cannot be weighed and measured. It will rather lead us to believe that the wonders and subtleties of possible existence surpass all that our mental powers allow us clearly to perceive . . . We must ignore no existence whatever; we may variously interpret or explain its meaning and origin, but, if a phenomenon does exist, it demands some kind of explanation.

The Principles of Science
William Stanley Jevons (1835-82)

CONTENTS

1 APPROACHING THE SUPERNATURAL

In 1956 *Life* magazine introduced some traditional but dressed-up American ghost stories with the caption: "The old beliefs die hard, even in this skeptical age." No one can doubt the age is skeptical (or anyway sees itself as being skeptical), in the sense that rational man in the first half of this century has done his best to believe that the boundaries of the world's reality are set by the limits of his own knowledge. But it can be doubted whether the old beliefs are really on their deathbed. The truth may be that they are very much alive. Perhaps Paul Tabori, a Hungarian-born author and expert on supernatural matters, gave a more accurate general picture when, in *The New York Times* in 1963, he remarked, "how little progress materialism has made against the vast body of beliefs, fears, suppositions, mis-information, and half-conscious practices we usually and loosely label superstition." Many of those beliefs, fears, and so on are often given another but equally loose label—that of our title: the supernatural.

This book is an account of some modern excursions into the realm of the supernatural—and also of some of their roots and antecedents in history and prehistory. But the account must begin by making it clear, as far as possible, what will be covered by the term "supernatural" in these pages. As everyone knows, the word literally means that which lies outside the reality of nature as understood by man in terms of his ordinary experience of life on this earth. (Hence "unearthly" is a frequent synonym—as is, sometimes, "occult," meaning secret or hidden.) In everyday speech, "supernatural" refers to anything that stretches or breaks or otherwise violates what we commonly think of as the laws of nature—the normal, accepted, natural processes and phenomena of day-to-day living. By this definition our title would be the second most inclusive that could be imagined, after "nature." (It is interesting that in English the word "supernatural" must do service as both adjective and noun; there is "nature" but no "supernature." Perhaps this is a real, and not merely a linguistic, truth. After all, no one can claim that our knowledge of the laws of nature is complete.)

To get away from the looseness of colloquial meanings: by the supernatural we mean, first, those instincts and perceptions about the universe that make no sense in rational terms but that, over many centuries and in many countries, have never been lost or eradicated. We mean those unseen powers and influences whose existence has been acknowledged by most people at most times—not only by those who, claiming special knowledge, have been said to be able to make direct contact with the powers, but also by those who, without personal contact, continue to believe with unshakable tenacity. And we mean the stories and lore about such matters that can be found throughout the world since history began to be recorded, and the accounts of spontaneous manifestations of such powers and forces.

That is a general description of the territory in which we shall be moving for most of this book. But in the face of an inquiry of such enormous breadth and inclusiveness some narrowing of focus is necessary. And we shall be more intelligible if we begin the narrowing process with a series of negatives—with what the supernatural, as this book sees it, does *not* include.

First, we shall leave aside mythology. Though the gods and demi-gods of the ancient world certainly do not belong in the natural order as we know it (and thus are truly supernatural), there will be no sections wholly and directly devoted to their biographies. At the same time, it will become clear that all supernatural belief derives from a view of the world that is basically religious—and these basic religious beliefs will appear and flavor our theme fairly often. For instance, there will be occasional glimpses of the old gods when we consider the Egyptian origins of ceremonial magic; or the reverence of unseen divine powers that underlies the practice of voodoo in Haiti; or the ancient fertility-cult forebears of the white-witch covens that meet today in modern suburban living rooms.

Secondly, the spiritual teachings of the great organized religions—Christianity, Judaism, Buddhism, Islam, and so on—will be largely bypassed. At the same time, again, there will be some unavoidable trespassing into Christianity when we come to look at witchcraft as a heresy, or at the Devil worshiped by diabolists. But no direct, specific examination will be made of the belief in the supernatural that is implicit in religious faith and doctrine.

Probably no one will be surprised at these exclusions, if for no other reason than that several more volumes would be required if these aspects of the supernatural were to be done even an approximate justice. By the same token, we must make a third exclusion, perhaps a more surprising one: that of extrasensory perception (telepathy and clairvoyance). Today many respectable scientists in many countries have accepted that some form of ESP *does* exist—an acceptance largely due to 25 years of extensive research by scientists like J. B. Rhine and S. G. Soal. And so, in order to remain strictly faithful to our definition of the supernatural, ESP can legitimately have only a tangential place in this book.

So much for negatives. Now we can spell out more specifically the range of our selective account of the supernatural. The subject can be divided into two aspects: first, the powers; second, the beings.

The supernatural powers are those that people have believed, throughout history, that they possessed in themselves or could be given or could learn (as initiates into a kind of religio-mystic awareness)—powers by which they could acquire hidden knowledge and could achieve some non-physical control over physical nature. They are usually all lumped together under the general term "magic" (or sometimes, confusingly, "witchcraft"). There are other terms, more or less synonymous: sorcery, wizardry, and so on.

The supernatural beings are those that, again throughout history, people have believed to inhabit darkness and the night, and that generally have inspired both fear and fascination in their believers. These are the ghosts, spirits, demons, and devils; the blood-sucking vampires, werewolves, and other evil and terrifying inhuman monsters.

Add to these the human beings—the magicians and the

witches, the mediums and the ghost hunters, the devil worshipers and the cultists—and the scope of this book has been
defined.

Perhaps our territory could be defined another way. If you
were to see on a library shelf a book entitled *Tales of the
Supernatural*, you would not be surprised if it turned out to
be a collection of ghost stories. Nor would your sense of
propriety be disturbed if some of the tales concerned witches,
or vampires, or black magic, or any of the other beings and
powers mentioned above. "Horror fiction," the genre to
which such stories belong, usually and traditionally restricts
itself to the very limits that we have set ourselves here. And
defining the scope of our investigation in terms of this branch
of fiction has its advantages: it places our definition on a
more familiar level. For a great many people—even in this
skeptical age—have some familiarity with supernatural fiction.

Of course, the supernatural has always crept into literature—classical plays and chronicles, medieval and Renaissance poetry and drama. (The works of Shakespeare, as we
all know, are rife with ghosts and witches.) But it really
came into its own at the height of the 19th-century Romantic
movement, when a craze developed for the so-called
Gothic tale of terror. The craze reached a peak in Britain,
after the mode had been established by such German writers
as Schiller, Wieland, and even Goethe. One of the first British
writers to venture into the supernatural was Horace Walpole,
whose *Castle of Otranto* appeared in 1764. Equally famous
as a pioneer of horror fiction was Matthew Gregory Lewis,
who produced *The Monk* in 1796. The early years of the
19th century brought an increasing flood of haunted castles
and supernatural fears—including *Frankenstein* (1818),
Mary Shelley's imaginative tour de force, which was
apparently sparked off by a dream.

Throughout the century, to shorten the story, horror fiction
dominated the market: there were Edgar Allan Poe, Wash-
ington Irving, and Nathaniel Hawthorne in America; there
was Pushkin in Russia and Hoffmann in Germany; in Paris
at one time practically every theatre was running a play
about vampires following the huge success of Charles No-
dier's *Le Vampire* (1820); and in Britain all amateur authors
(including a great many clergymen) and many professionals
(including Bram Stoker, the Irish author of *Dracula*, dis-

cussed in Chapter 8) were ringing the changes on the horrors.

After the turn of the century the peak of the craze for horror fiction leveled off, though there remained a demand for it among the reading public. New names were cropping up—names that are today acknowledged as the modern (rather than Gothic) masters of horror. America's H. P. Lovecraft dominated the genre with the incredible mythology he created (monsters of ancient evil released on this world by dabblers in forbidden arts) and with the disciples and imitators he gathered. In Britain, M. R. James produced his handful of perfectly constructed ghost stories, which became classics almost overnight, while that strange individual Arthur Machen gained fame more slowly with his unique visions of the macabre. (In the end his popular fame is due to an accident: he wrote a story during World War I about angelic hosts assisting the British forces; the people and the soldiers, hungry for a miracle, seized upon the idea and insisted that it had really happened—that the soldiers had seen the "Angels of Mons" with their own eyes.)

Often the great literary men would make excursions into horror fiction and the supernatural—among them Dickens, Kipling, Walter de la Mare, Henry James, and D. H. Lawrence. Perhaps it is partly due to their presence in the field that the supernatural story has retained its relatively prominent place on our bookshelves. But another reason is that the modern horror story (with certain modifications that usually offend traditionalist lovers of Gothic) forms an important branch of "fantasy and science fiction"—which, in the realm of popular fiction, now ranks second only to the detective story. Science fantasy today owes much to the imagination of H. G. Wells—but it is not all interplanetary strife, time traveling, and similar technological marvels. Much of it owes a debt to Poe as well. For instance, one of the most acclaimed masters of this sub-genre is the American writer Ray Bradbury, whose unique poetic style embraces spaceships and the future on the one hand (*The Martian Chronicles*) and witches, vampires, and magic on the other (*October Country*). Similarly, August Derleth (also American) is at once an indefatigable anthologizer of the spaceship type of science fiction and a leading disciple of H. P. Lovecraft.

And the trappings and creatures of the weird tales have found another niche in the modern world—and one in which they are just as popular as they ever were in the pages of books. They have been translated into visual terms—in "horror films." This macabre branch of the film industry has roots going back to the silent era, to those German visions of man-made monsters in *Der Golem* (1920) and *Homunculus* (1915-16). Then Hollywood spread visual horrors around the world in the 1930s with the first great versions of *Frankenstein, Dracula, Dr. Jekyll and Mr. Hyde,* and others. These had tremendous successes, which naturally produced a host of sequels throughout the 1940s. In the 1950s the American film makers shifted most of their monsters out of crumbling Transylvanian castles and into spaceships *(It Came from Outer Space)* or offered terrifying mutations (the giant ants of *Them*) or ancient monsters sprung on civilization *(The Creature from the Black Lagoon)*. Hollywood's old-style horrors were given a second brief, if uninspired, lease of life with hybrid attempts like *I Was a Teenage Werewolf,* as well as some intentionally comic treatments involving Abbott and Costello and other comedians.

But the 1960s have seen a new and startling revitalization of the originals. "A whole new generation," as *Look* magazine put it in September 1964, was able to see "the great old movie monsters." The horrors of the 1930s were re-released by Hollywood, or else remade—as in Britain, where film makers have gone back to the books themselves and begun afresh. Hollywood also searched the 19th-century writers, and adapted many a Poe tale for technicolor treatment. Vampire films seem especially popular (possibly because of the technicolor): they have drawn record audiences in France (as with Roger Vadim's *Blood and Roses*) and Italy, and even in Mexico and Argentina. Also in the 1960s television has jumped onto the supernatural bandwagon (and the science fiction one, for that matter): a top American success in 1964 was a series entitled *Bewitched* that blended situation comedy with magic.

Along with the supernatural's translation into films came an equally popular development, especially in the U.S.A. and Britain: the controversial "horror comics." Ostensibly for children, these cartoon books could hardly be less comic—and, many parents and educationalists have thought, hardly less suitable for the young audience they were aimed at. Publishers of horror comics vie with one another for first place in the repulsiveness of their drawings; relatively commonplace horrors like werewolves and ghosts take a back seat to twisted and fearsome "things from the grave" and so on.

As well as comic books, horror toys of various kinds (dolls, masks, games, costumes) provide another means for capitalizing on the new craze. *Look* estimates that American children spent $20,000,000 on such playthings in 1964. And—as a final indication of the new demand for horrification—in the late 1950s a magazine appeared in America entitled *Famous Monsters of Filmland.* Intended as a "one-time-only" issue, it proved so popular (especially among pre-teenage children) that it was continued; and by 1964 it was appearing bimonthly with a total readership estimated at a million.

Even so, can we go on to claim that the modern popularity of horror fiction implies any slackening in the grip of rationalism on this skeptical age? Perhaps not—from one point of view—for after all horror fiction is still fiction, and people do not think themselves less civilized and reasonable because they like to read untrue stories about non-existent people. Clearly a lover of ghost stories need not be a believer in ghosts; all he does, when picking up his favorite reading material, is to make no more than the same "willing suspension of disbelief" that we all have to make when faced with any kind of fiction, whether it is novel, short story, or drama.

But is that all there is to it? Surely our disbelief must be suspended a good deal higher in the case of supernatural fiction than with those other stories in which the known laws of nature remain untransgressed (as they usually do even with the most astounding feats of fictional detectives, cowboys, or secret agents). In the latter sort of writing, the events may be unlikely—but they are only extensions, exaggerations, of humanly plausible happenings. In supernatural fiction the events are (to the rational mind) totally impossible. Yet we read it.

Obviously there must be many tangled reasons why people set aside their 20th-century skepticism in this way. But possibly, among those reasons, we could postulate the existence of something in us (though we may be unaware of it) that has nothing to do with the straightforward appeal of works of fiction—something that allows us or helps us to accept the apparently impossible premises on which stories of the supernatural are built. To test this working hypothesis we can identify this "something" as a kind of *half-belief* (usually underground, unacknowledged) in the powers and beings of the supernatural. Then, if this idea holds water, such a half-belief should be found operating elsewhere, outside our reading habits. And it can be: in the popular "superstitions" from which this age is by no means free.

The British student of folklore Christina Hole describes the half-belief when she notes that while ". . . most people would hotly deny that they believe in magic, many frequently resort to it in luck-bringing rites, precautionary words or actions against misfortune." Most of us may know a person (or may *be* a person) who, after asserting that a certain rather unpleasant occurrence has never happened, will then "knock on wood" ("touch wood" in Britain)—probably a relic of the ancient belief that woods such as elder and oak have magical, protective powers.

The modern knocker-on-wood may do so with a mocking laugh, or some other outward disclaimer, in case his associates (or employer or wife) suspect his maturity and sanity. Nevertheless, he performs the ritual. He may also carry a rabbit's foot, or similar "lucky charm," though he may deny that he believes that it contains any magical power to bring him good luck. But he makes sure, when he goes out, that he has it with him. He is a half-believer; he is trying to hedge his bets.

Incidentally, some of the superstitious magical practices we still indulge in are often not recognized as such. We know it is "foolish" to believe that a broken mirror will bring bad luck (one's mirror image supposedly contains one's soul, and breaking the mirror prevents the soul's return to the body). We may not know that the enjoyable modern ceremony of throwing rice (or its up-to-date substitute, confetti) over a newly married couple is in fact an ancient fertility ritual—the scattering of products of a plentiful nature being a symbolic and magical act intended to make the marriage equally fertile and productive.

So the half-beliefs continue. Christina Hole assures us: "Living superstitions are much more numerous today than is sometimes supposed, nor are they found only among the foolish or uneducated." Recently a number of American college students were questioned on this subject: 40 per cent of the men and 66 per cent of the women admitted to superstitious beliefs or practices—and of the others of both sexes, 61 per cent admitted to having previously held such beliefs. And it is conceivable that these figures may understate the case for superstition, for people (especially men, who are theoretically anyway supposed to be the logical, practical sex) may deny that they are superstitious while in fact secretly retaining

some of the beliefs. As the British psychologist Peter Mc-
Kellar says, in his discussion of half-beliefs, "many who
would intellectually reject a superstition nevertheless allow it
to influence their thinking and actions." In a series of inter-
views undertaken by some British students of psychology in
1960, several people denied that they were superstitious but
admitted under further questioning that they did touch wood
and perform other rituals—but only "for fun." So to avoid
asking the questions that put people's defenses up, the students and their professor, Kenneth Garwood, tried an experiment.

They leaned a ladder against a wall so that pedestrians had
either to walk under it or to step into a narrow and traffic-
heavy street. (Walking under a ladder is thought to be unlucky because ladders were seen as bridges for spirits between
this world and the next—and anyone walking under one
might thus meet a spirit and perhaps impede its progress.) In
the first part of the experiment a window cleaner was on the
ladder. In only two minutes the students counted 6 people
who went under the ladder and 29 people who stepped off
the sidewalk, risking the traffic, to avoid it. But perhaps they
did so fearing that the man on the ladder might drop something on them? Another ladder was set up on a similar street
elsewhere and left empty: 14 people passed under it, 37 people stepped into the road. (Of these, incidentally, 9 were
women and 28 were men—and there were 3 clergymen.)

Now an isolated little experiment like this hardly provides
satisfactory scientific proof of superstition's strength. But it is
certainly suggestive. For further evidence, it would be easy
for anyone to arrange a few small-scale trials. Set up a ladder
and count people for yourself. Or buy a black cat and watch
guests' reactions (in Britain black cats are thought to be
lucky; in America, unlucky). Or spill salt at a dinner party.
Or check, the next time you are in a hotel or a hospital, to
see if there is a Room 13 (in many such institutions the room
in question is discreetly numbered 12a—or else is just miss-
ing). And so on. You may be surprised at how much half-
belief in magic there is among the people around you. Alternatively, you may not—for you may half-believe it yourself.

In the chapters to follow, discussions of wholehearted belief in the supernatural will add to the impression that these
brief looks at horror fiction and superstition were intended to
create: that the supernatural is doing very well for itself in

the 20th century—as it always has done. So we naturally ask: why? And, equally naturally, we turn to psychology for a few answers—to find, of course, that some of the most widely accepted and frequently cited of these answers are those offered by Freud.

It is clear from Freud's writings on the "occult" (as he calls it) that his own scientific and materialistic orientation produced in him a strong resistance to the subject. In a thesis published in 1920 entitled "Psychology of Occult Phenomena," he admits that "my personal attitude toward such material remains one of reluctance and ambivalence," and suggests that this attitude is made up partly of his scientific predilections and partly because of the harm such material might cause to the new science of psychoanalysis. For one thing, for many people the idea of the unconscious still smacked of mysticism and supernaturalism—so Freud was somewhat unwilling to confirm the prejudices of his opponents by writing about the occult. Still, he sought to maintain in himself the qualities of objectivity and impartiality; so he gathered his courage and plunged into a consideration of the occult—through ESP. (In recent years, since ESP has come to be considered more respectable and less supernatural, it has become quite fashionable to explain apparently supernatural occurrences in terms of telepathy and clairvoyance. Here, too, Freud paved the way that others followed.)

His consideration was limited to a few cases of patients under analysis who had been affected by some aspect of the supernatural—and to a few cases of apparently prophetic dreams. We can omit the latter, for no belief is essential on the part of the dreamer, and we are trying to find out what Freud said about the reasons for belief in the supernatural. As for the patients: briefly, all had visited fortune tellers and had received messages that had impressed them. The messages impressed Freud too, not because they had come true (in two cases they had not) but because their nature showed that the fortune tellers had a more intimate knowledge of these particular clients' lives than seemed possible. For example, a married woman of 27, who desperately wanted children but whose husband was sterile, visited a palmist. Though she did not mention her desire, or even that she was married, the palmist reassured her and told her that she would have two children within a few years. As it turned out, she did not; but the question Freud was asking was how the palmist knew what to say.

He suggests the possibility that the woman's powerful wish was telepathically communicated to the palmist. And that the prophecy could have been simply a transference of *wish fulfillment*. Similarly, a young man who felt rivalry with his brother-in-law gave the latter's birth date to an astrologer—and no other information. The astrologer cast a horoscope and predicted the subject's death. Further analysis of the young man revealed, as Freud remarks dryly, "that the content of the prophecy was congruent with a wish fulfillment."

It is possible, then, Freud suggests, that thought transference occurs most readily in cases where there are "strong emotionally colored recollections"; and elsewhere he tells us that at the back of apparently telepathic occurrences are "emotions belonging to the sphere of the Oedipus complex." Now we are down to the root of it. Wish fulfillment, the Oedipus and other "Freudian" complexes—not only are they spurs to telepathic communications, they also (in every case described by Freud in his papers on the occult) impel people, if unconsciously, to seek out fortune tellers and to turn to the supernatural. But in these papers Freud is hinting, thinking aloud, and not attempting to draw conclusions. He goes no further than to make the suggestion, in "Psychoanalysis and Telepathy" (1921), that belief in the occult is "an attempt at compensation."

But he does go further in his paper on "The Uncanny" (1919). He analyzes stories by Hoffmann involving animated humanoid dolls (automatons or robots), human monsters who rob people of their eyes, and the concept of the "double" (Doppelgänger). Also, from normal life, he refers to the sense of *déjà vu* (and his own experiences of it), to odd coincidences, and to the widespread belief in and fear of the "evil eye." All these call up in us the disturbance and fear that accompany experiences of the uncanny. And he asserts that the strength of these feelings is due to the fact that uncanny fictional or real occurrences are closely connected with the "repressed infantile complexes." The eye-stealing monster bears a relation to the "castration complex" (Oedipus put out his eyes as a symbolic castration). The double, a harbinger of death in folklore, is also related to castration, which is often represented in dreams by a doubling of the genital symbol—thus the doubling of the whole man implies death. He adds that the uncanny at its most potent (in fears of ghosts, demons, monsters, and so on, and especially in fiction) usually involves the elements of "silence, solitude, and darkness," which are "the most frequent accompaniment of the expression of fear in infancy." As for our feelings toward uncanny happenings in real life, like strange coincidences, Freud points to the close parallels and relationships between childish fears and primitive fears—and states, as his broadest conclusion, that repressed or vestigial elements of these fears remaining in our unconscious minds can be produced to explain (to use the terms employed before in this chapter) the popularity of horror fiction and the extent of half-belief in the supernatural among 20th-century men. In Freud's own words:

"It would seem as though each one of us has been through a phase of individual development corresponding to that animistic stage in primitive men, that none of us has traversed it without preserving certain traces of it which can be reactivated, and that everything which now strikes us as 'uncanny' fulfills the condition of stirring those vestiges of animistic mental activity within us and bringing them to expression."

("Animism" in primitive man, to put it simply, is the belief that the whole of nature is populated by spirits. This and other supernatural beliefs of primitive man will be considered in their own terms in Chapter 2.)

Freud's ideas go a long way toward answering the question "why do people believe?" But a few other possible answers are worth considering. For one thing, if the repressed infantile complexes centered around sex are at the root of some of our belief and fear, then perhaps certain other childhood remnants, not so much repressed as simply half-forgotten, might also play a part. For childhood is an age of magic; children in general are notorious accepters of the need for and efficacy of rituals, amulets, and incantations. Hundreds of such magic spells, existing as an amazingly universal, living, oral tradition going back for centuries, are listed and discussed in *The Lore and Language of Schoolchildren* by the British experts on folklore Iona and Peter Opie. As these authors put it, "it is in the nature of children to be attracted to the mysterious"; that is, to engage in magical practices, to believe that there may be such things as ghosts and witches (not to mention Santa Claus), and so on. And it is quite possible that the adult does not slough off all this attraction to the mysterious when he puts childish things behind him.

But this is a tangential addition to Freud's answers, not a contradiction. A psychologist may well say that behind the child's fear of ghosts and witches are, in fact, the infantile complexes. And he might add that behind the child's belief in magical power are indeed those vestigial unconscious remnants of primitive beliefs that Freud mentions. The relationship then would be: unconscious complexes (causing animistic fears) *plus* unconscious primitive relics (causing magical beliefs) *lead to* the child's acceptance and belief which *lead to* the adult's half-belief. Concerning the primitives, the Opies echo Freud in their remark that "the children here under observation are only at the stage of mental development sometimes ascribed to a savage tribe." And Christina Hole makes the same point: "Present-day superstitions are fragmentary remains of forgotten faiths, rituals, and systems of thought, left behind when these faded from human minds."

So, it seems, individual children pass through a "primitive" stage that inevitably produces in them superstitious beliefs analogous to those held by adult primitives, and that the archaic primitive past of the entire race has left fragments and remnants of itself buried in the unconscious of each of us, child and adult—fragments that can be activated in various ways to produce belief or half-belief. Many anthropologists and psychologists who might not be willing to accept the "infantile complexes" side of Freud's theory would agree with this line of reasoning. C. G. Jung, however, though apparently agreeing with the statement broadly, strongly objected to the idea of the vestigial fragmentary nature of our primitive leftovers. To Jung, these elements are still alive and functioning in our unconscious minds—functioning with a far-reaching effect.

Jung saw the unconscious as composed of several "levels": the barely subliminal level of unconscious memories, ideas, and so on, temporarily forgotten or ignored, which could as easily become conscious; the level of the personal complexes and repressed wishes, fears, and so on; and finally the *collective* level, the deepest and the most fully unconscious level of the instincts. On this collective level, common to the entire race throughout history, exist the deep instinctual tendencies that produced in primeval man (probably through dreams, among other means) his concrete belief in the supernatural. And these same unconscious collective tendencies, which Jung called the archetypes, exist in us today—no matter how much our civilized rationalism tries to repress them. Thus they produce in us today objective representations and beliefs similar to ancient man's. We are partly irrational beings, Jung is saying, and these unconscious tendencies cause us to respond to irrationalism—even if the veneer of civilized skepticism sometimes reduces that response to a weak half-belief. (Because we cannot as rational beings accept our own irrationalism, Jung always stressed, we therefore cannot control it. And because we cannot control it and live with it, it has got completely out of hand—and so to Jung, modern man remains an unbalanced neurotic, constantly in conflict with himself, going in search of a soul.)

Basically, then, Freud and Jung (along with a great many modern psychologists, sociologists, and anthropologists) would agree that there remain in men's minds certain elements that tend to produce, even in this skeptical age, supernatural beliefs and practices akin to those of primitive man. And that seems to be an acceptable answer to our initial question.

Freud's achievement—considering his work in its broadest terms—was his success in reminding men of something that for centuries they had allowed themselves to ignore: the fact that man is unconscious of a large part of his mind. Jung's achievement (again broadly) was to demonstrate that this "unconscious" was not separate—exclusive to and unique in each individual—but was collective as well: that beneath the personal area lay a level shared by all humanity; and that beneath *that* level, perhaps endlessly, lie other levels of consciousness or, in our terms, unconsciousness. These fundamental discoveries form the basis of all the more recent investigations of supernatural belief by "depth" psychology.

There is another basic idea at the root of many of these modern investigations—an idea offered by the American psychologist Erich Fromm, whose work and writings have gained a wide influence since the 1940s. Fromm stressed that it is a property of the human mind not to remain passive in the face of contradictions, anomalies, and incompatibilities in life, but to act on and react to them. It follows from this that religions, metaphysical systems, and all-inclusive ideologies like communism are attempts to resolve fundamental contradictions in human experience—to put things into a harmonious and comprehensive frame. Fromm thus argues that, while a religion is an outwardly acceptable form for such harmonizing impulses, a neurosis can be seen as an inner, disconnected, private attempt at forming a personal religion—a "non-socially patterned one designed by the individual to explain his relationship to life."

Much of current psychology is interested in pursuing the implications of this view—especially that growing branch of psychology known as "existential" psychology, which concerns itself with the person's basic *existence* rather than his apparent place in the outer world. In clinical terms, for instance, the neurotic is less often being asked to adjust to the limited framework of social living; more and more he is being encouraged to explore his "personal religion" and see whether he has got it straight—that is, to discover whether the view of life that he has formulated has any meaning and any value in terms of his own experience of reality.

In Britain in 1964 an interesting experiment was begun in a state-aided mental hospital: a small group of schizophrenics, rather than being urged to inhibit or repress their neuroses, are now being encouraged to live wholly in their inner worlds, to discover whether they "work" for them—and, if they do not, perhaps then to choose to direct themselves back toward sanity. In this connection the work and writings of the British psychiatrist R. D. Laing more or less sound the note of today's psychiatric avant-garde. Laing writes:

"We need not be unaware of the inner world. We do not realize its existence most of the time. But many people enter it—unfortunately without guides, confusing outer with inner realities, and inner with outer—and generally lose their capacity to function competently in ordinary relations. This need not be so. The process of entering into *the other* world from this world, and returning to *this* world from the other world, is as 'natural' as death and childbirth or being born. But in our present world, that is both so terrified and so unconscious of the other world, it is not surprising that, when 'reality,' the fabric of this world, bursts, and a person enters the other world, he is completely lost and terrified, and meets only incomprehensions in others."

It may be true, though, that "outer" advances in human knowledge manage to bring about some progress in our knowledge of the "inner." In terms of the body, as an analogy, the discovery of the principles of electricity was turned inward, applied to the brain and nerves, and man was seen as a being with a complex electrical system fundamental to his functioning. So the computer systems and communications theory ("cybernetics") of today reflect back into our knowledge of the human brain. And we can find an example (rather than an analogy) of this mutual outer-inner progress in the work of physicists exploring the basic constituents of matter and making discoveries (in the realm of subatomic particles) that defy our normal understanding of the world, in particular our familiar concepts of time and space. The modern French authors Louis Pauwels and Jacques Bergier (the latter is a physicist), writing in *The Dawn of Magic* about new breakthroughs in physics, state that elements of modern quantum theory have "overtones which seem to go beyond physics to rejoin the profounder regions of the human mind." Jung saw this as well and, with the help of the Nobel-prize-winning physicist Wolfgang Pauli, showed many ways in which modern physics and modern psychology might shed light on each other—and on these deeper levels of the mind. And, following his example, later psychologists have addressed themselves to the exploration of those profound regions.

With this kind of exploration going on, with the modern breaking-down of the old frameworks in both the sciences and the arts—with, in short, this whole new mood growing increasingly important in modern thought—we can see a clear reason for the enlarging interest in the supernatural. For there, recorded, are stories of other excursions into "unconscious" territory, into "inner space," at other times. They are, many of them, unselfconscious travelers' tales of other worlds and other forces, written down by people who did not inhibit their responses to make them fit outer knowledge. In a sense, then, although believers in the supernatural "knew" less than rational and scientific man, their freer responses gave them a contact with an inner reality, even a mastery over it, that might well be every bit as valuable as that external knowledge. It may well be possible for modern man to learn from them—by understanding the *processes* of their belief and perceiving the valuable elements and insights contained in them.

But such developments lie in the future—and also lie outside the general scope and aim of this book. Here we offer, more simply, an account of the major aspects of the vast subject of the supernatural—in terms of what has been believed and what still is believed and (wherever possible) why. It is offered as a general introduction (perhaps to whet readers' appetites) to one of man's most universal interests—or preoccupations, or obsessions—from his primitive, prehistoric days to this not-so-skeptical age.

2 PRIMITIVE AND PAST BELIEFS

Primitive man feels himself wholly surrounded by the supernatural, almost every moment of the day, every day of his life. His awareness of the supernatural, and his activities relating to it, are as familiar and integral to his life as are our recognition and use of the products of technology. When an Azande tribesman of North Africa sets out in the morning to cultivate his crops, he will carry a charm to assist his hoe. Going on a hunt in the afternoon, he will leave behind him a protective spell to guard his fields, and will take with him a "medicine" to guide his spear. He may beat a drum at a dance in the evening, and will therefore wear around his wrist a magic whistle to improve his musical technique.

For most primitives, magical rites are indispensable for enterprises ranging from hut building and cooking to funerals and war. Later in the chapter some examples will be given of varying attitudes to magic as well as varying uses of it. Here the important point is that the existence and efficacy of a supernatural power, magic, is invariably accepted in the societies that we class as primitive, whatever their level of development. And, inevitably, with this belief in magic there is always a belief in the pervasive presence of supernatural *beings*—that is, of various kinds of spirits.

(Incidentally, the term "primitive" has lately fallen out of favor with anthropologists, ethnologists, and sociologists, who usually prefer to classify such societies as "simple" or "small-scale." But since these phrases seem more unwieldly and no less condescending than the word "primitive," the latter will be used here. Still, no condescension is intended. Just as "civilized" man can display a rich streak of savagery, so "primitive" man usually possesses a high degree of sophistication in many aspects of his social organization. So the anthropologists give us a perspective on ourselves. The study of modern primitives—from the Australian or New Guinea tribes still embedded in the Stone Age to the highly developed societies of the North American Plains Indians—teaches us a great deal about our own social evolution in the unrecorded past. At the same time, such studies show that in many ways—such as the nature and strength of our belief in the supernatural—we have not changed so much after all.)

To the primitive, spirits populate all nature. Australian aborigines believe that every tree, river, and rock is the home of spirits and that every natural phenomenon is the work of demons. But these "nature" spirits are not the only ones inhabiting the primitive's world. There are others—like the spirits who attend births and initiations—that are directly involved in the life of the individual and his tribe. Often, however, the line between these two classes is blurred. Sometimes a rain spirit can be induced by, say, a ceremonial dance to act directly on man's behalf, and a river spirit, if annoyed, can produce a flood that will cause considerable harm.

Differences between spirits become even more shadowy when one tries to distinguish the disembodied spirits of the dead—ghosts—from spirits that never had human form. Many primitive societies believe that the soul of a dead man becomes demonic. The Caribs of British Guiana say that the soul goes into the forest and becomes an evil spirit; the Maoris of New Zealand regard a ghost as hostile even to those who had been its close friends. Thus, as with the American Sioux, fear of a malignant ghost often acts as an excellent deterrent to murder. And many primitives share the belief that the ghosts of shamans or witchdoctors are the worst of all evil spirits.

Not surprisingly, most of these supernatural beings—from the ghost of a neighbor to the demon that brings famine or disease—inspire only fear and horror in primitive minds. But there is one branch of the spirit world toward which the living sometimes feel almost friendly: the spirits of departed ancestors. Many North American Indians pray (or once prayed) to the spirits of their fathers to make the winter mild, to produce abundant game, and to grant various other favors. The Zulus of Africa and the Maoris of New Zealand traditionally believed that the ancestral spirits brought them strength in war.

When a tribal or familial ancestor is accorded supernatural power, he becomes, in fact, a deity—though his position in the divine hierarchy varies. In some communities, his divine authority is restricted to providing protection for his own family (as he did in life); in many more, it involves the power of life and death over a whole people. In Tonga the dead chiefs are lesser gods, who intercede with the greater gods on behalf of their descendants; in the Papuan Island of Tanna the dead ancestors are the *only* gods.

The worship of dead ancestors as divinities is an important and fairly widespread form of religion. It formed an integral part of the religion of the people of ancient China, where it persisted until fairly recently. Hindu traditions also include offerings to ancestors to ensure their continuing favor. The ancient Romans worshiped their ancestors as household gods and made offerings to their statues. And the Shinto beliefs of Japan are largely based on the worship of ancestors.

Since in primitive societies the ancestral ghosts are thought to have the power to look after the family or tribe, the living do all they can to please them—usually by regular offerings of food and drink. Generally (as among the Nagas of Assam) these offerings are placed by the graves, though some tribes of the Congo go even further—they pour food and drink down a channel through the grave right to the corpse's mouth.

Aside from the regular offerings—made sometimes monthly, sometimes daily, sometimes at every meal—major festivals and ceremonies are often held in honor of the dead ancestors. The Ashanti of West Africa celebrate a festival called *adae* approximately every 21 days. The chief and the elders enter the sacred house containing the seats where the ancestral spirits are believed to dwell. A sheep is slaughtered and a portion of the meat is placed on each seat, while the chief prays for tribal prosperity, fertility, and longevity. For drink, a few drops of rum are poured on each seat, and the prayer is repeated. The climax of the *adae* is a public ceremony with dancing, singing of songs and sagas, and a chorus of praise addressed to the chief as the living representative of the ancestors.

Generally, the spirits of all the dead chiefs, elders, and heads of families of the entire tribe are worshiped. But sometimes each family in a primitive community prays also to its own particular patrilineal ancestors. The Zulus, for example, look to the tribal fathers for collective assistance and care, but turn to the familial fathers for special favors. And usually the ancestors who are worshiped in this familial way fulfill the particular function of enforcing, by threat of punishment, the tribe's laws, rules, and taboos.

As might be expected, the ancestral spirits seem predominantly interested in ensuring that they receive due honor from the living. They impose swift punishment upon any of the living who forget to make offerings or who fail to comply with all the ceremonial rules of worship. The penalty may be disease, even death, or it may be less drastic. An Algonquin who once forgot to offer some of his food, and who later fell into the fire, was thought to have been pushed by an ancestor as punishment for his neglect. Desecration of ancestral graves or shrines incurs stiff penalties. Among the Malagasy of Madagascar even accidental damage to a tree branch near an ancestral grave will bring disease or death to the transgressor.

As for the ancestors concerning themselves with general rules of behavior as well as their own welfare: most societies prohibit incest, and on the Pacific Island of Yap the ancestors punish it by the illness or death of some member of the family (though not necessarily of the guilty couple). Other tribal taboos are safeguarded by the ancestors with equal strictness. (But of course it must be made clear that the ancestral spirits—or the spirits generally—are not seen as the sole enforcers of tribal prohibitions in the widespread primitive concept of taboo. The spirits *may* be involved, just as they may be involved in the working of magic spells and charms—but not necessarily. A violation of a taboo can just as well bring retribution automatically, in the way that *mana* or magic, to be discussed shortly, can operate automatically. For example, among some South African tribes sexual intercourse was held taboo during a war, not only for the soldiers but for the whole community; if the taboo was broken, thorns would impede the warriors and cause their defeat.)

When disaster occurs, whether to an individual or to an entire tribe, the ancestral spirits must be placated, or propitiated. Sometimes their goodwill can be regained simply by extra large offerings of food and drink, perhaps with the addition of a few ornaments or other valuables. This is the reaction of the Kol tribes of Chota Nagpur when disease strikes. The Toradjas of the Pacific try to end drought by drenching ancestral graves with water, and the Zulus sacrifice oxen to the spirits of their grandfathers to stave off disease.

This pattern of prayer and propitiation as a way of appeasing the dead is common both to ancestor-worshiping societies and to those that make no distinction between ancestral and other ghosts. Another means of appeasement is simply to give the spirits the rest they seek—the lack of which can cause their malevolence. The Maoris, the North American Iroquois, and the Karen of Burma all share the idea that ghosts wander and harm the living only when their bodies have not had proper burial. (The idea recurs throughout history, notably among the ancient Greeks—as in the story of the shade of Elpenor in the *Odyssey*—and it persists today, as Chapter 3 will show.)

Harmful also are the ghosts of victims of unavenged murders; these, as many of Australia's aborigines believe, take out their wrath more on the relatives who have failed in their duty of revenge than on the actual murderers. And many peoples especially fear the ghost of anyone who died violently, whether or not vengeance by relatives is considered necessary—because they believe that the ghost itself will seek vengeance on the killer. Thus many ways have been developed of either appeasing the ghost of a slain enemy or driving it off. In the island of Timor, according to the British anthropologist Sir James Frazer, when the headhunters return from battle carrying their trophies of victory the leader of the expedition must not return to his ordinary life in the village until he has undergone a two-month process of "purification"—which includes his being unable to touch food with his own hands (someone must feed him) and sexual abstinence. At the same time the other members of the community offer sacrifices to the souls of the men whose heads were taken, and hold ceremonies of song and dance in which their deaths are lamented and their forgiveness is sought. After these precautions the ghosts are thought to leave the killers in peace. Elsewhere, where it is believed that ghosts must be actively driven away, as among some New Guinea or some American Indian tribes, the process is noisy—beating of drums, shouting, shaking of rattles, and so on—in order to frighten the vengeful ghosts out of the village.

Other primitives, unwilling or unable to appease ghosts with burial or vengeance, try in different ways to prevent their return. Tribesmen in Thailand and elsewhere break an opening in the wall of a house to carry out a dead man, and then seal up the opening so that his ghost cannot find its way in. Siberian tribesmen fling a blazing coal out of the door after removing a corpse, to prevent the ghost's re-entry. But at one time South African tribes took less elaborate precautions to avoid being troubled by visitations from ghosts: they simply abandoned a house in which a death had taken place.

Now to look briefly at the supernatural beings who have never had human form—the "natural" spirits who were never incarnate. Some primitives regard them all as evil demons; others see some of them as good, some as evil. (The Iroquois, for instance, attributed all good fortune to benign nature spirits, all misfortune to evil spirits.) Still others believe they can be both—good if pleased, evil if angered. Therefore propitiation is again necessary. A native of Guinea tries to leave some kind of offering anywhere that he feels a spirit might dwell—including deep rivers, caves, great rocks, or even hollow trees.

Friendly spirits include the individual's guardian or patron spirit believed in by some Australian aborigines, or, to take an allied concept, the witch's "familiar" spirit (see p. 139). Evil spirits are more varied. Sometimes they are described simply as vague but dangerous beings who inhabit the darkness. Often any dangerous natural feature, like a volcano, is regarded as a demon's home—and so usually are deep lakes and forests. (Individual tree spirits are often kindly, as in the beliefs of the Gallas of Abyssinia; though natives of tangled forests and jungles, like the Brazilians, see a demon in every shadow.)

Animals too are often believed to have spirits of their own; many North American Indians would make offerings to, say, a dead bear in apology for having killed it. But just as often animals are seen simply as the dwelling-places—or personifications—of other spirits: good spirits in useful animals and evil spirits in dangerous ones. Peruvians prayed to the kindly spirits of fish, and tribes in India feared the deadly spirits that manifested themselves as tigers. C. G. Jung noted the primitive belief in the "bush-soul," personified by an animal, with which an individual spiritually identifies himself. And of course many primitives worship "totem" animals who personify the tribe's patron deity and symbolize tribal unity.

Where there is a belief that all natural phenomena are produced by spirits, it follows that there is a tendency among the
believers to seek ways of urging the spirits (or forcing them,
or helping them) to fulfill their function—whether that function is sending quantities of game animals, or causing many
healthy children to be born, or (most often in agricultural
communities) sending rain. The urging, forcing, or helping is
usually accomplished by means of some traditional, established, and complex ritual or ceremony—which must be
carried out with absolute correctness in every minute detail in
order to succeed. Ceremony, then, becomes an integral part
of the natural phenomenon itself, and of course an equally
integral part of the primitive's daily life, which is so bound
up with nature. As the American anthropologist Ruth Ben-
edict writes, concerning the Pueblo Indians of New Mexico:
"Their interest is centered upon their rich and complex
ceremonial life. . . . No field of activity competes with ritual
for foremost place in their attention. Probably most grown
men among the western Pueblos give to it the greater part of
their waking life." The Pueblos, in their generally arid lands,
devote a considerable amount of their ceremonial activities to
rain making—which, in their case, is a process of urging the
spirits to do their jobs.

In the Pueblo rain-making procedures many different rituals can be employed at different times, or interwoven
together in different ways, to achieve the same object. We can
look briefly at some of these procedures separately, but it
must be remembered that they are only an indication of how
the Pueblos bring rain, not an accurate detailed picture of the
whole ceremonial tradition. First, then, rain can be summoned by means of "imitative" magic (which is a form of
"sympathetic" magic, which we shall be discussing later).
The priests will roll round stones on a floor to simulate thunder, sprinkle water on the ground like rain, and place a bowl
of water on an altar to represent full springs and pools;
tobacco smoke is blown skyward and soaplike "suds" are
whipped up to imitate (and thus to produce) clouds. Another
ritual procedure is a ceremonial dance, in which the priests
impersonate the spirits—by wearing paint and masks—and
imitatively fulfill the rain-bringing function, thus impelling
the spirits to fulfill it in actuality. And, of course, incantation
and prayer play an important role. A priest will go into an
eight-day "retreat" during which time he addresses the gods
with requests such as one that begins:

From wherever you abide permanently
You will make your roads come forth.
Your little wind-blown clouds,
Your thin wisp of clouds
Replete with living waters,
You will send forth to stay with us.
Your fine rain caressing the earth. . . .

Rituals and ceremonies closely parallel to these of the Pueblo, addressed to the spirits of nature, can be found all over the world, in all primitive communities who share the belief in these spirits.

But few primitives see the natural world solely as the work of spirits. There is something else in operation: a mysterious all-pervasive power that modern anthropologists usually call *mana.* The word has been borrowed from the Melanesian peoples of the South Pacific, among whom the belief in this force was first noticed by the British missionary R. H. Codrington. Here is how Codrington describes mana in his book *The Melanesians* (published in 1891):

"There is a belief in a force, altogether distinct from physical power, which acts in all kinds of ways good and evil, which it is of great advantage to possess or control. This is *Mana.* The word is common, I believe, to the whole Pacific. . . . It is a power or influence, not physical, and in a way supernatural, but it shows itself in physical force, or in any kind of power or excellence which a man possesses. This *Mana* is not fixed in anything, and can be conveyed in almost anything. . . ."

Though appearing under a variety of names and guises, this power is believed in throughout the world. The Stone Age Papuans of New Guinea and the Karen of Burma see mana as a wholly impersonal, automatic force, and the primary cause of all unusual or inexplicable events. Other communities regard it largely as the property of spirits, who use it to continue nature's processes and to do man harm or good. Mana is widely believed to be the source of power that must be tapped when men turn to working magic. The tapping can be done directly but is often done through the agency of spirits. And the tapping requires special knowledge and techniques, which are monopolized to some extent by witches (or sorcerers or magicians) and of course witchdoctors (or shamans or medicine men). (A witchdoctor, as will be shown shortly, is usually the tribe's official magic worker with considerable authority; a witch is more often in private practice.)

These beliefs may seem confusing, because impersonal force, the power of spirits, and human magic are all inextricably mixed, and are in many cases even called by the same name. Remember, though, that the primitive mind generally tends toward synthesis rather than analysis; in the words of the French anthropologist Gustave Walter, "where we see confusion, primitive man sees fusion." One helpful way out of the confusion is to think of this supernatural power in the way that the modern layman thinks of the concept of energy: as a latent or potential "power" existing in all things. Energy can become kinetic quite impersonally, as in ocean waves or avalanches; but in some forms it can be tapped by man, as with hydroelectric power; while in others it can be directly possessed and used by man, in his own physical activity. The parallel is precise: magic, to modern practitioners as well as to primitives, is supernatural energy.

The spirits' role in the operation of magic varies widely. Often they are used to explain the origin of the power. The Dyaks of Borneo, tribes in Uganda, and many more, believe that long ago the spirits gave man the knowledge of magical techniques to help him survive. The Australian aborigines, among others like the Eskimos and the Zulus, believe that the spirits not only gave magic to man at the beginning of things but transmit the power to him whenever it is used. And for many primitives the spirits must be cajoled or even forced into providing the power. Sometimes an offering or a sacrifice will suffice: Borneans and others sacrifice fowls to the spirits to cast a spell that will protect the crops from vermin. Elsewhere an outright threat is necessary, as when a magician of the Kuraver tribes of southern India sets out to kill an enemy with a wax image; he invokes a spirit's help and vows to tear the spirit to pieces if the magic fails to work.

The practice of magic has always been considered a difficult and dangerous activity, largely because of its links with spirits and demons. And while amateurs and laymen among primitives may often dabble in magic to various degrees, it is mostly left to the professionals (who of course encourage this arrangement), especially in the case of major rites like rain making or murder. And among the professionals, as mentioned earlier, are all the witches, magicians, sorcerers, etc. Usually the three words can be used interchangeably to fit most primitive conceptions, though the British anthropologist E. E. Evans-Pritchard found, during his study of the Azande of North Africa, that to them witchcraft is one thing and sorcery quite another. (The terms will be seen, in Chapter 6, to be distinguishable in another way in later European conceptions.) Here it is worth looking at the Azande in some detail, for not only are their ideas of magic highly developed, but they are also in many ways typical of all primitive beliefs—while magic itself to some extent relates to every aspect of their culture.

Azande witches and sorcerers have one basic characteristic in common: their malevolence. They are assumed to be the authors of all misfortunes, especially the more inexplicable kind such as accidents, disease, bad luck, and even death. But they differ in the methods they use. A witch, Evans-Pritchard says, "Performs no rite, utters no spell, and possesses no medicines. An act of witchcraft is a psychic act." (Sorcerers on the other hand do perform rites and do use "medicine" or magical materials.) The witch's power derives from a "witch-substance" in his body—though the Azande are vague about its exact appearance or nature. The substance is inherited, but a witch's descendant can let it lie dormant if he wishes; in other words, it does not confer power automatically.

The Azande is concerned with witchcraft only on a personal level. If he falls ill or injures himself, he finds out who might be using witchcraft against him, and then employs witchcraft against his enemy. Only if a witch kills a man will other tribesmen take a hand—that is, the dead man's kin will avenge his death, as their familial duty, by killing the witch. (In the past the avengers used a spear; today they are more likely to set out to kill a murderous witch with more acts of witchcraft.)

An Azande witch commits his worst deeds—especially murder—at night. His witch-substance sends out a psychic emanation—in effect "the soul of his witchcraft"—which removes from the victim "the soul of his flesh." This the witch will eat—and the victim will fall ill and will eventually die unless counter-witchcraft is used. (A man who dies *suddenly* is thought to have been killed by sorcery; witchcraft causes lingering diseases.)

But unless they have committed murder, Azande witches are accepted as members of the community. Sorcerers, however, are ostracized. It is a crime to own the evil medicines and know the spells (which are presumably passed on secretly from elder sorcerers to apprentices). The medicines, made from plants, are put to work through ritual. A sorcerer planning murder goes by night under a full moon and places

the medicine *menzere* on the threshold of the victim's house
with an appropriate incantation. When the victim steps over
it he will immediately fall ill and die—unless, again, some
strong counter-medicine is quickly brought into action.

Counter-medicine falls into the category of good (or
white) magic, and as such can be practiced by anyone. Thus
most Azande know some spells of good magic and how to
collect a few helpful medicines. But good magic is not used
only as an antidote to evil or black magic; it also plays a part
in everyday life—to protect homes and fields, to improve
hunting, to increase virility or fertility, and so on. To take
one example: Azande gardeners tie vines infused with magic
around their gardens to protect them from theft.

But for his major magical needs—which include thwarting
a witch or sorcerer—the Azande will probably turn to a spe-
cialist: the witchdoctor. Witchdoctors can find the witch who
is harming a tribesman; they then either prevent the harm, or
cure it (in the case of disease), or if it proves incurable,
they punish the witch. Witchdoctors usually operate after a
ceremonial dance, during which they dance and sing themselves into a frenzy (or an apparent trance state). They are
then able to answer questions put to them by spectators and
to effect magical cures or punishments.

The Azande distinction between white and black magic is
not shared by every primitive society. Among some Papuan
tribes, for instance, there is only one kind of magic, though
there are two ways of looking at it. It is good magic if one of
your tribe's magicians is working against another tribe; it is
bad magic if a foreigner is working against your tribe. (In
these communities magicians never turn their powers on to
their fellow tribesmen.) But whatever type of magic is used,
the basic concepts of its nature and operation would seem to
be fairly universal.

One of these basic concepts is the belief that the qualities
of objects or creatures can be magically transmitted. Some
African tribesmen eat (or once ate) lions' hearts to obtain
the animals' strength and courage; British Columbia Indians
rub a baby girl with the body of a beaver, to make her indus-
trious. Transmissions may work negatively: Marshall Is-
landers say that if a man eats a fruit that has fallen from a
tree he too will fall when climbing. The transmission idea
also involves cures: a Kagoro tribesman of Nigeria, suffering
from a spear wound, will try to have the spear found and
washed in water. He will then drink the water and be healed.

Sometimes the transmission ensures protection: some East Africans wear the claws or teeth of dead leopards to protect themselves from living ones.

One important use of the transmission principle is the well-known and widespread method of harming an enemy by obtaining some of his nail parings, hair, saliva, urine, or other bodily cast-offs, and working black magic through them. These are thought to retain the qualities of the man, over which the witch gains power. Usually such materials are included in an image of the victim (like the wax doll of black magic); the image is then stabbed or burned or drowned and the victim dies in the same way.

The transmission of qualities also forms the basic idea of what is called "contagious" magic. As the modern American anthropologist Hutton Webster points out, primitive man reasons that if ice is cold and makes you cold and if fire is hot and makes you hot, the beaver's industriousness or the lion's strength should rub off as well. But with the use of nail parings and wax dolls contagious magic shades into what is known as "sympathetic" magic, based on the idea that whatever happens to part of something, or its image, will happen to the whole, or the reality.

Many prehistorians believe that the primeval artists who decorated cave walls at Lascaux and elsewhere were practicing sympathetic magic. They drew antelopes without ears so the real animals would fail to hear the hunters; they hurled spears at a picture of a buffalo to ensure a kill in the next hunt. And today a Cora Indian of Mexico, wishing to increase his herd of cows or goats, makes a small image in wax or clay (while making an appropriate incantation) of each additional animal he wants.

Amulets, too, can be in the form of sympathetic magical images, but more usually they are simply objects that are thought to confer magical protection. Some of the protective objects carried by primitives are active, designed to fulfill a specific purpose—like the phallus-shaped piece of lava, smeared with a special paste, carried by a young tribesman of the Torres Islands to ensure his success in love. But most amulets are passive, carried as protection from black magic or bad luck. Any object can become an amulet—a stone, a plant or part of a plant, a part of an animal or of a man—as long as it is believed to contain mana. (Fetishes on the other hand are a special class of amulets, for they are thought to contain actual spirits, personalized beings, and not just an abstract power.)

Many verbal spells are also used protectively, to ward off black magic. Gestures too can be magical. The Bathonga of Mozambique, among others, believe that a witch can curse a man by merely pointing at him with the index finger. And the Melanesians believe that some sorcerers can kill with a look—one example of the notorious belief in the "evil eye," which is still widespread in many communities.

But, as with the Azande, the primitive's best protection against magic is another magician. Thus the witchdoctor acts as a kind of supernatural policeman. More often, though, he cures rather than prevents. His magic neutralizes the magic that has made a man fall ill; alternatively, where another's magic is not the cause of illness, his rituals drive away the demon that has possessed and diseased a body. As official magic worker, he alone is usually responsible for such large-scale operations as rain making, increasing game, ensuring large crops, guarding the chief or king, divining the future, and maintaining the favor of the spirits or gods by the performance of religious ceremonies and rituals.

This brief outline of the main features of primitive belief in the supernatural has left little space for any detailed examination of the nature of magic or the characteristics and functions of spirits, demons, witches, or magicians. These details will emerge more fully in later chapters specifically devoted to these subjects. For the beliefs of later "civilized" societies in ghosts and magic and witches and devils are often merely variations on basic beliefs common to most primitives. It is as if each society, each culture, developed for itself the idea of the soul and the idea of impersonal supernatural power and from them developed and ramified complex but parallel sets of supernatural beliefs.

Some such theory may be necessary to account for the similarity of beliefs in primitive cultures that seem never to have had any kind of contact. (Though some authorities think contact could have been made, prehistorically, by means of widespread migration.) But the existence of parallel beliefs existing through time—from prehistory to today— could be explained by simple social evolution and inheritance. A small-scale primitive culture struggles up to comparative complexity, reaches impressive heights of civilization, and influences other peoples around it on various rungs of the sociological ladder. These peoples acquire its beliefs, and in turn later pass them on.

It was by means of this evolutionary process that the great civilization of ancient Egypt influenced (supernaturally and otherwise) the whole of later antiquity, and later spread its concepts of the supernatural—both directly and by means of the classical and Arabic tradition—throughout the Western world. And Egypt's "occult wisdom" still influences, quite explicitly, the nature of occultism and belief in the supernatural today.

In ancient Egypt the cult of the dead and the concern with life after death dominated the lives of the people as powerfully as in primitive societies. This domination was particularly strong in the later period of Egypt—the Empire, or the New Kingdom, which lasted from about 1567 to 1089 B.C. During these centuries it seems almost as if the Egyptians cared little for this life, pinning their hopes only on the next, so preoccupied were they with preparations for death involving ceremonial, rite, and magic. In earlier dynasties much more interest was taken in life as it was lived beside the Nile, in spite of the fact that the Old Kingdom (roughly from 2780 to 2610 B.C.) saw the construction of the great pyramids. Life after death and ceremonial magic did of course mean a great deal to these earlier Egyptians, but it did not have the priority that it later acquired.

In the later Empire, it was the immense power and influence of the priesthood that largely contributed to the obsession with death and the dead—since many and expensive funerals and funerary rites meant a wealthy priesthood, and so were encouraged and propagandized. The priests' authority derived from their position as the sole spokesmen for the gods—without whose blessing few enterprises succeeded. And, allied to this monopoly, the priesthood was a repository of an immense amount of learning, including the knowledge of writing, astronomy, and the occult. They had practically cornered the market on most important forms of magic—both the ceremonial magic that brought supernatural forces into beneficent action, and the black magic that would be turned against transgressors. For in Egypt, in the words of the 19th-century British Egyptologist Sir Wallis Budge, "magic was made to be the handmaiden of religion."

Magic talismans and amulets proliferated, though the knowledge of their nature and use was not always a priestly monopoly, since many of the best-known amulets had existed a good deal longer than the priesthood's predominance. Amulets were (and are) protection from both natural and supernatural dangers—and were buried with the dead for the same purposes. The preservation of the corpse was vitally important to the immortality of the soul; and so a corpse could be given a guardian amulet for every organ and limb, as well as others to ward off such dangers as putrefaction, worms, tomb robbers, and mildew.

When a corpse was prepared for burial, the heart was preserved separately from the rest of the body, and its place in the mummified body filled by a carved stone amulet, often heart-shaped, intended to prevent the theft of the heart by a demon. But from quite early in Egypt's history the heart was usually replaced by the most important and best-known amulet: the scarab. This object was modeled on the lowly dung-beetle—but that was the only lowly thing about it. The scarab was one of the symbols of the god Khepera, the invisible creative force that (among other things) kept the sun on its daily path. In later times, and especially after the pharaoh Ikhnaton had established the monotheistic religion of sun worship, the scarab became identified as the symbol of the Supreme God itself.

Above all, the scarab amulet stood for life. Its presence in or on a dead body represented the potential life in the body. Like most Egyptian amulets, a scarab usually had a magical spell carved on it—usually an address to a god, requesting immortality for the bearer. The living as well as the dead eventually came to wear scarabs to gain divine favor and protection. And even the beetle itself acquired some of the power of its magical image: childless women dried and powdered the insect, mixed it with water, and drank the mixture to achieve fertility.

Though not an amulet, another magical object of great importance in Egypt should be mentioned here. This is the *ankh,* the strange cross-like shape that appears in so many inscriptions and sculptures. The ankh is thought to have been primarily a symbol of life, but also variously of the universe, of man, or of all these things and more. It was therefore invariably carried like a scepter by the great gods who directed and guarded the life of the universe and the activities of man.

By their extensive use of magical images, the Egyptian priests turned sympathetic magic into literally a fine art. To them the statue of a god contained the spirit of the god and the image of a man contained the soul of the man. Images, therefore, could become magically animated—like the *ushab-ti,* a stone or wooden image of the deceased placed in the tomb to do all his physical work for him in the next world. (The tomb of King Seti I—about 1300 B.C.—is supposed to have contained 700 of these wooden laborers.) Other portrait images of the dead were placed in the tombs to serve as a dwelling place for the *ka,* which is thought to have represented a man's supernatural "double," his spiritual self as it were (though some authorities feel that the ka was a separate entity, a protective spirit or kind of guardian angel). The ka inhabited the spirit world, and dying meant joining one's ka. Yet at the same time the ka lived in the tomb with the mummy. (The dead man was similarly thought to live in both the after-world and the tomb. The Egyptians, like the primitives, tended to see fusion where we see confusion.) It was to sustain the ka that food offerings were left in the tomb—or sometimes these gifts were merely images of food, which by priestly magic could be made real and edible.

Whatever the ka represented, it was not the soul as most peoples have conceived of it. The soul of the dead took the form of a human-headed hawk called the *ba* (or ba-soul, or *bai*), images of which stood near the mummy. After death the ba lived almost entirely in the after-world until the day of resurrection, though it was thought to visit the mummy occasionally in the tomb. Images of the ba were therefore usually inscribed with spells, or "words of power"— inscriptions that mostly took the form of exhortations to the gods to preserve the dead from harm.

All these images were infused with ceremonial or white magic. But the Egyptian practice of the black art also involved the use of images. As an example of black magic, Budge tells a story of a conspiracy against Ramses III (who reigned about 1200 B.C.) in which a treasury official used wax dolls to try to kill the king. (The plot was discovered and thwarted.) And a later Greek tale concerns the Egyptian king Nectanebo II (about 350 B.C.) who fought his battles with wax figures. As a real enemy marched or sailed against the Egyptian forces, Nectanebo would animate wax soldiers or ships representing the opposing armies, and would see to it that the wax Egyptians won. When the figures of the enemy fell, so did their real-life counterparts. But one day the gods took a hand, counteracting the king's magic, and the wax enemy won the day. So Nectanebo realized that, as king, he had lost the gods' favor; he fled to Greece, where he set up practice as a professional physician and magic-worker.

In Egypt (as everywhere since) spells and incantations animated images and worked magic in general. The gods knew the words and used them, living priests and magicians knew them, and the dead knew or learned them in order to complete their journey to the next world. The words themselves seem to have had an intrinsic power. Many of the spells gave mortals power to command gods or demons. The dead especially needed such power to ensure a safe and easy transition from life to afterlife, and papyri containing the necessary magical formulas were often buried with them, like the book that accompanied King Teta (about 3260 B.C.) to his tomb, containing words of power that were intended to have, according to an inscription in the tomb, "effect upon the heart of the gods."

Known as "Books of the Dead," Egypt's vast collection of religio-magical papyri contained hymns and incantations to the gods as well as a great many spells and formulas to satisfy the wants of the dead. Some of the chapters serve as ceremonial formulas in funeral rites; one gives the incantation to be spoken over a picture of the sun-god Ra's boat, which accompanied the deceased so that he could journey forever with the god; others were recited to ward off demons, to infuse objects with magical power, and so on.

Magic was also used by the Egyptians to cure certain diseases (though not all, for they knew that some needed medicine only) believed to be caused by demonic possession. Magical pictures and spells were also effective in divining the future, and magic played an important part in warding off ghosts.

The ghosts and apparitions that troubled the Egyptians may have been manifestations of the ka or the ba-soul or some other spiritual component of the dead; no one can be sure. Probably, though, a ghost was a ka, for many authorities point out that if regular offerings were not forthcoming to feed the ka, it would venture out of the tomb to find its own food—and, presumably, to plague its forgetful relatives. The Egyptians also believed that evil men and women would invariably return after death to haunt the living.

If a man felt himself to be haunted, he often concluded that some deceased member of his family was angry at him. If he had neglected his duties to the dead, he would hurry to make offerings. He might also write a letter to the dead, asking forgiveness, explaining his neglect, and begging the ghost to leave him alone. He would put this letter in some obvious place near the tomb, or perhaps on an outer portrait image, knowing that it would be read and hoping it would mollify the ghost.

The Egyptians' overwhelming concern with life after death, and therefore with funeral ritual dominated by ceremonial magic, is unparalleled in any other ancient civilization. The various cultures that rose to dominate Mesopotamia, for instance, showed an entirely different attitude to things supernatural—an attitude nearer to that found in some primitive communities. To simplify the comparison, the Egyptian sought to provide himself with a happy life in and beyond the tomb while the Mesopotamian primarily sought to protect himself, in this life, from those who returned after death.

Of course, the Mesopotamians had a sizable tradition of magic. Ancient "Chaldea" (or Mesopotamia) was, after all, the birthplace of the divinatory arts—especially of astrology—which have always been closely linked to the practice of magic. Black magic apparently thrived. The traditional images and dolls would be burned to harm others or to ward off such harm—with an exhortation to the fire to "burn the man and woman who bewitched me." But the Mesopotamian use of magic and fear of witches took something of a back seat to the deep and all-pervading fear of ghosts and evil spirits.

These beings haunted burial places and ruined buildings; they lurked in the desert or the mountains to seize travelers; they moved abroad in the form of ravens, owls, and other dark creatures. Anyone whose body had not been buried, or whose remains were disturbed, would wander the earth as a ghost. In about 650 B.C. the Assyrian king Ashurbanipal purposely desecrated the tombs of the ancient kings of Elam so their spirits would have no rest, though he apparently received no harm from them as a result. Anyone who died in a horrible or inexplicable way was thought to become a restless ghost. As an Assyrian incantation points out, these included people who had died from supernatural causes, such as

He on whom an evil Spirit hath rushed,
He whom an evil Demon hath enveloped in his bed,
He whom an evil Ghost hath cast down in the night.

The Mesopotamians seem also to have been expert in the black art called necromancy—the art that involves conjuring up demons and calling up the dead in order to work magic or divine the future. An Assyrian magician or sorcerer was usually given the title "Raiser of the Departed Spirit"; and at one point in the Babylonian *Epic of Gilgamesh* the hero calls up (with the help of a god) his dead companion Ea-bani. (The Gilgamesh story has a famous parallel in Homer's story of the seer Tiresias, who was summoned by Odysseus from the underworld to indicate what the future would hold.)

In such a ghost-haunted society the exorcizer would naturally be an important personage. Many Mesopotamian clay tablets contain enormously long lists of ghosts exorcized by sorcerers, each ghost fully described and the reasons given for its return. Other tablets describe rituals for "laying" a ghost. One ritual includes the symbolic (or sympathetic) burial of an image of a dead man whose ghost is being laid. Various spells are recorded for protecting oneself from ghosts; but, as in the primitive world, the best protection was apparently to make sure that the dead were safely buried with all the proper offerings and then to leave the graves alone.

The Chaldeans, Babylonians, Assyrians, and of course Egyptians all bequeathed, in one way or another, various aspects of their culture to later civilizations, Greece among them. And of these legacies, beliefs in and concepts of the supernatural were naturally prominent. But, interestingly, these beliefs barely affected a people who had had *direct* contact with both Babylonia and Egypt—the ancient Hebrews.

In their most primitive past, of course, magic, soothsaying, and the rest were widely practiced among the Jews. Moses and his brother Aaron humbled all the sorcerers of Egypt with their miraculous power. But after Moses had led the people of Israel out of Egypt and had imposed on Hebrew culture the idea of the One God, and the ten commandments of Yahweh, magic lost its importance. Later, it was outlawed: "A man also or a woman that hath a familiar spirit, or that is a wizard, shall surely be put to death. . . ." (Leviticus xx: 27). The making of images of people and objects was forbidden; and King Saul's visit to the witch of Endor (I Samuel xxviii), to call up the spirit of Samuel, was highly illegal—which explains the witch's terror on discovering Saul's identity.

In ancient Greece, however, it was not monotheism that counteracted an obsessive concern with the supernatural but a sudden and amazing upsurge of the spirit of scientific rationalism, which began about the fifth century B.C. and dominated the Greek world-view until at least the second century. But this period—the classical period of the Enlightenment—had been preceded by what is called the "archaic age" of Greek culture. And in those centuries (which included the time of Homer, who is thought to have lived in the ninth century B.C.) the supernatural was as prominent as in any primitive society. The rise of rationalism that followed deprived the supernatural of much of its influence, and probably drove it underground to some extent. But later, when Eastern influences grew stronger, it regained a great deal of its former authority and respectability.

Even without touching on the complexities of the orgiastic mysteries and Dionysiac cults, plenty of material exists to prove that Greece tempered its well-known rationalism with some correspondingly irrational ideas. As far as their ghosts were concerned, the Greeks took a page from Egypt's book and believed that, on death, the soul went to the heavenly Elysium, but that the "shade" (called the *eidolon*) went to the underworld—where it lived a shadowy, semi-conscious existence (unless strengthened with a drink of blood, as were the shades in the *Odyssey*). Yet at the same time (and here the Greeks echo the old Egyptian inconsistency) the shade was thought to remain linked with the body as long as the body stayed intact.

But the Greeks were more hardheaded about the dead than some others before them; they made little of the embalming process, and often cut the shade off from this world entirely by cremating the dead. Again, if a body had no proper funeral—cremation or burial—its shade was compelled to wander and to haunt the living. In Homer's *Iliad* the ghost of the warrior Patroclus visits his friend Achilles in a dream to complain of being unburied. A similar story concerns one Eukrates, whose wife had died and had been duly cremated together with her clothing and ornaments. But shortly after the ceremony the wife's ghost appeared to the husband; she was unable to rest because one of her sandals had not been burned in the fire. Eukrates found and burned the sandal, and the ghost never returned.

Greek magic managed to achieve considerable importance —enough for Plato and his *Laws* to suggest that men who harm others by "enchantments" should be put to death—although he praised and, like many others, practiced the allied art of divination. Aggression by black magic was also common—either by the use of the universal wax image or by a technique that developed extensively in the fourth century B.C.: one could control a man, or kill him, by inscribing on a tablet "the curse of the underworld Powers" (as the modern British classicist E. R. Dodds calls it) and placing the tablet in an occupied grave. And at about the same time love potions and amulets with magically protective properties were gaining a much more widespread use among the populace—though, Dodds says, "if you wanted a really potent witch you had to buy one from Thessaly."

Perhaps the people of Greece came to react against the detached academic system that rationalist Greek thought eventually became; perhaps they came under the growing influence of Eastern culture (especially of Egypt); or perhaps they were just troubled men seeking some kind of security in troubled times. Whatever the cause, in the second and first centuries B.C. Greece wholeheartedly embraced irrationalism and the occult. Shortly thereafter the Roman Empire embraced Greece—and occultism with it. The addition of Egypt to the Empire increased the inflow of what skeptics like Cicero, in the waning days of the Republic, had scorned as "superstition." But such voices were generally ignored; Rome was impressed by the "ancient wisdom" of the once-great civilizations she had conquered, and swallowed it whole.

Yet Rome did not lack her own supernatural traditions. For instance, in the middle of May, a kind of exorcism ceremony known as *lemuria* was performed. Originally a ritual to drive away evil ghostly influences, it became, during the Republic, a domestic laying of family ghosts. Rising at midnight, the head of the household would walk through the house scattering a trail of black beans to attract the ghosts. These would then be expelled by repeating nine times the formula "spirits of my fathers depart."

Some of the world's best ghost stories originated in Rome. The historians Plutarch and Tacitus have told many, thus providing a goldmine of material for later writers. But one of the best (variations of which occur time and again in anthologies of such tales) was told by Pliny the Younger, at the end of the first century A.D., and concerns an apparition that haunted the philosopher Athenodorus. He had rented a house at a suspiciously low price; during his first night there he was disturbed by the clanking of chains, and looked up to see "the spectre of an old man, emaciated and filthy, with a long flowing beard and hair standing on end, wearing fetters on his legs and shaking the chains on his wrists."

The old man beckoned to Athenodorus, who rose and followed him into the courtyard. Here the apparition suddenly vanished. Athenodorus carefully marked the spot, then went to bed. The next day he and the authorities started digging at the marked place, and found a skeleton with chains at wrists and ankles. These remains were given a proper burial—and the ghost of the old man never appeared again.

In A.D. 77 Pliny the Elder had deplored the practice of magic in Rome, declaring that magicians were either charlatans or fools. He praised the Emperor Tiberius for suppressing magicians, and cited Nero's skepticism based on his own invariably unsuccessful experiments with magic. (Yet both these emperors had often consulted astrologers.) Other Roman writers followed Pliny in condemning magic; still others (apparently including Tacitus) took the opposite side. And while the intellectuals raged in controversy, wizards, soothsayers, dream interpreters, and astrologers crowded the streets of Rome—or else crowded the outlying provinces of the Empire, where some emperor's edict had banished them. One of the greatest and most famous of the provincial "magi" was Apollonius of Tyana (in Asia Minor), who, born within 20 years of Christ, was thought by many as late as the fourth century to be his superior as a prophet, miracle-worker, and philosopher.

Much of Apollonius's fame derived from his prophecies. In Alexandria, for example, he foretold that the Emperor Vespasian would rebuild the great temple of Jupiter at Rome—though at the time no one in Egypt knew that the temple had burned down. Other stories concerning his miracles (many of which are undoubtedly legends attached to his name after his death) include a case of raising the dead: Apollonius met a funeral procession of a young girl, presumably took pity on her family, and called her back to life simply by touching her and whispering a few words in her ear.

A modern British writer, Ralph Shirley, suggests that Apollonius's prescience might have been telepathy and his raising of the girl an intuitive knowledge that she was still alive. But whatever the explanation, Apollonius was often called a sorcerer while he lived, and at one time was arrested by the Emperor Domitian for practicing magic against him—magic that, according to the emperor's prosecutor, included the sacrifice of a boy. But Apollonius was acquitted and later in Ephesus was able to see, in a vision, the

assassination of Domitian at the exact time it was happening
in Rome.

But for all his fame, the name of Apollonius was
eventually overshadowed, and Roman occultism more or less
eclipsed, by the growing influence of Christianity. Pagan
supernaturalism and religion were condemned as heresies by
the early Christian fathers; Hippolytus, Bishop of Rome,
wrote in the third century a *Refutation of All Heresies* that
listed and exposed the techniques of fraudulent necromanc-
ers. Magic and sorcery were thought to be evil, inspired by
demons; and all the gods and spirits of the Greco-Roman
pantheon were now indiscriminately classed as demons.

But this condemnation still allowed one element of ancient
supernaturalism (found in every preceding society from the
primitive to Rome) to survive or even develop—the practice
of exorcism. If the pagans' mythological beings were all evil
demons, then the Christians—to ensure the spread of the new
religion—had to battle with them. In the second century, the
Christian philosopher Justin Martyr wrote of "many demo-
niacs all over the world . . . whom none other exorcists, con-
jurers, or sorcerers have cured, these have many of our
Christians cured . . . and still do cure." Origen, writing in
the third century, says that even the simple pronouncement
of the name of Jesus had the power to exorcize demonic possession.

In general, though, the Christians were the sworn enemies
of what have always been known as the occult arts. Yet these
survived in many places—survived, we might say, in read-
iness for their full-scale comeback in medieval and
Renaissance Europe. They were maintained, for instance, by
the mystic beliefs and practices of the Neoplatonists, who
formulated a secret and complex lore concerning the workings of magic through supernatural agencies and beings—
though it was carefully distinguished by them from demon-
dominated sorcery. Occultism was kept alive also in the Arab
world, whose scholars saved many other valuable portions of
classical thought and culture. All through the period now
called the Dark Ages, the Arab intellectuals—the ninth-
century Albumasar, Alkindi, and others—compiled huge treatises on magic, on amulets and incantations, based on the ancient knowledge. And from their stronghold in southern
Spain the Arabs poured this accumulated material—together
with the mysteries of the Hermetic tradition and alchemy—
into medieval Christian Europe.

Alchemy (which we shall discuss in Chapter 5) deserves a brief mention here. Its significance as chemistry's forerunner (comparable to the relationship of astrology to astronomy) is of less interest here than its predominant position in medieval and Renaissance occultism. Alchemists were not simply seeking to transmute lead into gold; as C. G. Jung has suggested, the more serious alchemists were religious philosophers, seeking to penetrate the mysteries of both matter and spirit, and their relationship to each other—which they expressed in many cryptic and symbolic ways.

Nevertheless, the hope of transmuting metals dominated the desires of less serious alchemists, and drew many people in the Middle Ages to squander their time and money in the search for free gold. By the avarice of such men the spiritual content of alchemy was reduced to the level of back-street magic. As the 15th-century occultist Agrippa wrote (after he had renounced such practices), these alchemists "at length grown old in chemical impostures, are compelled to live in the lowest degree of poverty, and in such calamity that they receive nothing but contempt and laughter."

Many of the Arab writers whose works were a major source of occult and alchemical practice were dismissed by later medieval skeptics as mere magicians. The same accusation was often leveled at the Jews, whose studies in religio-mystic philosophy—called *cabbalism*—perhaps left them open to such charges. The esoteric teachings of the Cabbala do in fact seem to include practices akin to magic (as we shall see in Chapter 5)—and were accepted as such by many medieval occultists including Agrippa (before he recanted), Pico della Mirandola, and Guillaume Postel.

Essentially the Cabbala is a mystical system by which the student can penetrate the profoundest secrets of God, the universe, and the nature of life. These hidden meanings are unraveled by specific means, including (to put it simply) the manipulation of letters and numbers containing divine power. But here, as with alchemy, lesser practitioners found not mysticism but magic; the letters formed words and anagrams that acted as charms and spells. Legends of supernatural achievements abounded. A 16th-century Jewish cabbalist, called Elijah of Chelm, was reported to have modeled a man in clay and to have brought the figure to life by writing the secret name of God on the figure's forehead.

Alchemy, Hermetics, cabbalism, astrology, and the rest preoccupied practically every great medieval scholar—even many within the Church. These learned men were also sometimes involved in practices that were less reputable, even expressly forbidden—like sorcery and necromancy. The Italian physician Peter of Abano (Peter of Padua) published among many other texts and translations a work on the elements of magic; but eventually his enormous and largely esoteric learning gave an enemy a chance to denounce him as a heretic and he was burned at the stake in 1318. Another scholarly Italian doctor, Arnold of Villanova, employed cabbalistic signs, amulets, and other kinds of ceremonial magic in his treatments (though at the same time denouncing necromancy and witchcraft). He too was arrested by the authorities (about 1300), though his punishment was lighter: only his books were condemned to be burned.

Others followed similar paths of study—famous scholars like Robert Grosseteste and Roger Bacon, William of Auvergne and Thomas of Cantimpré. One of the greatest was Albertus Magnus, Bishop of Ratisbon (who was canonized in 1932). Primarily a scholar and philosopher, Albertus nevertheless knew his magic—"natural" magic, concerning the power of herbs and stones. To take a few examples: emeralds can be used in a test for virginity; the plant verbena acts as a love charm; agate will drive away phantoms, snakes, and melancholy.

In many ways, medieval men almost matched the Egyptians in their overwhelming preoccupation with the next world. The world in which they lived was virtually reduced to the position of a battleground where Good and Evil fought for the possession of man's soul. The Devil walked abroad, seeking and tempting, waiting for the one error that could condemn a man for eternity. And so the Church found itself fighting a constantly defensive action against the incursions of Satan's minions—that is, the heretics of all sorts, the unbelievers, the theologians who turned away from dogma and arrived at their own doctrinal interpretations of Christian belief, and others. In the climate of hysteria to which this defensive attitude contributed, a new heresy was born: the heresy of witchcraft, of devil worshipers with supposedly magical powers devoted to evil. And this new threat to the Christian Church was fought and persecuted in medieval and especially Renaissance Europe with a fanaticism, depravity, and cruelty almost unparalleled in human history.

But here we must end our account of the supernatural's past. The chapters to follow, however, will pick up many of the threads that have been introduced here, and will carry them on in terms of the history of the Western world as well as the present day. The brief allusions above to the Renaissance witch persecutions, for instance, will be elaborated in some detail and thus will give a sufficiently extensive picture of the supernatural in that period of history. Some of the less materialist preoccupations of the 19th century—such as the birth of spiritualism, and of such allied forms of occultism as Madame Elena Blavatsky's Theosophy—will be examined against the background of their age. And so the story will continue to be traced up to the present day, where there have been some comparatively new developments—and where also it will be found that the ancient beliefs not only show an amazing staying power in our so-called skeptical age, but may even be widening their sway, increasing their effects on modern society.

3 GHOST STORY

"The wind had fallen, and there was a still night and a full moon. At about ten o'clock Stephen was standing at the open window of his bedroom, looking out over the country. Still as the night was, the mysterious population of the distant moon-lit woods was not yet lulled to rest. From time to time strange cries as of lost and despairing wanderers sounded from across the mere. They might be the notes of owls or water-birds, yet they did not quite resemble either sound. Were they not coming nearer? Now they sounded from the nearer side of the water, and in a few moments they seemed to be floating about among the shrubberies. Then they ceased; but just as Stephen was thinking of shutting the window . . . he caught sight of two figures standing on the grav-elled terrace that ran along the garden side of the Hall—the figures of a boy and girl, as it seemed . . .

"Whilst the girl stood still, half smiling, with her hands clasped over her heart, the boy, a thin shape, with black hair and ragged clothing, raised his arms in the air with an appearance of menace and of unappeasable hunger and long-ing. The moon shone upon his almost transparent hands, and Stephen saw that the nails were fearfully long and that the light shone through them. As he stood with his arms thus raised, he disclosed a terrifying spectacle. On the left side of his chest there opened a black and gaping rent; and there fell upon Stephen's brain, rather than upon his ear, the impres-sion of one of those hungry and desolate cries that he had heard resounding over the woods of Aswarby all that evening. In another moment this dreadful pair had moved swiftly and noiselessly over the dry gravel, and he saw them no more."

The quotation is from a short story by the British writer M. R. James (1862-1936), an acknowledged master of horror fiction—a literary genre that (as we saw in Chapter 1) had been with us from antiquity but that gained especially wide popularity in the 19th and early 20th centuries. Today, the supernatural story forms an important element of the literary movement called science fiction or, more broadly, science fantasy. Modern writers like America's Ray Bradbury or Richard Matheson seem able to turn their pens from rocket ships to ghosts within the same anthology with an ease that seems to be shared by their readers. And it is on such stories—both old and new—that most people today base much of their conception of the nature of ghosts.

The rest of the conception derives from the amorphous collection of legend and fantasy that is generally termed folklore. Fiction and folklore are themselves somewhat interdependent. M. R. James once wrote: "I have tried to make my ghosts act in ways not inconsistent with the rules of folklore." The word "rules" may dignify the subject more than it deserves; but the *ways* of folklore, anyway as far as ghosts are concerned, do seem to be more or less stereotyped. Aside from the perambulating bedsheets and chain-rattling skeletons that have mostly been relegated today to the level of children's so-called comics, legend seems to do little but ring the changes on familiar notions of misty figures of noble ancestors in European stately homes; of hooded monks or nuns in ruined medieval abbeys; of headless horsemen or equally headless ex-queens of England. But entertaining as fiction and folklore may be, they rarely resemble the results of more or less "scientific" investigations into the nature of ghosts. Yet, as often happens, the results of such investigations are less well-known than the tales of the legend-mongers.

Scientific investigations of ghosts are undertaken by psychical researchers, parapsychologists, and the like—devoted specialists, scrupulous about the need for objectivity and double or triple checks. They follow up reports of ghosts, subject the observers to searching examinations, and seek to verify the information as far as possible.

Most psychical researchers avoid the word "ghost" because

of its overtones of folklore. Instead, they talk about "apparitions." This is a much wider term: a ghost, according to the Concise Oxford Dictionary, is "a dead person appearing to the living"; but an apparition can be of the living as well as of the dead. Many hundreds of cases were collected in the late 19th century by the British pioneers of psychical research F. W. H. Myers, E. Gurney, and F. Podmore in their *Phantasms of the Living*—which is still a basic textbook for students of the paranormal. These and later authorities agree that by far the largest number of such apparitions occur at a crucial time in the life of the person who appears. So they are called "crisis apparitions." Most of these apparitions are perceived by someone (a relative or friend) emotionally close to the person who appears but far away from him in space. Quite often the crisis is in fact the moment of death; but it may sometimes be a serious but non-fatal accident. The apparition may or may not reveal the nature of the crisis: for instance, the "percipient" may see an apparition of his son lying unconscious after a crash at the very moment that the son is in that position miles away; or he may merely see his son standing there, looking perfectly normal, while miles away the boy has been flung from a smashed car. The following is a condensed account of a point-of-death apparition that gave no hint that a fatality had occurred.

A young Englishwoman living in India reported that on March 19, 1917, she had been playing with her baby when she looked up to see her brother—who was an airman—standing in the room. Pleased to see him, thinking he had been unexpectedly sent out to India, she turned to put the baby down. When she turned back to greet her brother, he was not there. She called out, and looked all over the house, but there was no sign of him. Only then did she realize that she had seen an apparition. Two weeks later she learned that her brother's plane had been shot down in France on March 19, 1917.

There is no need to go into detail concerning the nature of apparitions of the living, for their most important characteristics parallel, in general, those of a major group of apparitions of the dead. The latter fall roughly into two groupings: first (the major one), those apparitions that appear, usually to friends, relatives, and associates; second, the "haunting" apparitions, which are tied to specific places rather than to percipients. We will take them in turn.

Like apparitions of the living, *post-mortem* apparitions

have no physical, material presence. In this way they are true to folklore; they do seem to walk through walls. Nevertheless, they generally have an extremely lifelike appearance; like the airman, they may not even reveal themselves as apparitions until they vanish inexplicably. A story of such a ghost has attached itself to the name of the 19th-century American novelist Nathaniel Hawthorne. As a regular visitor to a Boston club, Hawthorne frequently shared the reading room with members whom he knew by sight and by name, but with whom, as convention demanded, he never communicated. One such was a Dr. Harris, who often sat reading his paper in the chair next to Hawthorne's. Hawthorne returned one day from a journey and took his seat beside Harris in the reading room, with, as usual, not even a nod exchanged between them. Nothing seemed out of the ordinary—until later that day Hawthorne heard that Harris had died and been buried during his absence. For several days, Hawthorne saw Harris in his accustomed chair, and though he examined the figure carefully (but discreetly) he noticed nothing ghostly about its appearance. Harris looked perfectly normal. The ghost never appeared again; and Hawthorn always regretted that he had not spoken to it, or even touched it. But, he felt, how could he? They had never been properly introduced.

Over the years psychical researchers have been able to build up a fairly useful general picture of apparitions and their attributes. Perhaps Britain's G. N. M. Tyrrell provides the best picture with his description of "the perfect apparition," of which he writes (in his book *Apparitions*, 1953): "Each of its features rests on solid evidence; but they are not all to be found in any actual single case, although there are cases with a good many of them." And though exceptions can be found—even in Tyrrell's own book—the principles of the "perfect apparition" can be applied fairly readily to all apparitions, living or dead, though they cannot be applied so neatly to haunting apparitions in general. So before we turn to haunts as a class by themselves, here are the most important points of Tyrrell's description.

First of all, an apparition would seem as real, solid, and clear in every detail as a human being. The percipient would be able to hear the apparition breathing, and the scuffle of its shoes on the floor. (As a frequent exception to this point, many researchers report cases in which the apparitions seem to "glide" quite noiselessly.) The apparition might in turn seem aware of the percipient, turning its head, smiling, or even speaking, though seldom for long. In short, the apparition would succeed, as Tyrrell puts it, in perfectly *imitating* a human being. (As we shall see, haunts provide a number of exceptions to this "natural behavior" rule.)

Nevertheless the imitation is not wholly complete. For example, a percipient might feel a sensation of cold at the touch or approach of an apparition, and if he tried to grasp it, his hand would go through it. Tyrrell adds that in a few cases people have been able to touch and feel an apparition, but usually it avoids physical contact by disappearing. An apparition leaves no physical traces such as footprints, and, it seems, cannot be photographed or its sounds recorded on a tape. Sometimes it loses its lifelike character by appearing luminous or unnaturally clear at a distance. And after a while, an apparition will disappear, either suddenly or gradually.

Some qualifications can be added to this picture of an apparition. Sometimes only part of a person may appear—a pair of hands, say, or a head. And not all apparitions are human figures. There have been a few cases of apparitional animals, and even of inanimate objects: a phantom ship was seen by reliable witnesses in 1923. But folklore contains many more Black Dogs, spectral horses, and ghost trains, than do the files of psychical researchers.

And now haunts—the apparitions that are alleged to appear again and again in a particular place or locality, no matter who is watching. Here is where folklore and fancy really come into their own, partly because a reputation for being haunted has become something of a status symbol—especially in terms of the tourist trade. The British Travel and Holidays Association has recently compiled, as an enticement to visitors, a list of many hundreds of ghosts complete with histories and descriptions. (It seems to indicate that Britain's castles, churches, and manor houses have as many ghosts as mice. No wonder the modern French writer Cyrille de Neubourg has called Britain "the country of ghosts.") And so, while it may be difficult to shake the testimony of someone who swears he once saw his long-dead Uncle George walking in the garden, it is quite easy to dismiss the statement of an over-excited tourist who, primed by his guide-book, claims that he did see the White Lady that appears on the castle battlements at midnight.

Even so, the psychical researchers have managed to dig out

some general principles on haunts. They find that haunts are often former occupants of the haunted locale—usually those who died or underwent some crisis there. Some appear to re-enact their death or crisis: for instance, for many years a house in New Orleans, U.S.A., had a haunted roof on which during cold weather the ghost of a beautiful woman was said to appear, invariably nude, invariably shivering and huddled as if trying to keep warm. Tradition says she was the part-Negro mistress of a wealthy man who, for a joke, had asked her to prove her love by spending the coldest night of the year naked on the roof. She took it as a command, obeyed, and died.

The most ordinary kind of haunt is that which appears, walks along a given route, and disappears—like the spectral policeman, seen in Britain around the turn of this century, who regular patrolled part of a country road at night. In other cases, haunts simply appear, and do very little, much like other apparitions. But with two definite differences. One is obvious: haunts recur again and again, unlike other apparitions. The other difference has been alluded to before: the behavior of haunts in general is less "natural" than that of apparitions tied to the percipients; they go through their repetitive actions more like automatons than actors. For one thing, they pay little or no attention to observers—though a 19th-century British haunt tried to strangle a temporary resident of its house. For another, haunts' actions seem vague, even semi-conscious; a word often applied to them is "somnambulistic."

Tyrrell states that, while all apparitions are to some extent like somnambulists, haunts are more so. He adds that many sleepwalkers are able to recognize other people, and even to speak to them—though not for long, and usually in a somewhat disjointed, vague way. Living somnambulists, too, often appear quite purposeful, with a definite object in mind. And so do apparitions. Apparitions of the dead sometimes even seem anxious to get a message to the living. In the 1920s a North Carolina farmer who had hidden his will appeared after his death to one of his sons and directed him to the hiding place. In many cases apparitions are said to appear because the people vowed, before death, that they would "come back" afterward if they could—to prove survival. Haunts, too, are often said to appear because they were murdered, or killed themselves, and were buried improperly or not at all (a notion that has lasted for thousands of years, as we saw in

Chapter 2). Or, as in most fiction and much legend, some ghosts walk to avenge themselves or for similar melodramatic purposes.

We have by no means exhausted the subject of what ghosts can be like, but we now know in general what it is that people think they have seen when they say they have seen a ghost. Now the question "What have they *really* seen?" poses itself. There is no shortage of answers. Obviously, the skeptic's explanation is that every percipient, if he is not faking, is either fooling himself or is temporarily insane. An exponent of this view is the British writer D. H. Rawcliffe, the title of whose book—*Illusions and Delusions of the Supernatural and the Occult*—speaks for itself. The American psychologist Joseph Jastrow includes ghosts in what he regards as "a grotesquerie of deluded prepossession, a weakly rationalized, mainly self-hallucinated projection of fancy presented as facts." There is no need for further examples. Where the paranormal is concerned, skepticism flourishes. Its standpoint is unvarying: anyone who claims to have seen a ghost was deluded, dreaming, drunk, or deranged.

Firmly entrenched on the other side of the fence are the various subscribers to some branch of spiritualistic theory—those who believe not only in survival after death but in communication and visitation between this world and the next. Recently, some sophisticated explanations of apparitions have been offered by spiritualist writers—as for example the theory put forward in 1950 by the British writers Phoebe D. Payne and Lawrence J. Bendit in their book *This World and That*. They base their explanation of haunting apparitions on the idea of the *psychon*—apparently a particle of the mind shed in a haunted house that retains enough potential energy to generate a re-creation, or "memory picture," of the event.

Those people who wish neither to dismiss the whole subject of ghosts with a skeptical snort, nor to accept the spiritualist view in its entirety, may find a satisfactory explanation in psychology—or parapsychology. Freud, for instance, saw in the belief in ghosts a continuation of the primitive fear of the dead. In his paper on "The Uncanny" he wrote: "There is scarcely any other matter upon which our thoughts and feelings have changed so little since the very earliest times." And though modern civilized man may claim disbelief in ghosts, in most cases he has merely repressed rather than dispelled the primitive notions. They return readily when something happens to recall them—like the "mysterious recurrence of similar experiences in a particular place or on a particular date . . . deceptive sights and suspicious noises."

The idea of the unconscious mind as a receptacle for repressed feelings, memories, and wishes (which can emerge to affect conscious awareness and existence) provides a basis for Freud's view of ghosts—as it does for C. G. Jung's. But Jung sees the unconscious as being, besides this container for personal repressions, at bottom *collective*—containing the products of "innate forms and instincts" common to mankind. Where repressed contents of the personal unconscious may have been conscious at one time, the collective contents have never had any association with consciousness. Thus they are autonomous; they can appear in dreams or even be "projected into space" as visions or hallucinations; and because of their wholly unconscious origin, when the consciousness becomes aware of them they seem "strange, uncanny, and at the same time fascinating." Jung has written of one of his own strange experiences—as he calls it, a "haunting." One night at his house in Bollingen he awoke to hear music, talk, laughter, footsteps around the house, and seemed to see "a visual image" of many dark-clad figures. At this point he really awoke, and looked out of the window, of course seeing nothing. He had been dreaming; but he had in fact *dreamed of himself waking* and hearing the sounds.

Perhaps this experience might shed a different light on all those well-attested cases of apparitions that begin: "I woke to discover a figure standing beside my bed." But it would be wrong to leave Jung here, assuming that he dismissed apparitions as invariably explicable in terms of dreams or waking hallucinations. In later years he wrote: "I doubt if an exclusively psychological approach can do justice to the phenomena in question." In this subject as in others he refused to be dogmatic, asserting that the full nature of the human mind "reaches into obscurities far beyond the scope of our understanding."

Many years earlier another great pioneer psychologist had turned away from the purely psychological approach—which was (and still often is) to dismiss apparitions and similar phenomena as the emissions of disturbed minds—and chose instead to investigate the subject in terms of parapsychology and psychical research. This was the American psychologist William James. We shall see in Chapter 9 his importance in forming and directing societies for scientific psychical research. And he filled this role not as a fanatical believer in ghosts but as one who held the opinion that "so long as the stories multiply in different lands, and so few are positively explained away, it is bad method to ignore them."

Having worked closely with Myers and Gurney in establishing Britain's Society for Psychical Research, James seems to have shared their tendency to explain apparitions as *objective* hallucinations caused, as he puts it, by "the invisible segments of our minds [that is, the unconscious] . . . being acted upon by the invisible segments of other conscious lives." James's principal interest, in the field of parapsychology, was in mediumship; and here, too, he was convinced that the true medium (a rare creature) operates by means of some form of mind-to-mind, telepathic communication. Many psychical researchers besides James have turned to telepathy to explain the phenomena they investigate. But before going on to the variations of the telepathic theory of apparitions, a word about telepathy itself.

Briefly, a great deal of investigation has been done concerning telepathy and the allied subjects of clairvoyance and precognition by methodically scientific men like, notably, J. B. Rhine and his associates of America's Duke University. The results of the many experiments in extra-sensory perception (ESP), evaluated statistically, are claimed by many today as convincing evidence that man is telepathic. Others reject the evidence, perhaps asserting that the experimenters were too predisposed to findings that favored ESP. Controversy rages. Meanwhile telepathy has become, in the 1960s, a fairly respectable subject for scientific and academic research. American university institutes of parapsychology go on patiently setting up experiments, collecting and collating evidence. Both the U.S.A. and Russia have recently investigated ESP in connection with their space programs, possibly thinking of it as an easy means of communication between astronauts.

Most fair-minded commentators on the value of psychical research agree on two points: first, more facts are needed before sweeping conclusions can be drawn; second, the gathering of these facts is by no means a waste of scientific talent and time. And most of them would probably agree on a third point: that evidence accumulated so far shows that telepathy and clairvoyance *do exist*. But when this statement is made the qualification immediately follows that virtually nothing is yet known about ESP's origin, nature, and function. They seem to have proved that something is there without discovering what it is.

Whatever it is, it is a far cry from the infallible mind-reading of a stage conjuror or the instantaneous, controlled mental conversations between characters in a science-fiction novel. The ESP faculty that has shown itself in hundreds of experiments is extremely weak, and above all *unconscious*—which means that it is spontaneous, uncontrollable, unreliable. With these facts in mind, we can now look at some telepathic theories of apparitions.

During the 1880s both Myers and Gurney put forward the theories whose basic tenets have dominated psychical research thinking ever since. Myers stated (to simplify his theory) that the agent—the person whose apparition is seen—while undergoing some crisis, sends a telepathic message to the percipient, who embodies or exteriorizes the message in a form apparent to the senses. This idea may not seem to explain post-mortem apparitions or haunts, but then Myers offered it in the context of his "phantasms of the living." Yet even in these terms objections were raised, principally the great bugbear of all telepathy theories: the evidence that many apparitions are seen simultaneously by more than one person.

Gurney, sharing Myers's acceptance of telepathy, suggested that the agent gets his message to percipient A who then telepathically "infects" percipients B, C, and so on—so that they see the same thing. Myers countered with the idea that some apparitions (including those collectively perceived) are caused by the agent's effect not on the percipients' minds but on a *portion of space*. But most commentators, noting that Myers was trying to correlate his belief in the non-physical nature of apparitions with their invasion of physical space, saw confusion here rather than solution.

Tyrrell begins his explanation—one of the most influential—from the Myers-Gurney starting point of telepathic communication. First, he points out that we do not perceive our surroundings directly. Our eyes, for instance, register a "sense-datum" (a splotch of color with a definite shape) that our brain then translates into a perception (a familiar object of some sort). This may seem a philosophical quibble; but Tyrrell's point is that the process can be altered. One level of the mind (presumably the unconscious) can, under certain stimuli, impose sense-data on the sensory organs, which as usual the conscious mind translates into perceptions—or subjective hallucinations.

A subjective hallucination would occur (like the proverbial pink elephants of *delirium tremens*) when the mind and/or body provide the stimulus for the imposition of sense data on the senses. But when *another* mind, elsewhere, telepathically provides the stimulus the result is objective. And the telepathic process, to Tyrrell, works like this: the "mid-level constituents" of the agent's personality (which clearly exist, for Tyrrell, on an unconscious level of the mind) reach out and touch similar constituents in the percipient's mind, and the two minds interact to produce an objective hallucination. To put it another way, the agent's mind provides the stimulus (a telepathic "idea-pattern") for the percipient's mind to create a little scene (the "apparitional drama") of which his own consciousness is the startled audience. The point that the apparition rises out of the joint efforts of two minds explains its apparent awareness of surroundings; the point that the joint efforts take place on an unconscious or semi-conscious level explains the apparition's occasional lapses or "somnambulistic" behavior.

In terms of crisis apparitions Tyrrell makes it clear that the "idea pattern" that is telepathically projected has some definite connection, in the mind of the agent, with a conscious idea—the crisis. Tyrrell suggests that in the case of merely somnambulistic haunts there is a very tenuous connection, or none at all, between the mid-level idea pattern and a conscious idea—that the agent may be, so to speak, transmitting an unconscious memory or the like, which explains the haunt's lack of awareness of the percipients (in most cases) and its automaton-like repetition of a routine.

On the problem of collective percipience, Tyrrell argues that the apparition produced by the two conjoining minds of percipient and agent tries to do a good job of imitating normal behavior. So, if other people are awake in the room, then their minds, too, must be stimulated by the agent to produce the apparition. They see the apparition in order that it may seem as real as possible. Any failure by people who are present to see an apparition seen by another can be explained in the same way as can be lapses by some apparitions from "normal behavior": the telepathic connection between minds is not infallible; sometimes it is imperfect or erratic, or cannot be made at all.

But the investigators who reported on apparitions in 1956

for the International Project for Research on ESP Projection were not satisfied with Tyrrell's (or indeed anybody's) theory. The report itself is a near masterpiece: a full statistical breakdown of 165 cases involving apparitions of every kind, followed by a review (with comments) of the leading theories propounded—with special attention paid to Tyrrell. And finally the report proposes some starting points for a development of a new theory—one that would account without strain for all the available data.

First, the authors of the report ask us to suppose that every physical thing (humans, animals, and inanimate objects) has a non-physical counterpart—which they call an "etheric object." Etheric objects exist in "psychic space," but this can sometimes intersect physical space. A man's conscious awareness and action can function within the vehicle of his physical body *or* his etheric counterpart, and—most important—a man's etheric counterpart can be *projected* by means of ESP while carrying with it full consciousness. An etheric object such as an apparition, therefore, has some degree of objective reality—it is not a hallucination when perceived. And, the report stresses, only a theory that allows an apparition to be a semi-substantial reality (with an emphasis on "semi") can accommodate all the facts.

This brief summary may not have done the report justice, but it at least contains its major suggestions concerning the nature of apparitions and the role of ESP. One question, which has been omitted from the account of each theory so far, remains: do apparitions prove survival after death? Gurney said no: apparitions of the dead were telepathic messages sent by the agent at the point of death that had somehow been delayed. Tyrrell said yes: because apparitions of the dead generally differ only slightly, if at all, from those of the living, the agent must be assumed to be the same in each case. So he boldly asserted that telepathy could cross the gap between living and dead, and that a post-mortem apparition was created by telepathic cooperation between the mind of the living percipient and the surviving mind of the dead agent. In the same way, the "etheric-object" theory presupposes belief in ESP projection from the surviving dead.

One last word before we leave the subject of apparitions. No matter how else they disagree, all theorists have made the point that, while their explanations are based on all the available evidence, they are at best interim hypotheses. They emphasize that the need for further research and for the ac-

cumulation of more facts is far more important than the
creation and defense of theories. The subject, in other words,
is still wide open.

Apparitions are often heard and felt as well as seen; some
authorities in fact include under that general heading ghosts
that are *only* heard (for instance, recurring footsteps, music,
or shrieks) or only felt (such as blows or taps on the shoul-
der). So it is often hard to tell where such manifestations
stop being apparitions and become another familiar kind of
ghost—the *poltergeist*.

Poltergeists (the word is German for noisy ghost) have in
most cases a clearly distinguishing hallmark: they leave physical traces. The common poltergeist that throws objects
around a house leaves them where they fall, and thus provides evidence—of a sort. For example, in Calais in 1964 a
woman and her two children were driven out of their flat by
a series of frightening occurrences. Butter, tomatoes, and
eggs flew around the rooms, curtains and clothing were torn,
crockery and flower pots were smashed, and to cap it all the
toothpaste arose and drew crosses on the ceiling. Clearly the
resulting chaos remained for all to see, including presumably
the police and the journalists from the newspaper that reported the incident.

As the British poet Robert Graves said, writing on the subject in 1958, "poltergeists everywhere show an appalling
sameness of behavior; humourless, pointless, uncoordinated."
He might have said "anytime" as well, for poltergeists have a
long history. A case that reportedly occurred in A.D. 355, at
Bingen-am-Rhein, is said to be the oldest recorded example;
it consisted of the familiar stone-throwing, rapping, and people being dumped out of bed—and it was not surprisingly explained as the work of the Devil. History reveals sporadic
cases in every succeeding century, always on the same lines
and usually with the same explanation. (One interesting variation appeared in Pembrokeshire, Wales, in about 1190: the
stone-throwing poltergeist began to speak, and had a habit of
relating in public some of the more embarrassing episodes of
various citizens' lives.) No country has been free of them;
and in the 1960s the poltergeist is just as ubiquitous and just
as stereotyped.

Still, though poltergeists behave in much the same
way, within their limits they do achieve a certain variety of
effect. Their activities can range (sometimes even in one

case) from mild noises in the woodwork to violent but petty destructiveness, to downright dangerous hurling of heavy objects, knives, or scalding water—and even to the extreme of arson. The gentle poltergeist (more mischievous than malevolent) seems to be fairly common: this category would include oddities like the 55-gallon water barrel on a farm in Missouri that, in 1950, was mysteriously filled up every day for several months: or the somewhat suspect poltergeist that wrote on the walls and sang its own lyrics to pop songs in a house in Stow-on-the-Wold, Britain, in 1964. But besides these exceptional incidents, the mild poltergeist is often noisy and little else, making sounds like thumping footsteps, or ringing doorbells, or (especially) rapping and knocking. In fact, in 1848 a rapping poltergeist in a house in Hydesville, N.Y., inhabited by a family called Fox, was directly responsible for the birth of that remarkable movement called spiritualism. The story of the Fox sisters is told in detail in Chapter 4; as a preview to it, we should note that a great many spiritualist mediums receive their "spirit messages" by means of poltergeist-like raps, knocks, and furniture-lifting. And one little-known fact should be added: the house in Hydesville had been the scene of rappings and poltergeist phenomena *before* the Fox sisters moved in.

In most cases, poltergeists are not content with mere rapping and knocking but prefer noises like moving furniture, shattering crockery, and so on. Sometimes the objects are simply thrown around indiscriminately, as were the groceries (and especially the bicarbonate of soda) from the shelves of a British supermarket in 1962. But quite often the objects move more strangely, apparently in violation of all natural laws. The famous poltergeist that plagued a house in Seaford, Long Island, New York, in 1958—a case that was investigated by parapsychologists from Duke University—caused (among other things) bottles to slide slowly to the edge of a table and fall, in front of two most reliable witnesses.

Though poltergeists seem particularly fond of throwing objects like dishes, kitchenware, vases, and ornaments, they are not averse to shaking, overturning, or lifting heavier objects. In a case in Hartville, Missouri, in 1958, which was investigated by the American parapsychologist W. E. Cox, a heavy pail of water, a full washtub, and other sizable objects were among the missiles flung around the house (some of which Cox himself observed in action). In fact, according to Cox's "Comparative Analysis of Some Poltergeist Cases" (to which these pages owe a great deal), about a quarter of the cases he has studied have involved the movement of particularly heavy objects.

Some poltergeist violence, far from being erratic and aimless, seems to be directed toward specific members of the terrorized household—as, for instance, in the case of the so-called Phelps poltergeist that in 1850 haunted the Stratford, Connecticut, home of the Reverend E. Phelps. Here the activity was "attached to" the clergyman's 11-year-old son, whose clothes were ruined and who was once picked up by an "unseen power" and carried across a room. In 1926 a 13-year-old Romanian girl was repeatedly attacked by a biting poltergeist, which left (according to eye-witnesses) clear teeth marks on her flesh. The phenomena followed her to London, where she was taken for investigation by psychical researchers. In her case no permanent injury was caused; and only rarely do poltergeists actually harm people, in spite of the danger from heavy objects hurtling through the air. As an exception, several injuries were inflicted on a member of a poltergeist-ridden family in Sciacca, Sicily, in 1890; at one point the mother was knocked unconscious by a flying object. The poltergeist does not, on the other hand, flinch from the destruction of property, even going so far as to burn the house down. Several fires occurred, for instance, during the "great Amherst mystery"—the poltergeist that invaded a home in Amherst, Nova Scotia, in 1879.

So these are the most important of the poltergeist's characteristic activities. And, as with apparitions, the explanations offered are about as varied—and often as predictable—as the activities. First place goes to the skeptic's automatic cry of either "hallucination" or (more usually) "fraud." And the skeptic can make out quite a strong case. Often a poltergeist scare has grown out of a strange noise (not uncommon in old houses) that the household has termed a "haunt," thus planting the idea in the mind of someone—usually a disturbed child—who then provides all the violence that anyone could expect of a poltergeist. Undeniably, people are credulous enough to find poltergeist activity everywhere once they have come to expect it. And the skeptic's case is further strengthened by historical precedent: one of the great poltergeist cases—the Cock Lane mystery that had all London agog in the 18th century—was eventually proved more or less conclusively to have been produced by the daughter of the house, possibly encouraged by her father, who was enjoying some of the fruits of publicity.

The British psychical researcher Frank Podmore (an author of *Phantasms of the Living,* mentioned before) dismissed all poltergeists as trickery. "We have, speaking broadly, no good evidence for anything having been done which could not have been done by a girl or boy of slightly more than the average cunning and naughtiness." And he adds: "The peculiar difficulty of investigating the ordinary poltergeist is that the phenomena cannot as a rule be produced to order; and that any insistence on conditions or even betrayal of suspicion is liable to stop them altogether. . . . Actual exposure of the fraud practised becomes therefore extremely difficult."

Podmore was writing in 1902; since then, considerable further investigation has taken place. But before we come to that, a quick look at another explanation produced in 1955 by the British psychical researcher G. W. Lambert. In this theory the physical disturbances ascribed to poltergeists are explained painstakingly by the effects of tidal patterns, subterranean rivers, slight earth tremors, and so on. For instance, Lambert states that when the mouth of a subterranean river (where it discharges into the sea) is blocked by a high tide, pressure is created and the layers above the river forced upward, acting like a "hydraulic jack" on any houses that happen to be above it. So the houses' contents get shaken up. Lambert adds that about half of the poltergeist cases that he investigated occurred within three miles of tidal water. "It is not easy," he comments, "to account for that distribution on the basis of population density."

This summary has, of course, done more than injustice to the complexities of Lambert's "geophysical theory," and so it must be stressed that the details of the theory are worked out with care, precision, and objectivity. But it should also be added that in 1961 two equally painstaking authors, A. D. Cornell and Alan Gauld, cast some doubt on the applicability of Lambert's theory to more than a few poltergeist cases. As one example, the challengers point out that any tilting of a house great enough to cause a heavy chair to slide might also severely damage the house's structure (rare with poltergeists); and that many poltergeists cause only one object in a room to move, which seems unlikely to happen if the whole house was being shaken. Nevertheless, Lambert's ideas remain a sound method of separating phenomena that are caused naturally from those that are inexplicable.

In recent years some poltergeist cases have been investigated by professional parapsychologists, like Cox or J. G. Pratt, also of Duke University. And in many cases the experts have been present when certain phenomena occurred—as Cox was at Hartville—and so could verify with their own eyes that no trickery was afoot. At the same time they did not accept the belief that a poltergeist is an invisible spirit. Instead they noted the two most common and striking features of poltergeist cases—two features that are really one.

First, the violent activities of the poltergeist, invariably wanton, senseless, harassing, and annoying, are the kind of thing that an irresponsible, destructive, and possibly mentally disturbed *child* might do—in a hysterical rage, or for the malicious fun of it, or in order to draw attention to himself. Secondly, almost all poltergeist activity takes place in a house where there is a child or an adolescent. Usually the child is a girl at the age of puberty who is in some way psychologically disturbed—perhaps mentally deficient, or perhaps exceptionally intelligent, but at least showing symptoms of hysteria and nervous malaise, which are not uncommon during early adolescence.

Clearly the implication is that the disturbed child causes the phenomena. And most experts will admit that often the child does so as a conscious fraud. Or that the child creates the effects unknowingly—perhaps while in a hysterical state followed by amnesia, or perhaps while sleepwalking. But, still, there are those uncomfortable cases where the child in question (at Hartville again, for instance, where there was a young girl) was under close observation by an unimpeachable witness when the phenomena occurred. Other cases include phenomena—like the hurling of heavy objects—that a child could not physically have caused. How, then, does it happen?

The answer most often offered is that some form of that intangible mental force called "telekinesis" (or "psychokinesis") was in action—that the maladjusted child had, unconsciously, the power to move physical objects with his or her mind—"as though," Tyrrell writes, "a certain subconscious level of the personality, of a sub-intelligent character, may be able to express itself by exercising a physical force of an unknown kind which is dependent on an abnormal physiological condition." Psychokinesis (usually shortened to PK) has, like telepathy, been studied in this century in quite respectable institutions, again notably by J. B. Rhine. The results of Rhine's famous tests with dice, begun in the 1930s, seemed to show that there was some basis for the long-standing myth among gamblers that they could "will" the dice to fall a certain way. The results were immediately claimed by many as proof of the power of "mind over matter," but a careful look at Rhine's methods seemed to uncover some flaws in the experiments—for instance, a failure to consider the nature of the dice. Many dice are made by slightly hollowing out the spots, making the "six" side minutely lighter than the "one"—a difference that, over the vast number of tests that Rhine held, might account for the thrower's achievement of a score slightly higher than that which chance should produce.

But then followers of Rhine in America and elsewhere instituted new tests, again usually with dice, but with better safeguards. And some surprising results emerged. First, evidence began to accumulate (involving a great deal of complicated statistical analysis) that was difficult to explain without accepting some form of PK hypothesis. Secondly, even if the British psychologist and parapsychologist R. H. Thouless is right in asserting that "evidence for the reality of the PK effect is strong," PK itself appears to be even more unreliable than telepathy—and evidence from experiments seems to show that it fails when directed at anything but dice. Nevertheless, there it is. Many hard-headed psychologists admit that psychokinesis is the best explanation they can find for those dice coming up "above chance." But it is still a long step from stopping a pair of dice on a certain side to lifting a heavy table off the floor. Perhaps it could be suggested that poltergeist PK, like apparitional telepathy, works unconsciously. But at the moment, as far as explanations of any kind of ghost are concerned, it is safest to echo Sacheverell Sitwell: "What, by all the powers of good and evil, are these sights and sounds! No one can tell. It is still, and may ever be, a mystery."

Not everyone who has been the victim of a ghost, of one kind or another, has been satisfied with merely having it investigated and explained, however convincingly. They might also want to get rid of it. Perhaps they might attempt to drive away—or "lay"—the ghost themselves, using the do-it-yourself processes supplied by folklore. A fair sample of amateur ghost-laying methods can be found in the old beliefs and legends of Brittany. Ghosts there are thought, for exam-

ple, to be powerless against three people together who have
been baptized, or against anyone carrying work implements.
In one legend a ghostly priest who haunted a chapel in
Bourg-de-Batz, celebrating a mass each year, was finally laid
to rest when a courageous man attended the spectral service
and gave the responses; apparently this was what the ghost
had been waiting for. Some legends echo the maxim about an
ounce of prevention: a cross should be erected near the scene
of a fatal accident to prevent a ghost's returning; victims of
an assassin are said to walk until the assassin has met his end,
but can be prevented from haunting if the shoes they wore
when they died are buried with them.

And so on. Folklore is always with us—even in its most
primitive forms. We saw in Chapter 2 that most primitive
peoples placate ghosts with offerings of food; and still in the
early 20th century, in suburban Ilford, England, a woman
tried to appease a poltergeist by leaving some food and a bottle of beer on a table overnight. And, just as the primitives
turned to their witchdoctors and shamans for help in the
case of a stubborn ghost, so today many people who believe
themselves haunted turn to organized religion and its representatives. Sometimes a layman's prayers, or the sign of the
cross, will apparently be enough to discourage the ghost. But
often the case requires the assistance of a clergyman and the
ceremony known as exorcism.

Throughout history exorcism has been used by every religion to drive out evil spirits and demons that have possessed
humans. And in the past, as we have seen, haunts and poltergeists were seldom differentiated from demonic activity. So
they were exorcized. During the witch-hunt hysteria that in-
fected all Europe during the Middle Ages and after, many
priests devoted all their time and efforts to exorcisms. Since
then the demand for this service has died down—but not out.
In recent years there seems to have been something of an
upswing—enough of one, in Britain anyway, to cause the
1960 Church of England Assembly to order vicars and cu-
rates to refrain from exorcism without their bishops' permission.

Today the only established form of exorcism is that found
in the Rituale Romanum—a book of services to be used by
Roman Catholic priests. So the Protestant churches have had
to improvise. Some of the formulas evolved (often by clergy
who have studied the occult) invoke the Trinity and the
Cross and command the ghost or evil spirit to "depart into

outer darkness." But a London vicar uses a gentler form of words, telling the ghost to "depart into the realm of light instead of into outer darkness, from which the pathway of return is long and painful." And still others feel that simple prayer is quite sufficient. Father Thurston, the Jesuit expert on poltergeists, points out that the Catholic ritual is designed not to drive haunts out of houses but to drive devils out of people. Nevertheless, the Rituale Romanum does contain ceremonies for blessing and consecrating a particular spot—and cleansing it from evil influences—and this might be used for a haunted house. But Father Thurston adds that he discovered an exorcism formula employed in the 17th century by the Spanish Inquisition that was designed for places rather than people. In full it is lengthy; but its core is a powerful adjuration that is worth quoting alone:

"I adjure thee, O serpent of old, by the Judge of the living and the dead; by the Creator of the world who hath power to cast into hell, that thou depart forthwith from this house. He that commands thee, accursed demon, is He that commanded the winds, and the sea and the storm. He that commands thee, is He that ordered thee to be hurled down from the height of heaven into the lower parts of the earth. He that commands thee is He that bade thee depart from Him. Hearken, then, Satan, and fear. Get thee gone, vanquished and cowed, when thou art bidden in the name of our Lord Jesus Christ who will come to judge the living and the dead and all the world by fire. Amen."

Incidentally, exorcism apparently does not always work. In 1963 poltergeist activity at Leigh, England, ignored the efforts of the local vicar; though it was reported that the singing of hymns brought temporary peace. And a poltergeist at Coonian, Ireland, reported by the Irish ghost hunter Sir Shane Leslie in 1914, not only ignored the exorcising priests but actually drove them and the family out of the house. Leslie adds that the priests got far the worst of the encounter: "One had a nervous breakdown, another spinal meningitis, and the third facial paralysis."

Many people plagued by ghosts, instead of calling in the exorcising clergyman, turn to the professional ghost hunter or the scientific psychical researcher. These are not much concerned with laying ghosts; their interest is in investigating ghosts—or adding the case to their collection and writing an article or book about it. One well-known modern American collector, Dr. Louis C. Jones of Cooperstown, N.Y., has over

700 case histories in his files—and once pointed out that only about 10 per cent were of malevolent ghosts. Another American ghost hunter, Hans Holzer, suggests that ghosts are surviving mental faculties of people who died traumatically, and that they can be laid by being in a sense "psychoanalyzed." France, according to Cyrille de Neubourg, has no professional ghost hunters; there the people simply call the police. In 1951 a French police commandant, E. Tizané, published a book entitled *On the Trail of the Unknown Man* that described over 400 investigated cases of allegedly haunted houses.

Britain, being the country of ghosts, has ghost hunters galore—among whom are the members of the Ghost Club, founded in 1862 as an amateur organization devoted to the study of paranormal phenomena. The Club primarily sponsors lectures and discussions, but occasionally it sets out on an expedition to visit, say, a haunted stately home. Another group in Sussex goes ghost hunting armed with every kind of detecting device known to modern technology: microphones, cameras, even radar,—and several ingenious ways of detecting human intervention as well. And Britain can also boast the most internationally famous ghost hunter of them all—Harry Price.

Price, who died in 1948, had been a ghost hunter for 40 years and in that time had built up quite an organization. He began his career with a youthful interest in conjurors, stage hypnotists, fair-ground mediums, and similar professionals. Fairly early he developed considerable expertise as a conjuror himself, though he never performed on the stage. Instead, he used his conjuring skill in the investigations that first made his name in psychical research—the investigations and exposure of fraudulent mediums who used sleight of hand to produce their spirit noises and materializations. In 1926 he opened, under his own direction, the National Laboratory for Psychical Research, through which he devoted himself to the study of mediumship—and to examining reports in newspapers and magazines. He was becoming known as an authority on psychical matters; he then extended his reputation around 1930 by his lengthy investigations of the Austrian medium Rudi Schneider. International interest focused on Price and Schneider, for both had gained considerable fame by the time they met. After several séances, Price announced that Schneider was genuine; but in 1932 he claimed to have discovered trickery in another séance. Controversy sprang up immediately, enhancing public interest in the matter; Price was said, even by associates in his laboratory, to have made unfair and misleading accusations. Others charged him with publicity seeking. The question was never satisfactorily solved, but Harry Price had made his name as a psychical researcher.

Price's investigatory technique was usually fairly simple. Although his National Laboratory was well stocked with apparatus and gadgets—cameras, microscopes, X-ray equipment, thermometers, stop watches, and exotica like "luminous plaques" for use in séances—in most of his ghost hunts he relied on his own observation. It was enough, if psychic phenomena occurred, to be an on-the-spot eye-witness—and, of course, to guard against fraud by, for instance, scattering powder on a floor and sealing doors and windows of a room with thread or adhesive tape.

It was through his investigations and publications on the notorious case of Borley Rectory—which he called "the most haunted house in England"—that Price achieved his greatest fame. He had investigated many ghosts and poltergeists before Borley, but never had he had the chance, as it seemed, to investigate practically every form of paranormal phenomenon under one roof. The rectory was then a decrepit, rambling 19th-century house in Suffolk with a considerable amount of ghostly legend attached to it before Price ever heard of it. Legend said the rectory was built on the site of an ancient monastery, from which developed a story of a ghostly nun—who, along with black shapes and a spectral coach, was duly seen many times during the late 19th and early 20th centuries. (Later the monastery idea was proved false.) The ghost of the Rev. H. Bull, who had built the rectory in the 1860s, was also said to haunt the place. Finally, in 1929 "queer happenings" were reported in a newspaper, and Harry Price was asked to investigate.

Price went to Borley, and the happenings became queerer. For instance, in none of the local gossip and legend had there been any mention of a poltergeist; yet full-scale poltergeist activity started up on Price's arrival—bells ringing, stones flying, and so on. Things got so bad that the rector, Eric Smith, gave up and left; 14 months later, in 1930, a new incumbent moved in, an elderly man maned Foyster, with a young and attractive wife. Things got worse. No day or night went by without some violent phenomena, as well as more developments like ghostly writing on the walls. Various phantoms appeared, including the nun, a headless man, a coach and horses, a black hand, and a girl in white. In 1935 the Foysters left; and the rectory lay fallow (but not quiet) until 1937, when Price rented it. He lived there studying the unabated phenomena—and writing about them—until 1938. In 1939 the rectory was burned to the ground, but without deterring the ghosts. Later the foundations were torn up to leave no trace of the old building.

Price then compiled his famous books, *The Most Haunted House in England* and *The End of Borley Rectory,* using data gathered from the residents, from his own experiences, and from a corps of amateur investigators that he had recruited by advertising in a newspaper. Not even the war diminished public interest in the story; and Price was hailed as the greatest, most fearless, and most thorough ghost hunter in the world. But the story didn't end there. Price had made a few enemies, partly because some of his techniques were somewhat unorthodox, partly because of his apparently insatiable hunger for publicity. The S.P.R. was among those who frowned on Price for fear that his often popular-journalist approach and occasional lapses into sensationalism would bring scientific psychical research into disrepute. And it was under the auspices of the S.P.R.'s journal that three experts produced a careful analysis of the Borley case that seemed to shatter the legend built up by Price.

Unfortunately, the three authors— E. J. Dingwall, K. M. Goldney, and T. H. Hall—produced their study after Price's death, when he could no longer reply. And so the mystery has never finally been cleared up. But the three authors indicated, in a meticulous, scholarly way, that doubt could be cast on about 90 per cent of Price's evidence—and that Price himself may have created some of the phenomena to make a good story. To select just a few points from the structure of facts that they erected: none of the investigators Price collected was knowledgeable about psychic matters, and all had been thoroughly primed with suggestions of what to expect; Price's notes and reports, when compared with the published material, showed that Price had suppressed some facts and distorted others toward sensationalism; acoustic tests on the rectory indicated that most of the auditory phenomena could be attributed to natural causes; the poltergeist activity during the Foyster incumbency centered around young Mrs. Foyster, who hated the uncomfortable and isolated rectory and wanted to move; she was almost never in view while the phenomena were occurring. There is, of course, much more. Not all of the trio's suggestions and innuendoes add up as conclusively as their case against Mrs. Foyster; but one is left with the overall impression that a reasonable doubt was cast on most of the occurrences—which make them all seem to some extent suspect.

A reasonable doubt is in most cases quite enough to make the academic researchers of the Society for Psychical Research discard the case as unproved. In Chapter 9 we shall deal further with organizations for psychical research in Britain, America, and Europe today. But it is worth indicating here the kind of precautions that an S.P.R. investigator would take when on a ghost hunt—precautions against fraud, and against his own possible vitiation of the investigation by lack of scientific detachment and objectivity.

The precautions are outlined in an S.P.R. pamphlet entitled "Notes for Investigators of Spontaneous Cases." After noting various classifications of phenomena that the investigator must distinguish between, and offering a few hints as to the kind of tact and diplomacy required in interviewing percipients, the pamphlet makes its major point: beware of distortion by imaginative additions or exaggerations or imposed interpretations after the event. So the "Notes" insist that percipient and witnesses should immediately write down their observations. As a bad example, most experts quote the world-famous "adventure" of the Englishwomen Miss Moberly and Miss Jourdain, who in 1901, during a visit to the Petit Trianon at Versailles, saw apparitional 18th-century scenes and people, including Marie Antoinette. This may be an even more famous ghost story than Borley; it is just as controversial. But perhaps the controversy would be less hot if the ladies had not written down their observations for the first time some *nine years* after the event.

When all the immediate, first-hand, and detailed evidence has been gathered and sifted, the expert investigator tries to find in it a "significant pattern" (and usually tries to relate the case to others of its kind). Also necessary are a knowledge of the percipient's state of mind at the time, of his previous attitudes to such phenomena, of his health (especially eyesight in cases of apparitions), and so on. Again, tact and patience are prerequisites. These qualities are also stressed in the description of an ideal researcher given by the British psychical researcher Hereward Carrington. As examples of other qualifications offered by Carrington: a grounding in normal and abnormal psychology; keen powers of observation; training in sleight of hand; shrewdness, resource, and a sense of humor; an the ability to withstand bigotry, whether scientific or religious.

With these stringent requirements, it is not surprising that investigators as well as witnesses often lose their objectivity and ruin a case's value as evidence. Many once-accepted cases (like the lengthy haunting of a house in Cheltenham, England, in the 1880s, called the "Morton case," or the supposed poltergeist activity in the home of John Wesley during the 18th century) have now largely been discredited due to flaws detected in the witnesses' testimony. Some psychical researchers have hinted that almost always some doubt can be cast on the witnesses' veracity; but they add that, even though one might question every case separately, one has (as Immanuel Kant said of ghost stories) "some belief in them all taken together."

At any rate, the need for a great deal more reliable evidence is the most pressing problem facing psychical research today. Most researchers feel the surface has barely been scratched, and that the theories they have built up have been erected on an insufficient foundation of fact. Thus the serious researchers are not primarily interested in convincing the public that ghosts exist; their main objective is to prove that their researches are worthwhile. Undoubtedly they receive more acceptance today than a generation ago; undoubtedly, also, they have a long way to go. In the meantime, as far as belief in ghosts is concerned, one can only endorse the attitude of M. R. James, with whom this chapter began. In the introduction to his *Collected Ghost Stories* James writes: "Do I believe in ghosts? . . . I answer that I am prepared to consider evidence and accept it if it satisfies me." Who could do more?

4 VOICES OF THE DEAD

Just over a century ago a movement began in America founded, basically, on a belief in life after death. Spiritualism—as the movement came to be called—is convinced that it demonstrates that the soul survives the death of the body and that communication between living and dead can and does take place. This belief has been wholeheartedly embraced by countless people all over the world—in part, it can be assumed, because of the hope and comfort that it offers to the lonely and the bereaved. For in spiritualist belief, the emphasis is on light, joy, hope, and solace; the dark places of the soul are rarely paraded. In the words of a pamphlet produced by Britain's Psychic Press—a publishing company that specializes in spiritualism and in other allied subjects:

"The dead come back to guide, help, cheer, sustain and inspire us with glad tidings of another life, where injustice is redressed, where rank and station no longer hold sway, where mankind is given a second chance. And so they come back, not a privileged faithful few of the orthodox, not the haloed saints, but human beings, men and women of all colours, classes, races, of all creeds or none."

Spiritualists believe that the natural, visible universe has a supernatural, spiritual counterpart that exists beyond it and is inhabited by the disembodied spirits of men. As well as his earthly body, every living person has an etheric body, or double. This double, which is normally invisible (and, incidentally, is said by some to weigh approximately two and a half

77

pounds), is linked to the physical body by a cord. Sometimes the etheric may leave the physical body temporarily—a phenomenon (known as "astral traveling") that is said to occur particularly at times of crisis. But normally the etheric is separated from the physical body only when the cord is finally cut. For the physical body, this is the moment of death. For the etheric, which lives on as a spirit, it is merely the moment of parting from material things. Though death does not change the character and personality of the individual, there is no longer the same need for food, sleep, or exercise. At first, spirits often cling to old habits: for example, they tend to wear replicas of their earthly clothes. Later they discard these for more comfortable "spirit robes."

The spirit world is conceived as having its own hierarchy—an ascending scale of successive states, or spheres, of consciousness that form layers above the earth, with the higher spheres invisible to the lower. Nearest the earth are the spirits that are still earthbound because of old attachments, habits, or ignorance of their state. These spirits are said to be responsible for haunts, and spiritualists sometimes organize "rescue circles" to help them to an easier place. Spirits who bring news to the living of friends and relatives who have "passed on" also exist in a sphere near to earth, and know little more of conditions in the spheres above them than we do. Farthest away from earth are the celestial spheres—worlds of light and harmony inhabited by beings spiritually far in advance of earthly consciousness. One of these spheres is called "Summerland"; to judge from descriptions received in séances, it is a blissful place with all life's pleasures and none of its drawbacks.

Information about life in the spirit world is always communicated to the living through a *medium*—conventionally a woman, though in practice just as likely to be a man. The medium, the central figure in all spiritualist activity, seems to be rather like a human radio receiver. To borrow again from a Psychic Press pamphlet: "Mediums register the subtle and delicate vibrations of the spirit world which is round and about us."

Most mediums can be fitted into one of two distinct categories. The first—and by far the larger—comprises mediums who produce only what may be called *mental* phenomena. Usually operating in trance, they "hear" or "see" the spirits (by what is called clairaudience or clairvoyance) or produce written messages from them; or they may be healers, who are guided to detect the presence of disease, and perhaps to cure it. In the smaller, second category—which is far more open to charges of conscious fraud—are the mediums in whose presence the full repertoire of *physical* phenomena occurs—knocks, lights, sounds, shaking, rushing winds, levitation, and spirit materializations.

None of this is new. The Witch of Endor, when (in the Old Testament story of King Saul) she called up the spirit of the prophet Samuel, was acting as a medium. The ancient Greeks were in constant communication with the spirit world through their oracles. And evidence suggests that during the early days of the Church, trance speaking by the faithful was commonplace. Tertullian, one of the early Latin Church Fathers, writing toward the end of the first century, describes the activities of a trance speaker in terms that might well be applied to many modern mediums:

"There is a sister amongst us who possesses the faculty of revelation. She commonly, during our religious service on the Sabbath, falls into a crisis or trance. She has then intercourse with the angels . . . hears divine mysteries, and discovers the hearts of some persons; and administers medicines to such as desire it; and when the Scriptures are read, or psalms are being sung, or prayers offered up, subjects from thence are ministers to her visions."

Similar phenomena have occurred all over the world. Practices very like spiritualist séances have been reported among the people of Haiti and among North American Indians. One of the founders of Britain's S.P.R., Andrew Lang, described (in 1894) a Maori séance in New Zealand at which a "medium" sat in a dark corner, became entranced, and in the voice of a dead chief revealed the hiding place of the dead man's lost journal. Many spiritualists claim that Joan of Arc when she heard her "voices" was in that sense a medium. The Middle Ages teemed with manifestations of spirits of quasi-human form; probably many of those who were then persecuted as witches would now be practicing as mediums. In fact, instances of some form of communication with the dead through prophet, priest, or oracle can be found in the records of almost every religion from the shamanistic cults of northern Asia to the Shinto beliefs of Japan.

In its modern form, this belief in survival and communication after death has become the keystone of a worldwide movement claiming millions of followers. Every Sunday evening in Britain, for example, about a quarter of a million people attend spiritualist meetings. In London alone there are three large spiritualist organizations as well as scores of small societies and groups. In 1963 over 8000 visitors went to the Spiritualist Association of Great Britain for séances and spirit healing. Spiritualism still has a large following in America too. In 1956 *The American Journal* stated that there were about 150,000 spiritualists in the U.S.A. and a prominent medium estimated recently that there were at least 500 practicing mediums in New York. The number of French spiritualists has been set even higher, at 200,000.

In Brazil a variant form of spiritualism enjoys great popularity. According to the official 1950 census, some 900,000 Brazilians declared themselves to be "spiritists"; today it is estimated that the figure is nearer to 10 million. Spiritualism in Brazil is compounded of elements from the religious beliefs of slaves transported from Africa in the 19th century and the principles propounded by Allan Kardec, the French authority on spiritualism (see page 84). What is more, its existence is officially endorsed: in 1957 the Brazilian Government issued five million stamps portraying Kardec with the legend: "Brazil—Correio—1957—1st Centenary of Organized Spiritism." There are nearly 200 spiritualist societies in the country; Kardecian spiritists maintain schools, hospitals, clinics, and a large variety of social services. Physicians in the hospitals are said to be selected by spirits. Trained mediums are employed as assistants to the doctors who run the hospitals and clinics: their diagnoses, often startlingly accurate, are confirmed by standard methods like X-ray and laboratory tests.

Yet spiritualism as an organized *movement*, for all its present-day size, is comparatively young, since it came into existence only in the middle of the last century. At first sight, this sudden upsurge of interest in non-material spirits might seem surprising in an age generally thought to have been dominated by skeptical and materialist thinking. But perhaps it is not so surprising, if one sees the sudden birth and spread of spiritualism as examples of the deep-rooted belief in the "irrational" that always seems to flourish privately—as a sort of inevitable counterweight—in any period that places a heavy public emphasis on the material and the rational. For spiritualism emerged at a time when the workers were beginning to hope for a better life on earth; when the British evolutionary theorists Darwin and Huxley were disseminating powerful rational ideas about the here-and-now; and when the authority and teaching of the Church (which had always successfully struck a balance between things spiritual and temporal) was suffering serious challenges from the scientists. In fact, it was 1848, the year of the democratic revolutions that attempted to introduce a heaven on earth in the Old World of Europe, that saw the formal beginnings of the spiritualist movement in the New World of America.

Europe, though, had paved the way. In Sweden in the mid 18th century the philosopher-scientist Emanuel Swedenborg developed, at the age of 55, extraordinary psychic abilities. Swedenborg claimed to have communicated with spirits and—while never losing his grasp on the affairs of this world—made supernatural journeys to the next, and reported what he had experienced. Once, while dining with friends (who verified the incident), he "saw" a fire 300 miles away in Stockholm at the exact moment that it happened.

A few years after Swedenborg's death in 1772, the Austrian physician Friedrich Anton Mesmer was gaining enormous fame in the drawing-rooms of fashionable Paris by carrying out a series of astonishing cures. Mesmer attributed his healing powers to "animal magnetism"—a mysterious curative force similar to the magnetic property found in minerals. During Mesmer's demonstrations, patients crowded around a tub, from which protruded iron rods. Those in the front row, touching the rods, kept in contact with those behind by holding hands or moistened cords. Mesmer, in a delicately colored silk robe, walked around majestically with an iron wand in his hand. Tunes were played on a piano. Almost all the patients went into trances, convulsions, or some sort of ecstasy. Not only were many patients cured; often they read the magnetizers' thoughts, found hidden objects, and predicted the future.

Meanwhile, such trance activities were being initiated in America by similar "mesmeric" healers. The best known of these was Andrew Jackson Davis, known as the "Seer of Poughkeepsie," who claimed in 1844 that Swedenborg had appeared to him in a trance and had told him he had a mission to mankind. Three years later, at the age of 21, Davis was living in luxury in New York on the proceeds of his mesmeric healing, and had written (in trance) a book called The Principles of Nature, describing the spiritual and physical workings of the universe.

All this prepared the ground for the spiritualist movement. The final impetus for its launching was provided by a series of events that took place a year after the publication of Dav-

is's book—events that, because of their consequences, are
worth looking at in some detail.

In 1848, a family called Fox was living in a small tumble-
down house in a village called Hydesville, in Wayne County,
New York. The Fox parents were Methodists, and at the time
had been living in the house for a year with their youngest
daughters, Margaret, aged 15, and Kate, 12. As was pointed
out in Chapter 3, the house already had the reputation of
being haunted. The previous tenant had heard rappings and
bangs—and so did the Fox family. Sometimes the noises
were simply knocks; at other times they sounded like heavy
furniture being moved. The children were so frightened that
they insisted on sleeping in the same room as their parents.
This is how Mrs. Fox described one incident in an affidavit
sworn after all the fuss and fame began:

"On Friday night, March 31, 1848, . . . it commenced as
usual. I knew it from all the other noises I had ever heard
before. The children, who slept in the other bed in the room,
heard the rappings, and tried to make similar sounds by snap-
ping their fingers. My youngest child said: 'Mr. Splitfoot, do
as I do,' clapping her hands. The sounds instantly followed
her with the same number of raps. When she stopped the
sound ceased for a short time. Then Margaret said, in sport,
'Now, do just as I do: Count one, two, three, four,' striking
one hand against the other at the same time; the raps came as
before. . . . I then thought I could put a test that no-one in
the place could answer. I asked the noise to rap my different
children's ages, successively. Instantly each one of my children's ages was given correctly, pausing between them sufficiently long to individualize them until the seventh, at which
a longer pause was made, and then three more emphatic raps
were given, corresponding to the age of the little one that
died. . . . I then asked: "Is this a human being that answers
my questions . . . ?' There was no rap. . . . 'Is it a spirit? If
it is, make two raps.' The sounds were given as soon as the
request was made."

After a while, the Foxes and their visitors evolved a code:
a certain number of raps for each letter of the alphabet and
for yes and no. Using this code, the invisible rapper claimed
to be the spirit of a murdered man who had been buried in
the house. He gave them his name and the name of his murderer as well. Later, human bones were unearthed in the cellar, although the complete skeleton was not found until further excavations were made in 1904. A tin box was also

found with the skeleton. This fitted in with the spirit's story of a pedlar's visit to the house and subsequent murder—a visit that was confirmed by a maid who had lived in the house before the Foxes' arrival.

But on most points of the story—as in many reports of spiritualist phenomena—it is impossible to separate objective fact from subjective coloration. In 1855 both Kate and Margaret Fox confessed in public that they had made the rap themselves by cracking their toejoints. Later they withdrew their "confession," and said they had been bribed to make an untrue statement.

Yet despite the doubt that surrounded their testimony, the Fox sisters soon had their imitators. The word "spiritualism" was coined—it was called "spiritism" in most of Europe—and the movement snowballed. In 1852, only four years after the Hydesville rappings, the movement held its first gigantic convention at Cleveland, Ohio, and petitioned the American Senate for scientific recognition. Many newspapers hailed spiritualism as a "religious and social revolution," the beginning of a new era in the history of the world. The owner and editor of the *New York Tribune,* Horace Greeley, helped enormously to publicize the movement; the Foxes even lived in his house for a while. People started to receive messages from their dead relatives. Mediums found themselves speaking in strange languages; for example, the daughter of the President of the Senate, Judge Edmunds, was said to have spoken (while in trance) in Greek, Polish, Spanish, Latin, Portuguese, Hungarian, and several Indian tongues. Some, claiming to be controlled by the spirits of dead composers, gave masterly performances on instruments that they could barely play in normal circumstances. Mediums became social assets. In America, the Fox sisters were the most popular guests, and it was the ambition of many to entertain Mrs. Fox and her three daughters—three because the spirits had manifested themselves to a third, married sister.

The contagion spread from America to England, France and Germany. Mediums were discovered in their thousands, and séances were held as frequently as tea parties. The language of the spirits grew in scope. They no longer simply replied yes and no, or composed sentences by making raps for each letter of the alphabet. Pencils were tied to table legs, and the spirits wrote for themselves. The *planchette* was invented in France: a small board holding a pencil rested on castors, which, with the medium's hand placed lightly on it, would write spirit messages or draw spirit pictures.

In France, spiritualism spread quickly, largely popularized by the writings of Allan Kardec. Kardec, whose real name was H. O. Rivail, founded in 1856 the *Revue Spirite*, which still thrives today. He also wrote, at the "dictation" of spirits *The Book of Spirits*—a handbook that is still a standard work on spiritualist doctrine. In Germany, spiritualism caught on more slowly than it did in France, but in the 1850s there was a fair amount of table-turning and rapping in Berlin. Over the years it took root in other countries: for example, it was introduced to the Turks by an American visitor to Constantinople in 1858. The feverish spirit activity of this period is summed up by the modern French writer and psychical researcher René Sudre in these words:

"They [the spirits] gave . . . various messages, from cooking recipes to the most lofty reflections on the immortality of the soul and the beneficence of providence. Joan of Arc and Napoleon graciously condescended to manifest themselves. There were solemn spirits and facetious ones; there were even obscene ones. These last were evil spirits from low spheres. . . ."

Of the thousands of mediums who flourished in the second half of the 19th century, the most celebrated was the Scotsman Daniel Dunglas Home, who claimed that his father was the illegitimate son of the 10th Earl of Home. Like Davis before him, Home's activities as a medium started early, in 1850, when he was only 17. Home's career began in America, and continued in England and the Continent, where he lived almost entirely on the patronage of rich and distinguished clients who, at the height of his success, even included the emperor of France and the Russian tsar. Home's feats were often spectacular: he could reputedly elongate his body by 11 inches, levitate himself, and float around the room below the ceiling. On one famous occasion, in 1868, in the presence of Lord Adare and the Master of Lindsay, he is said to have floated out of one window and in again at another.

As widely famous as Home's levitations were the feats of a young illiterate peasant girl named Eusapia Palladino, who was born in 1854. She, like Home, achieved international fame. Heavy objects floated at her glance or gesture; extra "limbs" extruded from her body and moved objects in the room while she herself was bound to a chair. These phenomena took place in the presence of some of the most celebrated psychical researchers of the day, including the Director of Milan Observatory, Professor Schiaparelli.

Few mediums today achieve the fame of Home or Palladino. But in almost any country there is a group of mediums with a high reputation. Mrs. Eileen Garrett, for example, the president of America's Parapsychology Foundation, is deeply respected. As the promotor of numerous academic conferences and impartial inquiries, she reflects the modern, experimental approach to spiritualist phenomena—which includes investigations using hypnosis and drugs such as mescalin and lysergic acid (LSD). She is both articulate and analytical about the possible nature of her psychic gifts.

Not everyone, of course, is confident of spiritualism's efficiency or value. Dr. D. J. West, in his *Psychical Research Today* (1954), writes:

"Spiritualism thrives on simple souls. The average small Spiritualist service has all the crudity of meetings of any fundamentalist sect. Middle-aged women make up the bulk of the audience. After the set number of hymns, they settle down to the address and clairvoyance given by the visiting medium, who pours out a stream of verbiage about vibrations of harmony, astral bodies, attuning with the Godhead, or whatever else may be the patter of the moment. She begs her hearers to make themselves receptive to the loved ones on the other side, who are waiting to communicate. . . . Nothing could be more pathetic or boring."

This is only one possible view (and an unsympathetic one), since it is hard to generalize about spiritualist meetings, which differ enormously in size and quality. The word séance simply means "sitting" in French, and there are few hard-and-fast rules on how proceedings should be conducted. Any number of people may be present: sittings of more than 20 have been reported, but the usual number is six or seven. Séance rooms generally contain small tables, suitable for tilting, and also a "cabinet"—usually a corner curtained off from the room—from which the spirit forms materialize. Sometimes trumpets are blown or moved (often they are marked with luminous paint so that their movement can be seen) and a tambourine shaken.

Séances at which physical phenomena are produced usually take place in darkness or in a room lit at most by a dim red light. Spiritualists advance several reasons for this, aside from the obvious one that darkness offers less distraction. They point out that some phenomena are luminous and can therefore be distinguished only in the dark. And many believe that darkness is as necessary for the production of spirit manifestations as it is to the germination of plant and animal life. Skeptics, of course, offer a simpler explanation—darkness conceals the practice of fraud.

But despite the theory that darkness is needed to produce all physical manifestations, the literature of psychical research includes many cases where spiritualist phenomena occurred in rooms that were fully lit. In 1894, for example, Eusapia Palladino caused a table to rise into the air at a séance conducted in broad daylight. And in January 1964, in Southampton, England, in the full glare of the lights of a BBC television camera unit, two tables rocked violently and moved vigorously around the room.

In materialization séances, the outer forms of the spirit are re-created in a mysterious substance called ectoplasm. The materializations may take the shape of a face, a limb, or (rarely) a whole body. This strange material is defined in Norman Blunsdon's *A Dictionary of Modern Spiritualism:*

"A subtle living matter present in the physical body, primarily invisible but capable of assuming vaporous, liquid, or solid states and properties. It is extruded usually in the dark from the pores and various orifices of the body, and is slightly luminous, the more so when condensed. The temperature of the room is usually lowered when ectoplasm is produced; it possesses a characteristic smell and is cold to the touch. This substance is held to be responsible for the production of all phenomena classed as 'physical'."

As well as materializations, the medium may produce other physical phenomena—levitation of persons and objects such as furniture; noises such as raps or music; lights and scents from no apparent source. According to Blunsdon, ectoplasm is in action in all this too, forming "elastic or rigid rods to produce movement in objects, raps and noises; artificial 'voice-boxes' for the phenomena of the direct and independent voice. The levitation of tables and heavy objects is accomplished by building extensible columns under them." Also included under the heading of physical phenomena are "apports"—the materialization of small objects like stones or coins (or even birds or animals)—and the transportation of such objects through solid walls. In 1928, the British medium Mrs. Samuel Guppy, for example, produced large quantities of plants and flowers, and on one occasion even claimed to have transported herself to a house three miles away. The activities of a Frenchwoman, Madame Elisabeth D'Esperant (who died in 1919), were even more dramatic: her apports included a golden lily seven feet high, and on one occasion she herself melted away into thin air from the waist downward.

Few sensational activities of this kind have been reported recently. Today it is extremely difficult for an investigator to gain admittance to a séance for physical phenomena, since most mediums dislike the presence of possibly hostile observers. But during the early part of the century, when spiritualism aroused far more controversy than it does now, the scientific investigation of "physical" mediums was often exhaustive; sometimes the medium was stripped completely naked, subjected to a searching physical examination, and securely tied to a chair. Modern techniques of investigation are less crude—and more effective: Britain's S.P.R. offers £250 to any medium who will allow infra-red photography at a physical séance. No one has yet accepted the offer.

Today the majority of séances are simply sittings for two, between medium and client, and the procedure can be as simple as a visit to the dentist. The medium will probably begin by chatting about the weather or some equally non-committal topic to put the client at his ease. Sometimes the medium will ask if there is someone in particular the client would like to contact—but normally not, for it is part of a medium's task to find out. A first sitting is often a hit-and-miss affair, but if the client returns and a rapport grows up between him and the medium, more information is likely to "come through." The importance of the sitter's attitude has been emphasized by the famous modern British medium Mrs. Osborne Leonard (whom we shall meet again later): "How greatly, the sitter can help one's mediumship to develop! The wise, cautious, even skeptical sitter, if he has an *open* mind, gets the best results, and is a great factor in building up, little by little, the psychical and mental forces of the medium."

At the other end of the scale from an intimate sitting for two is a public spiritualist meeting conducted, before a large audience, by some well-known medium. Usually the medium will begin by calling out a name, which some member of the audience will at once identify as that of a friend or relative. The medium then delivers his message. At a recent meeting of this kind (which was attended by one of the authors) the medium called out: "I have someone here called . . .

Boody." Knowledge of Boody was claimed from the audience. "Yes, well," the medium went on "he says do you remember a black purse and kippers? Yes, *kippers*."

To spiritualists, the very meaninglessness and triviality of such messages is evidence of their authenticity. A message that is detailed and personal is far more convincing than generalities or ambiguities that anyone might invent. As a good example of this kind of intimate detail an incident is often cited from the career of the celebrated American medium Mrs. Piper. It took place in 1889 at the home of Sir Oliver Lodge, then Professor of Physics at Liverpool University. To test Mrs. Piper's psychic abilities, Lodge had written to America to ask for a relic of his uncle's twin brother, who had died about 20 years before. He was sent an old watch, which he gave to Mrs. Piper, who in trance described such boyhood incidents as swimming in a creek, nearly being drowned, killing a cat in a specific field—many of which were confirmed by Lodge's surviving uncle.

How do mediums achieve such results? In spiritualist terms (we shall come later to those of psychologists and others) the most usual methods are clairvoyance—the "seeing" of visions—and clairaudience—the "hearing" of messages, either in the state of trance or not. But as well as clairaudience and clairvoyance many mediums prefer to receive their spirit communications "automatically"—usually by putting themselves at the end of a pencil. Messages obtained in this way are often incoherent and incomplete. (According to Kardec, these may be evil spirits trying to get through.) And sometimes the meaning is obscured because the message is written backward, in anagrams, or in mirror style. (To Kardec, indications of the spirit's sense of humor.) To streamline the automatic process many mediums use a planchette (described on p. 83) or an ouija board. An ouija—from the French *oui* and the German *ja*, both meaning yes—is a small wooden board with a pointer, which, placed under the medium's hand, rests on a polished surface bearing the letters of the alphabet.

Perhaps the best-known case of automatic writing is the remarkable performance of the American Mrs. Curran, whose alter-ego claimed to be the spirit of a 17th-century English spinster called Patience Worth. Mrs. Curran began her spirit-inspired literary career in 1913 with an intimate account of life in Elizabethan England, which she followed up with a number of other novels set in even earlier historical periods including a description of life in Jerusalem at the time of the Crucifixion. Mrs. Curran herself had never crossed the Atlantic, nor was she interested in history, though in her youth she had had literary ambitions that had come to nothing. She had been introduced to spirit-writing as a parlor game at a party, took it up herself, and astonished everyone by her apparently accurate compositions.

Spiritualists of course accept that Patience Worth was what she claimed to be; others have suggested that Mrs. Curran had unconsciously noted and stored every scrap of information she had ever heard and read and then, writing automatically (and uninhibitedly) by means of some kind of "short circuit" or channel from her unconscious, had "dramatized" the material into long and detailed stories. And though few mediums have emulated the achievements of Mrs. Curran, the same explanation has been applied to many of the phenomena attributed to spirit intervention. It is thought, for example, that a similar process of mental dissociation followed by a dramatization of unconscious material occurs when mediums appear to acquire what are known as their spirit guides or controls.

When a medium falls into a trance during a séance, spiritualists maintain that his body is occupied by the wandering spirits of the "astral plane," using the medium as a vehicle. These spirits speak through his mouth but otherwise generally behave in a manner very different from that of the medium. When not in a trance, the medium "sees" or "hears" a spirit, and reports. But in most cases, the medium makes contact with a controlling spirit, whose function is rather like that of the chorus in a Greek play, to usher the various characters involved in and out of the proceedings. These spirit guides often tend to have outlandish names and styles—a usual psychological explanation being that the medium picks from her unconscious a name with connotations of strength, guidance, the unknown, and the like. This is probably why so many early American mediums found themselves with guides with Indian names like Sparrow Hawk or Red Eagle. Chinese and African guides are also common—possibly for the same reason. Mrs. Osborne Leonard's guide was a six-year-old girl called "Feda," who was said to have married one of the medium's ancestors in India and to have died in 1900. A Hungarian medium, Mrs. Lujza Linczegh Ignath, was perhaps unique in claiming as a control a "pure spirit" called "Nona," who had never been incarnate.

Controls and guides also play an important part in the healing activities of spiritualists. For just as mesmeric healers were prominent in spiritualism's early development so there are many mediums who claim to carry out cures in collaboration with spirit guides operating inside the movement today. Much of this healing work is done with the patient present—by prayer and the laying on of hands. But more often, healers will invoke the aid of their spirit guides to heal unknown people whose names they have been given.

These then are some of the phenomena attributed to spirit intervention—in all of which the medium plays a key role. But how does a medium discover an ability to establish contact with the spirit world? In some families, a psychic faculty can be traced back for generations. D. D. Home, for example, was the son of a clairvoyant. And there are villages in Poland and Russia that are famous for the number of mediums they produce. But apart from heredity, many investigators believe that mediumship nearly always starts with some physical or psychological crisis: a fright, accident, or illness. (This applies not only to mediums, but almost invariably to anyone who seems to possess paranormal powers of any kind.) Mrs. Piper, for example, suffered from illness as a young married woman. She consulted a psychic healer who not only restored her to health but also undertook to develop her powers of mediumship. It has been suggested that such people are jolted by shock or illness out of the conventional framework of their everyday lives, and as a result become conscious of responses and perceptions of which they had been unaware.

Once a medium feels she possesses some psychic gift, she may undergo specific mediumship training. She will probably attend a "development circle" where, in a friendly atmosphere, she develops confidence in her ability to communicate with the spirit world. Sometimes a novice medium will go into trance at her first attempt; for others, the process may take months. Such circles are always led by an experienced medium, who guides the novice and shows her how to allow the spirits to take over. The process has been described by the modern British medium Muriel Hillier in a widely used textbook of *Practical Mediumship:*

"After the sitters have been attending the development circle for some time . . . there may be signs of control by a spirit entity. The leaders should encourage this entity to speak, and much patience is needed now for it may take a few weeks before sufficient is learnt by novice and spirit-friend. . . . It is quite likely that a novice will be controlled by one after another spirit-friend, until trance can be achieved. The spirit operators have to become familiar with the mental and spiritual capacities of the medium, so as to produce cooperation. When they are satisfied, instead of a control who has up to then been manifested through the medium, another stronger entity will take over, and will thereafter act as what is known as the guide."

In such a permissive group, of course, a lot of self-deception can arise—which even an alert and conscientious teacher may not be able to prevent. And certainly self-deception or unconscious fraud is a common feature of trance psychology. There is also an obvious temptation for the medium to produce phenomena so as not to disappoint her sitters. In the case of the 19th-century American medium Ada Bessinet, for example, Professor Hyslop of the American Society for Psychical Research concluded after 70 sittings that the medium herself was responsible for the phenomena but, since she was functioning as a "secondary personality," she was not morally liable for fraud.

However, apart from such unconscious trickery, the history of spiritualism—like every other branch of the supernatural—is riddled with cases of deliberate fraud. Over and over again in the history of spiritualism it has proved to be ridiculously easy to practice the most bare-faced deceptions on people who long for marvels. Even alert and unbiased observers have been found to differ enormously in their impressions of the same events. Dr. West describes how a psychical researcher, Theodore Besterman, once set up a mock séance with a fake medium and, telling all the sitters what he had done, asked them to describe what happened. Most of those present failed to notice many of the incidents, including the medium's leaving the room and returning.

Fraud practiced by mediums is often a streamlined process: there are accomplices, card indexes, and bribes to switchboard operators to eavesdrop on telephone conversations. Some countries have taken legal steps to prevent such frauds: for example, in 1951 Britain passed the Fraudulent Mediums Act, and in New York, police attend séances in their pursuit of bogus mediums.

The most obvious incentive for fraud is, of course, money. In 1958, the British medium William Roy admitted in a confession that appeared in the *Sunday Pictorial* that he had collected "£50,000 [about $140,000], mostly from bereaved women who wanted the comfort they thought I could provide by putting them in touch with loved ones beyond the grave." Roy used stooges, faked trances, and even altered his pulse rate by breathing techniques. He learned a smattering of foreign languages, so that he could greet sitters who had lived abroad in a tongue familiar to them. He was ingenious in tricking his way out of tests imposed by investigators. For example, when they tied his hands to the arms of his chair and fixed sticking plaster over his mouth to prevent him speaking, Roy merely bent his head forward under cover of darkness, pulled aside the plaster with his bound hands, and spoke.

A common trick of fraudulent mediums involves an accomplice who searches handbags and briefcases left in the entrance hall by the sitters (who are asked not to bring them to the séance room for fear of spoiling the "vibrations"). The accomplice uses a small radio transmitter to pass on his findings to the medium, whose receiver is concealed in his shoe and wired to a tiny speaker in his ear.

Equally sophisticated are many of the methods used by modern scientific investigators of physical phenomena. Nevertheless one of the most indefatigable fraud detectors in the history of spiritualism was not a scientist but the famous magician and illusionist Harry Houdini. Houdini had a curiously ambivalent attitude to spiritualism: always anxious to establish that spirit communication was in fact possible, each successful exposure seemed to sadden him. His close friendship with Sir Arthur Conan Doyle was broken when Lady Conan Doyle (an automatic writer) produced a message from Houdini's dead mother. Though at first much moved by the message, Houdini later rejected it as false on the grounds that it was the sort of message *any* mother might have sent and that it showed a greater command of English than his mother possessed.

Houdini also figured in an investigation conducted by the magazine *Scientific American*, which, in 1923, offered $5000 to any medium who could satisfy a committee of scientists that he was genuine. Houdini was a member of the committee, which tested several mediums. One, claiming to produce "independent voice" phenomena, was shown by a galvanometer (an instrument that detects any unseen movements) to have been walking around the room producing the manifestations himself. Another slipped his bonds and produced phenomena with his free hand—except when Houdini took 45

minutes to tie him up. Then nothing happened. But not all
the frauds were so blatant. In the end there was no award
because the committee could not agree in the case of one medium. This was Mrs. Margery Crandon, who managed to
produce, among other phenomena, the spirit fingerprints of
her dead brother, Walter. (Later the prints were discovered
to be those of a Boston dentist.) The same kind of disagreement and controversy among experts still continues today
over séances that took place more than 80 years ago. Opinions still differ, for example, about the phantom Katie King
and the medium she controlled, the Englishwoman Florence
Cook.

Katie King is one of the rare examples of a spirit that materialized entirely. During the séances, the medium, wearing a
black dress, sat inside the cabinet, while the white-clothed apparition emerged from behind the curtain and chatted amia-
bly to the sitters. Although some sitters noticed a close resem-
blance between medium and apparition, no dramatic attempts
at exposure were made until a sitting held in December 1873.
Then a Mr. Volckman, deciding that both were one, seized
Katie by the waist. Far from disappearing, Katie struggled to
re-enter the cabinet. In the confusion, the gas lamp was put
out and, when it was relit, Florence Cook was found in her
cabinet, tied to her chair by a sealed tape.

After this incident, Florence Cook asked the celebrated
chemist William Crookes (later president of the Royal Society), who had conducted experiments with D. D. Home, to
investigate her mediumship. When a galvanometer revealed
no movement by the medium during the séance, Crookes announced that there had been no fraud.

Controversy has raged ever since. Many writers have held
that Crookes's investigations were not sufficiently thorough;
some have suggested that Florence's sister Kate, also a medium, might have been acting the part of the phantom. The
debate reached a climax in 1962 when the well-known British
psychical researcher Trevor H. Hall published a book called
The Spiritualists. Hall not only challenged Crookes's findings
but also questioned his integrity, claiming that he had con-
spired with Florence Cook to produce the apparition, and
that the sittings had been a cover-up for a secret love affair
between them.

These accusations may be hard to believe of Crookes, who
was an eminent and respected scientist. He was in this way
typical of those men of high professional standing—like Pro-

fessor Henry Sidgwick and Frederic Myers—who, at a time
when the intellectual climate was totally hostile to psychical
research, risked their reputations to conduct investigations
into all forms of paranormal phenomena.

Today the aims of psychical researchers are rather
different than they were in the days of Florence Cook.
For on the whole, modern investigators are concerned to
evaluate spiritualist phenomena less in terms of possible spirit
inspiration (or alternatively fraud) and more in the light of
newly evolved theories of ESP. We have already mentioned
in Chapter 3 the experiments into ESP carried out by Dr.
Rhine and his followers—experiments that finally succeeded
in establishing the existence of telepathy. And though this
telepathic faculty was found to be generally weak and erratic,
it nevertheless provided investigators with an acceptable explanation of the often equally erratic "clairvoyant" activities
of mediums. Some have even claimed that these extra-sensory
powers operate more successfully in altered mental states.
The Czech biochemist Milan Ryzl, for example, has discovered that by hypnosis the telepathic faculty not only of mediums but of normally non-"sensitive" subjects can be increased. Similarly the modern British psychiatrist Humphrey
Osmond, one of the pioneer experimenters into the effect of
drugs on the human mind, has reported the establishment of
more-or-less sustained telepathic contact by two people under
the influence of lysergic acid (LSD)—a drug that releases
much latent, unconscious material.

But even if one finds an explanation of mediumship based
on ESP as hard to swallow as the spiritualist hypothesis of
spirit intervention, it is still possible to reconcile most paranormal powers ascribed to mediums with more conventional
psychological theory. This is particularly applicable to phenomena, such as spirit writing and spirit messages, that come
under the general heading of automatism.

The term automatism was first used by Frederic Myers,
whose influential theory of telepathic communication to explain living apparitions was discussed in the preceding chapter. In his *Human Personality and its Survival of Bodily
Death* (1903), Myers considered the trance speech and
"spirit writing" of mediums, which he then went on to explain in terms of the then-revolutionary idea of the unconscious mind. For he concluded that in many cases the so-
called spirit writings were in fact dramatizations of material
from the medium's unconscious—a theory that many claim

was strikingly demonstrated in the case (described earlier) of Mrs. Curran and her spirit guide, Patience Worth.

Myers also noticed that the spirit-guides in their writings and messages often assumed a definite style and character of their own—a sort of secondary personality. Today these secondary personalities are also seen as dramatizations of repressed tendencies; it is just because they are repressed that they are often characterized by qualities opposite to those displayed by the individual in normal life. This theory is neatly illustrated by the experiments during the 1930s of the British psychical researcher Whately Carington with the medium Mrs. Osborne Leonard, who (as we have seen) claimed to be controlled by the spirit of a child called Feda. By giving both Mrs. Leonard and Feda the Word Association Test—by which a person's psychological make-up is evaluated by his reaction to certain words—Carington showed that the results were not those to be expected from two entirely different individuals, but those of contrasted but complementary personalities.

Such theories, though helpful in explaining the psychology of mediumship, still leave unchallenged the validity of spiritualist aims and theories. And many people believe that the answer to this problem should be sought in religion rather than in psychology or parapsychology.

Established Christianity has in fact often been embarrassed by spiritualist views, which, though basically Christian, often have an unorthodox flavor. For example, some spiritualists refer to God as "The Great White Spirit," and see the divine will as delegated to successive hierarchies of spirits. Many spiritualists see Jesus as an outstanding Jewish medium, healer, and preacher, who after his death materialized to some of his followers. Nor surprisingly, such ideas find little favor in the Roman Catholic Church. On April 24, 1917, the Vatican issued the following statement (which has never been revoked) on participation in spiritualist activity:

"In full plenary session it was asked . . . whether it was permitted through a medium, as they are called, or without a medium, with or without the use of hypnosis, to watch any spiritualist manifestation, even presented with honesty and piety. . . . The most Holy and Reverend Fathers have replied 'No' on all points."

The Church of England, however, is cautiously becoming friendly with spiritualism. Here is an extract from a report by a committee of Anglicans appointed in 1955 to investigate spiritualism:

"There is nothing inherently improbable in the account of the conditions involved in . . . the communications. It is, however, no more than a hypothesis, incapable of scientific proof, nor does it assist us in determining the authenticity of the communications themselves. The verification of these, if it is possible at all, must rest upon ordinary scientific tests. . . . Many alleged communications seem to fall below the highest Christian standards of understanding and spiritual insight and mental capacity shown by the communicants while they were still alive."

The report goes on to discuss other explanations for spiritualist phenomena, such as telepathy, and allows that it is legitimate for Christians to take part in research into these things. It warns, however, of the danger of allowing "an interest in spiritualism, at a low level of spiritual value, to replace the deeper religion which rests fundamentally on the right relation of the soul to God himself." But it also admits that the Church has in the past been too cautious in its references to the departed. An interdenominational Churches Fellowship for Psychical Study was in fact set up in 1953.

And so communications between living and dead, the basis of spiritualist belief, has never been conclusively proved, though some people think they have found such proof in the extraordinary series of "cross correspondences" that for 30 years were found in the writings of a group of mediums scattered all over the world. The messages began shortly after the death in 1901 of Frederic Myers, who had said while he lived that he intended to show, if he could, evidence for his survival. Shortly after his death, messages signed by Myers (and others) turned up in the automatic scripts of a number of mediums in England and America, and one in India. The messages were extraordinarily complicated, full of references and cross-references involving obscure literary and classical allusions unknown to many of the mediums. Many have claimed that a controlling theme became clear, but how far this may be attributed to the mediums' differing acquaintance with Myers and how far to the interplay of the mediums' minds, it is impossible to say.

What then emerges from all the controversy? Very little, most modern psychical researchers would say, in the way of concrete evidence for the existence of paranormal phenomena. Few would deny, however, the importance of spiritualism in the development of modern psychical research. For it was largely as a result of spiritualist activity during the last half of the 19th century that the attentions of scrupulous and unprejudiced observers was first drawn to the possible nature of all types of psychic phenomena.

So the riddle is still unsolved. For, after allowing for spiritualism's connections with conscious and unconscious fraud, there still remains a small percentage of phenomena that seems not wholly explicable in non-spiritualist terms. This residue, reinforcing the geniune spiritual easing and joy that the movement seems to provide for its followers, is perhaps what continues to make it the most widespread exercise of the supernatural in the world today.

5 THE SECRET ARTS

The study of magic tends to be as tantalizing as it is attractive. It tantalizes mainly because there seems to be so little objective information on the subject, for while books on magic may hint portentously of marvels, they generally reveal little of them. As the modern British magician W. E. Butler remarks in *The Magician, His Training and Work,* "Books on magic seem to be largely made up of quotations from and comments on other books on magic." Even so, the unyielding nature of every book on the subject has never managed to destroy the attraction that magic has for most of us. In the words of the American author Kurt Seligman, who wrote a *History of Magic,* "No one can say he is entirely free from magical thought and action." And, according to the Polish anthropologist B. K. Malinowski: "There is a certain desire in every one of us to escape from routine and certainty. . . . Even the most skeptical at times rebel against the inevitable causal chain which excludes the supernatural and, with it, all the gifts of chance and good fortune."

We have already discussed, in our introductory survey of the supernatural in Chapter 1, the continuing prevalence in the world today of half-beliefs in personal "magics": private spells to ward off danger, private formulas to encourage desired results. We also pointed out that surveys and experiments have shown that the incidence of these half-beliefs is probably higher than might be thought. You can try an experiment yourself by introducing the subject of magic at a party. No matter how rational and enlightened the guests may be (in fact, the more open-minded they are, the more they are likely to respond to this challenge) probably only the most unimaginative will fail to volunteer the most surprising confidences. But these admissions will not be made casually: they will be made only when people for a while relax their conversational guard and uninhibitedly reveal their innermost feelings. And the fact that we *feel* rather than *think* about magic gives us an important clue to its nature. A belief in magic has its roots in the emotions and in the imagination. It comes from the *inner world* of the individual.

With this in mind, we can begin to see why so many writers on magic have failed to make the subject objectively meaningful. So, as a possible approach it might be helpful to recall the time in one's own life when there was no clear dividing line between this inner world and the outer; or between supernatural and natural; when everything in the physical world seemed to contain a mysterious power of its own; when rituals, spells, and incantations, demons, fairies, and spirits were as real as the living-room furniture—in other words, in childhood. Next, one should assume that what was true of oneself as an individual may also be true of the childhood of the human race. As the French psychologist Jean Piaget has so often stressed, everyone, until the age of six or seven, seems to live in a magical world in which he shares the beliefs of the remote past and of the modern primitive.

In a similar way the magic worker, though an adult, does not, when operating, divorce the inner world from the outer. Bound up both inwardly and outwardly with the magical event, he will not attempt critically to *understand* what he is doing (at least, not while he is doing it). In this way he is unlike the scientist, who isolates himself from an experiment, clearly sees the processes at work, and assumes that the results will be the same whether he is present or not. If the magician is not present (and not only physically but emotionally present) he can achieve nothing. For this reason spells and incantations tend to look inert and meaningless when printed, like a cross between a cookbook and the jottings of a madman. To be understood, let alone be used, they must be enlivened by the imagination and the emotions.

The scientific comparison is valid, for magic is commonly described as the science of the primitives. Just as a chemist observes and deduces the properties and qualities of the substances he studies, so the ancient magician observed the properties and qualities of the universe and embodied his findings not in scientific laws but in myths of gods and supernatural beings. To take the parallel further: a modern scientist might change the properties of a chemical by heating—an objective method since anyone can put a match to the flame. The magician can be said to have been attempting to achieve a similar result but by a subjective method of "heating": he is trying to influence the invisible powers or beings that he believes to exist in the universe. And he himself is the crucible. (Incidentally, the Elema tribe of Eastern New Guinea actually used a word meaning heat to denote the "fire" of the magician. Similarly, among the Mailu, also of New Guinea, the sorcerer chews pepper leaves or wild ginger root in order to acquire "heat" or power.)

The magic worker's processes—his rites and spells and incantations—express in symbolic form his attempts to control or be in touch with the supernatural beings and powers that populate his world. Symbolism, as C. G. Jung notes, is constantly used "to represent concepts that we cannot define or fully comprehend." Jung adds that this is why all religions employ symbolic language or images. It is also why magic does. The magician feels that the truth is greater than he can see or comprehend, but that by acting on that which he *can* understand he may perhaps influence other things associated with it. So all spells are symbolic acts as well as concrete ones. And a symbol, to the magician, is like a drop of water that has condensed in visible form out of the nebulous swirl of vapor in the air—vapor that is widely diffused about the world in different forms and places and times.

Everyone, of course, uses symbols. Most obviously, symbols populate our dreams. We share many other important ones with members of our own generation and culture; others with the whole human race. Jung, at the beginning of his *Symbols of Transformation* (1912), has this to say about the symbolism of dreams and its interpretations:

"That dreams should have a meaning, and should therefore be capable of interpretation, is certainly neither a strange nor extraordinary idea. It has been known to mankind for thousands of years; indeed, it has become something of a truism. One remembers having heard even at school of Egyptian and Chaldean dream interpreters. Everyone knows the story of Joseph, who interpreted Pharaoh's dreams. . . . According to the old belief, a god or demon spoke to the dreamer in symbolic language, and the dream-interpreter had to solve the riddle. In modern speech we would say that the dream is a series of images which are apparently contradictory and meaningless, but that it contains material which yields a clear meaning when properly translated."

Most of us have at some time played Joseph to our own Pharaoh and cracked the symbolic code of a dream to reveal its inner meaning. Magicians have always paid great respect to dreams, believing that the dreaming self "knows" more than the limited, waking self—an idea comparable in some respects to magic's two worlds of inner and outer. And today—after long neglect—the value of dreams as a method of achieving self-knowledge is beginning to be widely recognized.

Magicians believe that outside their dreams, as well as in them, they can make symbols yield up a magical power and meaning. The symbols we use today are intricate and sophisticated, but long ago man was also using symbols to express his approach to the world—an approach that made no distinction between religion and magic.

Anthropologists use the word *animism* to describe primitive man's world-view and term the kind of magic that developed from this view "sympathetic magic." As was pointed out in Chapter 2, this usually means an imitation of, or borrowing from, the qualities or persons to be influenced. And it seems reasonable to suppose that primitive magic of this sort (in which what happened to a part—a nail paring—would happen to the whole—the person it had come from) arose because to primitive man everything around him was alive, as he himself was alive. Plants, animals, the earth itself, went through cycles of birth, reproduction, and death similar to those of man himself. And so it must have seemed natural to feel that every object was animated by the same life forces. The Italian medical historian Dr. Arturo Castiglioni, author of *Adventures of the Mind*, puts it this way: "The ego [of primitive man] is not a limit . . . but it embraces all things surrounding him and participating in his life, even those which, after a brief contact with him, detach themselves from his body." And so nails, hair, footprints, clothes, and weapons remained part of a man—and might be used as a substitute for him. The ancient Egyptians believed that even a name could be identified with the man who bore it. They would write the names of hostile tribes on pottery, which they would then break.

This, then, is the earliest form of magical activity and the first step in symbol making. To follow primitive man's development to the next phase, called *anthropomorphism* by anthropologists, we might again refer to the developing mind of the child. In early childhood, as in animism, everything is infused with a separate life of its own; only later a child begins to see that certain objects have properties in common. At this point, he starts to group things together. He evolves the concept of women, as opposed to his mother and other individual females; he imposes the concept of trees onto his familiarity with the growing things in his garden. Similarly, early man began to see that the forces that animated his world acted identically in many different things. He came to associate reproduction and fertility, for example, with everything that lived and grew. He saw that it was a female quality, which was to his eyes most profound in woman herself and in the earth that sustained all plant and animal life. So the image of the Earth Mother was slowly formed in the minds of men.

Gods probably evolved in a similar way in every culture of the ancient world. They were conceived by man anthropomorphically—that is in his own image—because, though the gods' powers were much greater than man's own, man seemed nearest of all creatures to the divine. (Not all gods, of course, assumed human form; the ancient Assyrians revered winged bulls, and the divinities of ancient Egypt often combined attributes of animals and men.) So, in his gods, man embodied the power that he felt to exist all around him. And often these deities outlived the cultures that had created them. Civilizations rose and died, but the gods remained, perhaps merging with the gods of the succeeding conquerors and settlers. Even today, the power of the old gods can still excite a response in us—like, for example, the images immediately evoked in us by the Roman gods Mars and Venus.

As man developed further, anthropomorphism was replaced by another way of thinking, which can be classified as *abstraction*. Fertility, for example, becomes an *idea* removed from the fertility of an object in animism or fertility as a female attribute in anthropomorphism. Good and evil here become concepts, divorced from the visible world or no longer personified by benevolent or evil spirits or gods, as they were in the dualistic mythology of the ancient Akkadian world. Seligman suggests that this development probably took place some 2000 years before the Christian era. He writes: "By contemplation of the night sky, Chaldean priests conceived a supreme God who sprang from other deities. This God was a creative power chained to the eternal law which he embodied and submitting to his own decrees."

At this point in history, supernatural power began to be concentrated in the hands of a powerful priesthood, educated and qualified to use a power that was stronger and more complex than that which had formerly been available to everyone. (Again we can draw a parallel with a maturing child. An ability to think in abstract terms gives a child new power: he can predict and calculate.) The priests were masters of the art of divination, predicting the future from the livers of slaughtered animals, from fire and smoke, from the brilliance of precious stones, and from the weather. They began, in short, to study the workings of the universe in an orderly manner—to develop systematic ways of looking at the stars, at words, or at numbers.

And as man's view of the world became systematic and abstract, magical thinking began to achieve the intricacy that it has today. One of the most influential (and most complex) of the mystical systems that this kind of thinking produced was the Cabbala, which had a profound influence on Western magic in the Middle Ages. The word Cabbala means "tradition" in Hebrew and originally referred to the body of Jewish doctrine that was handed down by word of mouth from one generation to another. By the 13th century, this body of teaching had been developed by Jewish mystics into a system of occult philosophy. The cabbalists attached great importance to the symbolism of letters and numbers, each of which had a particular significance in divination or evocation. Castiglioni calls it "a speculative, fantastic and mystic superstructure of religion," and points out that many later magicians and occultists resorted to its words, formulas, and symbols (such as the pentagram) as a means of working their magic.

The cabbalists' most famous symbol is the glyph known as the Tree of Life. It is a meditation symbol that is said to contain not a facet of the truth, as smaller symbols may do, but a way to truth itself. Every possible correspondence between all branches of knowledge is said to be compressed into it. There are 10 points on the tree, and 22 paths between them; and, cabbalists say, it is possible (by meditation) to reach the knowledge and power contained in them in a way similar to the revelation that occurs when we understand the meaning of a dream.

Gnosticism was another ancient body of religious doctrine whose teachings came to be associated with the practice of magic. This system of spiritual thought developed in the Near East side by side with Christianity, reaching the height of its influence toward the end of the second century. Its philosophy was based on the belief that the path to salvation lay in *gnosis,* a secret and higher interpretation of the gospels, rather than in *pistis,* the ordinary beliefs of Christianity. As in cabbalism, this religious knowledge was contained in mystical rites and formulas, at first known only to initiates, many of which later became assimilated into the body of traditional occult knowledge—the astrologers, for example, took over the association of each of the seven planets with a particular metal.

The intermingling of magic and religion that is found in the Cabbala and in Gnosticism can, as we pointed out at the beginning of this historical survey, be found throughout the development of magical thought. For until the growth of Christianity, very little distinction was made by the practitioners themselves. A religious view of the world was in a sense an ordinary view of the world—a view that could without strain comprehend the possibility of marvels and miracles. The Old Testament, for example, teems with magic and sorcery. But with the division between ordinary and extraordinary that grew up with the development of Christianity, religion began to assume two different aspects: first, the laws and "rules" for behavior in this world; second, the individual path of the mystic that takes him from the deep inner self directly toward God. At this point, the magician who is not necessarily a priest makes his appearance. Two useful words sum up the difference in roles: the *theurge,* the priest-magician, has become distinct from the *thaumaturge,* or sorcerer, who uses magical power for non-religious ends. In other words, *within* religion, the priest-magician uses his magical powers as the agent of the supernatural forces and beings that activate his universe. *Out* of religion, the individual magician begins to use his powers for himself—to bring good or bad luck, to ward off evil, to secure riches and power, and so on. And it is largely these "unofficial" forms of magical activity that we shall be discussing.

Having classified men's differing attitudes to the forces of the universe as animistic, anthropomorphic, or abstract, we must now concede that these distinctions are somewhat artificial, and made largely for the sake of clarity. From now on, none of the magical processes that we shall be examining is likely to fall neatly into one or another of these categories. Most spells contain elements of all three—though much simple "sympathetic" magic is still performed today. In 1955, for example, a Moroccan financier was reported to have stuck pins into photographs of his business rivals. But however we may classify them, all magical processes are simply means of tapping the occult power that is believed to inhabit everything—people, plants, precious stones, stars, planets, and so on.

Vestiges of magical power in *people* can be felt even today. We speak of a man's "powerful" personality—which is analogous to the kind of power that in the past was thought to be possessed by, for example, people with the "evil eye." This personal power was at its strongest with priests and magicians. The modern religious historian Mercia Eliade writes on the particular quality of "occult power" in people: "Shamans [priests of the religious cults of northern and central Asia] are of the elect, and as such they have access to a region of the sacred inaccessible to other members of the community. . . . It is the Shamans who, by their trances, cure the laity, accompany their dead to the 'Realm of Shades,' and serve as mediators between them and their gods." Men with such power have existed in the civilized Western world—men like the Georgian-born G. J. Gurdjieff, an occult "teacher" who came to the West after the Russian revolution, and acquired many followers. The quality of his attraction has been described in the following way: "You could not help being drawn, almost physically, towards him . . . like being sucked in by a vast, spiritual vacuum cleaner."

Occult power was also believed to exist in the mineral world—the source of magical remedies since ancient times. As might be expected, precious stones such as emeralds, sapphires, and pearls predominate as magically powerful objects. For example, diamonds (which have always been prized for their beauty and value), were thought by De Boot, a 17th-century Dutch authority on precious stones, to repel poisons, witchcraft, madness, and the terrors of the night. Metals too played important roles, especially as methods of warding off harmful influences. For this reason, the ancient Chinese believed any medicine containing gold leaf to be particularly effective. Copper and bronze also contained magical power, but they were generally considered to be less effective than iron for keeping evil away.

Similar magical power was thought to be found in plants. Knowledge of herbs whose medicinal and poisonous properties are today generally recognized was once the exclusive property of magicians—herbs such as rue, wormwood, mugwort, and the castor-oil plant. But for the magician the herbs he used had powers other and greater than those resulting from their natural properties. To him their power was also symbolic. A good example of a plant thought to have such magical properties is the mandrake.

Stories of the mandrake as an aphrodisiac, a narcotic, and for easing pregnancy, can be found in literature from 3000-year-old Persian legends to the works of Shakespeare and Machiavelli. Recent chemical research has to some extent confirmed this long-standing tradition, for the root has been shown to contain a substance with a sedative and stupefying effect. But there was something more to its magical function: the roots were often seen as representing male or female bodies, partly because of their forked structure and perhaps partly because of their aphrodisiac properties. And so the mandrake came to be used as an amulet and was fastened to warriors' shields or wrapped around babies' necks.

The power contained in plants therefore operated at different levels. One might be an entirely natural remedy; another might be part-natural, part-symbolic; yet another wholly symbolic. And this brings us to an important point about all magical thinking. Among the cabbalists, the Gnostics, the Hermeticists (the sect that followed the teachings of the mythical Hermes Trismegistus), and the alchemists, a vital phrase keeps recurring: "as above, so below." Implied in this phrase is a vast system of *correspondences* between all natural objects.

This correspondence between like things, between microcosm and macrocosm, underlies all magical reasoning. It is also an important ingredient in the magical power of amulets and talismans. These two words are often used interchangeably to describe all kinds of magically protective objects. So much so, that some authorities, including the American author of *Studies in Magical Amulets*, Campbell Bonner, maintain that it is impossible to make a distinction between the two. Others, however (including many writers on magic and a large number of occultists themselves), do separate amulets from talismans, usually on the basis of the materials used and the purpose for which they are intended. This particular method of classification is summarized as follows by Marianne Verneuil in her *Dictionnaire Partique des Sciences Occultes:*

"The amulet has the power of passive protection against 'influences.' The talisman, on the other hand, introduces us into active magic, but is still protective in many respects. . . . The amulet utilizes natural objects . . . and operates through its own inherent virtu whilst the talisman is the product of intellectual speculation and magical fabrication. It is directed towards a specific end, and therefore only has value within this context. The making of a talisman requires knowledge of analogies and their magical correspondences."

According to this definition, the amulet derives its efficacy from one of the basic sources of magical power—the power inherent in any object. Any substance, animal, vegetable, or mineral, can be used as an amulet. Sometimes, as we have seen with the mandrake, an amulet was made from plants or stones that had some natural, medicinal property; others acted symbolically, like the peach stones worn by ancient Chinese to ward off evil spirits.

If an amulet is worn for general protection, a talisman acts in a more specific manner—to ward off a particular kind of illness or misfortune—like, for example, the miniature canoes carried by Iroquois Indians as a safeguard against drowning. Sometimes the talisman was deliberately "charged" with magical power by ritual and incantation. The *lilissu,* the bronze kettle drum used by the ancient Assyrians to expel evil spirits, was produced to the accompaniment of ritual sacrifice and incantations begging the gods for their aid and intervention. The holy relics of medieval times were also talismans: if they were touched after appropriate prayers were uttered their curative powers were believed to be almost unlimited.

Inscriptions too could impart magical power to a talisman, like the ancient talismanic formula inscribed in Hebrew characters on the magic Assyrian bowl known as the "Devil's Trap." This was buried under a house to entice evil demons down to the deepest bowels of the earth.

Many such magical inscriptions come under the heading of pantacles (also known as pentacles)—figures that are usually in the form either of a square or of the five- or even six-pointed star known as Solomon's Seal (familiar today as the star of David, the symbol of the Jewish people). The pantacle was an essential part of ceremonial magic, since it was believed to express in visual form the mystical systems of correspondences that were to link together all parts of the universe. According to Marianne Verneuil:

"The root *pan* which figures in this word indicates its universal essence and its orientation towards the macrocosm. Astrology and its macrocosmic symbolism holds a very important place in the content of pantacles. The pantacle is a kind of fluidic transmitter; its compilation must take place according to the rules of a complex art which at once takes into account: (1) the symbolic and magical value of the figures, letters, and words inscribed on it; (2) the symbolic and magical value of its form and the form of the designs inscribed on it; (3) the time when the pantacle is put into operation; (4) the state of preparation of the person who puts the pantacle into operation from the point of view of suitable fluidic harmonies." In Solomon's Seal itself—formed by two equilateral triangles—the occult power was thought to reside not only in the figure itself, but in the characters, symbols, and inscriptions incorporated in it. The hexagram (which was often incorporated into magic circles) was sometimes drawn on parchment and attached to the vestments of the magician.

From occult power in people and objects we come to the most fundamental and important source of magic: the power contained in words and numbers. The reasoning behind the use of words and numbers is the same as in all other types of magic—that they "reverberate" through the universe, connecting with all similar (though unseen) things. As Castiglioni notes: "Among primitive peoples the power of signs and geometric figures is limited to simple numbers and figures, but countless combinations and associations of numbers and figures, of numbers and stars, of numbers and letters were soon formed. . . In its earliest forms, the alphabet made a new and important contribution to symbolic formulae: every letter, either in itself or because of the position assigned to it, in connection with numbers or geometric forms, assumes a special significance, and every one of the elements mentioned contributes to the formation of a complex magical ritual, which differs in time and place, but is identical in its fundamental lines."

It is easy to see that words would readily lend themselves to magical use, since they exist on two definite levels: first, as objects; and second, as concentrated symbols or communicators. And there can be no doubt about their extraordinary force. For by putting our thoughts and feelings into words, we define them and give them reality. In fact, "to name" in Hebrew means to "make appear"; and in English to "in-form" means the same—to *give form* to something that was previously vague and indefinite. The notion that to name is to in-form lies behind many myths of the Creation. At the beginning of Genesis, for example, we read: "God said, let there be light: and there was light . . . and God divided the light from the darkness. And God called the light Day, and the darkness he called Night."

For this reason, it is not surprising that in magic certain words were thought to have such enormous power that they were taboo. "The evocation of the name of the divinity," writes Maurice Bouisson, the French author of *Magic, its Rites and History*, "was, indeed, an attempt to dominate that divinity, to cause it to appear and to subdue its will." Such taboos existed among the Egyptians and the Jews. In an Egyptian "Book of the Dead" we read: "He who resides in Amenti [the land of the dead] detests that his name be pronounced." And in the Book of Exodus: "Thou shalt not take the name of the Lord thy God in vain."

Nor is it surprising that people's names should be kept secret, or replaced with aliases or nicknames, as they frequently are in children's fairy stories. In the Christian religion, novices in monasteries or nunneries are given new names. Similarly, each Egyptian had two names, one of which was known only to himself and his parents. In India, during the naming ceremony of a child, the infant receives two names, one of which must remain secret, to be revealed only to relatives. In all these cases of secrecy, the primary object is protection: an evil magician can harm a person through his name, as through his nail parings, hair, and so on.

The written name is as powerful as the spoken. As an example, there was an old Jewish tradition (which originated in the Prague ghetto during the Middle Ages) of the *golem*. The golem is an image of a man that the rabbi, having brought himself into an ecstatic state, "animates" by writing on its forehead the word *AMTh*, which means "truth" or "reality." When he rubs out the first letter A, there remains MTh, meaning "dead," and the golem crumbles into dust. Similar rites involving the use of words have been performed all over the world, and are particularly common in the magical traditions of Egypt and Tibet.

Sometimes the shape of letters can contain a secret meaning. For instance, the form of the Hebrew letter *aleph* (א)

according to the Zohar (one of the chief books of the Cabbala), represents the division between the male and female principle. Another Hebrew use of letters, which clearly expresses the power of words, is a spell in which a devil's name is written out, and then, beneath, rewritten lacking a letter, again rewritten lacking another, and so on until no letters are left. Thus the devil was thought to shrivel up as one by one the letters of his name were eliminated.

In magical incantations the power of the word was often united to that of numbers. Belief in the magic power of certain numbers, such as 1, 3, 7, and 12, is found in many civilizations of the ancient world, especially in the metaphysical systems erected by the Pythagoreans in Greece. Each letter of the alphabet had a numerical equivalent—as it still does in some languages in use today (in Arabic in particular). So that the "number" of a name was the sum of the numerical values of the letters composing that name. The tetragrammaton of Yahveh (YHVH), the Hebrew name for God, for example, had the value of 10-5-6-5, or 26.

Words, numbers, and objects—the whole universe, in fact, is seen by the magician as a potential source of magical power. And as magical thought developed, the intricacy of its interlocking systems increased. Now we must look at the ways in which the magician uses this complex knowledge: how magic is actually worked. And the first method is, of course, the spell, which can bind, break, make, or mend; which can harm an enemy, make rain, banish ghosts, or raise the spirits of the dead.

The power of the spell derives from the power of words and of incantation. As was pointed out earlier, the spell itself, when written down, may appear prosaic or repetitive, but its effectiveness lies in its associations and in its method of delivery, and in the repetition of ritual that allows its impact to be built up and reinforced. Secrecy is also an important factor in spells. Eskimo magicians used a secret language that was known only to initiates. The more esoteric the spell, the more powerful it was. And the more powerful, the greater the need to keep it secret from those who had not attained sufficient wisdom and knowledge to wield such strong magic. Every child is told the story of the sorcerer's apprentice who tried out one of his master's spells, but was overpowered by it, because he did not know enough to stop it.

Secret formulas for spells, compiled in little hand books or "grimoires," have always been jealously guarded by sorcerers.

These spell books, handed down from one generation to another, assumed (and still do assume) an almost sacred character. In fact, in nearly every grimoire an extra precaution to ensure secrecy will have been taken: the magician will usually have transposed or omitted some part or step. The reasoning was simple: if someone knew enough to spot the error and to correct it then he was knowledgeable enough to work the spell. If not, no harm was done. So, as the ancients said, in one way or another, "all secrets are open." But they meant open only to those who were capable of understanding them.

This kind of secrecy, however, leads to red herrings trailed left and right through the pages of the grimories, with explanations and glosses and commentaries adding further complications. The French expert on folklore Claude Seignolle recounts (in his book *Les Évangiles du Diable*) an instance of this compounded confusion. While engaged in research in a rural community outside Paris, he met an aged sorcerer. Seignolle wanted to see the grimoire used by the old man, and so persuaded him to produce it—only to find that the alleged grimoire was one of his own works on the survival of magical traditions in France.

A glance at any grimoire will show that a spell is seldom used in isolation but will be worked in conjunction with a prescribed ritual, which is usually set out in great detail. This is as true of the most awe-inspiring conjuration as it is of the more everyday spells, like a simple Spanish recipe for gaining someone's love. Here the spell is merely ritually recited three times while the magic worker burns three shoots of rosemary (supposed to induce warm feelings in the beloved). Spells, of course, can involve less attractive procedures, like a 16th-century formula for invisibility that involved, among other things, boiling a black cat in a pot.

The importance of ritual can be seen (to return again to our earlier analogy) in the world of the child. He attempts to control the outer world by devising games and ceremonies: "If I walk on every paving stone between here and home, the letter I want will be waiting." An obsessional adult personality attempts the same thing: by ordering the outer world (by making frequent lists or placing objects in geometrically neat patterns on a desk) he strives to control the inner (to gain peace of mind or the ability to concentrate on work). We might ask, *which* world exactly is this obsessional personality trying to control? But there is no clear answer to this question—just as there is not in the world of the magician, where inner and outer are one.

If the spell employs the occult power of the word, the charm makes use of the magical properties of objects. (Incidentally, the term charm was originally applied to magical songs and chants. In the Greek myth, Orpheus by playing his lute caused even inanimate objects like trees and stones to follow him. Similar legends are found in many primitive communities: the Ona of Tierra del Fuego believe that the chants of their ancestors could draw whales out of the sea onto the land.) In the modern sense of the word, charms may consist of anything—from, say, a wolf's tail to precious stones. They may be worn or carried by individuals for some specific purpose, such as averting the evil eye (beads set out in the shape of an eye have been used for this) or with the more general talismanic function of bringing good luck. Charms, like spells, may be limitless in power. In Hindu magic a charm called the "charm of the figure twenty" grants the user anything he desires: he need only write a certain set of signs on 120,000 tiny scraps of paper, fold them, and throw them into a swift current of water.

Charms and spells can be effective entirely by virtue of the power of letters, numbers, or objects contained in them. But as soon as any society begins to evolve a cosmogony involving supernatural powers or beings, charms and spells are likely to invoke the aid of a spirit or god, especially when a magical operation is difficult or dangerous. In an Assyrian spell to appease the evil spirits of the dead who have returned to plague the living, a libation of wine and the offering of a lighted censer is made before sunrise to greet the sun god. He, in return, will then liberate the victim from his tormentors. In more ambitious enterprises, the magician may conjure up a whole host of spirits to do his bidding. A famous treatise on magic called *The Clavicle of Solomon* sets out many involved and detailed rituals for summoning supernatural entities to carry out the desires of men. This famous "key," traditionally believed to have been first compiled by the great biblical king, was revised many times, and has been a standard reference book for professional magicians since the 14th century. And because "tampering with" spirits has always been considered a dangerous business, minute instructions are given for every stage in the ritual, which must be rigidly observed. It describes in detail the pantacles that should be made, the exact diagrammatic symbols that should be inscribed on them, the methods of making and perfuming all magical instruments such as the wand and the staff, and so on. The priest must undergo strict disciplines of fasting and purification before he is ready to begin the rite of conjuration.

The rite begins with the ceremonial drawing of the circle with the appropriate cabbalistic names, and continues with a series of complicated incantations addressed to the spirits. Spirits can be summoned up in this way for a number of purposes, but most often they were invoked to discover the hidden treasures of the earth. And here, in this request, we can see most clearly the difficulty of setting any clear dividing line between so-called black and white magic.

Treasure *can* be used for the greater glory of beneficent supernatural powers; but it can also bring out the blackest instincts in man. And so any incantations addressed to the angels are not essentially different from those for invoking demons. The difference is solely one of *intention*. Any magical operation that taps the universe's occult power can do so for good or evil ends—depending on the magician. If the ends are evil, or black, it will be through demonic agencies that they are accomplished, through invoking evil spirits. And the operation becomes truly satanic only at the point when the magician signs a pact with the infernal powers, binding himself to them in return for further powers. The Romanian-born biblical scholar Moses Gaster, in *The Origin of the Kabbala* (1894), tried to distinguish between the "white" power of the cabbalist (drawn from knowledge of sacred writings) and the "black" power of the wizard (drawn from the Devil, and less powerful). But as Professor E. M. Butler—who wrote *Ritual Magic* (1948) and who is not to be confused with W. E. Butler, who was quoted earlier—remarks, any line thus drawn is as arbitrary "as all classifications of magic . . . are doomed to be; white and black are continually mingling and fertilising each other; and the ineffable names of the Kabbala were used and misused by the magical confraternity quite as profusely as those of the divinities of Egypt, Greece and Christendom."

Another magical practice that is associated with both black and white magic is the use of effigies—images of people to be harmed or spellbound. Whatever the motive behind the ritual, however, the use of effigies is a straightforward branch of sympathetic magic (based, remember, on the principle that an image or copy of something is the same as the thing itself,

and harm done to it causes harm to what it represents). The
most common form of effigy is the doll made (usually of
wax) to resemble the victim, often with parts of the garments
belonging to him, or with his hair or his nail parings, worked
into it. The doll can be wounded in a number of ways, including the obvious one of piercing it through the heart with
a needle. Indian sorcerers tied the doll to a stake and covered
it with a poisonous oil for over a week. In modern technological times, according to the French magazine *Réalités* in
1960, some Parisian sorcerers electrocute dolls or shatter
them with pneumatic drills.

Not all effigies are material. A man could be harmed if his
shadow was walked on, spat on, and marked with evil signs.
This practice was particularly prevalent in ancient Egypt,
where the shadow was regarded as one of man's several souls.
And as for the white or beneficent uses of effigies, an ancient
Assyrian formula for laying a ghost included burying the
effigy of the dead man, and washing in pure water the person
to whom his ghost has appeared—symbolizing the proper
burial of the former and the purification of the latter. Many
of the functions of magic that have already been looked at fall
clearly into either the black or the white camp: harming people is obviously black; protecting oneself is white. Also white
are curative remedies and the like. But two all-important
functions are by their nature invariably at the disposal of any
magician, whatever his color. Of these two, the first is *divination*—a magical operation that expresses most completely
man's desire to rationalize the forces of the universe. The divinatory arts comprise the many methods of predicting the
future and of discovering hidden things—methods like alectryomancy (divination by poultry) and oneiromancy (divination by dreams).

Alectryomancy was widely used in antiquity: a circle was
traced on the ground and divided into sections—each corresponding to a letter of the alphabet. These sections were
sprinkled with grain. A cock was then released, and the sections in which it pecked revealed the word or name that
answered the diviner's question.

A surprising number of the ancient forms of divination
still persist in the Western world today. The most common of
all (there must be few people without some experience of it)
is chiromancy or palmistry. Astrology also flourishes, as does
cartomancy, divination by cards. And here the Tarot pack represents one of the most interesting links between divination

past and present. It is a pack of playing cards of uncertain
origin, which first appeared in 14th-century Italy (where it
was used both for card games and for divination). It comprises 78 cards of which 56 were called the "minor arcana"
and the other 22 the "major arcana." The 56 are divided into
four suits (the origins of our modern hearts, clubs, diamonds,
and spades), which were usually called cups, wands, pentacles, and swords. In the major arcana, called trumps, each of
the 22 cards corresponds to an allegorical figure, and contains
a complicated symbolic meaning. It is said, for example, that
into each card is coded what is virtually a book, and that
anyone possessing knowledge of the keys to decode it can un-
lock a wealth of wisdom from every single picture.

There are endless ways of dealing the Tarot for the purposes of divination. One example, picked from hundreds, is
known as the Cross. Fifteen cards are drawn, three of which
are set out side by side in the center; they represent the present life of the consultant. Three above these consist of the
answer to the question that has been put. Three below indicate the consequences of action taken. Three to the left show
the life of the emotions, and three to the right, the social life.
But whatever method is used, the art of the Tarot apparently
consists in allowing the cards to stimulate the unconscious of
the person attempting the divination, rather than in reading
the meanings too literally. This can be said to be the basis of
all divinatory methods. The most successful operator is often,
for this reason, a clairvoyant who uses cards, words, hand-
writing, palms, or horoscopes as a focus and a mediating
channel between his "intuition"—the unconscious mind—and
the world outside. Thus the Tarot and other divinatory tools
may be seen as yet another example of the way people have
found it necessary to contain the complexities of life inside
symbols, in order to gain an understanding of them—whether
that understanding can be called "intuitive," "irrational," or
not.

The second of the black-or-white functions of magic is perhaps less familiar, that of causing material *change*. Most
magic involves change of some sort, but an enormous amount
of it is aimed at producing a specific type of change. Here we
are referring to *alchemy*, which was concerned with changing
base metals into gold and the search for the "philosopher's
stone" by which this transformation might be effected. The
quest was carried on with varying degrees of intensity from
antiquity to the Renaissance.

All writings on alchemy are difficult and devious, and to make any sense of them, we must remind ourselves of the dictum "as above, so below." We must also remember that, as in other magical enterprises, the search was conducted on a number of different levels at once. As we have already briefly noted, metals have many correspondences in magical thought—with parts of the body, with the planets, with stars, and with aspects of the earth. The careful sifting and purifying of base metals into gold could therefore be seen as a vast mystical analogy. As Idries Shah, Grand Sheik of the Sufis (a widespread system of mysticism generally associated with Islam), has recently written: "The methods of concentration, distillation, maturing and mixing, endowed with chemical names, is none other than an organisation of the mind and body to produce a human, not a chemical, effect. That there were imitators who practised physical chemistry is in no doubt whatever. But it is equally true to say that there were until fairly recently (and they still linger in some places) people who believed that physical things had a spiritual parallel." He adds that the originator of alchemy was traditionally thought to have been the Greek god Hermes, who guided the souls of the dead to the underworld—who represented, in other words, the link between the human world and the divine.

So in alchemy the attempt to achieve material transmutation went hand in hand with a quest to reach spiritual perfection. For it was thought that by attaining a Christ-like state a man would automatically acquire the power of transformation—the power revealed by Christ when he performed the miracle of turning water into wine. But since the loftiness of this ideal made it all but unobtainable, it might at first sight seem that alchemy was at worst a greedy search for gold and at best an allegorical process that never contained any actual metallurgical knowledge.

Two modern French writers Louis Pauwels and Jacques Bergier (who were mentioned in Chapter 1) have shed new light on this old subject. After studying alchemical books and manuscripts, they concluded that alchemy is the only para-religious activity that has contributed to our knowledge of science. To quote from their book *The Dawn of Magic:*

"We have heard a learned scientist affirm that since repetitions of the process of refining and purifying metals and metalloids do not in any way alter their properties, the recommendations of the alchemists in this connection could be considered as a kind of mystic lesson in patience, a ritual gesture, like telling the beads of a rosary. And yet it is just by such a refining process and the technique described by the alchemists, known today as 'zone fusion,' that the germanium and silicon used in transistors is prepared. We know now . . . that by purifying a metal very thoroughly and then introducing minute quantities, some millionths of a gramme, of impurities . . . the substance thus treated is endowed with new and revolutionary properties."

So Pauwels and Bergier argue that experiments did take place in alchemy that yielded material results. And as examples of alchemists who were also pioneer scientists, they cite Albertus Magnus (1193-1280), who was the first to describe the chemical composition of cinnabar, whitelead, and minium; Paracelsus (1493-1541) who introduced the medical use of chemical compounds; and Johann-Baptiste della Porta (1538-1615) who recognized the existence of gases. But they also believe that a spiritual "transmutation" sometimes took place during alchemical experiments—that the change that occurred in an alchemist's crucible also occurred in his soul. They say: "All the traditional texts stress this phenomenon and evoke the moment when the 'Great Work' is accomplished and the alchemist becomes an 'awakened man.' It would seem that these old texts describe in this way the final stage of all real knowledge of the laws of matter and of energy, including technical knowledge."

These days, the usual concept of the alchemist is of a man with a long white beard devoting his life to a task incapable of solution; absorbed among his retorts and crucibles and dreams. Our idea of the magician is often similar (the cloaked old man in the pointed hat, like cartoon versions of Merlin); but it also tends to evoke the image of a stage illusionist or perhaps the witch-doctor of simple societies. Several hundred years ago the position was different. The magician represented and reconciled many different practices. He possessed knowledge of the magic arts; he was a physician, theologian, philosopher and, if astrologer, also astronomer and if alchemist, also chemist. If he was prevented from exercising his art (or more usually, killed) by the representatives of whatever the current orthodoxy happened to be, it was probably less for his heresies than for an unconventional and disturbing view of the world that was thought to constitute a threat to the established order.

One of the most notable examples of this kind of magician was the Swiss alchemist and physician Paracelsus. Though chiefly a healer, it was his knowledge of alchemy that led him to explore the possibility of extracting medicines from mineral substances (as opposed to traditional herbal remedies). Paracelsus is credited with having performed many astonishing and miraculous cures, which he always insisted were not entirely due to his medicines, since he was convinced that the health of the body could not be achieved without the well-being of the soul that dwelt in it. Thus Paracelsus, by reason of his concern with spiritual welfare, could be said to resemble the theurge rather than the more conventional image of the sorcerer or thaumaturge.

In contrast, a man who epitomized the thaumaturge was Count Cagliostro, who in 1743 was born Guiseppe Balsamo in Palermo, Sicily. He was a flamboyant and mysterious figure, who claimed to be master of every branch of magic. Among his alleged exploits was the manufacture by alchemical means of a huge and brilliant diamond, which he offered to the French Cardinal Louis de Rohan. In London, he convinced a large following of his magical powers by forecasting several times in a row the winning numbers in lotteries. Not surprisingly, Cagliostro, as an alchemist, seer, and magician who was famous throughout Europe, ran into trouble and was imprisoned many times and in many countries for fraud and witchcraft. But so great was his name among the people of Paris, that when he was released from the Bastille, in 1786, a crowd of 10,000 turned out to acclaim him. Another more modern example of a magician whose notoriety caused him to fall foul of the authorities was Britain's Aleister Crowley. During the 1920s in Britain, America, and Europe, Crowley's activities got him into the kind of trouble that ended in exile and poverty.

Crowley, the son of a devout member of the English sect of the Plymouth Brethren, shocked the Western world by his newspaper accounts of Black Masses and sexual orgies. A monstrous legend grew up round him; he was proclaimed by the press on both sides of the Atlantic as "the wickedest man in the world," "a cannibal at large," and "king of depravity." Serious occultists, however, have questioned the basis of this legend, claiming that Crowley, a prolific writer and poet, was essentially a seeker after spiritual truth. Certainly he had studied the occult philosophies of India and Tibet; and could have been said to be attempting through sexual indulgence to achieve higher states of consciousness and knowledge. Even so, the legend was largely manufactured by Crowley himself:

he adopted the title of "the Beast," after the Beast of the
Apocalypse, the false prophet of the New Testament Book of
Revelations. He initiated into his ceremonies a large number
of women whom he styled Scarlet Women, and whom he
branded with the "Mark of the Beast." Some of them, unbalanced by Crowley's demands, ended their lives disastrously,
in poverty or suicide. Crowley founded a community in Ce-
falu, Sicily, which was broken up by the police after one of
his followers had died, allegedly as the result of imbibing the
blood of a cat that had been ritually killed. But though he
was expelled from the island and his temple became deserted,
it was rumored, as late as 1947, that disciples of Crowley
were still living there.

Though Crowley provides an extreme case of damaging
publicity, it would seem that any magician who wants to survive must be prepared to operate in secret, since the unorthodoxy of most magical systems usually makes them unaccepta-
ble to society. The alternative, of course, is to pursue magic
publicly only in theory or in writing—which was the method
adopted by the 19th-century French occultist known as Eli-
phas Lévi.

Lévi started his career by training for the priesthood, but
soon abandoned theology for magic. His reputation as an occultist spread fast; he had a wide circle of disciples, some of
whom he initiated by correspondence. His admirers claimed
that he possessed the secret of the philosopher's stone, and
his exposition of high or "transcendental" magic, as he
named it, aroused immense enthusiasm for both magic and
the study of the Cabbala. But Lévi was not merely a theorist.
There exists a fascinating account by him of his conjuration
of the 16th-century magician Cornelius Agrippa. For years
he had written about and studied the magical arts, but apparently without achieving anything very much in the way of results until comparatively late in his life. And when the materialization *did* occur, Lévi, in spite of all he had written and
learned on the occult, fell down in a faint of terror.

If Lévi's work seems to have been more theoretical than
practical this would seem to underline the theory that magicians are usually born and not made. All practicing magicians
seem to have been started on their careers by a common se-
quence of experience. It is a ritual pattern of isolation, suffering, death, and resurrection—a pattern found throughout the
history of magic. Sometimes this process takes place as a series of external events; sometimes it is experienced inwardly,

though no less really, in the loneliness that the candidate must endure. Certain initiations of Australian witchdoctors, for example, are supposed to involve the candidate's ritual death by mutilation—an act performed either by spirits or souls of the dead. Among the Smith Sound Eskimos, an aspiring magician is shut up alone at night in a cave, which he cannot leave until he has "died" and is, with the aid of spirits, reborn. Similarly, the ancient Egyptians entombed their candidates for elevated grades of the priesthood, and dug them out again after several days. Even if they emerged sane, they would have been "changed"—which means, of course, initiated.

Modern experiments in weightlessness carried out in space research laboratories indicate some of the effects of these lonely and terrible rituals. The modern human "guinea-pigs" are deprived of all sensory stimuli (which is very like being incarcerated in a dark, silent cave) and within 20 minutes at most they lose their sense of identity and begin to hallucinate. In magicians' initiations something similar must have happened, and through the days of isolation the candidate would have wandered in an inner world, with the spirits and demons and angels that inhabit it, and would have had successfully to make his way back to the outside world.

In a society that has no organized priesthood or caste of magicians to set the form of initiation for the aspirant, the pattern is the same, but it takes place in private. As we have already seen in Chapter 4 (and shall see again in Chapter 7) the start of the career of a medium or of a voodoo priest is usually marked by an illness, accident, or trauma of some sort. So is that of the magician. As Eliade writes of the shamans: "More or less pathological sicknesses, dreams, and ecstasies are . . . so many means of reaching the condition of Shaman."

Once initiated, the magician will have to be taught and trained by his masters in the art. And it is a long and arduous apprenticeship. But what happens when there are no apparent teachers around, as in civilized Western societies? The journeys apparently can still be made, alone; though again it becomes clear, from W. E. Butler's guide book on how to do it (p. 98) that this is no easy or swift matter. Butler's book is based on the Cabbala, and contains information that has been made public in the West over the last 50 or so years by the writings of a number of famous British students of the Cabbala—among them Macgregor Mathers, A. E. Waite, and Al-

eister Crowley. Essentially, Butler's instructions to the stu-
dent-magician concern the techniques that may be used to
link, "deliberately and consciously, a symbol with its appropriate force, and to become so expert at it that the mere
fact of the symbol rising in consciousness brings with it a
surge of emotional energy of the type associated with that
symbol of the Tree" (the Tree being the famous and beautiful glyph mentioned on p. 103). The achievement of this
state, says Butler, is like learning "the alphabet of a new language," though its attainment is clearly a laborious and ut-
terly absorbing journey toward self-knowledge and self-
control.

It also becomes clear from his book that in the 20th century as in the 10th, the *tools* of the magician are the same.
One set of tools is to be found in the magician himself, his
emotions and his senses, so that what he hears and sees, what
he feels, how he moves, the direction of his energies all are
an essential part of the whole. The important role played by
the emotions accounts for the frequent connection between
magical activity and sexual orgy (as in some ancient Greek
cults where priestesses ritually "prostituted" themselves—or
perhaps even in the scandals associated with Aleister Crowley
in Britain in the 1920s). It also explains the important part
played by scents and colors and sounds in magical rituals.
The second set of tools—for example the cup, the wand, and
the circle—reinforces the first. The magic circle (usually
traced by the magician's wand) is, in fact, the simplest form
of pantacle. Inside it, the magician is protected against all
hostile occult powers.

The magicial way of thinking has by no means disappeared
from our lives in the 20th century—in spite of the outwardly
prevailing attitudes in the West of rationalism and objectivity.
And magic's tenacity in the inner life of the individual today
is to some extent matched by its continuing presence in some
highly respectable institutions—such as, especially, the
churches. Though the organized religions long regarded magicians as blasphemers and heretics, they retain at their hearts
living relics not of thaumaturgy certainly, but of theurgy, in
their approach to the mysteries of the universe. How else can
the ceremonial invocations and incantations to be found in the
services of almost every religion be explained?

There has also been some indication in recent years of secular attempts to reanimate magic's old bones, to discover the
life that may still linger in them. As we pointed out in Chap-

ter 1, the 1960s have seen the beginning of a growing revival of interest in religion, mysticism, and the occult. Increasing attention is being paid to the work of Jung, who writes of marvels and magics embedded in our unconscious minds. Wide interest is being taken in drugs like mescalin and LSD 25, which seem to produce much the same effect as the old magical rituals were once said to have done. A new approach is also being made to the study of mental illness by doctors and psychiatrists who are beginning to examine the kind of picture of the world that is built by the disordered mind. To quote again from Dr. Laing's paper to the 1964 International Congress of Psycho-Therapy (p. 23): "Experience is mad when it steps beyond the horizons of our common, that is, our communal sense. . . . [The madman's] centre of experience moves from ego to Self. Mundane time becomes merely anecdotal, only the Eternal matters. The madman is, however, confused . . . nevertheless, he often can be to us, even through his profound wretchedness and disintegration the hierophant of the sacred." He goes on to suggest that the sane can learn from the mad; that the psychiatrist must use the schizophrenic as his guide to this inner world.

So as psychology (along with the other sciences, even physics) begins to look beyond the previously well-defined frontiers of our knowledge, can we continue to deny the possible existence of a reality that lies outside our present area of comprehension—a reality that, if it exists, may not behave according to the rules that govern the world that we do comprehend? It may well be that we are on the verge of an enormous breakthrough in understanding, whose results will include evidence that the old magicians were not all superstitious and ignorant dabblers but were in their own way testifying to the presence of a power or force that really exists.

6 IN SEARCH OF WITCHES

In the Western world today our conception of a witch, if we have a conception at all, is probably little more than a vague amalgam of the Weird Sisters from *Macbeth*, the children-eating crones that inhabit forests in Grimms' Fairy Tales (and in Walt Disney's cartoon treatments of them), and the beak-nosed hags wearing conical hats and riding broomsticks that children pretend to be on Halloween. We picture the witch casting spells on her enemies, stirring loathsome animal parts into a cauldron, and dancing on stormy mountain tops in the moonlight. In fact, if we were to put all our ideas on witches together, we should probably arrive at something like this:

"A witch or hag is she which being deluded by a league made with the devil through his persuasion, inspiration, and juggling, thinketh she can design what manner of evil things soever, either by thought or imprecation, as to shake the air with lightnings and thunder, to cause hail and tempests, to remove green corn or trees to another place, to be carried of her familiar (which hath taken upon him the deceitful shape of a goat, swine, or calf, etc.) into some mountain far distant, in a wonderful short space of time, and sometimes to fly upon a staff or fork, or some other instrument, and to spend all the night after with her sweetheart, in playing, sporting, banqueting, dancing, dalliance, and divers other devilish lusts and lewd disports, and to show a thousand such monstrous mockeries."

That rich and rolling sentence, written by a 16th-century English lawyer named William West, seems to sum up the witch fairly definitely, and also to conform closely to our modern conception. The only difference is that West, like other writers of his time, makes a strong point of the witch being *in direct league with the Devil*.

Not so today. Modern newspapers, for instance, when producing a story about witches (which they do remarkably often, either semi-facetiously or semi-salaciously), treat "witchcraft" and "black magic" as synonymous terms and make little or no reference to Satan. An article in the British magazine *Punch* in September 1958, for example, refers to "a witch who cured men and beasts and made faulty cars go when garages were baffled." Another story in the French paper *L'Express* in October 1963 quotes an old farmer on witches he knew who could prevent hens from laying. And *Time* magazine, in May 1953, described witches in Arizona who killed by "hexes."

Clearly the word "witch" has today lost most of its satanic associations, and has gone back to the older, pre-Christian inter-changeability with words like "sorcerer" (or "sorceress") and "magician." In the *Odyssey*, Circe, who changed men into swine among other things, is called sometimes a witch, sometimes a sorceress. So is Medea, the evil protagonist of Euripides' play. So, for that matter, are the Three Witches in *Macbeth*. And in the same way two European women who figured in two sensational 20th-century cases were called indiscriminately witches and sorceresses in the news reports.

To digress for a moment: women have always predominated in the history of witches, and a host of more or less unsatisfactory explanations of this fact could be cited. For instance, 16th-century writers felt women were more credulous and impressionable than men, and so more easily tempted by Satan. Others felt that Satan, being a male personification of evil, preferred women assistants. Later authorities like the 19th-century French pathologist J. M. Charcot saw that demonic possession was in fact a form of hysteria (from *hystera*, the Greek word for uterus), and considered it primarily a female sexual disorder. Anthropologists, recalling the female shamans of many primitive tribes, suggested that the supposedly "irrational" tendencies of the female left an opening for occult and quasi-religious belief. Probably the real explanation (if there is one) will somehow be connected with the fact that women were for so long thought to be inferior beings, and thus were considered more susceptible to foolishness and sin; also, they were less able to protect themselves against accusations leveled at them by the entirely male and officially celibate Church and Inquisition. Anyway, just as there are many male mediums today, there were many male witches in the past, though outnumbered by the women. Here we shall avoid the terms that have been coined for the male witch—such as the confusing *wizard* or the somewhat affected *warlock*—and call a witch a witch, indiscriminate of sex. Now back to the two present-day female witch-sorceresses.

One of these women lived in Naples, and (as a British newspaper put it) had been "practicing sorcery for most of her 77 years, dispensing spells, charms, and love potions from herbs, birds' feathers and beaks, and animals' bones and skulls." Her name was Marianna Castellano, and she died in 1957 in remarkable circumstances. Twenty years earlier she had been hired by another woman to cast a spell on the latter's relatives. The "witch's" fee was about a dollar a month for life; but after the war inflation set in, and she demanded a larger monthly payment. Her client paid the higher price for some years, but in 1957 decided to pay no more. So Marianna set out to collect, using as an inducement a pan full of blazing gasoline. But somehow, so the newspapers reported, the panicky client got hold of the pan and threw its contents over the "sorceress," who was burned to death.

A less dramatic story, recounted by the *Parisien Libéré* in 1963, featured a 72-year-old woman named Madame Marie Moreau, who was accused of using witchcraft to create discord within a family in a small village in France. She denied the charge, asserting that she had never committed an evil deed. Her work (which was reportedly much in demand) involved only good deeds like curing sick animals and people, removing spells from fields, stables, and houses, and so on. She used salt to work her magic—ordinary salt, which she infused with power through incantations. Though most of her customers would call her a witch, she is more frequently referred to as "the good lady of Château-Ponsac."

As a "good lady," she belongs to a class of witch that has gained predominance in recent years—that of the so-called white witches. Most of the self-professed witches that are heard of today claim to be on the side of the good—like Mrs. Sybil Leek, head of an English group centered in the New Forest, who told London's *Daily Express* in 1964: "I am a white witch and come from a long line of white witches, who exist only to do good."

Although white witches appear very often in the witch headlines of the present, they appear only rarely in the witch legends of the past. It is most useful to think of them as a branching-off from the main stream of witchery. Nor can they simply be classified as sorcerers, for while they (like their black opposites) use many of the techniques of sorcery, their activities also seem to resemble many of the quasi-religious ceremonies of witches. So they are not merely sorcerers; nor are they satanists; nor Christians. (They claim to be the inheritors of a pagan tradition that antedates almost any known religion.) Because they seem therefore to be unique, to stand on one side of the European-American witch tradition, we shall leave them on one side for a while and concentrate on the witch proper (or improper)—the wicked witch of folk tale and history. And here it must be emphasized that the witch to be discussed here is an entirely *Christian* phenomenon (though having some things in common with witch-sorcerers of non-Christian societies) and so will be looked at primarily within the confines of the Western Christian world.

A medieval representation of a common conception of the Devil. A 16th-century Italian illustration shows the Devil carrying off a witch to help him with his infernal enterprises. (From *Historia de gentibus septentrionalibus* by Olaus Magnus, Rome, 1555.)

Some authorities see the witch tradition as a very short one, lasting for about 300 years, from the mid 15th century to the mid 18th. These authorities are using the word "witch" in a very restricted sense, to mean only those unfortunates who were persecuted by civil and ecclesiastical authorities during the peak of the witch-hunt frenzy. To these writers, the witchcraft that people believed in during the 1400 years of Christian history that preceded the frenzy was simply sorcery. The line is apparently drawn firmly: sorcery is magic at work, and is about as old as mankind; witchcraft was magic plus a great deal more, and lasted only briefly.

But to differentiate between the two by means of a historical dividing line is poor definition and worse history. Much more useful is the distinction drawn in terms of *intent*. The sorcerer or black magician (remember that we are leaving white magic on one side for a while) may cast spells, charms, and hexes, and stir up love potions and other "eye of newt, toe of frog" mixtures; he may conjure up demons or even Satan himself, and may (like Faust) "sell his soul" to the Devil by means of a pact. But all these activities are directed toward a *selfish* end; the sorcerer's motive is to gain riches or power or pleasure for himself, in this world, by means of evil magic and demonic assistance.

The witch's activities, as far as magic is concerned, may exactly parallel the sorcerer's, but her motive is different. Her magicial power is operated to serve the *Devil's* purposes, not her own. Her principal function is the worship of the Devil, which involves the conscious repudiation of God and the Christian faith. Thus witches, as distinct from sorcerers, must be seen as part of the dark side of Christian belief. They are the human emissaries of hell, exactly as the clergy of most persuasions are the human representatives of heaven.

The overall distinction, then, can be put very simply. Every witch is something of a sorcerer, but not every sorcerer is a witch. And this chapter will examine all witches' supposed activities—of which sorcery is only one.

As is always the case with history, no matter how many watertight compartments we try to divide it into, there is overlapping and confusion. The idea of the witch as the Devil's emissary doing the Devil's work arose almost with Christianity itself; but the confusion between sorcerer and witch lasted for centuries. Most of the pre-Christian beliefs about sorcery thus came to be imputed, unchanged, to the Enemy of the Christian God—the Devil, with his legions of fallen angels. (In the same way, among the early Christians the pagan deities came to be identified with Satan and his demons; hence any continuing worship of the gods was tantamount to devil worship.) Satan led people to commit sorcery

exactly as he led them to commit other sins, and so, naturally, the early Christians legislated (in ecclesiastical and civil
law) against it. Christian emperors who ruled over the crumbling ruins of the Roman Empire passed laws like that of
Theodosius (in 381) forbidding meetings and magical sacrifices in old temples—and showing a typical confusion between witchcraft and remnants of the Greco-Roman religion.
In England in 690, Theodore, Archbishop of Canterbury, issued edicts against sacrificing to demons and casting spells.
Similarly, laws throughout other parts of Europe opposed the
operation of witchcraft. But the penalties were never savage;
in France in the sixth century, a witch who had killed by
magic was merely required to pay a specified fine (though if
the murderer failed to pay, he or she could be burned).

In these centuries, then, the so-called Dark Ages, witchcraft was sorcery and both were illegal and more or less sinful. But later, in the Middle Ages, the Church gradually
began to take more careful looks at the idea of magic; gradually the authorities began to suggest that evil magic was the
Devil's work, and that the practitioners must therefore be
somehow in league with the Devil and in explicit opposition
to God and His Church. So gradually, witchcraft came to be
named a heresy.

Heresy can be defined as religious error persistently adhered to in the face of the truth as defined by the Church.
The various inquisitions of the Middle Ages, which had been
busy pursuing all kinds of heresies, had occasionally probed
into sorcery, seeking heresy—and finding it. In the early 14th
century in southern France about 600 people were accused of
heretical sorcery (sorcery for the Devil's purposes) and were
convicted and burned. But this was an isolated case, and
there were rarely others until the 15th century. (Also, in these
rare cases the charge was *sorcery;* the other "crimes" of
witchcraft that we are about to examine, such as the pact and
the sexual orgy, did not crop up in these early trials.) Then
in 1484 came the bull of Pope Innocent VIII that unequivo-
cally defined witchcraft in *all* its aspects and practices as a
heresy; and this marked the Catholic Church's declaration of
war against the practitioners of that heresy.

We shall return to the Inquisition and its pursuit of heresies later, when we deal in detail with witch-hunting and
witch trials. The main point here is that it was the witch's
consorting with the Devil, or the way in which she was believed to consort with the Devil, that branded her as a here-

tic. A conscious and willing *pact* made with Satan was the principal means, the witch-hunters believed, by which a person acquired a witch's powers and gained admission to witches' activities. But here it must be noted that the traditional pact of legend and folklore, a contract written or at least signed in blood, appears infrequently among witches. Such documents were usually drawn up by black magicians, who would call up the Devil to strike a bargain with him—so many goods and services to be delivered by Satan in exchange for the consignee's soul at death. No question of Devil-*worship* was involved. But witches were not trading their souls in the afterlife for riches or power in this life; they were committing themselves, body and soul, before and after death, to the Devil's work. They were Satan's servants, not his customers. And so their pacts took the form of ceremonial entry into a kind of secret society devoted to evil.

A would-be witch's initial approach to the Devil was often made through a practicing witch, part of whose work was to seek out converts. The neophyte would be taken along to a witches' meeting known as a *sabbat* and there presented to the Devil, who was alleged to preside at such meetings. Then followed the ceremony of initiation—sometimes simple, sometimes complex, but always managing to blend sacrilege and obscenity. One of the simplest ceremonies on record comes from the testimony of a young French girl given at her trial in 1594. When she was presented to the Devil by her lover (who was a witch) she was required merely to make the sign of the cross with her left hand, in front of the celebrants at a sabbat. Then, apparently, she was in; and she joined in the general orgiastic veneration of the Devil that followed.

A more involved ritual was described by a 17th-century Italian demonologist, Francesco-Maria Guazzo, who lists 11 separate stages, as follows:

1. A spoken denial of the Christian faith.

2. Rebaptism in the Devil's name, at which point the novice gained a new name in place of his Christian one.

3. Symbolic removal of the baptismal chrism (consecrated oil mixed with balm) by the Devil's touch.

4. Denial of godparents and the gaining of new sponsors.

5. Gift of a piece of clothing to the Devil, as a token of submission.

6. Oath of allegiance to the Devil made while standing in a magic circle.

7. Inclusion of the initiate's name in the "Book of Death."

8. A promise to sacrifice children to the Devil.

9. A promise to pay annual tribute to the Devil (black-colored gifts, etc.).

10. Marking the initiate with the Devil's mark—a strangely-shaped area on the skin that became insensitive.

11. Various vows of special service to the Devil, including destruction of holy relics and, especially, keeping the secrets of the sabbat.

Other accounts of pacts give special emphasis to two further stages: a female initiate was usually required to have sexual intercourse with the Devil; and often all initiates were required to conclude the ceremony by kissing the Devil's buttocks.

Of course sex played a fundamental role in all witch celebrations, as did various involved perversions and obscenities. And apparently most female witches were regularly required to have intercourse with their master, as a sort of reaffirmation of the evil bond between them. (Invariably the witches asserted in their confessions at trials that the experience was unpleasant, in fact highly painful; in this way the prosecutors may have been ensuring that sexual pleasure did not come to be seen as a devilish enjoyment.) Also, sexuality was a means of gathering to the witches' fold new recruits who would not come willingly—waverers, perhaps, who both yearned and feared. An already committed servant of Satan might seduce a girl first to his bed and then to his sabbat; girls who surrendered sexually may have found the next step, into full witch-hood, a natural one. But the Devil, it was believed, did not rely entirely on human seducers; certain of his demons were especially empowered to conscript souls through what prosecutors at witch trials loved to call "the lusts of the flesh." To women, Satan sent demons called *incubi;* to men, those known as *succubi.*

The devils themselves were thought to be sexless, and often a lesser demon would at different times take either form. It was generally thought that the incubi outnumbered the succubi nine to one—probably because chastity was more important in women (though perhaps, as a few medieval authors suggest, because women were thought to be more licentious). The task of these demons was thought to be, simply, to lead people into sexual sin. Naturally they took on human form to do so; but the sin itself was aggravated by the fact that demons were not considered to be human, and therefore sexual intercourse with them was an act of sodomy (in its widest sense). The unfortunate victims of such demons, especially the women visited by incubi, were often punished whether they submitted willingly or not. But usually distinction was made between the witches who were willing, the waverers who were seduced, and the innocent who were raped.

Before and after the peak of the witch fear, a few men had suggested that the incubus-succubus idea arose largely out of highly charged erotic imaginations. Indeed, there was often some confusion, in the minds of the witch-hunters, between evil sexual dreams sent by demons and evil sexual acts perpetrated by them. But some authorities drew a distinction between nightmares and incubi: the former inspired only terror, the latter as often as not caused pleasure. Many a woman seemed strangely reluctant to be separated from her incubus by an exorcism. The reason was often that the incubus-succubus provided an excellent loophole in the strict prohibitions against sexual relations outside marriage. Demons were thought capable of impregnating humans, and so had fatherhood by rape attributed to them in many awkward illegitimacies. An unfaithful wife could assure her husband that she had been assaulted by an incubus; and similarly for a straying husband. A man accused of seduction or illegitimate paternity could swear that an incubus must have assumed his shape. And so on.

But the belief in the sexual demons had an even darker side. A girl using the incubus as an explanation of pregnancy might find the trick backfiring when she was beaten or burned for consorting with demons, if no one chose to believe her story of having been raped. Stories circulated about the monstrous creatures that incubi fathered on women; and so any baby even slightly malformed came to be suspect. And, as one more example, the incubus offered husbands a vicious way of getting rid of unwanted wives; one simply accused one's wife of sleeping with a devil and even if she escaped torture or death, the marriage could then be annulled.

Sex being a perennial human obsession, and especially so in an age of repression like the Middle Ages, it was naturally insisted upon by the persecutors as a main feature of an accused witch's confession. But there were a few other ways by which the Devil was said to draw people into his clutches. Greed, for example—the Devil's offer of riches to witches—supposedly caused a few to fall. And sheer malice must have tempted a few to enroll at their local sabbat, in the hope of acquiring magical powers with which to wreak havoc among their neighbors and enemies.

Also it was believed that if one would not come willingly, and would not succumb to any of the foregoing blandishments, the Devil had a last resort—or means of revenge. One of his demons would forcibly gain control of the human in question, a takeover known as *demonic possession.*

The possessing devil enters the person's body without displacing the soul, and makes the person speak and act as it wishes. A demonic personality asserts itself; the victim is therefore rarely held responsible for his or her words and acts. (Nor is the victim held responsible in cases of *obsession,* where the Devil and his agents besiege the person from without—as St. Anthony was terrifyingly and subtly besieged.) Nevertheless, virtuous people were usually thought to be immune from demonic possession, which is why the beleaguered early saints like Anthony or Hilary were only obsessed. To some extent, then, victims of possession did not win unqualified sympathy, for it could be felt that they had, by their sins, left the door a little ajar for the invading devil.

But at the same time possession was thought to be most frequently caused by witchcraft. Witches were believed to force a demon's entry into a person by means of spells— necessary in those cases where people's blameless lives barred the way. In this way the witch could gratify her desire to degrade the victim by sending a demon to drive him or her to the most blasphemous and obscene speech and actions. Thus, the theorists suggested, did a witch harm the enemies of Satan, those good people who avoided sin and resisted the witch's attempts to recruit them. For this reason inmates of monasteries were especially open to demonic attacks in the 15th and 16th centuries.

When a demon made his entry and took control, a fairly stereotyped pattern of behavior resulted. The victim's face and body would go into startling contortions (which were often impossible for an unpossessed person to imitate); the expression would take on a definitely devilish look. The voice would change, even young girls speaking in coarse, gruff tones, and in this new voice the victim would often scream invective against God in the foulest of language, or speak in foreign or unknown tongues, or simply foam at the mouth and speak gibberish. And stranger things were reputed to happen. Victims would vomit quantities of strange objects—needles and pins, broken glass or pottery, hair, bark, stones; they would make animal noises, perform feats of superhuman strength, and even rise several feet into the air.

While these last somewhat excessive signs of possession occur again and again in accounts of witches and witch trials, many of them can be written off on the grounds of inaccuracy (due to excitement) or over-credulity (due to prior suggestion) on the observers' part. But there is no need to dismiss the entire concept of possession and its symptoms. Undoubtedly many people did change, facially and vocally, did rage and rant and curse, did speak strangely or make animal noises, did become terribly strong and uncontrollably violent in their convulsive actions. These are nothing more than the symptoms of hysteria (though epilepsy and similar afflictions were also often ascribed to devils). Similar symptoms can be found among primitives like the Azande (mentioned on p. 36). There the witchdoctors' dancing and singing induce hysteria in themselves and their audience, producing tremendous physical feats, strange cries, gibberish, and hallucinations. In much the same way, among some of the extreme religious sects in America and elsewhere, the effects of music and hypnotic oratory and chanting by preacher and congregation send the latter into ecstatic, hysterical convulsions, "speaking in tongues," and more. It is not surprising, then, that hysterical possession was prevalent, and highly contagious, in the Middle Ages and after. The persecution of witches was itself a mass hysteria, to which judges and prosecutors and witch-hunters succumbed—just as, on the other side, mentally disturbed people succumbed to suggestion and auto-suggestion (aided by the repressive nature of society and the dominance of an ascetic religion) and became possessed.

But widespread hysteria cannot be held solely responsible for the frequency of cases of possession. Often fraud was perpetrated and found out; presumably it was just as often perpetrated successfully. People might pretend to be possessed if they felt they were in danger of being accused of witchcraft (because strange actions would not be held against them if they were seen to be in a devil's control). Or they might simulate possession in order to bring a charge of witchcraft against an enemy. Or they might do so merely to draw attention to themselves, to be briefly the center of attraction.

As far as the non-fraudulent cases are concerned, many authorities today (not surprisingly, especially within organized religion) reject the "hysteria" explanation and still hold the Devil and his minions responsible for possession. Nor are such authorities considering the subject historically only; as pointed out by the French writer Monsignor L. Cristiani in *Satan and the Modern World* (1959), many cases of possession occur today; and the Church today deals with these cases just as it did centuries ago, by *exorcism*.

We saw in Chapter 3 how clergymen exorcise ghosts from haunted houses. The procedure is similar in the exorcism of devils from occupied bodies. Monsignor Cristiani gives a detailed account of how a devil was driven out of a woman in 1954. Like most exorcisms, it was a dramatic and at times terrifying duel between demon and priest. It is told mostly in dialogue, between the priest and the devil (speaking through the woman); the devil is seen to resist, to mock the priest, to lie and blaspheme—trying in every way to distract the priest and to make him give up. But the priest is adamant. He sprinkles the woman with holy water, touches her with a crucifix and with his stole, and recites prayers and litanies over her (knowing that this procedure causes devils great pain). This exorcism continued over a period of many months, but was eventually successful. (Of course, there is always the danger that the devil might return, as apparently happens occasionally.)

Some theologians have recently suggested (to sum up rather crudely their complex argument) that a literal and anthropomorphic belief in the Devil may no longer be possible. In the light of this suggestion it might be said that exorcism succeeds (in those cases where it does succeed) in the same faintly baffling way that various forms of psychoanalysis and psychotherapy succeed: that is, for certain individuals religious exorcism seems to be the correct method of approaching and curing (or at least relieving) mental disturbance. And, interestingly, accounts of dialogues between psychiatrists and schizophrenics show a marked similarity to dialogues between exorcists and those possessed by devils.

But all these somewhat digressive points are merely intended to underline the fact that, whatever we choose to call it—schizophrenia, hysteria, demonic possession—and whatever its cause, natural or supernatural, the phenomenon has existed and still exists. Cases from the 1550s and the 1950s show parallel symptoms; and other, rather more startling, resemblances occur between medieval and modern accounts. For example, concerning the methods used by a witch to wish a devil on to an enemy, most Renaissance experts believed that entry was principally gained through food. The witch's magic put the devil in the food, and the victim ate it. Often a major aim in exorcisms of the past was to force the victim to vomit the original devil-bearing food. Today we can read an account by Monsignor Cristiani of an exorcism performed in 1920 in which the demon inhabiting a woman admitted that "he had entered into her, by means of a sortilege [spell] contrived by a wizard, in the form of a bolus [pellet] of salt pork, washed down by a glass of white wine." In this case, we are told, the woman was freed when she vomited the bolus, "a little ball of salt pork, about the size of a nut, with seven horns."

The ability to infuse food with demons is one of the many magical powers conferred on witches by their satanic master. Without exception, the witch's powers were both conferred and used for the purposes of harming humanity, scorning God, and worshiping Satan. Obviously, almost any act of witchcraft managed to fulfill all three purposes at once. Also, many of the witch's magical acts—her spells, charms, potions, and hexes—are simply those of the evil sorcerer, with the difference of *motive* mentioned earlier. Chapter 5 has given an introductory look at magical acts and what lies behind them. Here we need only outline briefly some of the special effects for which the witch would aim, according to legend, in the exercise of her magical skill.

Witches were generally supposed to be avidly engaged in harming people directly, and not only by putting demons inside them. Disease and untimely or accidental deaths were often laid at a witch's door, just as in primitive communities. A wife's barrenness, or a stillbirth, or a drying-up of a mother's milk, or impotence or sterility in a man, were all often ascribed to witchcraft. Even minor mishaps like soured milk or burned food might be blamed on a witch's petty spite. In short, for hundreds of years the witch was the scapegoat for all the ills that might befall men.

Witchcraft was also blamed for harm done to a man's house or property. Witches were thought to injure or kill cattle and other animals and to destroy crops, often by spreading a powdered essence boiled up in a cauldron. They set fire to people's houses; they brought plagues of locusts; they called up mighty storms to ruin harvests or sink ships. (Their control of the weather is frequently mentioned in witch trials, various accused people confessing—under torture—to riding the tempest and hurling bolts of lightning.)

Also, witches sometimes acted as consultants for people engaged in some nefarious deed, of which by far the most common was seduction. The manufacture of love potions seems, by the accounts we have of indictments against witches, to have been a very profitable sideline, as was poisoning. Again, these are age-old preoccupations of sorcerers, which the witches supposedly took over to wage their master's war against God and man.

Incidentally, there is little doubt that a few people, called witches or magicians, *were* able to cause disease or death in men and beasts, and to produce love potions or poisons. These effects (if not the more dramatic ones like thunderstorms) could be produced by natural means. Many witches had a sound knowledge of drugs and herbalism, in spite of some of the irrelevant or apparently ridiculous beliefs that were bound up with it. We may not be able to believe that the "eye of newt" kind of potion could produce a correct vision of the future; but we can certainly recognize that a love potion will work when it contains, among other things, a powerful aphrodisiac like Spanish fly. And many did. In the same way, a concoction put together by a witch for would-be murderer (or used by the witch herself) will be quite successful when it contains (as did some of the formulas revealed to the Inquisition in France) a mixture of hemlock, belladonna, and arsenic. No magic here.

We shall come back to some of the implications of witches' knowledge of drugs. Turning again to the witch's harmful activities, we find that a very widely accepted method of bewitching or killing required little effort on the witch's part, no incantations or cauldron stirring—just a straight look. This is the power of the "evil eye," firmly believed in among witch-fearing communities from ancient Egypt to modern America (where it functions within voodoo, as well as witchcraft). Witches with the evil eye could cause disease or bewitch with a glance, either because of the evil within them that shone through their eyes, as some theories suggested, or because of evil spirits that actually issued from the eye. Sometimes this attribute attached itself to non-witches—innocent people (today we should call them "accident-prone") who seemed to carry bad luck and misfortune around with them, which they inflicted unwittingly upon anyone within reach. But more usually it was another of the witch's Devil-given powers; and a mother whose children fell ill or a farmer whose cows went dry would recall the old woman who had gazed strangely at the child or cow, and another witch-hunt would begin.

Two other magical abilities seem more often to belong to the real witch than to the mere sorcerer. These are the power of metamorphosis and the power of flight (which is often called *transvection*). The best-known kind of metamorphosis—man into wolf, or werewolf—will be discussed in Chapter 8; though it has connections with witchcraft (some witches assumed wolf form), there are marked differences, as will be seen. More usually a witch chose to assume the shape of some common and acceptable animal—a dog, cat, rabbit, toad, or bird—because the purpose of the disguise was to hide her activities and thus prevent people from recognizing her. Also, metamorphosis was one useful way of, say, getting into a house (through a high narrow window as a cat, under a door as an insect) to work evil magic on its occupants.

Metamorphosis was sometimes thought to be a special power reserved for witches who proved themselves especially zealous—something of a reward for achievements above and beyond the call of duty. Flying, however, was part of every witch's repertoire, although the theorists sometimes disagreed about how it was accomplished; three different ways were suggested at various times. Some felt the witch could simply fly through the air, unaided; others believed she flew with the aid of a magic implement, which might be a broomstick but was more often a cleft stick, a hayfork, or even a shovel. The third suggestion was that a devil, or the Devil himself, came to the witch in some demonic or animal form and carried her through the air.

Almost always the flights took place at night; and though sometimes a witch flew on one of her evil missions to harm her neighbors, most often she took to the air to get to witches' sabbats, which were often held in inaccessible places like the tops of mountains. (German witches, for instance, were supposed to gather on May 1 on the summit of Brocken, once called Blocksberg, a high peak in the Harz mountains.)

Whether the witch subscribed to the cleft stick or broom method or flew unaided, most authorities were certain that she could not take off without first applying a magic flying ointment. Usually she was thought to cover her entire body (witches always attended sabbats naked) with the ointment, though some theorists suggested that she merely touched certain key spots, perhaps her breasts and arms. Witch-hunters and other knowledgeable persons usually seemed vague about

the ointment's composition, revealing only that it was made
up of various noxious substances and that it was either black
in color or a repulsive green. Some of the wilder persecutors,
perpetuating the idea that witches killed and ate children,
suggested that children's blood might be a basic ingredient. A
similar ointment, it must be noted, conferred the power of
metamorphosis—a power that was often used by those who
had it for changing into a bird in order to manage the night
flights to sabbats.

Certain facts about the nature of this ointment, culled
from some of the less vague reports, indicate that neither
metamorphosis nor flight can be entirely dismissed as old
wives' tales confessed under torture. Though witches (or people who sincerely thought themselves to be witches) are
hardly likely to have possessed these powers, it is undeniable
that many of them were convinced they did, thanks, in part
at least, to the properties of the ointments. The anthropologist Dr. Margaret Murray (in her book *Witch Cult in Western Europe*) gives several formulas for the flying ointment,
and lays particular emphasis on one containing the drugs
aconite and belladonna—drugs that acted on the witches, it is
suggested, like narcotics and hallucinogens. (It had often
been suspected in the past, by a few clear-headed medieval
writers, that witches merely imagined or perhaps dreamed
that they had flown—and, for that matter, that they had
taken part in a sabbat. Even a few witch-hunters later subscribed to this view—like Sir George Mackenzie, the king's
advocate in Scotland in the 17th century—but since they believed that such fantasies were sent by the Devil, the dream
was considered as bad as the act, and the dreamers punished
just as severely.)

Even small doses of aconite produce excessive excitement,
belladonna causes delirium, and so on. And rubbing such
substances into the skin would, experts say, be as effective as
swallowing them. So witches roamed the night as black cats,
or flew naked through the air, in their drug-induced
dreams—prompted, no doubt, by a considerable amount of
prior suggestion and aided by some adjustments of memory
when giving a waking account.

Of course, few of the witches' sworn enemies would have
accepted this explanation—or, if they did, would simply have
claimed it was all the Devil's work anyway. Others played
down the ointment in their theories of witches' flight, and
played up the idea of a demon who acted as beast of burden.

Often this role was thought to be part of the job of the witch's *familiar* (or familiar spirit, or imp), her personal demon. The familiar acted sometimes as the witch's aide in working magic, sometimes as her personal servant. Though it was capable of harmful magic itself (since it was a demon, although usually a low-ranking one), its primary function seems to have been to focus and strengthen the witch's power.

Most witches had only one familiar—a dog, a cat (not necessarily black), a rabbit, sometimes an insect or a more unpleasant animal like a toad. It appears that multiple familiars were usually attached to those accused witches who were less visibly poor—which is the same thing as saying that the only people who kept more than one pet were those who could afford to. To this it must be added that the stories of familiars were most widespread in Britain, traditionally the land of animal lovers and pet owners. (That they harbored the most repulsive creatures as pets is less likely: but how many poverty-stricken old women in 15th-century England would be able to keep the odd spider, beetle, or even toad out of their hovels?) According to the tales, the familiar was rewarded for its work by food—ordinary food, or special tidbits, or (most often) some of the witch's blood sucked from her body. The place on the witch's body from which the familiar fed was known as the "witch's mark" (not to be confused with the devil's mark); both this and the presence of an animal were considered incontrovertible proof of witchery.

As the witch-hunting frenzy built up in the 15th century and after, people were provided with a means of ridding themselves of possibly dangerous witches: they turned suspects over to the Inquisition, which was considered to be the appropriate body for dealing with such evil-doers. But long before inquisitions were born, and also long after they disappeared, ordinary people had their own private ways of combating the Devil's emissaries. Folklore and tradition provided a knowledge of countermagic—spells, charms, and amulets that kept the witches at bay. For instance, a whip or switch of elder or mountain ash would drive a witch away; if these were unobtainable, garlic, bay branches, or witch hazel would do as well. (But better than all of these, if you could get it was holy water.) In Britain, stones with holes through them were worn as anti-witch amulets; or they were attached to doors to keep witches out of the house. Other widely used objects to prevent entry included "witch balls" (spheres of green glass) hung in windows, knives buried under doorsteps (witches cannot pass over cold iron), horse brasses, and horse shoes.

For personal protection against possible bewitchment or the evil eye, the precautions taken ranged from simple gestures (fist closed, thumb and little finger extended—or index and little fingers; or thumb pushed between index and second fingers) to wearing a waistcoat that had been spun on Christmas Night by a virgin in the name of the Devil. Some people carried the Lord's Prayer written on a piece of paper in their shoes; others relied on religious medallions or crucifixes, or simply on making the sign of the cross at a witch.

Traditional and virtually pagan ways of opposing witches thus mingled with approved Christian methods. One might steal a tile from the witch's roof, sprinkle it with urine and salt (salt is a prime ingredient in white magic), and heat it in order to lift a spell; or one might recite an anti-witch incantation containing references to the Father, Son, and Holy Ghost. Often, no doubt, both kinds of preventive measure would be taken, just to make sure. Matching sorcery with sorcery was considered illegal in most places, but it was seldom punished as strictly. Then, too, few people would turn informer against an amateur who had defeated a witch at her own game.

Some people, who either distrusted countermagic or knew none, found that threatening the witch's life was a most effective way of lifting a spell, especially if the threats were accompanied by a sound thrashing. Or the beating alone was thought to be sufficient; in Britain, if a witch was thrown onto the ground until blood issued from her eyes, any spell she had cast would be broken. So would it be if her house was burned down. The best way, though, to prevent witches from harming you was the Christian way—which meant not amulets nor medallions nor crucifixes nor prayers in the shoe, but an unblemished life of righteousness and good works. The 16th-century French demonologist Jean Bodin stressed charity above all the virtues; no witch could harm a charitable man, no matter how sinful he was in other respects. (Gentler voices like this, however, tended about that time to be drowned by the sound of the Inquisition polishing their instruments of torture, firm in the belief that an ounce of cure was worth a pound of prevention.)

In information offered by authorities past and present, sorcery and other magical practices of the isolated witch and her familiar are generally overshadowed by witches' collective activities. To put this another way: the idea of the witch as principally a magic-worker became transformed (as heresy hunts got well under way) into the idea of the witch as devil-worshiper. And the witches worshiped in groups—called Witches' Sabbaths, or *sabbats*.

Many strange etymologies have adhered to this word. Montague Summers, the British writer on the supernatural, suggests that the word derived from an ancient Thracian god, Sabazius, who was "worshipped with frantic debaucheries." Among many of the controversial theories offered by Dr. Margaret Murray in her famous *The God of the Witches* is the derivation of sabbat from the French *s'esbettre*, to frolic. Other authorities, including the British professor and encyclopedist Rossell Hope Robbins, reject these ingenious derivations, and suggest the most obvious one: sabbat is the Hebrew word for seventh day, "transferred," Hope Robbins says, "by hostile association to witches—Jews, witches, and Mohammedans were three traditional targets for Catholic opposition." And, he adds, "in early works, even the word *synagoga* was often used for sabbat." Today most reliable authorities, including the weighty Oxford English Dictionary, accept the Jewish Sabbath, and medieval anti-semitism, as responsible for the origin of the word.

Strangely, however, though the Jewish Sabbath is on Saturday, no one day (or night, because sabbats were nocturnal) of the week seems to have been especially singled out for witches' gatherings. Thursdays and Fridays perhaps occur most often in accounts of sabbats; but the witches were apparently quite willing to meet on Sundays as well, or any night they pleased. But on certain days of the *year*, it seems that meetings, especially large-scale meetings, always took place. That is, a small group of witches from one neighborhood might meet at a weekly sabbat nearby, but on special nights they would fly off to a larger gathering embracing many such groups. These large sabbats were thought to occur on the nights of four seasonal festivals: February 2 (the winter festival, Candlemas); June 23 (spring festival, Eve of St. John the Baptist); August 1 (summer festival, Lammas Day); and December 21 (autumn festival, St. Thomas). In 17th-century Scotland something of a variation took place; there were sabbats on Candlemas and Lammas Day, but the spring and autumn meetings occurred on May 3 (Holy Cross) and November 1 (All Saints' Day).

Aside from the seasonal dates, two world-famous nights would have been heavily marked on any witch's calendar: April 30, the eve of May Day, and October 31, All Hallows' Eve (which children, costumed as, among other things, witches and demons, now celebrate as Halloween). The night of April 30 was the *grand sabbat*, known as *Walpurgisnacht*, Walpurgis Night, so called because it was the feast-day of the English saint Walburga, who is said to have died in Germany in 777.

References to earlier pagan traditions throw light on the development of the whole sabbat idea—a development that took place, some authorities insist, entirely in the minds of the witch-hunters and demonological theorists of the 15th and 16th centuries. Briefly, then, the sabbat as such was unknown before witchcraft became named a heresy—that is, before sorcery was supplanted by Devil-worship. Accounts of sabbats (in witches' confessions at trials, or in the writings of theologians and experts) appear for the first time and only occasionally in the early 1400s; by the later part of that century and throughout the next, no witch trial was complete without a lip-licking description of the proceedings. It seems that this development took place because, as a heresy, witchcraft had to be seen as an organized form of worship, as were the Albigensian or Waldensian heresies that cropped up at the end of the 12th century and after.

Because witchcraft was of its very nature anti-Christian, theologians came to associate it with most other sacrilegious ideas and practices. They saw inversions or parodies of Christian ritual (and thus unwittingly encouraged the growth of the Black Mass idea—see p. 148); they saw elements of other heresies (the Waldensians, for instance, were said in the 1380s to conclude their services with wholesale sexuality, as did the witches); and they saw, or thought they saw, pagan elements (nocturnal feasting and dancing, as in the ancient rites of Bacchus and Priapus described by many Roman writers). From sources such as these the witches' sabbat took its form—the form that was later to be embellished and then fixed by the expectations of witch-hunters, judges, and the public. So here we must examine in some detail the procedure of the sabbat, which (in spite of individual variations offered by tortured prisoners or over-excited prosecutors) had assumed a fairly definite pattern by the end of the 15th century.

First, the witches assembled on the chosen night. (Married

witches usually put spells on their spouses so that they wouldn't be missed.) They met in a specified place, in most cases a hilltop, but sometimes a forest clearing or a field well away from human habitation. (The big festivals drew witches to places like the Brocken peak in Germany, the top of the Puy-de-Dôme in Auvergne, France, or a meadow in Sweden called the Blocula.) Sabbats were attended by an equal number of male and female witches; but if one sex was outnumbered, demons (usually incubi or succubi) would even things up. On rare occasions, and mostly at small local sabbats, some interested but uninitiated humans would be allowed to join in to equalize the sexes or just (literally) for the hell of it.

No special number of witches was required at a sabbat. Some accounts describe village meetings where fewer than 10 attended. Others give enormous (and certainly wildly exaggerated) figures. Near Ferrara, according to a witch's confession in the mid 16th century, the congregation numbered 6000; earlier, in the 15th century, a confession estimated the assembly at Valpute, France, at 10,000; and the wild-eyed 17th-century French demonologist Pierre de Lancre spoke of sabbats gathering "some one hundred thousand devotees of Satan." But the consideration of numbers brings us to a question of etymology considerably more important than the derivation of the word *sabbat* mentioned earlier. Many authorities, among them principally Margaret Murray, have subscribed to the idea that witches organized themselves in covens, composed of 12 witches led by a devil or a man disguised as a devil. (The parody of the apostles is obvious.) The word *coven* has clear links with words like "covey" and "convene" and, though originally at first meaning any assembly of people, came to be applied specifically to witches.

Since Dr. Murray announced firmly that "the number in a coven never varied, there were always thirteen, i.e. twelve members and the god," many other writers on the subject have taken up the idea and given it currency as a part of the witch legend. Thus it became confused with the sabbat. When a local coven met, the meeting would be a sabbat; at the grand sabbats a number of covens would combine to form the congregation. But aside from their participation in the sabbat revels, the covens were said to serve as organizational nuclei for the witches' war on man and God. They functioned, in other words, rather like the communist "cells" that meet secretly (in fact and fiction) in Western nations today.

Witches allegedly met in their coven to pool information, to work powerful magic in concert, and to receive new orders from their leader—all this besides the usual worship and orgy.

Now there can be no question but that covens do exist in the 20th century. That is, people calling themselves witches band together in groups of 13 and dance in the nude around a magic circle. And more. If these people call their groups covens, then they are covens. And so we shall call them covens when, later in the chapter, we come to look at their organization. But in spite of Dr. Murray's evidence, strong doubt has been cast on the existence of the coven in the Middle Ages and Renaissance. Dr. Murray herself admits that "there is only one trial in which the number thirteen is specifically mentioned" (and that one in 1662), but adds that in other trials all you have to do is count the accused and you get 13. Unfortunately, those other trials number only 18. Not very satisfactory statistically, suggests Hope Robbins; he estimates that more than 200,000 witches were executed during the persecutions, which would seem to give at least 15,000 *potential* covens—of which only 18 came to light in the whole period?

Similarly, the British writer Alex Keiller had a look at Dr. Murray's sources and found that in many of the trials where she had made her calculations she had added up wrongly. Others counted for themselves and agreed with Keiller. The British historian G. L. Kittredge stated flatly: "There is not the slightest evidence that [witches] were ever organized at all," let alone in groups of 13. Dr. Murray's opponents in this controversy believe that her error grew from her willingness to accept as fact confessions dragged out of prisoners by torture—confessions designed by the inquisitors to prove their own prejudices. Very few people today who have looked at Dr. Murray's sources (rather than swallowing her theories on faith) will deny that the coven idea was spawned in the minds of a few persecutors and demonologists, wishing to foist on the heretic witches the sin of sacrilegiously parodying Christ and the 12 apostles. Just as, centuries later, the similarly manufactured sacrilege of the Black Mass was also to be imposed on older notions of witchcraft.

(A word, at this point, of warning and reminder. Much of the information about witches collected in this chapter has, like Dr. Murray's coven idea, been drawn from accounts of witch trials and the evidence obtained by torture. But the authors here have not accepted this material as the "truth about witchcraft." They accept it, and offer it, simply as the truth about *what people believed* about witchcraft. The inquisitors and witch-hunters, apart from those who were hypocritical sadists, were firmly convinced that certain horrors and blasphemies always formed a part of a witch's activities. Therefore, they felt, any accused witch who failed to confess was holding back, and so they tortured her until she produced the evidence they sought. It rarely occurred to them that the accused might be innocent; it never crossed their minds that their own assumptions might be false.)

If there is little evidence before the 20th century for widespread belief in the coven as a center for highly organized witchcraft, there is a vast amount of evidence for belief in the sabbat as a gathering place for witches. So to our description of this gathering we must return. We have seen the witches assemble. Once gathered together, their naked bodies (greased with flying ointment) shining in the light of a fire or of black candles held in their hands, they were supposed to fulfill certain rituals, in homage to the Devil.

Satan was usually thought to be present in person, especially at the major annual sabbats. At other times the proceedings might be presided over by a lesser demon, or even by an important witch masked as the Devil, who acted as the Devil's deputy. The Devil himself appeared most often in his favorite guise of a black goat or ram, though he sometimes manifested himself in demonic form, with the traditional horns, leathery bat wings, and cloven hoofs, or in human form (though often pitch black) wearing a fearsome horned mask and headdress. He sat on a black throne, or stood on an altar around which the witches gathered.

Usually the Devil began the proceedings by reading a roll call (from a red book, claimed witches of Bamberg in Germany); there, according to some demonologists, the witches reported their activities and successes. If any newly introduced neophytes were present, they would be accepted and initiated in the manner described on p. 129. Then the entire company would line up to pay homage to the Devil, giving him gifts (such as black candles) but especially performing the ultimate act of abasement: kissing his buttocks. This was known as the *osculum infame*, the kiss of shame; it features in practically every account of the sabbat. (It was probably a carryover from earlier inquisitional investigations, for the Waldensians were accused of performing the kiss, as were the

Knights Templar in the early 14th century.) A few sophisticated accounts tell us that the Devil, Janus-like, wore a second mask "under his tail," perhaps symbolic of a dualistic nature (like that imputed to certain pagan gods) comprising the
principles of both good and evil. But this may be complicat-
ing the subject needlessly; in the kiss of shame, symbolism
was seldom as important as plain obscenity.

When the homage (which as well as the kiss included the
more usual forms of abasement, bowing and scraping, and
was sometimes said to include the sacrifice of an animal,
often a goat) was concluded, the witches proceeded to the
banquet, where they gorged themselves gluttonously. Some
demonologists, visualizing orgiastic feasting, wrote of luxu-
rious wines, with aphrodisiacs added, and stronger liquors, of
huge platters of meat (some thought it was the flesh of children stolen by the witches) and quantities of rare delicacies.
But other writers were anxious to play down the propaganda
value of these pleasures, and insisted that the food was always foul and disgusting and that no matter how much was
eaten it satisfied no appetites. Most authorities, however,
agreed that, whatever was eaten, the witches ate riotously,
seldom using utensils (and never iron ones, because of their
aversion to that metal); and that salt, because it was so often
used in white magic, was never available.

The feasting concluded, the witches began the dance that
invariably formed the central feature of a sabbat (if not its
climax). A few experts believed that the dancing came before
the feasting, perhaps because not even witches were believed
able to dance their best with full bellies. Then again, the
order of these two events undoubtedly varied from one sabbat to another. At any rate, the dance was of major importance to the sabbat. The witches occasionally were said to
dance ordinary folk dances of the locality; more often they
were thought to dance various kinds of ring dances, around a
central object—usually the Devil himself, or a phallic pillar
or maypole. In one ring dance the witches danced back to
back, which was considered especially indecent. In another
they did a version of the Conga line. But whatever they did,
they did it with such incredible abandon that many experts
today believe them to have been in a state of high excitement
or hysteria. Since the dances were preceded by excessive
drink as well as food, and were accompanied by emotion-
stirring music (provided by those witches who could play instruments), and since in most reports the dancers were

naked, it is not surprising that the participants should have felt some of the trance-state excitement induced by similar dances in primitive communities.

Most authorities compare the sabbat dancing with primitive ritual dancing; many also actually connect the nocturnal frenzies and dances of older pagan cults (the *saturnalia*) with the witches' revels. The modern British author Pennethorne Hughes described dancing in general as "the origin of almost all expression—religious, dramatic, poetic, mimetic or to invoke superhuman aid by pantomime"; and after reminding us that the witches' main object at a sabbat was to worship, he points out that until the 17th century there was a considerable amount of ceremonial dancing in European churches. So the witches' dance served several purposes. It was at once a means of expressing adoration for the Devil, of parodying an older Christian tradition, and of scandalizing the more austere members of the Church (and, later, the Puritans) by indulging in what they would probably call sinful wantonness. And, presumably, the excitement of the dances loosened the witches up in preparation for the climacteric to follow.

The sabbat concluded with a general, uninhibited sexual orgy. At some sabbats the Devil himself began this part of the proceedings by systematically copulating with every woman present. In most of the confessions that included this act, the women announced that intercourse with the Devil was extremely painful, generally because his sexual organ was ice-cold. Nevertheless, they submitted, as part of a witch's duty. (Here, as with the feasts, certain demonologists were making sure that no one got the impression that sabbats might be enjoyable.) After the Devil had been given his due, the witches, both male and female, and any demons present, indulged in indiscriminate copulation with one another. Of course, in the confessions and the demonological treatises no form of sexual activity was excluded from the final stages; incest, sodomy, and bestiality seem to be featured in almost every account, to satisfy the expectations of the witch-hunters.

The pre-dawn crowing of a cock usually brought the proceedings to an end, and the presumably exhausted witches returned to their homes till next time. The basic procedure that has been described is repeated over and over in trials and treatises. In all these accounts, the activities seldom vary; the only difference was the amount of exaggeration involved in describing the obscenities. But in the later years of the witch

persecutions certain new variations began to creep in more
regularly. These added new breadth to the element of conscious parody of Christian ritual that had always been present
in some form. There would be inverted imitations of the
Church's ceremonies, such as the assembly repeating the
Lord's Prayer backward, or the Devil delivering a mock ser-
mon or chanting a liturgy of evil. And above all, according to
later demonologists, there would be a sacrilegious travesty of
the Mass. From these variations grew eventually the concept
of a fearsome ritual that is today so well loved by sensational
newspapers—the Black Mass.

Hope Robbins, that exploder of popular delusions, has
asserted that "the black mass, as something that historically
occurred, is one of the biggest intellectual frauds ever imposed on the lay public." He explains it thus: isolated instances that occurred in the 14th, 15th, and 16th centuries of
sacrilegious parodies of the Mass or parts of it, added to
more frequent accusations against witches that desecration of
the Host was part of their heretical practices, gave later writers material with which to construct their stories of satanic
masses. During the 18th century Black Masses began to be
held in some sophisticated circles, and by the 19th century,
long after the witch frenzy had died away, the Black Mass
came into its own. But these later versions can be said to be
derived from the earlier writers, rather than from a continuing tradition. Thus, Robbins states, "the satanic mass was
virtually a literary creation"; and therefore it apparently did
not grow directly out of witchcraft. Still, in spite of Robbins,
the witches were seen as satanists and so were the celebrants
of the Black Mass; the parallel cannot be denied.

On the other hand, a great many modern newspapers (and
probably most of their readers) continually confuse witchcraft and the Black Mass, and black magic as well. So perhaps it might be worthwhile to repeat and underline the correct view of these activities. Black magic is occult power used
for evil ends and for the magician's self-aggrandizement. The
Black Mass is a parody and perversion of the Mass indulged
in ostensibly for the purpose of mocking God and worshiping
Satan. Heretical witchcraft of the 16th and 17th centuries included some elements of black magic (though always with
the difference of *motive*) and of Devil-worship, though rarely
a full-scale Black Mass.

So much for reiteration. Black Masses themselves vary im-
mensely in different accounts, largely because some writers or

practitioners stress the sacrilege and others the obscenity. (And Black Masses in popular fiction, as in the novels of the British writer Dennis Wheatley, serve only to cloud the issue more, and to add to the confusion with witches and magic.) To take an example of the variety possible, different substitutes were used in different places for the sacramental wafer, the Host. One mock ceremony elevated a slice of turnip stained black; others used ordinary bread, "consecrated" in the devil's name: still others went to the length of making pseudo-wafers stamped with the name of Satan. In later years the imitation was often said to have become direct desecration. Satanists would go to a real Mass (sometimes with alum in their mouths to prevent salivation) and would retain the consecrated Host in their mouths, removing it later for profanation in a Black Mass. (Incidentally, around the 15th century, before witches and sorcerers were distinguished, this theft of the Host was thought to be a common practice, but primarily for black magic purposes, not for satanist ceremonies.)

Satanism and the Black Mass, as was said before, came into their own as separate practices from the 17th to the 19th centuries, principally among people (who would then have been called "profligates") looking for a new thrill, like the members of England's notorious Hellfire Club. Actually there were several hellfire clubs throughout England, Ireland, and Scotland; but the principal one met regularly at fashionable addresses in London in the 1720s. Montague Summers hints darkly at Black Masses being held in a Dublin Hellfire Club in 1730s. The idea was taken up by Oxford undergraduates in the 19th century; Summers recounts a horror story, which he seems to accept as true, about the death of a student and devil-worshiper at the hands of a demon, apparently conjured up in one of their ceremonies. Again according to Summers, a satanist club also met at Oxford in 1912, and another was organized in London in 1934.

The modern American author W. B. Seabrook is less given than Summers to hints and warnings; he alleges that he has seen Black Masses in New York, Paris, Lyons, and London. (Like Summers, though, Seabrook confuses witchcraft and the Black Mass.) In his account the basic pattern is clear. The Black Mass requires an unfrocked or apostate priest, a consecrated host, a prostitute, and a virgin. The last is stretched naked on the altar, and over her is a crucifix upside down. Parts of the true Mass are repeated backward, with "evil" substituted for "good" and "Satan" for "God." The prostitute serves as the acolyte, assisting the priest. A wine goblet (the chalice) is placed between the virgin's breasts, and some wine is spilled over her; the host is debased, not elevated, and defiled in ways that Seabrook leaves unnamed.

In versions from other sources, variations occur. Sometimes the Mass is held in a ruined church, sometimes in cellars or in ordinary rooms. The virgin is a standard feature, but, as in the Black Mass described in the Marquis de Sade's *Justine*, she seldom stays unviolated. Various parodies of holy water are used, and various nauseous mixtures replace the wine in Seabrook's account. The following description of a more horrific ceremony is given by the modern British author Julian Franklyn:

"The Black Mass . . . is carried out at midnight in a ruined church with a renegade priest officiating. His assistants must be public prostitutes, and the Holy Eucharist befouled with human excrement. He wears a black surplice cut in three points, and burns black candles. The holy water must have been used to drown an unbaptized, newly-born bastard, and the altar decorated with owls, bats, toads, and creatures of like ill-omen. Standing with the left foot forward, the officiating priest reads the Roman Catholic Mass backwards, after which the congregation indulges in all kinds of orgies and excesses. A crucifix is usually trampled and spat upon, and sexual perversions performed before the altar."

In all fairness to Mr. Franklyn, it should be mentioned that he does not claim to have seen such a ceremony, strongly doubts that these conditions are ever fulfilled, and suggests that the orgies following the ceremony are the main attraction. He also adds, "no wholly sane person would adhere to such a cultus." Yet, like many other experts on the subject, he is sure that many people today do meet and hold Black Masses of one kind or another. And some fairly convincing proofs are available to back him up. For example, a Presbyterian minister in Ayrshire, Scotland, found in 1964 that Black Masses were being held in a ruined 17th-century church; among the evidence were a mutilated Bible, a broken chalice, and an upside-down cross chalked over the altar. In 1963 Princess Irene of Greece (the wife of the anthropologist Prince Peter) wrote a sensationalized story for a British magazine about a Black Mass that she had personally seen in a Paris cellar; included in the ceremony was the ritual sacrifice of a black cockerel.

The Black Mass is said to be especially rife in southern

England, and became equally rife in the headlines in 1963 when a cemetery was desecrated and graves opened in Bedfordshire. Reports said that the graves were in the burial ground of a ruined 10th-century church, and that the remains of a woman were removed from one grave and were found on the church altar. Also found were the body of a cock that had apparently been sacrificed, and crosses chalked on the wall. A similar desecration of a graveyard occurred in Sussex, England, in 1964; but in this case the rector of the parish struck back by pronouncing a powerful curse on the desecraters. The following night, according to a newspaper report, much of the damage was cleared up. Gravestones were righted, the debris cleared away, and the Black Mass signs erased. In spite of the fact that most people thought the damage was just vandalism, not satanism, and that it was later found to have been the police who tidied up, the rector stated that he was satisfied, and lifted the curse.

Black Masses may abound, and witches may band together and dance by firelight, all over the 20th century world, but no one seems deeply concerned. The witches gain the attention of the authorities if they infringe certain laws (for instance, laws pertaining to public order or to sexual offenses) but they are seldom prosecuted simply for being witches. Britain repealed its laws against witchcraft in 1951; West Germany instituted in the 1950s a campaign of education, not legislation, to reduce the estimated 60,000 witches operating in rural areas; most states in the U.S.A. have repealed their old laws against witches and, like France, retain only laws against fraudulent mediums and fake diviners to protect the credulous. In short, no one pays much attention to the Biblical injunction, "Thou shalt not suffer a witch to live." Yet a few hundred years ago this was the motto of thousands of people all over Europe and in America, and resulted in hundreds of thousands of deaths. Before considering the methods and results of the witch-hunters, then, we must try to answer the question: how did the witch-hunting hysteria get started?

Early laws against witchcraft, as we saw at the beginning of this chapter, were in fact laws against sorcery, and were neither particularly stringent nor zealously enforced. A Church Council in the early 14th century forbade divination, conjuring, and so on; but it was not until the 15th century that practitioners of sorcery were excommunicated. The ecclesiastical laws began to tighten only when sorcery began to get tangled up with pacts with the Devil, and repudiation of God and Christian teachings. And most authorities today agree that the tangling was produced by the inquisitions themselves. As Hope Robbins puts it, "Were it not for the Inquisition, the Catholic tribunal charged with exposing and punishing religious unorthodoxy, not one person would have died for witchcraft."

He may be stating his case too extremely; we have seen that ordinary people had ways of taking the law into their own hands if they felt some minion of the Devil had bewitched them. But basically the point is clear. The Inquisition, formed to pursue the Church's enemies, to a great extent created the enemies it pursued.

Not all of them, of course. About 1200, when the first inquisitions were appointed directly from the Vatican, the Church could be said to have been surrounded by heretics. Its position was insecure, partly because of the anticlerical reaction to its own notorious immorality and authoritarian methods were producing. (Complaints against the profligate clergy can be found in the writings of many great medieval figures including St. Bernard, St. Bonaventura, and St. Catharine of Siena.) Add to this the surviving remnants of the pagan Roman religious practices and the start of contact with the heathen East and Arab world, and it becomes clear that the Church's doctrinal sway was no longer absolute. Men were beginning to ask questions, and the answers they were giving themselves were heretical.

Sporadically, various heretical sects were formed and were attacked and persecuted by local Church authorities. Then the trickle became a flood, and a series of papal bulls created the Inquisition for the investigation and examination of heretics. After exercising on a few small deviations, the Inquisition began in the early 13th century in southern Franch to wage war against one of its greatest enemies, the Manichaean heretics in Albi (hence also called Albigensians), believers in a dual God of good and evil. The Inquisition became a crusade; the object was extermination. In the same area was another group of heretics called Waldensians (also known as Vaudois), who believed among other things in the ultimate authority of the Bible, not the pope. They too were persecuted during the Albigensian crusade; some fled and formed a community in Piedmont. In the late 15th century the Church once again sought their extermination—not only as Waldensian heretics then, but also as witches.

Isolated cases of inquisitorial witch-hunting can be found as far back as 1245. Perhaps the first person to be executed as a witch was a woman (suspected of having relations with the Devil) condemned to be burned in 1275 by the Inquisitor of Toulouse. During the 14th century, French inquisitors wrecked the Knights Templar, accusing the members of this secret society of exactly the same acts that were later ascribed to witches: worship of the Devil (including the "kiss of shame"), profanation of holy objects, and so on. When the major heresies had been crushed in the 14th century, the Inquisition came to realize that it had done itself out of a job. Its enemies were exterminated or in disarray. But at the same time more and more theologians found themselves unable to emulate the tolerance of their predecessors. (In the 13th century and earlier, to repeat, sorcery was a misdemeanor not taken too seriously except when it ended in murder.) They saw in the sorcerer's art a perpetuation of heathenism, and worse—and a threat to the Church. The theologians saw in magic the Devil's hand, produced a mass of demonological works, and created a new heresy. The Inquisition turned from mopping up small pockets of Vaudois, and went into action.

The demonological works set the pattern of what the inquisitors were looking for. And chief among these was the terrible *Malleus Maleficarum,* or "Hammer of Witches," first published in 1486—a "handbook for witch hunters," as Robbins calls it, that retained an immense authority among Catholics and Protestants alike until the late 17th century. Works like this listed and described as facts all the witch practices, magical and satanist, that we have outlined so far; and these works also set out the proper procedure for securing convictions of witches in the inquisitional courts.

The courts may originally have been set up as committees of investigation, but in their examinations there was only one side to the question; the dice were cruelly loaded against the accused. For one thing, the judges unvaryingly assumed that an accused witch was guilty until proved innocent. And there was almost no chance for one to prove his or her innocence. Both the prosecutor and the judge were inquisitors, and no defense was allowed (since anyone who defended heresy would be guilty of it). Torture was used regularly and often; its use had been sanctioned by Pope Innocent IV in 1257 by a decree that was confirmed and strengthened by later popes; it was not officially abandoned by the Vatican until 1816.

Through torture the inquisitors sought confessions, but these were really unnecessary. The so-called evidence by which people could be brought to trial for witchcraft was usually quite enough to convict them. The Inquisition encouraged informers, but half-formed suspicions and gossip were sufficient for an arrest to be made. Strange behavior or unexplained acts were indications of sorcery to the authorities and the witch-conscious public. If you threw water into the air, Hope Robbins tells us, you were assuredly a witch trying to stir up a tempest. Ugly old women and deformed people of all ages were suspected; but then, so were attractive young girls, who were considered most literally to be "bewitching."

An infallible proof of witchery was the presence of a pet in the accused's home. But the search for familiars went much further than this. The accused at a trial would be trussed (usually naked) in a chair in an empty room, and the prosecutors would watch through a peephole to see if her demon came to her. Any spider or beetle or mouse that came into the room (and the odds were all for it in the vermin-infested buildings of the time) was seen as the witch's personal demon, especially if it could not be caught and killed. And such creatures are hard to catch.

The theorists developed several tests and ordeals that could be applied to an accused in the search for proof. Of these, ducking (or "swimming") was a popular method of testing. The theory was that the witch would float (since the water would reject servants of Satan who had themselves rejected the baptismal water). Therefore, if you sank you were innocent; in all probability you were also drowned. The accused might have been tossed into ponds or rivers with ropes attached to pull them out if they sank; but since guilt was usually presumed, only rarely were precautions taken against drowning an innocent prisoner. The accused witch was tied hand and foot in most cases; so (except in legend) those who floated were few.

The authorities generally came to reject ducking as a test by the 17th century, although it continued to be a favorite of the hysterical mobs that the Inquisition's Reign of Terror was producing. But the search for witch's or devil's marks was always a favorite. The witch's mark, to make the distinction clear, was a small protuberance (often a supernumerary nipple, or resembling one) at which she was supposed to suckle her familiar. The devil's mark could be anything—a birthmark, scar, mole, wart, any kind of blemish—that the witch-hunters could convince themselves was the brand put on new witches at their initiation. Many of the uglier stories of the witch trials involve these marks—stories of women, old or young but preferably young, stripped naked in a crowded court or on a public platform and their bodies examined for the telltale signs. Obviously, there are few people on whose bodies some blemish cannot be found, so the prurient searchers were usually successful.

With the devil's mark especially, the test called "pricking" was developed. It was believed that a pin stuck into these marks would cause neither pain nor bleeding. Also, to give suspects no chance at all, the idea grew up that some devil's marks were invisible, and could be discovered only by use of a sharp instrument. It is well known now that many points on the skin are relatively pain-free, and that healthy skin may close up behind the small wound a sharp pin makes and allow no bleeding. It is also obvious that scars and other common blemishes are usually insensitive. Finally, it is understandable that anyone, but especially a woman, would be in a state of shock after having been man-handled, stripped naked in public, shaved all over her body (thus was the search facilitated) and perhaps previously tortured—so that she simply would not feel the pinprick even in unblemished flesh. And to cap it all, some of the professional witch-finders who came into being at the height of the frenzy carried special instruments for pricking witches—instruments like ice-picks with hollow handles and retractable blades that slid back when pressed against a suspect's skin and caused no pain.

Probably the most vicious of the professional witch-finders was Matthew Hopkins, who operated in Protestant England in the mid 17th century. He was a demagogue who knew a good thing when he saw it; how could he fail to succeed when accusation was enough, when proof consisting of lies, rigged tests, and torture-produced confessions was perfectly acceptable to the Puritan judges? He first achieved fame by sending 32 people to trial at Chelmsford, Essex; with his new reputation and several assistants he traveled the country (often by request of local authorities) finding witches and riches wherever he went. Ducking and pricking were favorite tests of his; he also employed starvation, prevention of sleep, and other tortures that left no visible marks (for the English tribunals were on the whole less fond of torture than the European inquisitions). He is said to have been responsible for more executions in the year and a half that he held sway than all the English persecutors had achieved in 160 years. But finally his methods caught up with him; he had accused too many and too wildly, and judges began to doubt his sincerity and suspect his sadism. Fourteen months after his first accusations he was discredited and forced to retire; a year later he was dead, of tuberculosis.

Inquisitional courts were never established in England; and English courts generally refused to countenance torture, hanged witches instead of burning them, and executed many fewer witches than European countries. Also, the American trials were seldom as terrible as those perpetrated on the continent of Europe. And these could be very terrible. As an indication, the following are the main features of typical witch trials, based on accounts from various places all over the 15th-, 16th-, and 17th-century Christian world.

First, a suspect was necessary. Perhaps several people would be accused together, but more often one person was accused and then forced to incriminate others. Often suspects were arrested because of an accusation made by a witness or an informer. (At the height of the witch-fear many people genuinely suspected others to be guilty of witchcraft; but just as often, accusations were made by spiteful neighbors, by paid informers, or by semi-crazed thrill seekers. Husbands accused wives, children accused parents. In 17th-century England, witch-finders persuaded children to act bewitched and then to accuse innocent people of bewitching them. In Salem, Massachusetts, a group of vicious teenage girls threw out accusations wholesale, and caused the deaths of 22 people, for the sake—as one of the girls later admitted—of "some sport." A threat of accusation put immense power into the hands of blackmailers, vengeance-seekers, and paranoiacs.)

Once arrested, the accused would then be taken into the court and interrogated. They would be asked about their familiars, about their pact with the Devil, their activities at sabbats, their magic. They would be ordered to confess to their heresy, and to produce the names of associates. If they answered all these questions with a denial of witch-hood, the interrogators stripped them and examined them for incriminating marks. Then again they were ordered to confess; if they still resisted, their tormentors resorted to other means. In England the other means went only as far as enforced wakefulness, imprisonment (quite bad enough, considering the state of the prisons), bread and water, and minor brutalities. In Scotland and Europe, however, the later stages of interrogation produced the most barbarous refinements of torture.

Seventeenth-century Bamberg, in Germany, has one of the worst histories of torture in all the annals of witch persecution. If initial methods, such as scourging or forced feeding of salted food without water, were ineffective, more brutal means were adopted, such as the thumbscrew, leg vises, the stocks with iron spikes, burning sulfur-dipped feathers applied to the armpits and groin, immersion in scalding water with lime added, and cutting or tearing off of limbs and breasts. *Strappado,* a common torture, involved hoisting the victim off the ground by a rope attached to his wrists and then tying heavy weights to his ankles. Most inquisitions applied fire or red-hot metal to the victim's flesh quite readily; it was thought, as the 16th-century French writer Jean Bodin noted, to be considerably milder than the tortures of hell soon to be endured by the accused witch.

Torture was applied to induce victims to confess and to inform on others. Once a confession was made in the torture chamber, the witch then had to stand up in court and repeat it to the judge, thus indicating to all that the confession was made "freely." Naturally, if the victim retracted the confession once out of the torture chamber, she was quickly returned. One of the most pathetic documents from witch trials is a letter that had been smuggled out of Bamberg prison in 1628, a letter from a man to his daughter, written in his last extremity before going to the stake, written in agony because his hands were crushed in vises and his joints dislocated in *strappado.* He concludes his account of the tortures, and the "crimes" that he found himself confessing:

". . . here you have all my acts and confession, for which I must die. And it is all sheer lies and inventions, so help me God. For all this I was forced to say through dread of torture beyond what I had already endured. For they never cease the torture till one confesses something; be he ever so pious, he must be a witch. . . . God in heaven knows that I know not the slightest thing. I die innocent and as a martyr."

And so did hundreds of others in Bamberg alone. Execution was the usual outcome of a witch trial in Europe, and almost invariably it meant burning alive. England, as has been said, hanged its witches, but Scotland applied the stake and flame. America, even Salem, sometimes only whipped and banished a convicted witch, but hanging was common as

well. The burnings were of course public; and usually, if one
victim incriminated several others, and they in turn under
torture informed on others, the executions were a vast spectacle. Any convicted witches who were not executed (before
the frenzy reached its peak, or after its decline) met a variety
of punishments, usually including confiscation of property; in
many cases the guilty ones had to wear "the cross of in-
famy," a yellow cross sewn on their clothing.

The witch-hunting epidemic in Europe killed thousands of
people; of this there can be no doubt. Though precise figures
are unobtainable, it is thought that 200,000 people had died
as convicted witches by the 17th century, and that is a con-
servative estimate. A minimum of 100,000 had gone to the
stake in Germany alone, where the frenzy reached heights
unmatched elsewhere in Europe. France and Scotland were
runners-up (one authority wrote in 1903 that the Scots had
burned 70,000 witches, but this is doubtful—the real figure is
more likely to have been under 10,000). England executed
only about 1000, according to most informed guesses; and although America (especially Salem) persecuted many, it killed
few—probably fewer than England. To the modern world,
remembering Auschwitz and Belsen, 200,000 deaths may
seem comparatively inconsequential. But the Reign of Terror
that produced them was not; fear of persecution made everyone its victim, for *anyone* (not just those suspected of belonging to a particular race) could find himself on the slenderest
evidence facing a sentence from which there was little chance
of escape.

In the 17th century, however, the mania began to die. Part
of the reason was that an atmosphere of terror was unhealthy,
as businessmen and governors began to see, for the flourishing of trade. There had always been a few brave men prepared to risk death by speaking and writing against the
witch-hunting horror; now kings and prelates and politicians
began to listen. Holland, whose prosperous middle class depended on the healthy flourishing of trade, provided a refuge
for opponents of the frenzy, and their voices grew in
strength. Holland executed her last witch in 1610; in England, the next country to see the light, the last official execution was in 1684. America put a stop to her killings in 1692,
Scotland in 1727, France in 1745. Germany beheaded her
last witch in 1775.

The rational atmosphere that began to pervade Europe in
the 18th century swept away most traces of the international

hysteria, and while in isolated rural areas mobs still ducked
or stoned or lynched suspected witches, in the major centers
witchcraft once again became identified with sorcery, and received little attention. In the 19th and 20th centuries, as previously noted, various laws have been passed or retained concerning fraudulent conjuring and similar confidence tricks;
but although the stories told at the beginning of this chapter
indicate that a certain amount of belief in evil witches still
flourishes all over the world, the civil authorities take little
notice. As for the religious authorities, there are indications
that wholehearted acceptance of the Devil, as an anthropomorphic personification of evil, is diminishing. Many theologians of various persuasions would agree with the British
theological writer J. S. Whale, who remarks that the idea of
the Devil is "difficult . . . for our thought" and is mostly a
handy image for the principle of evil.

Having thus come back to our starting point—the incidence of belief in witchcraft today—we are left only with
that curious anomaly, the 20th-century "white witch." There
are a fair number of reports of white (or good) magic in action today that parallel the story of the good witch of
Château-Ponsac (p. 125). But many of these reports have little to do with witchcraft as we have defined it; they are simply
cases of belief in magic—in the healing charms (the ashes of
a toad mixed with brandy forms part of a recipe to cure
drunkenness) or helpful remedies (to ease a baby's teething,
hang around its neck a tooth extracted from a live mouse)
offered by beneficent sorcerers or white magicians. The real
white witches are people whose activities are only in part
magical—that is, whose witchcraft is largely *worship* (as was
the witchcraft of the 15th-century black witch) but, in their
case, of a non-evil deity or deities.

These practitioners of modern witchcraft are organized, as
the black witches were thought to be, in covens of 13; at
their meetings they engage in certain religious ceremonies
that include dancing around a fire in the nude. White witch
covens flourish especially in Britain, but the secrecy that
usually surrounds them prevents an exact figure being given.
Estimates range from 400 to 5000 (the latter figure being
offered by Sybil Leek, the witch mentioned before, who dis-
likes the atmosphere of secrecy and has recently announced
plans for a Witches Incorporated in London that expects
5000 members). Several covens exist in America, especially
in the larger cities (in 1958 *Look* magazine published inter-

views with some New York witches), but again their secrecy is impenetrable, due largely to their quite understandable fears of misunderstanding, abuse, and mockery from skeptics.

Modern white witches claim to be the heirs of an unbroken religious tradition stretching back into primeval history—a tradition of worship of the Great Mother, the earth mother, symbol of fertility, oldest and most elemental of the ancient gods. In most cases the white witches make their deity dual, including along with the female goddess that male deity written of by Margaret Murray: the horned god, primitive symbol of power, but not an evil god; much closer to the Greek Pan than to Satan. The closest classical parallels to the female goddess would be Artemis (Diana) and Aphrodite (Venus), who were worshiped in rituals somewhat resembling witch ceremonies. But according to Gerald B. Gardner, until his death in 1964 the foremost British witch, the white witch religion antedates classical Greek religion, and in fact has its roots in the Stone Age. A connection is said to exist between witches' worship and the prehistoric painting of the "Horned God" (thought to be a shaman in a fertility rite) in the Trois Frères Caves in France. There are also parallels mentioned by Gardner with ancient Druidical belief. The Druids practiced a magical religion (Stonehenge is thought to be a ceremonial circle used for seasonal ceremonies), and a group of female magicians existed who were called Druidesses, and who had many of the characteristics that were later ascribed to witches.

Gardner suggests that the ancient religion was diffused and scattered throughout the world, becoming mingled in many cases with other religions. The ancient Norse sagas make mention of women riding staffs and metamorphosing; a pre-Columbus Mexican cult had meetings closely paralleling a sabbat, though led by a priestess rather than a horned god. Some aspects of Egyptian ceremonial magic and Greek fertility cults (of Dionysus and of Pan) got tangled with the witch mysteries; and in Celtic countries a connection was formed between the witch religion and the "Little People" (led by a priestess-queen, dancing in circles or "fairy rings," possessing magical powers).

So much for the possible historical background of modern white witchcraft. Its practitioners, insisting that it is a religion and not a cult of evil (they refer people to the derivation of the word "witchcraft" from the Anglo-Saxon *wiccecraeft*, "craft of the wise"), may introduce many variations of detail into their forms of worship. One group may virtually ignore the Horned God and direct their worship entirely at the Great Mother under one pagan name or another; many other groups worship a more abstract male and female principle. A coven may come together every Saturday night, or only on the days that mark the four seasonal changes—the two equinoxes and the two solstices. But it is worthwhile describing the events at a representative coven, even though every group of witches meeting today may not do all these things, or may do more, or may change the procedure in other ways.

First of all, the typical coven today has 13 members, six couples and a leader. The latter is often a woman, a high priestess. Meetings are usually held indoors, in members' living rooms, though some covens in Britain will in summer chance an outdoor meeting. And others have special rooms used only for meetings. The atmosphere, participants assert, is always relaxed, almost casual but dignified. On the ground or floor a circle is drawn, nine feet in diameter, usually with chalk, and then symbolically gone over with the witch's magic knife (*athame*). Then the participants remove their clothes and begin the ceremony.

According to Gardner, the evil magician draws a circle to protect himself from the spirits that he calls up to help him in his work; but the white witches draw their circle to focus their own power—not to keep spirits out, but to keep magic in. And their power, they feel, can be raised from their own bodies, which is why they worship in the nude. Clothing dissipates and obstructs the power. The power itself is often thought to be some form of psychic force. A British woman named Doreen Valiente wrote in 1964 of a clairvoyant experience that came to her during the rites; extra-sensory powers were also mentioned by two American witches in the *Look* magazine interview. The religious ecstasy that the rituals can produce are thought by the witches to bring them into contact with a supernormal power or force, which, by acting together, they can strengthen and direct to achieve their desired (and beneficent) ends.

The rituals themselves, of course, remain secret. We know that incense is burned and water and salt are consecrated; that the participants must be "purified" before they enter the circle; that the priestess invokes the goddess and the god with an incantation, and the members of the coven, holding their knives aloft, worship with incantation and prayer. At outdoor meetings a fire (sometimes in a cauldron) blazes in the center of the circle. The priestess may read from the ancient writings (said to be called *The Book of Shadows*). In most cases the members of the coven join hands and dance around the circle, singing or chanting. Where there is a fire, couples may join hands and leap over it. Then there is a symbolic feast, usually cakes or wine, and the meeting is concluded.

It must be added in fairness that while in the past the covens employed objects that reminded people of black magic—skulls, and dolls impaled with pins, and so on—today the magical knives are probably the most sinister-looking bits of paraphernalia. Modern covens use crystal balls or magic mirrors (for clairvoyant visions) rather than devil masks, broomsticks, or sacrificial animals. Also, in the concluding feast no hint of a parodied Mass must be apparent; if the cakes and wine have any Christian parallel, Gardner says, it in the early Christian love feast (*agape*). But more likely the white witches' feast can be related to similar feasts at pagan rituals.

Finally, and in spite of the tradition of nudity, modern covens reject entirely the black witches' sexual orgy. Of course, theirs being a fertility religion of nature, they claim to have a more healthy attitude toward sex than most people. As a young British high priestess told a newspaper in 1958, "we believe that sex is nothing to be ashamed of—nor should it be overdone."

White witches today therefore resent accusations of being participants in sexual orgies; but most of all they resent being confused with practitioners of black magic and satanism. Their power, they insist, is directed toward helping people, their own members or others. The same British high priestess claimed to be able to "heal sick persons, . . . influence people, . . . and to some extent make wishes come true." She adds that, were there enough white witches around, they could bring about world peace. Gardner tells of a witches' spell specifically devoted to this aim to prevent Hitler invading England after France fell. They channeled their power (Gardner's capsule description of it as "a sort of long-range hypnotism" is interesting) to Hitler's mind, telling him that he could not cross the Channel. He adds that British witches had done the same to Napoleon, and had tried to stop the Spanish Armada in the same way.

But many present-day witches see such tales as spurious. Their witchcraft is not magic as much as a serious form of religious worship, designed (as a British witch recently put it) "to conduct members through a path where there should be fire and energy, enlightenment and liberation." An article in the British sociological magazine *New Society* in December 1964 summed the covens up thus: "In our age of moral relativity, and with the growing respect for the 'irrational,' both as occasion and source of psychic activity, the witches' efforts at self-transcendence should be seen at least as a private exploration of the same region beyond the known which on occasions inspires scientific research, introspection, religious awe."

In the Middle Ages a few theorists had accepted the idea of beneficial magic and had thought that the white sorcerers were most useful in "unbinding," which meant curing illnesses that baffled doctors and that were therefore to be attributed to a black witch's spell. Most later writers, though, agreed with the 17th-century Salem preacher and witch-hunter Cotton Mather, who assured his flock that among witches there was "none that doeth good, no, not one." Today the situation has clearly been reversed. The only people whom we can properly call witches are good ones, and there seem to be none (or few) that are evil. For, remember, we have defined witchcraft as part sorcery and part religious worship (as it was thought to be by the persecutors during the years of the Renaissance witch delusion). Modern black magicians like Aleister Crowley seldom, if ever, worship the devils they try to conjure up; modern diabolists rarely try to work magic in their Black Masses.

The story of witchcraft and diabolism from ancient times to the 20th century is a long and complicated one, obscured further by lies, misapprehensions, delusions, and ignorance. We have tried here to straighten out some of the modern confusion by clarifying the distinctions between black magic and witchcraft, and between the Black Mass and black magic, that have been blurred by today's popular writers and newspapers. But the confusion is understandable, for our conception of the nature of witchcraft is based on an incredibly tangled skein of religio-magical threads: the ceremonial magic of ancient religions such as Egypt's; the rituals of pagan fertility cults from northern Britain to southern Greece; personifications of evil as defined by the tortured and hallucinated minds of medieval Christian ascetics and hermits; appalling, pseudo-religious, obsessively sexual practices dreamed up by equally tortured minds in this century and the last. And that is only a partial list of ingredients.

Things were simpler in primitive times, when everyone knew that witches existed, had certain powers from supernatural sources, and could be fought in known and definitive ways by people with equal powers. And while the comparatively clear-cut concepts of primitive magic and witchcraft had an indirect influence on the later development of European concepts, their direct inheritors, principally along the main line from Africa to the West Indies and America, form a separate system to be considered in the next chapter.

7 LAND OF VOODOO

Most people today think of magical practices and supernatural beliefs as things of the past, or, if existing in the present, as activities and ideas that exist only under sufferance on the fringes of conventional society. But in this chapter on voodoo in Haiti, we shall be examining practices that all take place today and in public. Voodoo priests are as accessible as doctors and a voodoo ceremony is as much a communal event as a local dance. Voodoo, in short, is a popular religion—the religion of a large proportion of the Negro peasants of the West Indian republic of Haiti, who make up roughly 97 per cent of the population.

The term voodoo probably derives from *vodun*, or *vaudou*, themselves corruptions of the word *vodu*, which in the West African lands of Dahomey and Togo is the term applied to deities and spirits. Today the word "voodoo" is commonly used to mean any New World African-derived Negro rite—though many scholars prefer the term *vodoun*, which avoids the popular image of primitive frenzy and dark, orgiastic rites that "voodoo" tends to evoke. This image has been created by past travelers' tales—tales that were brought back by visitors to Haiti, most of whom seem to have put the most lurid interpretation onto what they saw and heard. One such tale-bearer was W. H. Seabrook, the American author of a detailed account of the "black" legend of voodoo, in which he wrote of colonial masters who, while treating their slaves like animals, were at the same time terrified by their slaves' occult powers. The French anthropologist Alfred Métraux, writing in 1959, comments: "Perhaps certain slaves did revenge themselves on their tyrants . . . but the fear which reigned in the plantations had its source in the deeper recesses of the soul: it was the witchcraft of remote and mysterious Africa which troubled the sleep of the people in the 'big house'."

The legendary fear of voodoo was given added force by a book called *Hayti or the Black Republic,* written in 1884 by a British consul in Haiti, Spencer St. John. In it, he told of dreadful atrocities committed by voodoo sects, of cannibalism, and of voodoo worshipers who sought and lived for both blood and power. Much of the horror fiction written about voodoo in the land of Haiti is inspired by St. John's descriptions—descriptions that have spread the idea of Haiti as a savage hell where children are sacrificed and eaten. On a popular level this conception has remained more or less unchanged, perpetuated by highly colored newspaper reports that emphasize voodoo's more sensational activities. A more balanced view is of course taken by such serious students of voodoo as Métraux, author of *Voodoo in Haiti* (1959), one of the few authoritative and objective works on the subject; the American documentary film maker Maya Deren, who wrote *The Divine Horsemen* (a reference to the fact that the gods are said to "ride" their possessed worshipers); and the American Zora Hurston, author of *Voodoo Gods.*

Voodoo, of course, is not a phenomenon that exists only in Haiti. Similar practices involving trance and possession have existed—and still do exist—all over the world. In its old forms, voodoo continues in its African countries of origin. And in South America it flourishes still under the name of *macumba* or *candomblé.* Many stories of non-Haitian voodoo come from the United States. In 1959 the principal of the Cathmagy Elementary School in Wetumka, Alabama, Mrs. Francis Webb Smith, resigned from her post after an investigation of complaints that she was teaching "voodooism." In Phoenix, Arizona, in 1962, a woman shot her husband "under the spell of a voodoo doctor," and was given a year's suspended sentence. Also in 1962, the magazine *Newsweek* reported: "The day's bargains included bat's blood, graveyard dust to counteract a charming, and death-to-thy enemy candles. The market, however, was not a trading post in the African bush, but a stall in New York City's steaming Harlem. Alarmed by the open and growing sales of do-it-yourself voodoo kits—usually hawked alongside Madonnas and religious medals—the New York Market Commission ordered a crack-down." A few years before, the New York Public Health Service warned that Haitian "voodoo dolls," sold in America as novelties, were less harmless than one might imagine. They were capable of producing a poison-ivy type of rash, and might even prove deadly to infants.

But to most people voodoo means Haiti. And on its home ground voodoo is a religious system made up of a collection of beliefs and practices with African roots that has become adapted to the needs of life in Haiti. This religion is chiefly characterized by the worship of ancestors and of a hierarchy of gods who manifest themselves by taking "possession" of their worshipers. And why such a system should continue to exist in the 20th century, for the most part unaffected by prevailing ideas in neighboring countries, can be understood in part by taking a brief look at Haiti's history.

The slave trade from Africa to Haiti began in the early 16th century, when the island of Santo Domingo, of which Haiti occupies the western part, was a Spanish possession. In 1677 Spain ceded Haiti to France (while retaining the eastern part—known today as the Dominican Republic), and it became France's richest colony. As more and more plantations were established, the growing demand for forced labor was met by shipping Negro slaves from West Africa. But the slave ships brought across the sea more than agonized, uprooted human cargoes; they carried also the gods and the forms of worship of those cargoes. In the words of Maya Deren (who went to Haiti in the 1940s on a film-making expedition), the slaves "brought with them their particular traditions, their language, their gods, their rituals, their dances, their drum beats, the memory of their homelands and the names of their towns and rivers. Bokono [magicians] and vodû-no [priests] trained in Africa, taught the following generations, born in slavery, the names and characteristics of the gods and the sacrifices required."

The slaves must have suffered an unimaginable shock; first torn from their familiar background, then subjected to the misery of an ocean crossing in a slave ship, and finally, on arrival (for those who survived) separated from their families and scattered across the island. (The separation was probably deliberate on the part of the colonists who, vastly outnumbered, would have wanted to weaken their slaves' strength by splitting families.) Yet in spite of the horrors of forcible transportation and separation from their families, the slaves never allowed the religious beliefs of their homeland to deteriorate into a mass of incoherent superstition. The reason for this, Métraux suggests, is that these early batches of men and women that were transported across the Atlantic must have included a handful of priests, who in exile rekindled the religious practices of their native lands. Otherwise, he writes, it is difficult to explain the presence of "temples, organized clergy, a rather complicated ritual, sophisticated dances and rhythms."

A further reason for the preservation of the slaves' religion can be found in Haiti's social and economic background. In the centuries that followed their arrival, generation after generation of Haitians continued to live the same harsh and comfortless existence as their slave forefathers. The population of Haiti today is one of the densest in the world; and so the struggle to earn a living from his meager and infertile plot condemns the Haitian peasant to a lifetime of backbreaking labor. Add to these ills of poverty and hard work the dread of disease (malaria, tuberculosis, and hookworm are rife in Haiti) and it is easy to understand the powerful appeal of a religion such as voodoo. For voodoo not only satisfies the emotional need for social contact through its colorful ceremonies and the collective life of its sanctuaries, but it also supplies a practical method of alleviating physical misfortune. The voodoo worshiper not only petitions the gods for an end to his poverty and unhappiness but (in a country where medical services are minimal) he also relies on his voodoo priest to provide him with magical remedies in cases of injury and disease.

But the voodoo worshiper does not see his religion only in terms of relaxation or solace. It is a system of belief that is reflected in all the thoughts and actions of his daily life. Everything that happens has a double significance—that of the real event and that of the symbolic meaning that lies behind it. So a crossroads is never merely the visible intersection of two highways; it is also the representation of the meeting point between men and gods. An illness is never solely an arbitrary attack, but an act of divine retribution for some wrongful intention or action (or, as frequently, the result of an enemy's magic). The ocean is as much the home of the sea gods as it is a place in which to swim, sail, or fish. Twins are particularly revered, since they are not regarded simply as two children who happen to have been born at the same time, but as the physical expression of man's dual nature, half human, half divine. (In fact, so indivisibly are they thought of as two parts of a single soul that every effort is made to arrange for all their important activities, such as marriage, to take place simultaneously.)

This dual awareness of a visible and invisible world is clearly reflected in the voodoo idea of the "soul" that everyone is believed to carry within himself. This soul is conceived in the form of two spirits: the first is called the *gros-bon-ange* (the big good angel) and the second the *ti-bon-ange* (the little good angel). The ti-bon-ange (which is usually seen as a kind of guardian angel) might be said to represent a man's conscience. It is this spirit that, for example, prevents him from lying. The gros-bon-ange on the other hand is the sum of a man's personality, intellect, and experience. And after his death a man's family literally provides this disembodied soul with an alternative physical form in place of the body that has perished. For it is believed that after death the souls of the dead spend at least a year at the bottom of a stream or river. But after a while, they grow restless and begin to warn their friends and family that they wish to leave. Métraux tells the story of a voodoo priestess who, having repeatedly ignored the messages of her dead relations, one day fell ill. As she gradually grew weaker and weaker, she realized that her illness was caused by her impatient relatives as a punishment for her neglect, and that she could delay the fulfillment of her duties toward them no longer. She therefore immediately made arrangements for the ceremony known as *retirer d'en bas de l'eau* (extraction from the bottom of the water). During this ritual, the souls of the dead are called up from their watery home and placed in a clay jar or *govi*, which is a substitute for the "vessel" of the flesh. These jars are then revered as the containers of tutelary spirits who, in return for sacrifices, provide their family with protection and advice.

The reclamation ritual is no mere formality, as anniversaries of a death elsewhere often are. It is of real meaning to the believers—as can be seen by the fact that the ceremony of reclaiming an undistinguished relative may be repeatedly postponed, while an exemplary or unusually valued member of a family will be reclaimed as soon as possible. But postponement does not mean permanent neglect. Among poorer people (for reclamation is a costly ceremony), or for those souls not held in especially high esteem, a group ceremony will be arranged with the *hungan* (voodoo priest) at which a number of souls will be reclaimed at the same time.

Once reclaimed, the spirit inside the govi gradually acquires the status of a god. As the dead man's contemporaries die off and first-hand knowledge of his human personality begins to fade from men's minds, all that is left within the govi is the disembodied essence of some special characteristic. So, according to Maya Deren, "in time, the ancestor becomes an archetype. Where there was once a person there is now a personage. . . . The ancestor is transfigured into a god."

But these ancestral spirits make up only part of the voodoo pantheon. This enormous collection of gods and spirits—known collectively as *loa*—may be broadly divided into two categories. First, there are the "great" loa that are worshiped on a national level. These divinities are mostly of African origin and more or less correspond to the group of gods and spirits known as *rada*. (The word is probably a contraction of the name of the ancient capital of Dahomey, Allada or Arada.) The rada gods therefore represent the traditional gods of Dahomey, with, however, the characteristics and attributes that they have acquired in the New World.

But as well as these "great" gods there is a huge proliferation of divinities known as *petro* gods. (It is thought that the word is derived from Don Pedro, a powerful voodoo priest who lived in the early days of the colony.) These include some African divinities, but the majority are of more recent, or exclusively Caribbean origin. Many of these are conceived as the spirits of the ancient and powerful dead (especially of priests and priestesses) that have assumed the status of gods.

Most students of voodoo would agree that a complete catalogue of all these gods would be impossible to compile. For not only are new gods being constantly introduced and old gods forgotten, but their forms and characteristics are continually being modified and changed. So here we shall attempt to list only a handful of the most common and therefore the best defined.

First place in any list of Haitian divinities must always belong to Legba, the intermediary, without whom no contact could be made between men and gods. Most voodoo sanctuaries hang Legba's symbol—a crutch—on the wall. He is also the guardian of gates and fences, the protector of the home, and god of every place of meeting and of parting. And under the name of Maître Carrefour (god of the crossroads), he is a patron of sorcerers.

Agwé, too, has a clearly defined role. He presides over the sea and life in the sea as well as the ships that sail on it. So ceremonies in honor of Agwé are often held on the edge of water and sailors pray to him for delivery from storm and shipwreck. Offerings to Agwé are sometimes floated out to sea in a boat. If it returns to shore, it means Agwé has spurned the sacrifice and must be propitiated in some other way.

One of the gods who most frequently appears is Zaka, the patron of crops and farming. Anyone possessed by Zaka wears the tattered blue shirt and trousers, the shabby straw hat, and basket-work bag of the typical Haitian farm laborer. When he speaks, it is in the rough tones of a peasant.

Another well-known god is Damballah-wèdo, who, depicted as a great snake, is patron of the waters of heaven and of the springs and rivers they are believed to feed. Also associated with watery places is the Simbi family. It is believed that any child who goes to fetch water at a spring risks being kidnapped and enslaved by one of the Simbi. Other "nature" gods are Badé, the wind; Sogbo, the lightning; and Agau, a storm spirit.

As for the female loa, the most famous of these is the beautiful, flirtatious goddess, Ezili. Every sanctuary contains a room or a corner of a room dedicated to Ezili, where, according to Métraux, "Her red and blue dresses and jewels are kept . . . and, on a table, always ready to hand, lie basin, towel, soap, tooth-brush, comb, lipstick and orange-stick." Playing Mars to Ezili's Venus is Ogu the warrior, a deity of fire and power and wisdom. And to complete our brief sketch, there are the sinister Guédé, spirits of death, who terrify the worshipers with a kind of obscene and macabre humor. This family includes the notorious Baron Samedi, the keeper of the cemetery, who is both lord of eroticism and god of the grave. His attributes include the spade, pick, and hoe of the grave digger.

Most of the best-known gods have both rada and petro manifestations—differences in role that are usually indicated by an epithet tacked onto their name—like, for example, Ezili-coeur noir (black heart) or Guédé-l'orage (the storm). Broadly speaking, the rada loa represent the stable, protective, benign aspects of the powers; petro loa tend to be more aggressive, more stern, and less forgiving. Ezili, for example, in a rada rite is (as we have already described her) the essence of voluptuous femininity, and will speak (through the person she possesses) in sweet soprano tones. In her petro aspect, though, she has a gruff, almost animal growl.

But even within the two classifications of rada and petro, the handful of gods we have mentioned can manifest themselves in a multitude of ways. In rada, to take but one example, there is Ogu-balindjo, known sometimes as a sea god, at others as a healer; Ogu-badagri, who is connected with fertility, wisdom, and prophesy; and many more. Ogu is also represented in the petro loa—as, for example, Ogu-jé-rouge. (Any spirit called jé-rouge—red eyes—is invariably violent and cruel.) Here, however, his role is less important, since there are other petro gods with similarly unpleasant characteristics and functions.

Even more than most gods, the loa reflect the habits and characteristics of their worshipers. They drink, quarrel, and make love as the peasants do. They are often touchy and petty; so if they are ignored or slighted, they are likely to revenge themselves. Punishment may take several forms, and some loa are more severe than others. On the whole, the rada loa are usually less arbitrary and spiteful in their dealings with men than are the jealous and capricious petro spirits.

To further complicate this complex system of gods and spirits, there are in existence two different forms of voodoo practice: one domestic and the other public. The domestic kind had a far larger following in the days when most of the population lived in small, interrelated rural communities. Each of these "compounds" included a sanctuary, in which the head of the community would officiate at ceremonies in honor of his *loa racine* (or root loa)—the gods and spirits that were believed to protect his own family.

Today, however, for economic reasons that include a drift to the towns or elsewhere in search of better living, these closely knit family communities are beginning to disintegrate, and voodoo sanctuaries (called *humfos*), presided over by qualified priests, tend to serve worshipers who happen to live in the same district rather than those that are bound together by blood. (Incidentally, the word "humfo" is often applied to any place connected with religious activity—including trees growing near the sanctuary sacred to one or another of the gods, individual altar chambers, and all the ritual objects and accessories used in the ceremonies. But in this account we shall be following the example of Maya Deren, who uses the word "humfo" to refer only to the precincts of the voodoo sanctuary itself.)

Humfos vary enormously in size and style from one district to another. Sometimes they are simply small buildings divided into one or more altar chambers adjoining a covered area (known as a peristyle) for ceremonial ritual and dance. In rural areas, a humfo may be more elaborately constructed, with several peristyles. Or it may be small, plain, and unpainted, with a crude cement block to serve as an altar. Maya Deren suggests that this lack of uniformity is only partly explained by differences in wealth, taste, or tradition, and that it primarily reflects the varying status of the religion in different districts.

A representation of a Haïtian Guédé family spirit of death. A vèvè (or ceremonial emblem) of Baron Samedi incorporating his symbols of a cross and a skull. (From *Les Zombis* by C. H. Dewisme, Editions Bernard Grasset S.A., Paris, 1957.)

Each humfo is presided over by a priest or priestess (*hungan* or *mambo*). And though there are recognized grades in the priestly hierarchy, no hungan or mambo is responsible to any other. Each operates independently as the head of his own particular cult, with authority only over those who voluntarily choose to attend his sanctuary.

Métraux defines a good hungan as "at one and the same time priest, healer, sooth-sayer, exorcizer, organizer of public entertainments, and choirmaster." He is an important and influential figure in all community activities, secular as well as religious—partly because the initiation and training he will have undergone may well have given him a measure of psychological as well as spiritual understanding. (He is also likely to be the richest man in the district. In addition to the fees for organizing ceremonies, a hungan also receives payment for treating the sick, for fortune telling, and for remedies against sorcerers' spells and the evil eye.)

The British anthropologist Francis Huxley has found from questioning many voodoo priests that they have been directed to the priesthood through the familiar pattern of trauma, accident, or illness. In other words, at some period during which they have been forced to reconsider their lives, they have become initiated into voodoo—a process that requires time spent in solitary meditation. Priesthood may very often also be handed down from father to eldest son. But even so, it will not be confirmed except by the "call of the loa," by which the spirits who have chosen a man or woman to serve them are thought to make their intention known to him or her. This summons to the priesthood may be made through the utterances of the possessed or through a symbolic dream. Métraux mentions the case of a man called Tullius who, before he became a hungan, "often saw, in dreams, a gourd containing the beads and snake-bones covering the sacred rattle (*asson*) symbol of the priestly profession." The story of Tullius also illustrates the grave risks run by those who ignore the summons of the loa: "Some time after he had dreamed the dream which we have just mentioned, Tullius became seriously ill. He believed he had been struck down by the *mystères* [the loa] who had grown tired of his inability to make up his mind."

Training for the priesthood involves a course of instruction (lasting perhaps months or years) by the hungan or mambo. Candidates learn the techniques of the priestly profession by assisting the hungan in his religious duties and by taking an active part in the ceremonies. With regular attendants to the humfo (known as *pti-cay-yo*, children of the house) these initiates form a community around the hungan known as the humfo society. As members of this community, they serve successively as *hunsi* (meaning "the spouse of the god"), *hungenikon* (choir master or mistress), *la-place* (master of ceremonies), and *confiance* (the hungan's chief assistant who is in charge of the administrative details). In return for these services the hungan or mambo is regarded as the "father" or "mother" of his or her hunsis, and is responsible for their moral and material welfare.

During the ceremonies, the hunsis act as chorus and chief dancers. The hungenikon (a hunsi who has been promoted because of particular devotion to duty) is responsible for organizing the singing—for beginning and ending the song of salutation appropriate to each loa as it appears. As for the la-place, while the hungan may be leading prayers, he is performing such duties as preparing the sacrificial animal and checking to see whether the offerings have been assembled.

The initiation of a hunsi—who then becomes known as *kanzo*—takes the form of an inner event that is represented in outward terms very similar to those already described in Chapter 5. The candidate withdraws from the world and goes through a symbolic enactment first of death, and then of resurrection. The ceremonies that express this process are preceded by ritual cleansing and purification, after which the candidate is wrapped in a white sheet, like the shroud of a corpse. The initiates then withdraw into a locked room for a week—during which time a person's past is said to die and a new self gradually to emerge into being. To quote from Maya Deren's description of the process: "For four days the body is annointed with oil at noon, when the sun is highest. And in this nascent state the nourishment of the spiritual embryo is entirely liquid. . . . The neophytes may not communicate with each other, should there be several in the same room, but they may pray, and beside them is a bell for calling the houngan's assistant to tend to their needs. Outside the door, each day, the other hounsis come and sing, invoking the loa and their blessing upon those within."

During the retreat, locks of the novice's hair and nail clippings from his left hand and foot are placed in a pot, which is later put on the altar of the humfo. This represents the initiate's gros-bon-ange, which is now in the custody of the hungan. Another initiatory rite that takes place at this time is the procedure known as *laver-tête*. The initiate's head is washed and covered with a paste made up of herbs, rice,

bread, syrup, and blood. This is thought to place the novice
under the protection of a particular loa (*loa maît'-tête*) who
will from then on act as his personal protector.

At the end of the retreat, the new "soul" is led out to take
part in the ceremony of the burning pots (*bulé-zin*). These
are pots dedicated to various loa (including the initiate's
maît'-tête) set over small fires burning in the peristyle. Each
of these contains a mixture of flour and other ingredients
cooking in boiling oil. The initiate kneels down before each
pot, and is made to grasp a handful of burning hot dough by
the hungan. He then passes his left hand and foot through
the flame. The next day, the initiate emerges once more into
the world amid an atmosphere of triumph and rejoicing.

After this brief summary of the major aspects of voodoo belief, we are now ready to take a look at what happens at a
"typical" voodoo ceremony. There are of course not only a
great number of different rituals—including, as we have already seen, those of reclaiming the dead and of
initiation—but also enormous variations from humfo to
humfo in the celebration of these rituals. So it must be remembered that the following is only a sketch of some of the
basic elements common to most voodoo services.

The service is likely to be held on Saturday night, since
any voodoo ceremony is long and strenuous, and on Sunday
morning the peasants can sleep late and slowly recover. The
celebrants gather in the peristyle of the humfo in the early
evening, in an atmosphere that is friendly and casual rather
than solemn. Inside the sanctuary itself, the altar is covered
with offerings of fruit, bottles of rum and cold drinks, and
clay jars, some containing the spirits of the ancestors, others
the gros-bon-anges of living worshipers who have, like the
hunsis in the initiation ceremony, surrendered them permanently to the hungan's safe-keeping.

When everyone has assembled in the peristyle, the hungan
takes a jug of water, and lifting it successively to the four
cardinal points, salutes the loa. (He also salutes—for reasons
we shall come to later—the Father, Son, and Holy Ghost of
the Christian Trinity.) Next he puts three libations into the
ground at the entrance to the peristyle; he then makes a
drawing (called a *vèvè*) on the ground with sand or flour of
the emblems of the gods to be manifested at the ceremony.
Each vèvè is consecrated by putting on it small piles of
grilled maize and other dried foodstuffs, and some drink

(which may even be Coca-Cola). These emblematic drawings have a magical purpose: to summon the loa, and placate and honor them with food and drink.

After these preliminaries the hunsis and la-places emerge from the chamber of the humfo. They advance backward, revolving first one way, then the other, until they reach the center of the peristyle. The rituals that now follow may vary, but all include a combination of singing, dancing, and drumming to create an atmosphere in which the gods and their worshipers may come together and meet one another.

An approach to the gods is often made by a ceremonial "feeding of the loa." This ritual offering of food may take several forms, from the first fruits of the season to large numbers of slaughtered birds and animals such as chickens, goats, bulls, and pigs. After this ceremonial "meal" is over, the preliminary courtesies are considered to be complete, and the gods begin to take possession of their worshipers. As the moment of entry approaches, the classic symptoms of possession begin to manifest themselves: tremblings, convulsions, even feelings of terror and anguish. These mark the displacement of the gros-bon-ange of the person to be possessed. At this moment his body is taken over by a god, and it is the god's personality, not his own, that from then on is expressed in his bearing and words. His voice, his features, his gestures, and the words he utters all reflect a characterization of the god, who is said to "ride" him. In the words of a Haitian proverb, "the character of the loa is the character of his horse."

Very often the possessed thresh about wildly; but if they struggle too frantically they are restrained, and if they stagger too uncontrollably, they are prevented from falling. Possession may last from a few seconds to the length of the entire ceremony. Generally it ends spontaneously, but sometimes the hungan has to intervene to restore the gros-bon-ange to its owner. When it is all over, a person who has been possessed will remember nothing of what he said or did.

When the initial crisis is over and the personality of the god begins to become apparent, the gods' traditional accessories (like, for example, the sword of Ogu) are brought one by one to the possessed man. The possessed man now *is* the god—the physical expression of an invisible presence. Such a manifestation of one of the major loa is greeted by a special rhythm: the drums and the singers burst out with redoubled fervor.

From this description, it becomes clear that voodoo in-corporates many of the classic ingredients of religious cere-monial such as dance, music, and drama. The possessed man dresses up as the god who "rides" him; there is excitement and gaiety; and throughout the persistent beat of the drums. (The drummers are supremely important at a voodoo cere-mony, since upon their rhythm depends the fervor and con-centration of the dancers. A good drummer can even start or end possession by intensifying or breaking the rhythm. The drum itself is revered as a sacred object, and must be made from a particular kind of wood laid down by tradition.)

Some manifestations are dramatically more successful than others. One may well hear a possession commented on in ad-miring terms as a particularly fine performance. Nevertheless, to the Haitian, all cases of possession are genuine appear-ances of the loa, though, when describing them, objective ob-servers might well apply such commonly used psychological labels as "dissociation" or "hysteria."

But, as we pointed out earlier, though the Haitian may re-gard voodoo in a genuinely religious light, he does not set its practice apart from his everyday existence as in the formal, orthodox observance of less ecstatic religions. And when reli-gion occupies such an integral part of a man's life, it follows that his attitude to the gods will not remain on a consistently solemn level. This almost casual approach is reflected in the atmosphere of a voodoo ceremony, which may be simulta-neously awe-inspiring and obscene, frightening and matter-of-fact. To their worshipers, the gods are not only advisers and mentors, but also bullies and gossips.

The voodoo worshiper, in short, does not equate his reli-gious devotion with piety or purity. His instincts and feelings are given free rein even during the most sacred ceremony, without any self-conscious reflection that it might be inap-propriate to the occasion. For example, when the Guédé (whom, as we have already said, represent death and the un-derworld) make their appearance at a ceremony, they will not necessarily—as might be expected—be met with despair and gloom. Their entry into the peristyle (which usually hap-pens toward the end of a ceremony) may well be greeted with a series of broad jokes. In the words of Métraux, "[The Guédé] can be relied upon to introduce a vein of frank gaiety into the most serious ceremonies. [Their] habit of talking through [their] noses is by itself comic enough—even though meant to be like the speech of Death. . . . [They have] a fine repertoire of obscene songs. . . . In some *humfo* a huge wooden phallus is kept on the altar in case such an attribute is suddenly required by the god. The possessed masquerade with it, dance obscene dances. . . ."

Death can sometimes have this grotesque aspect, which the Haitians acknowledge as they do its more conventional associations by the manifestations of the Guédé that are blood-chilling and macabre. As an example of this versatility, a god may be talking in transcendental terms at one moment, and at the next be scolding someone for stealing a chicken. In the same way, during the ceremony of reclaiming the dead (mentioned on p. 169) as the souls rise from the watery abyss, they converse in a manner typical of them in life. The hungan may find himself cajoling an ancestor who is reluctant to enter the govi—an ancestor who displays all the stubborn and selfish qualities that he had on earth, to the amusement of the spectators.

Since the Haitian's response to their religion is so uninhibited, it is not surprising that there is another, less attractive aspect to voodoo. This is the "black" voodoo so beloved by sensational newspapers—the world of sorcery and black magic, of zombis and werewolves, murders and dreams of hidden treasure. The loa are in operation here too, since the grandmaster of spells and sorceries is Legba-petro, invoked under the name of Maître Carrefour—and invoked (as befits his name) very often at crossroads. Any rite involving sympathetic magic is also thought to be ineffective unless terms are first made with Baron Samedi—who, as we have pointed out, belongs to the Guédé family. It is believed that even the most powerful sorcerer cannot kill a man if the Baron has not first "marked out" the victim's grave.

And here, as in Chapter 5, we find the same lack of distinction between religion and magic. In voodoo, the role of the priest is not easy to separate from that of magician and sorcerer. "The *boko,* or sorcerer," says Métraux, "is only a hungan who 'serves with both hands'." And he adds: "A hungan worthy of the name knows all the techniques of sorcery since he is constantly required to counter them."

In a community that is still in many ways a primitive one, it is not surprising that many will resort to magic to achieve their dreams and aspirations. And in a society where life is often harsh, many of these ambitions are selfish or even wicked. So there exists alongside the gaiety, fervor, and gentleness of the Haitian, a mysterious, disquieting world of ma-

levolent and twisted desires. Nor is this sphere of darkness
and evil entirely African in origin. Many of the beliefs and
practices of Haitian magic are based on ideas of magic and
the occult that were popular in 18th- and 19th-century
France.

The practice of magic is in fact illegal in Haiti and for this
reason many of the tales of sorcery, enchantment, poisoning,
and magical murder that drift around the country may well
be invented—or the result of coincidence. The French writer
C.-H. Dewisme described (in *Les Zombis*, 1957) an example
of this so-called murder by magic that took place during the
American occupation of Haiti after World War I. A hungan
from Port-au-Prince cast a death spell against an American
lieutenant who was in command of the police department.
The spell was designed to take effect at the end of a week
and was greeted with ridicule by its intended victim. On the
evening of the seventh day, however, a gendarme returned
drunk to the station. While the lieutenant was unbraiding him
for his conduct, the drunkard seized his gun and shot his superior officer dead.

The best-known form of black magic—that of working
harm through a doll or some other object representing the intended victim—is prevalent in Haiti. But there are variations
on this classic theme. In one of these, the sorcerer first produces (by incantation) an image of his victim in a bucket of
water. He then stabs the reflection. If the spell "works" the
water immediately reddens, as with blood. There are also less
summary methods of magical murder: potions that cause
long, lingering and finally fatal illnesses: and, most dreadful
of all, the "sending of the dead." In this spell, the *boko* is
possessed by Baron Samedi who, speaking through his mouth,
orders the client to go to a cemetery at midnight, with special
offerings of food. There he must gather a handful of earth
for each person whom he wishes to kill, which he later
spreads on some path frequently taken by his victim. Alternatively a client takes a stone from the graveyard, which will
transform itself into a being ready to carry out his evil designs as soon as he throws it against the door of his victim's
house. Métraux comments: "Whoever has become the prey
of one or more dead people sent against him begins to grow
thin, spit blood, and is soon dead. The laying on of this spell
is always attended by fatal results unless it is diagnosed in
time and a capable hungan succeeds in making the dead let
go."

There are rituals and magic to carry out every evil or self-seeking purpose; to cause injury or death, to obtain riches, to bring bad luck to enemies and rivals or good luck to the client. But the most notorious and dreadful phenomenon produced by black magic is the *zombi*—a corpse that has been reanimated to live again as a mindless slave. Precautions are sometimes taken to prevent a sorcerer from raising the dead in this terrible way by "killing" the corpse a second time by poison or by strangling. Other methods include burying the body with a dagger to protect it and sewing up the corpse's mouth to stop it from answering when a sorcerer calls its name. Such superstitious practices may be scorned by the enlightened, but there are few among them who do not feel at least a twinge of belief in stories of zombis. A famous case that is still remembered is that of a society girl who, a few years after her death, was seen by some school friends at the window of a house in Port-au-Prince. The news spread all around the town and a warrant to search the house was issued, but no trace of the girl was found. Next her grave was opened and inspected, to reveal a skeleton that was too long for the coffin and without the clothes in which the corpse had been buried. These were found neatly folded beside the skeleton. Later, it is said, the girl was removed from Haiti by her family and sent to a convent in France, where she was subsequently visited by her brother.

In an atmosphere poisoned by such terrifying beliefs, it is not surprising that few Haitian peasants will dare to go out alone at night. For what is feared is not only ghosts or evil spirits but an encounter with a mob of sorcerers, members of secret societies devoted to magical gangsterism. Each region has its own name for these groups, which are called variously *zobop*, *galipotes*, "hairless pigs," "grey pigs," and *vlanbindingues*. To these "red sects" (as they are collectively known) every possible violent and sadistic act is ascribed, although in the garbled stories of their activities, it is difficult to disentangle fact from fantasy. Members of these societies are hard to identify, for they have no distinguishing badge or mark; they may even turn out to be apparently quiet and law-abiding citizens. Among other atrocities, the peasants accuse the zobop of changing their victims into beasts about to be slaughtered, and it is a widespread conviction on the island that among the animals that enter slaughter houses there are a few who are in fact human beings. One slaughter house in Port-au-Prince allegedly once took steps to prevent this

form of magical murder by giving the animals injections.
Whereupon a wretched beast who had been bewitched cried
out: "Now I am here, I remember my children!"

According to another popular belief, zobop often carry out
their nocturnal raids in motorcars. Métraux writes: "A few
years ago there was much talk in Port-au-Prince of a 'ti-
ger-car' that took people away by night to eat them. This was
no innocent folk-tale, as a friend of mine was able to witness.
He—Monsieur M. B.—was suspected of being the driver of
the phantom car and was almost lynched by a crowd which
surged round him, accusing him of having killed a chito
[child]."

Perhaps some of the tales of these gangs who roam
through the island at night beating up their victims or forcing
them to do their will, are true. For in this sort of atmosphere,
superstitious fear can easily be exploited by criminals or even
politicians. For example, Dr. Duvalier, the president and vir-
tual dictator of the island, is said to be in league with powerful spirits, and his personal bodyguards (called *tontons ma-
coute*—the name for wandering voodoo herbalists) are invoked as a threat in much the same way as Western children
are frightened by the bogeyman.

As we pointed out earlier, not all magic is black, directed
toward evil ends. As might be expected in an island where
life brings few material rewards and health services in particular are inadequate, much "white" magic is concerned with
easing misfortune and pain. The hungan is familiar with the
curative properties of herbs as well as usually possessing a
certain understanding of psychology. There are frequent tales
of Haitian peasants refusing hospital treatment even in cases of
obvious and urgent illness. Maya Deren cites the example of
her servant who, having been diagnosed as a case of acute
appendicitis, refused to go to hospital. Instead she went to
her hungan, who (by means of a ritual in which she, ill as
she was, had to play an active part) cured her completely.

Voodoo then, is far more complex and wide ranging than
its popular image of black magic and orgiastic rituals would
at first suggest. It also makes available to a whole society
many of the techniques that are used elsewhere as a means of
contacting the supernatural. Among these methods are trance
mediumship (in which state the hungan does much of his divination), acts of sympathetic magic, and speaking in
tongues (which occurs frequently during voodoo ceremonies). More specifically, voodoo incorporates many elements

of Christian belief. In fact, voodoo worshipers are often practicing Christians, though not surprisingly this dual allegiance is discouraged by the Church. It is however more or less helpless in the case of the voodoo worshiper who, in the words of Miss Deren, "sincerely insists that he believes in the Trinity, baptizes his children and his drums, places the saints on his private altar, and makes lavish use of the sign of the cross. . . . It is in the peculiar position of trying to convert the already converted."

In voodoo, moreover, many of the Catholic saints are equated with the loa. Like some loa, the saints were once human beings; and like the loa, they have acquired specific attributes. And so, all over Haiti, voodoo altars are decorated with illustrations of saints and biblical figures. St. Patrick, with the snakes at his feet, is identified with Damballah-wèdo, the serpent god; Lazarus, when depicted as an old man with a staff and dogs at his heels, is a representation of Legba, to whom dogs are sacred. St. Ulrich, who holds a fish, is Agwé, god of the sea.

If Christian tradition is interwoven with voodoo myth, voodoo ritual also borrows heavily from Catholic liturgy. Most services in honor of the loa are conducted by the priest or priestess in front of an altar covered with candles and surrounded by pictures of saints. Recitations of Paternosters, Confiteors, and Ave Marias are followed by hymns addressed to the Virgin Mary and to the Saints. Voodoo ceremonial also includes the use of holy water, which is sprinkled over worshipers by means of a leafy branch. As Métraux comments: "In giving a Catholic *cachet* to ceremonies which are not Catholic, Voodooists are in no way trying to pull the wool over the eyes of authorities or Church: rather is it that they are in fact convinced of the efficacy of Catholic liturgy and therefore wish their own religion to benefit from it. The singing, prayers and kneelings, which precede a service, are said to 'stir the loa up'."

This intermingling of Christian and pagan elements is only one of the many complexities and contradictions inside the framework of voodoo. The complications are so enormous that we have hardly been able even to hint at them. In fact, no one has yet succeeded in making the practice and beliefs of voodoo wholly intelligible. The consideration of any detail can lead to endless digression and speculation. Take, for example, Monday, Tuesday, and Thursday, which are seen as auspicious, "feminine" days, while Wednesday, Friday, and

Saturday are inauspicious, "masculine" days. For what reason? What is the thinking that lies behind the sacred numbers and colors that are to be found throughout voodoo belief? How do all these seemingly unconnected details fit into the whole pattern?

But these are minor puzzles that should not be allowed to obscure the simple central core of vooodoo belief and practice—the unquestioning acceptance that in ordinary, everyday life there exists a two-way traffic between the natural and supernatural. To the voodoo worshiper, every human emotion has a matching, answering emotion in the world of the divine, which can be manifested through possession. He is also convinced that on the quality of the believer's emotion—that is, the emotional potential that he brings to the ceremony—will depend the quality of what the loa give to him in return. And for some time now, the Haitians admit, manifestations of the "great" loa have been rare. They have a proverb that shows they are under no illusions as to the reason: "Great loa," they say, "cannot ride little horses."

8 HERE BE MONSTERS

Lyncanthropy means the transformation of a man into a wolf. A man with this power of metamorphosis is called a werewolf (from old English *wer*, man). Of all the supernatural monsters that haunt our fiction, folklore, and dreams, the werewolf dominates both in the ubiquity of its legend and in the terror that legend can produce.

Werewolf stories abound in the folklore of practically every country in the world. Germany has its *wer-wolf*, Spain its *lob ombre*, Portugal its *lob omem*, Italy its *lupo manaro*, and, above all, France and French-speaking nations have more than their share of the *loup-garou*. And the werewolf has its cousins in countries where wolves have never been: India has tales of were-tigers, Africa of were-leopards, were-jackals, and were-hyenas. Even in places where there are or once were plenty of wolves, such as Russia and France, tales exist of were-dogs, bears, cats, foxes—even toads.

The depth of terror the werewolf can inspire, and its hold on men's imaginations, will become plain as we progress through werewolf lore. But two factors underlying the fear are worth stressing from the start. First, wolves (the animals themselves) have been deadly enemies of men almost since each first evolved—perhaps the deadliest enemy, at least in the northern hemisphere, where they have been hunted relentlessly in an attempt to exterminate them. (Other dangerous animals are hunted to be controlled; it seems where wolves are concerned men grow hysterical and seek to wipe them out completely.) Extermination has succeeded in many places. There are no longer any wolves in Germany, Switzerland, Britain, or the U.S.A. (except Alaska). It was thought that France (which suffered more than any country from wolves in the past) was also free of them; but a small pack was seen there in 1963—and, indicating the widespread fearful fascination of the animals, made headlines internationally. Wolves have recently been seen in Northern Italy, and in Canada (where a man was attacked in Northern Ontario in 1963) as well as in Spain, Portugal, Poland, and Turkey.

But wolves are not only (in general) ferocious predators who hunt in packs and who don't mind what kind of meat they eat; they also have a certain eeriness about them that readily prompts a link with the supernatural. They are semi-nocturnal, silent, greyish in color; their catlike eyes glow red in reflected firelight, yellow-green in moonlight; and their chilling, banshee-like howl completes the picture of a not-quite-natural beast. They are animals, in other words, with something demonic about them. From there it is a short easy step to linking them with the Devil's legions, and with witchcraft.

Throughout the centuries of witch persecution in Europe, lycanthropy was seen simply as another activity of the witch—whose powers of metamorphosis have been discussed (p. 137). That is, transforming herself into a wolf and ranging the countryside at night terrorizing the people, killing and devouring wayfarers, was thought to be one way that a witch obeyed her satanic master's orders to wreak harm on man. Some commentators at the time thought that not all werewolves were witches—that some of them were lesser demons of hell. A few individual werewolves, whose depredations were exceptionally extensive, were actually thought to be the Devil himself. But even where the werewolves were not metamorphosed witches, but demons, the connection was clear. Many accounts of sabbats refer to witches being transported to the scene on the backs of wolves; at a few sabbats the whole assembly was said to transform itself into a wolfpack and spend the night ravaging the countryside. An old Latvian tale concerns a 12-day march at Christmas of a pack of thousands of werewolves led by the Devil, who was himself in wolf form.

Obviously, then, to the 16th- and 17th-century experts, if a werewolf was much the same as a witch then one became a werewolf the way one became a witch—through a pact with the Devil. Once the pact was concluded in the usual way (p. 129), the Devil conferred upon the initiate the power of magical metamorphosis. Now this power was just one of the talents acquired by a new witch. But in a great many tales and demonologists' accounts, it seems that a large percentage of werewolves were *only* werewolves; they lacked the witches' other powers—of sorcery, or of flight, for instance. It seems as if most werewolves had petitioned the Devil only for the lycanthropic ability.

Also, the folklore of most nations offers many methods of becoming a werewolf other than by entering into a contract with the Devil. Some of these semi-magical procedures did not directly involve any diabolism. In Italian folk belief, anyone conceived at the time of the new moon would become a werewolf; and so would anyone who slept overnight in the open on a Friday under a full moon. In the Balkan Peninsula—fertile ground for werewolf and vampire legends—a certain nameless flower would turn anyone who ate it into a werewolf. Drinking water from a real wolf's footprint, drinking from a stream where a wolfpack drank, or eating a wolf's brains—these are some of the ways, according to folklore, of becoming a werewolf, intentionally or not.

The 16th-century magician Paracelsus suggested that a man who lived a brutal or bestial life might return after death in beast form—usually as a wolf. (But not many tales concern *ghostly* werewolves; they are generally believed to be all-too-solid flesh and blood.) According to the modern French writer Claude Seignolle, old French lore contains stories of priests putting a curse on criminals to change them into werewolves for seven years. And other writers have mentioned unwilling or involuntary lycanthropy. At one time werewolfism was believed to be hereditary; and many writers (including, in this century, Montague Summers) firmly asserted that werewolves were invariably cases of demonic possession.

However, if a man or woman *wanted* to become a werewolf, any of the magical methods mentioned could be employed—or, for absolute certainty, a special ritual could be used. This ritual is essentially a black magic ceremony, resembling those in which sorcerers conjure up demons, but it has special lycanthropic features. The aspirant to wolfhood goes to a lonely wood or hilltop on the night of a full moon (or, some say, a new moon). There, at midnight, he draws a magic circle: an outer circle seven feet in diameter and an inner one three feet in diameter. Within the circle he makes a fire and boils up a cauldron into which he puts ingredients like hemlock, opium, henbane, and parsley. He then speaks an incantation, including these lines:

Wolves, vampires, satyrs, ghosts!
Elect of all the devilish hosts!
    I pray you send hither,
    Send hither, send hither,
The great grey shape that makes men shiver!

After this he strips naked, smears his body with an ointment prepared previously (like the witch's ointment, p. 137), and puts on a belt made of wolf's skin. Then he kneels down and waits. If he has carried out the ritual correctly, a demon will appear (sometimes said to be the Devil or one of his minions, sometimes just a non-satanic evil forest spirit) and will grant the aspirant the power of metamorphosis.

In many legends, metamorphosis into a werewolf can be accomplished only by some such complicated ceremony—in which the man must strip, smear on the ointment, say an incantation, and (always important) put on the wolf-skin belt or sometimes even an entire wolf hide. But often the process is simplified. Some folktales tell of men changing into werewolves merely by stripping under a full moon and rolling around in the dirt for a few moments. In others a man achieves the metamorphosis by removing his clothes under a full moon and urinating in a circle drawn on the ground. In still others all that is needed is to remove human clothing and put on a wolf's skin—or just the belt. As for changing back, a few authorities say that parts of the ritual need to be reversed—for instance removing the wolf-skin belt (and perhaps rolling in the dirt again, or bathing in running water). Others say that the wolf-to-human transformation happens automatically when the night is over.

During the night itself, a werewolf's activities are generally limited to the very wolfish practices of hunting, killing, and eating. (This is aside from those demonic wolves who spent their time at sabbats.) Some tales of werewolves have them limiting their ravaging to flocks and herds in the countryside; but most often lycanthropy means cannibalism—the werewolf hungers for human flesh. Though werewolves were seldom particular, they were generally thought to prefer the flesh of children (remember that witches were often accused of eating children at sabbats)—and especially of young girls. A self-confessed werewolf in 17th-century France, an imbecilic boy named Jean Grenier, boasted that he had killed and eaten many young girls, and was promptly tried and imprisoned by the authorities, who took him at his word. This link between lycanthropy and another tortuous word, *parthenophagy* (a delight in the flesh of girls), recurs again and again; and since the parthenophagous werewolf was usually a child rapist as well, here we have links between the werewolf myth and two age-old and almost universal human taboos: cannibalism and sexual perversion. (What these links indicate about the basis of the myth will emerge later.) Both figure strongly in a famous case of werewolfery in 16th-century Germany—the case of Peter Stubb, or Stump. It is one of the most detailed (and therefore, for us, most valuable) accounts of a supposed werewolf's activities ever written.

Stubb achieved werewolfhood by a pact with the Devil. His purpose (according to an English pamphlet on him published in 1590, whose spelling we have modernized) was to exercise "his malice on men, women, and children, in the shape of some beast, whereby he might live without dread of danger of life, and unknown to be the executor of any bloody enterprise which he meant to commit." The Devil gave him a wolf-skin belt ("girdle"); Stubb merely need to put it on in order to metamorphose. Then he began 25 years of terrorizing the countryside.

He killed and ate cattle and sheep occasionally; he killed many people who had at one time offended him (but seldom ate them if they were adult and male); and, especially, he raped, killed, and ate women and girls. The pamphlet says: ". . . he would walk up and down, and if he could spy either maid, wife, or child that his eyes liked and his heart lusted after, he would wait their issuing out of the city or town, if he could by any means get them alone, he would in the fields ravish them, and after in his wolfish likeness cruelly murder them. . . ." Thus, within a few years, "he had murdered thirteen young children and two goodly young women big with child."

The pamphlet goes on describing his evil. Stubb committed incest with his daughter (who had a child by him) and his sister, and had many other "concubines"—including, for seven years, a succubus sent by the Devil. Among all his murders during the years he was a werewolf, one was by far the worst: the pamphlet tells us he killed and ate his own son.

Finally the populace's attempts to catch and kill the terrible wolf succeeded. Pursued in his wolf form by men and many dogs, Stubb tried to shake off the pursuers by removing the belt and changing back into a man. But the pursuers, realizing what must have happened, "had him incontinent before the magistrates to be examined." Though the belt was never found, there was enough evidence: the fact that Stubb had suddenly appeared before the pursuers' eyes, the fact of his incest and other sins. He was found guilty, tortured horribly, and executed—and his head was mounted on a pole outside the town of Bedburg as a warning and a trophy.

Like most of the Devil's human servants, Stubb seems to have given his captors no trouble once he was caught; he was executed the way anyone, supernatural power or no, would have been executed if they had committed a capital crime. The way, also, that witches were executed (few witches were ever said to have escaped the Inquisition by exercising their magical powers). The experts said that the Devil left his servants to their own devices once they were caught (that is, once their usefulness was at an end), and simply waited for their souls to arrive in hell. So, no special means were necessary to put an end to werewolves. They merely had to be caught, the way ordinary wolves and ordinary heretics were caught.

Even where folklore did not relate werewolves to the Devil, plain means were often sufficient to destroy them— means that would be employed against real wolves. They were killed, then, in various accounts, with knives and clubs and guns. And usually when wounded or dead the wolves automatically reverted to human form. There is a 16th-century French tale of a hunter who beat off an attack by a fierce wolf, and, in the fight cut off one of the beast's paws. He put the paw in his pouch and set off home; on the way he met a friend, told the story of the battle, and reached for the paw to show it. But he found in his pouch a woman's hand, wearing a gold ring. The hunter thought he recognized the hand, and rushed home to find—as he suspected—his wife bandaging the bleeding stump of her arm. The wife was shortly tried by the local authorities and burned.

As would be expected, where the werewolf is thought to be demonically possessed, exorcism is the usual cure. But there are many non-religious, quasi-magical procedures that people can use to rid themselves of werewolves, when normal means fail. In many English and Scottish folk beliefs, the werewolf (especially if it is a metamorphosed witch) is immune to ordinary bullets and can be killed only with bullets of silver—or sometimes even of silver that has been consecrated in church. Sometimes a man can be cured of lycanthropy if three drops of blood are drawn from him, or if (when in his wolf shape) he is called by his human name. Involuntary werewolves will be cured if they abstain from human flesh for nine years. In French folklore, the *loup-garou* will be cured if he is pricked to bleeding-point during the night; and the werewolf created by the priest's curse (mentioned earlier) can be cured if wounded by that or any other priest. In these cases, the belief is that the wolf is wounded or killed while the man remains unharmed.

If the werewolf cannot be killed, or cured, there are a variety of materials that will at least keep him away. Rye, mistletoe, ash and yew trees have been considered good protection in Britain. Some authorities say that werewolves fear running water (perhaps relating lycanthropy to hydrophobia, seeing a werewolf in a real wolf gone rabid). And there are also ways of knowing that a man is a werewolf, and thus protecting oneself by keeping away from him. Such signs include: straight, slanting eyebrows meeting over the nose; long, curved, reddish fingernails; small ears set low on the head; an exceptionally long third finger on each hand; and, sometimes, merely extreme hairiness, especially on the hands and feet. There are no generally accepted ways of distinguishing a werewolf in his wolf shape from an ordinary wolf, except that the werewolf is said, rather vaguely, to be bigger, fiercer, and hungrier. But in some folk tales the werewolf is a human with a wolf's head, or a wolf with human hands. In one case related by Claude Seignolle, supposed to have occurred about the turn of the century, a French farmer saw two wolves and climbed a tree to avoid them. They hadn't seen him, however, and so he was able to watch and listen—and to recognize them very easily as werewolves. Not only did they converse in human voices; but one took a snuffbox from under his tail and offered it to the other. They dropped the box, and the farmer later recovered it and traced its owner—a local man. The farmer (who died in 1927) told the story often, but never revealed the names—until one of the two alleged werewolves died an apparently natural death some years later, and it was found that, every morning, his gravestone showed fresh scratches apparently made by the paws of a wolf.

Authorities on the supernatural, and especially witchcraft experts, have produced many theories of varying degrees of plausibility to explain how and why the werewolf legend first grew up and why it still persists in so many parts of the world. For instance, the origin of the legend, some say, was in various wolf myths and wolf cults of antiquity. Apparently an ancient Greek named Lycaeon became overzealous in his worship of Zeus, and sacrificed a human child—and was turned by the angry god into a wolf. (Some Greek writers embellished the story, adding that Lycaeon not only sacrificed but ate the child.) Anyway, a cult grew up for the worship of Zeus Lycaeus, wearing wolf masks and so on. The wild Maenads also wore wolf masks in their bestial ecstasies, when they would pursue an animal (or sometimes a man) through the woods and literally tear it to pieces when they caught it. So perhaps, the theory says, garbled accounts of such orgies resulted in a belief that such people actually metamorphosed into wolves before the hunt.

Presumably these ancient forerunners did contribute in some way to the European werewolf stories—just as, in Africa, the concept of the totem or "bush-soul" probably contributed to the growth of were-leopard stories. (A tribesman believes that he has identity with an animal—the bush-soul—that is not just spiritual or symbolic, but complete: they are one and the same.) Other parallels from European history also contribute—foremost among them, the stories of the wild, fur-wearing, barbaric warriors from the North. Some writers hint that legendary memories of such men and their attacks on peaceful settlements form part of the werewolf's background—memories especially of the Nordic *berserkers*, the warriors who fought in a blind, hysterical, and almost invincible fury. ("Berserk" comes, it is thought, from the old Norse for "bear-shirt"—for naturally these men wore furs.) The berserker was said to howl like an animal, foam at the mouth, and so on.

But the modern British writer Robert Eisler has produced a far-reaching anthropological theory concerning sadism, masochism, and lycanthropy based on his knowledge of ancient history and legend. To simplify greatly Eisler's ideas: first, he amasses evidence to show that man was not always carnivorous or aggressive—that, like most primates and many primitives today, ancient men were vegetarian and frugivorous, given neither to war nor to violence nor, especially, to sexual violence. But this idyllic state was altered by changing circumstances—such as the coming of an Ice Age. To survive, then, primeval man had to find new food, so he turned to meat; he had to cover his nudity, so he made fur clothing. He learned to hunt, and to do so in packs for better results. And the upheaval that this gradual transformation caused left its scars on man's collective unconscious (Eisler borrows the term from Jung) and produced sado-masochism, its related guilt feelings—and the werewolf myth.

Eisler's theory offers attractive explanations for many aspects of werewolfery. For instance, the sexual emphasis: primeval man in his wolf pack had the choice between fighting the pack leader in order to get a woman, or stealing a woman from a more peaceful tribe. Hence, later werewolves are seen as rapists. And as for cannibalism, presumably the ancient fur-clad tribes ate whatever they could find when the glaciers ruined the north land, and the human packs moved south—where people might still be frugivorous and peaceful. The same way that, much later, the berserkers moved south to pillage; and that the wolves themselves would move during a hard winter. And if you were an inhabitant of a southern community and had your village robbed and burned and your women stolen and raped by fur-clad, howling berserkers one day—and the next day were ravaged by a pack of four-legged wolves—would you not tend to see little difference between man and wolf? And assume that they could change their shape at will?

As for today, according to the modern American psychoanalyst Dr. Nandor Fodor, "The old, savage lycanthropic beliefs have been relegated to our dream life; where they are still active conditions and are exploited for the representation of criminal motives, while the transformation is used symbolically as self-denunciation for secret deeds, fantasies or desires." Some of the dreams that Fodor recounts to prove this point lend considerable weight to Eisler's idea that those scars on the collective unconscious are by no means healed.

This leaves us with only one more factor that may have contributed to werewolf tales: the pathological disease that is also called lycanthropy. A sufferer will be fully convinced that he is a wild animal; he will howl, desire raw meat, perhaps even run on all fours. It is possible, then, that many specific werewolf stories have grown out of cases of actual lycanthropy—which, according to Rossell Hope Robbins, were fairly prevalent in the 16th and 17th centuries. (The mentally defective Jean Grenier, mentioned before, may have been this kind of lycanthrope; the disease is often linked with defectiveness.) The disease gives the sufferer the hallucination that he has actually metamorphosed, or at least that his teeth and claws have lengthened. Some lycanthropes (in 17th-century accounts) assured people that they were actually wolves but that their hair grew on the inside. It is also possible, remembering the drugs employed by witches, that the ointment used in the metamorphosis spells, plus auto-suggestion, may have induced hallucination in would-be werewolves who did not suffer from the disease lycanthropy.

To sum up, then: adding together all the possibilities—unconscious archetypal fears and memories, garbled and exaggerated history transmitted orally, mental disease, hallucinatory drugs, and man's age-old fear and hatred of the wolf—it is no wonder that the werewolf legend grew up, spread so widely, and persists. And it does persist. In Bourg-la-Reine, France, in 1930, a farmer had a reputation as a sorcerer (his house was found to contain all the paraphernalia, including amulets and wax dolls), and was firmly believed by his neighbors to take the shape of a wolf at night. And in 1946 in America a trading post on a Navaho Indian reservation was terrorized by rumors of an Indian werewolf who raided flocks, dug up graves and robbed them, and killed and ate women.

If the werewolf is closely related to witches, the vampire is closely related to ghosts. Vampires are, most generally, corpses (living dead) that rise up out of their tombs and suck the blood of the living. The vampire legend is neither as old nor as widespread as that of the werewolf or other were-animals. The latter's basic pattern is found throughout recorded history, and all over the world from Siberia to South Africa; but the basic pattern of the vampire story developed into the form we know today only about the 16th and 17th centuries, and principally in the Balkan peninsula and neighboring areas. (In antiquity there were beings that seem to be cousins of the vampire—bloodsucking ghosts, magicians, or witches—but these have only a few correspondences with the vampire pattern.)

The word *vampire* is itself of Slavonic origin. Montague Summers tells us there is a Magyar word *vampir*, and finds close variants in Russian, Czech, Polish, and Hungarian. The word did not enter the English language until 1734; the 1730s were a period of great vampire activity in the Balkans, and apparently some English travelers heard and published

some of the stories. The word and the legend soon became
well known all over Europe, perhaps partly due to the efforts
of the French theologian Dom Augustin Calmet, who wrote a
study of vampires in 1746. (Although a 17th-century Greek
scholar, Leone Allacci, had preceded him by 100 years with a
similar, if more limited, study.) Still, the greatest road to
fame for the vampire was through fiction. Somehow vampires
have always inspired horror writers almost as much as
ghosts—and much more than werewolves. Perhaps a modern
psychologist might suggest that the attraction stemmed from
the sadistic eroticism that underlies every vampire story—and
more immediately than in werewolf stories, since the vampire
is in human form. (These sexual implications will be looked
at again shortly.)

The vampire came into his fictional own during the flood
of horror stories in the 19th century. Even great literary
names were attracted to vampire tales: Goethe, Gautier, and
Baudelaire among them. At the other end of the scale were
best-selling "penny dreadfuls" like Thomas Prest's *Varney the
Vampire* (1847). But dominating the vampire market—and,
incidentally, forming the usual conception of a vampire up
till today—was the inimitable *Dracula*, by the Irish author
Bram Stoker, published in 1897.

Stoker's biographer states that the idea for a book about a
vampire came to Stoker in a dream (the way Stevenson conceived *Dr. Jekyll and Mr. Hyde*, and Mary Shelley *Frankenstein*). But then Stoker, like all good horror writers, searched
for a measure of authenticity on which to base the fantasy.
And he found a 15th-century Wallachian nobleman named
Drakula—a great general who led and won many battles
against the Turks, but also a vicious and depraved sadist, tor-
turer, and murderer who used his feudal power to get victims
from the local peasantry. His castle was hated and feared; the
locals whispered tales of horror and thought that the man
was a (or the) devil; and one manuscript, telling Drakula's
story, called him a *wampyr*. So Stoker's masterpiece was
born. From then on, it was necessary only to find out a few
things about the Balkans (the story is set in Transylvania)
and the vampire legends that abound there. His research was
remarkably thorough—the novel incorporates a tremendous
amount of legitimate Slavonic folklore. But he added many
other elements from his own imagination—and through the
fame of the book these became imposed on the vampire leg-

end. Folklore itself, then, is a safer source of information concerning the vampire's nature and habits.

First, its nature. But to avoid pushing Bram Stoker out of the picture too readily, we can let the appearance of Count Dracula typify the general appearance of all vampires. Two points especially stand out from the description to follow: a vampire is always cadaverous, because he *is* a cadaver; and a vampire's diet of blood always makes itself apparent. Here is Count Dracula, as seen by the unsuspecting hero of the novel, who has just entered the Transylvanian castle:

"Within stood a tall old man, clean-shaven save for a long white moustache, and clad in black from head to foot, without a single speck of colour about him anywhere. . . . He moved impulsively forward, and holding out his hand grasped mine with a strength that made me wince, an effect which was not lessened by the fact that it seemed as cold as ice—more like the hand of a dead than a living man. . . .

"His face was a strong—a very strong—aquiline, with high bridge of the thin nose and peculiarly arched nostrils; with lofty domed forehead, and hair growing scantily round the temples, but profusely elsewhere. His eyebrows were very massive, almost meeting over the nose. . . . The mouth . . . was fixed and rather cruel-looking, with peculiarly sharp white teeth; these protruded over the lips, whose remarkable ruddiness showed astonishing vitality in a man of his years. For the rest, his ears were pale and at the tops extremely pointed; the chin was broad and strong, and the cheeks firm though thin. The general effect was one of extraordinary pallor.

". . . I could not but notice that [his hands] were rather coarse—broad, with squat fingers. Strange to say, there were hairs in the centre of the palm. The nails were long and fine, and cut to a sharp point. As the Count leaned over me . . . I could not repress a shudder. It may have been that his breath was rank, but a horrible feeling of nausea came over me. . . . The Count's eyes gleamed. . . ."

It should be said that Stoker made his vampire an old man because the Count was, after all, 400 years of age (he was supposed to be the *original* Wallachian nobleman, not a descendant). Most vampires look only as old as they did when they "died" and were buried. Otherwise, Stoker's description is full and accurate: the thinness and pallor, the red lips, sharp teeth, hairy hands (a connection, as with the eyebrows, with the werewolf here), great physical strength, rank breath (from the ingested blood), and burning eyes.

Stoker dresses his vampire in ominously black but otherwise fairly normal clothing. In folklore vampires usually wear their burial clothes—a shroud or winding sheet. The reason is that vampires rise from their graves or tombs to seek their food, and return to them when replete. Dracula returned to his coffin in the ancestral vault of his castle; when he visited his horrors on the people of London, he had to ship his coffin and a quantity of cemetery dirt to England. Most often the vampire must be back in his coffin before daybreak (though in a very few Balkan localities there have been tales of vampires walking by day). At the same time, there is rarely any indication that daylight would do a vampire any actual *harm* (the way it sometimes does in Hollywood horror films); it is apparently just one of the rules that a vampire can act only at night.

The legends are usually rather vague about how the corpse gets out of the grave and into locked houses to attack people—for a corpse is a material thing, not a ghost that can walk through walls. It has simply to be accepted that among a vampire's magical powers is the ability to pass through matter—or at least through very small spaces (keyholes, gaps under doors, the narrow slits between window and frame). In some tales a vampire's grave shows several small holes, through which the vampire apparently can filter. Here again, as so often in supernatural beliefs, and especially the older ones, there is a surprising confusion between corpse and soul. We have seen (in Chapter 2) primitives fearing the ghost but placating it by feeding the corpse; we have seen the Egyptians preserving the corpse yet believing in a separate non-material soul (or several souls). And so with the vampire. He also is a supernatural being returned from the dead, and is at once a material being and one who has non-material attributes—including, as well as the power to pass through small spaces, the inability to cast a shadow or be reflected in a mirror. Perhaps, then, this materiality exists in the old legends on a symbolic and a concrete level at the same time.

In many tales (and in *Dracula*) vampires have the ability to command destructive or noxious animals. Count Dracula had a wolfpack at his command; legendary vampires can summon wolves or dogs, as well as cats, owls, rats, even flies. And sometimes a vampire numbers werewolves among his minions. Also, a vampire has hypnotic powers; he is able to put his intended victims into a trance-like sleep—so that they awaken, weak and anemic, knowing nothing of what has happened (unless they believe in vampires, in which case they can probably hazard a good guess). Occasionally as in some old Romanian tales, vampires are believed to have the power of metamorphosis, being able to transform themselves into animals. Usually, again, they became wolves (it was sometimes thought that a werewolf automatically became a vampire after death); sometimes cats, dogs, or owls; very, very rarely, almost solely in Romania, did any tale, until the late 19th and 20th century show a vampire metamorphosing into a bat.

The reason is quite simple. Until about the 19th century, few people had ever heard of the blood-sucking bats of the South American forests; and before then even fewer had ever related the innocuous, blind, little flying mouse that was the European bat to any dangerous supernatural creature. (There were ancient tales, as in Ovid, of bloodsucking ghosts or witches that took the form of owls; but this is the closest parallel to the more contemporary vampire bat motif.) But when travelers began to bring back tales of a larger, uglier bat that settled at night on sleeping cattle, sheep, or men and drank their blood, and that retreated when replete to a dark place in the forest to rest by day, the connection was too good to be missed. So the vampire bat (as the creature came to be known, after the vampire of legend) took its place among other animals with sinister associations—and especially took its place in horror fiction, largely thanks to Stoker's giving Dracula the power of metamorphosis. (Dracula also, at various times in the novel, changed himself into a wolf, a cloud of mist, and motes of glittering dust.)

All the vampire's powers and activities were devoted single-mindedly to one goal: to satisfy his hunger for human blood. The werewolf sometimes sought to terrorize (doing the Devil's work) as much as to cannibalize; but the vampire was simply hungry. As an animated corpse (and in these terms the corpse is definitely a material thing, needing sustenance), the vampire gained its vitality and its powers from blood—which is, of course, traditionally the vitalizing life-giving fluid. Remember, among other parallels, that Odysseus had to provide blood to the underworld shades before they could become humanized again, able to speak or think or predict the future. In some folk legends vampires had a secondary purpose—sexual satisfaction. Usually the married ones returned, very properly, to their marital beds, but the unmarried visited any pretty girl in the vicinity. Generally, though, the kiss-cum-bite on the throat for the purpose of sucking blood had sufficient erotic content, and other forms of sexuality were omitted by the tale-tellers. They did, however, add that vampires usually first visited their loved ones upon their return from death, especially their wives (or husbands) or their betrothed. Also, many vampires show a predilection for youth, males preferring ripe young girls and females preferring handsome young men—which is explained, in respectable 19th-century accounts (in which murder and cruelty are fine but sex is considered shocking), by the fact that young people have richer, more succulent blood.

Men and women were thought to become vampires in several, mostly magical, automatic ways—rarely by means of a pact with the Devil. While many of the theologians who wrote on the subject felt it their duty to give the Prince of Darkness some part in vampirism, they usually contented themselves with hinting that all power for evil comes originally from Satan—and that some vampires were quite innocent corpses taken over and reanimated by demons. The most frequently mentioned way of becoming a vampire is to die in a state of sin, without the blessing of the Church and the prospects of salvation. Many Slavonic legends assert that any exceedingly wicked man (especially one who dabbled in black magic) would become a vampire—as a sort of punishment, the way that the wicked elsewhere are often thought to be punished by being made to walk the earth as ghosts, unable to find rest. To the Balkan peoples, a man returned as a vampire if he had died a perjurer, or under a curse by his parents, or excommunicated; if he had committed suicide; or, sometimes, even if through no fault of his own he had been buried without the full rites of the Church. And in places like Sicily and Greece where the law of the vendetta ruled for so long, a murdered man whose death went unavenged would rise up as a vampire.

All these beliefs parallel explanations from other parts of the world concerning how ghosts came to be. But there are some odd ideas that relate especially to the creation of a vampire. It has been mentioned that werewolves were often thought to become vampires after death. So, in all legends, does any victim of the vampire—not only the ones that he eventually kills by draining their blood, but even the ones he visits once or twice. In Greece and a few other countries, it was sometimes thought that any child born on Christmas Day, or between Christmas and Epiphany, would become a vampire. And a more widespread and equally strange belief maintains that any dead person over whose coffin a cat jumps (or dog, or even a hen) before the burial will be vampirized. This belief occurs in the folk tales of the Slavonic countries and of Greece, China, and Scotland. Because of this coffins were closely guarded before funerals. But even if the mishap did occur, if a cat got past the guards, there were ways of counteracting it—for instance, in the Balkans, by putting a piece of iron in the corpse's hand, or putting hawthorn or garlic in the coffin. And further, if these didn't work, there was still one saving grace: at least the people knew where to look when vampiric happenings began.

Of course, they had other ways of knowing—for instance, if a child should be born with teeth (another sure sign of an incipient vampire). People who looked like vampires, as we have described them, were shunned; and so were other innocent unfortunates. A vampire's teeth and disposition were thought to make him snarl; so anyone with a harelip was automatically suspect. In fact, where the vampire fear was strongest, anyone slightly unusual was under suspicion (as in those places where the witch hysteria took hold). Even, in Mediterranean countries, redheads or people with blue eyes were feared as vampires—because they were different.

And if a village came to think that a vampire was around when none of these conditions for his creation had happened, there were still other ways to find which of the dead had returned. A grave with a few small holes in it was a sure and simple sign; but some methods were more complex. The people could drive through the cemetery a white stallion who had never gone to stud and who had never stumbled; the horse would refuse to step over the vampire's grave. Sometimes this test was varied, and it was a virginal, sure-footed, but *black* stallion ridden by an equally virginal boy that was sent into the graveyard. As a desperate last resort, all the bodies could be exhumed until the vampire was found—that is, until a body was found that was not corrupted, no matter how old, but that was alive-looking, ruddy of lip and white of tooth, with perhaps a streak of blood oozing from the corner of its mouth. Often, the authorities say, the resting vampire seems, after a night's feeding, swollen "like a great leech" and often the coffin is found to be awash with blood.

During the vampire hunt, if it took some time, there were

various sure ways of protecting yourself against the creature. You could wear a crucifix at your throat, for the vampire (being evil, even if not directly allied with the Devil) feared all holy things—including holy water and relics. You could put hawthorn or whitethorn (a connection here with the crown of thorns) around your doors and windows—or, especially, you could put garlic. (No likely explanation has been offered for the protective power of this pungent herb; most authorities merely say vaguely that it is full of *virtu*.) Or you could sit up all night and wait for the vampire, and shoot him with a consecrated silver bullet.

But the best way was to trace him to his grave and, during the day, destroy him. The method is almost standardized; the destroyer must drive a wooden stake through the vampire's heart (at which point the creature emitted a terrifying shriek, and blood gushed from the wound). When this was done, the body rapidly decomposed—or, if the vampire was very old, simply fell into dust. Sometimes there were refinements: the stake must be of hawthorn or whitethorn; it must be driven with one blow only; the head must be cut off as well, and only with a sexton's spade; and, finally, head, body, stake, and coffin must be burned—as a permanent removal of the evil. Here again is the view of the vampire as both symbolically and actually material. The stake is a concrete "pinning" of the material corpse, to keep it in its grave—but a pinning that must also be symbolic, because a creature that can filter up through six feet of solid earth is not going to be held back by a short piece of wood unless there is some magic at work. The action of staking a vampire corresponds with the widespread tendency in the past to bury suicides or executed criminals (or sometimes witches) with stakes in their hearts and at crossroads. The stake symbolically kept the ghost down; the crossroads were an extra precaution, since if the ghost rose up anyway, it wouldn't know which way to go. (So crossroads are even today feared by some people as highly haunted places, crowded with ghosts that have been unable to leave their gravesides.)

Now, having outlined the basic pattern, with variations, of the vampire legend, we can do as we did with the werewolf and look at some of the theories advanced to explain its origins. A few theorists, including demonologists, have suggested that a link exists between the incubus demon (p. 130) and the vampire—obviously because the latter tends to come at night to sleeping humans and engages in sado-erotic activity.

But a more plausible basis for vampire beliefs can be found in an ancient primitive attitude to the dead, mentioned on page 27. Freud discusses this attitude in *Totem and Taboo*, pointing out that at later stages of development ancient man ascribed malevolence only to those of the dead who had reason for feeling resentful (because, say, they had been murdered)—but that "originally . . . *all* of the dead were vampires, all of them had a grudge against the living and sought to injure them and rob them of their lives." And, of course, robbing people of life is symbolized by robbing them of the life fluid, blood. Thus, it could be said, this ancient belief came to be altered and varied with additions of folklore—the magical conditions under which a dead man walks again to seek blood—and the vampire myth was born.

Here, then, is certainly one ingredient in the vampire's ancestry. There are others. Some are fairly rare and make only a limited contribution, such as Hope Robbins's vague reference to a "rare and abnormal" disorder that produced a maniacal hunger for blood. (An example of such a blood mania is given by Robert Eisler, in *Man Into Wolf*, in an account of a British "vampire" who in 1949 killed nine people and drank their blood.) Others seem stronger. In Europe's past, the many plagues or epidemics—especially of "wasting" diseases—might readily have spawned supernatural fears and added strength to rumors of vampirism. Then again, there is always the possibility that the erotic dream of fantasy—or some kind of sexual mania—played a role in developing the vampire. As with the werewolf, the vampire can be interpreted as a projection of oral sadism (Hope Robbins makes this point). One's repressed sexuality and sexual guilt thus breaks through into the consciousness by means of sadistic, erotic nightmares. And many psychologists stress the symbolic connection between blood-letting and sexuality; as just one fairly close parallel from anthropological studies, many primitives have made a definite ritual requirement out of the vaginal bleeding that takes place on a virgin bride's wedding night.

Another ingredient in the compound that produced tales of vampires was, undoubtedly, the prevalence of premature burial. It can happen today; it did happen with terrifying frequency a few hundred years ago—when people might enter a cataleptic trance or similar state of "suspended animation" and apparent death. Of course they would not live long after burial; but if they woke up in their graves and tried to claw their way out, and if later their bodies were exhumed in a vampire search, the searchers would surely find the evidence they wanted: the body's position disturbed, torn and bloody fingers and nails and, very likely, blood on the clothing and face.

Also, of course, if the body of a prematurely buried person were exhumed, then, because death had been delayed, it would not have decomposed as much as its finders would expect. Nevertheless, it is quite a long step from a corpse's remaining whole for a week after burial to decomposition being deferred for 400 years (as with Dracula.) Or is it? The French author Cyrille de Neubourg offers an interesting story from a French newspaper of an occurrence that took place in Italy in 1952. The story, in full, is as follows:

"Blood spurted from a corpse which had been buried since 1920 in the cemetery of Aberici di Montemarciano, in the region of Ancona. The corpse had just been exhumed in a perfect state of preservation. The clothes were also in very good condition. It was the corpse of a woman who had died at the age of 70 in February 1920. Blood flowed abundantly from the left knee, and it was only after this outflow that decomposition commenced. No explanation has as yet been found for this phenomenon."

Nor was any convincing explanation ever found. Nor, for that matter, will one be offered here.

Other perambulating corpses are found alongside the vampire in the ranks of supernatural monsters. These generally go under the name of *zombis*—a word probably derived from the Congolese *nvumbi*, meaning a body deprived of its soul. The vampire is the "living dead" or the "undead"; the zombi is merely the walking dead, a corpse called up by sorcery from the grave, but empty of soul or mind.

In Haiti, the land of voodoo, sorcerers are said to create zombis to provide cheap, uncomplaining labor, either for themselves or to hire out to local plantation owners. The sorcerer rides, backward, to his victim's house and sucks out the man's soul through a slit in the door. He then blows it into a bottle, which he corks immediately. The victim soon becomes ill, and dies. After the burial, the corpse is taken from its grave after propitiatory rites to the spirits of death and the bottle containing its soul is held under its nose. The dead man is immediately animated and, after being given a special drug, becomes the slave of the sorcerer. According to some accounts, the corpse can be raised only if it answers to its name. (We have seen before, in Chapter 5, the power that is thought to reside in a name.) And it is sometimes said that the sorcerer does not have to take the soul from a living victim; he can obtain it, through the connivance of the corpse-washer, from the body of a man who has died naturally.

The American author W. B. Seabrook, in his account of zombi tales he had heard in Haiti, mentions various ways of preventing sorcerers from making zombis out of the dead. An obvious one is to prevent the sorcerer from getting at the grave—by burying the dead under solid masonry, or close to the doorway of one's house, or beside a busy road where there are always passers-by. Or the grave may be guarded continuously until there can be no question that the body has decomposed into uselessness. Once a zombi has been activated, the sorcerer must guard against its eating meat or, especially, salt (which is almost universally believed to have strong beneficent or "white" magical power); if the zombi tastes salt, it regains its faculties, remembers that it is dead, and cannot be prevented from seeking its grave and dying again—this time permanently.

Seabrook, incidentally, was told that some laborers he saw were, in fact, zombis. They were working in a canefield like automatons, their eyes were "staring, unfocused, unseeing," their faces seemed "not only expressionless, but incapable of expression," and they neither responded to nor seemed aware of his presence or his touch. In his judgment they were merely total idiots; but his confidence was slightly shaken when he saw a paragraph in the Haitian *Code Pénal* stating the penalties for administering "substances which, without causing actual death, produce lethargic coma more or less prolonged"—and when he was told that people thus drugged into a death-like "suspended animation" were sometimes buried as dead, later to be secretly reclaimed and put to work as blank-minded laborers.

The zombi is not totally restricted to voodoo-ridden Haiti. Although there are no direct parallels in European supernatural belief, there is that unique monster tale, Mary Shelley's *Frankenstein*—in which a fanatical scientist steals dead bodies from their graves and assembles from them a creature that he activates by electromagnetism. Only something goes wrong, the monster comes to life mindless and malevolent, and eventually destroys itself and its creator.

But many parallels with the zombi can be found in African legend. In Gabon, for instance, natives have long believed that sorcerers are able to bring a corpse—the *wengwa*, according to the French writer C. H. Dewisme—out of its grave; and it is sometimes thought the wengwa can rise of its own volition. And turning to Asia, in Tibet, according to one credulous French traveller, Alexandra David-Neel, writing in 1931, master occultists are able briefly to animate a human corpse by a rather repulsive ritual. The magician lies on top of the corpse, and presses his mouth to its mouth, while repeating (mentally) an unspecified magic formula. The corpse—called a *rolang*—will begin to move, trying to escape, and will stand, leap, run around; the magician must keep his hold and concentrate on the spell. Eventually the corpse's tongue will protrude, and the magician must bite it off—at which point the corpse collapses and the magician has a most valuable prize, for the tongue contains powerful magic. (If the magician loosens his hold or relaxes his concentration the corpse will kill him.)

It is a short if not particularly attractive step from this belief to the widespread legend of another supernatural monster, the ghoul. Ghouls originate in the Middle East and Asia, where they are supposed to be evil spirits or demons who rob graves and feed on corpses. But the word *ghoul* has lost its original meaning, thanks to inaccurate horror fiction writers, and is now used (especially in the adjectival form "ghoulish") to mean anything monstrous, evil, blood-chilling. It is somewhat appropriate when applied to grave robbers, as it was when doctors had to obtain cadavers however they could in order to study anatomy. It is less appropriate when used, as it was by the British writer Eric Maple, to describe the vandals who rifled graves in Bedfordshire in 1963—for black-magic purposes or for no purpose at all.

Ghouls are, in many places around the world, closely related to more werewolf-like demons who also eat human flesh, but prefer it alive. Many Oriental legends tell of such demons, and in some the monster eats both living and dead bodies. In Haiti members of a particular secret society have been thought to turn into demons called *baka* and to feed on human flesh. Of course, most commentators relate such beliefs to the taboo against cannibalism (mentioned in connection with the werewolf) and to perversions like necrophilia (sexual intercourse with corpses) and necrophagy (eating dead bodies).

* * *

Not all monsters are repulsive. One legendary creature would, in fact, probably be on everyone's short list of all-time favorites—the so-called Abominable Snowman, or *yeti*. This is a hairy man-like thing, said to inhabit the Himalayan peaks, and a special favorite of newspaper editors the world over. A great many respectable people believe—or at least refuse to disbelieve—in the yeti, probably because there is undeniably no objective, scientific reason why such a creature should not exist. Skeptics, however, find ammunition for their scorn in wild theories offered to explain belief in the Snowman, as well as in statements like the following, made by the interpreter of King Mahendra of Nepal and reported in American newspapers in 1960: ". . . His Majesty is no expert, no anthropologist or zoologist, so he cannot say anything definite about this creature. But all the same it pays us to keep the mystery alive."

Nevertheless, some very interesting and reasoned theories have been advanced about the yeti. Some say he is a direct descendant of Neanderthal man, hiding in inaccessible mountains from the offspring of Cro-Magnon. Others suggest that he is a "hominid" (half-man) who evolved separately from *homo sapiens* and who, with a few others like him, ekes out a meager existence in out-of-the-way areas. Still others, perhaps basing their idea on Jung's concept of the collective unconscious, see in the Snowman legend a projection of an ancestral memory—and fear—of the hairy half-man from whom *homo sapiens* developed and with whom, it is then assumed, our more direct ancestors must have fought many battles.

These theories are attractive speculations simply because the Snowman belief is paralleled by similar legends all over the world—among Tibetans and Chinese, North and South American Indians, and more. In North America there is an especially close parallel among the Indians of Canada's west coast, who believed in a hairy man-like creature called the sasquatch. This hominid roamed the forests and sub-Arctic tundra of what are now called British Columbia and the Yukon. And the tale carried over into the legends of European settlers—many a miner, during the Klondike gold rush of the 1890s, told a story of a near-fatal run-in with the sasquatch.

Furthermore, almost identical demonic beast-men exist in Indian lore all down the west coast—among the Yaqui Indians of Mexico, the Chorti of Guatemala, and others throughout the Americas. And it is interesting to note the characteristics these creatures and the Abominable Snowman have in common. For one thing, most of them are said to have metal fingernails and reversed feet (that is, with the toes pointing backward). It is thought that to encounter one, even if it does not attack, means sickness or death. (The father of Tensing, the sherpa who accompanied Sir Edmund Hillary up Mount Everest, was supposed to have been a yeti and to have been ill for a year.) And finally all these beings are thought to be guardians of the wilderness—as were the "wild men" of Oriental and European legends and Pan and his satyrs in Greek mythology.

Perhaps the legendary giants that, in much folk mythology, once peopled the earth also have some affinity with these wild men or half-men. They, too, were generally beings of the forest or mountain, not shunning men but at the same time not seeking out their company—except (in the case of the man-eating Celtic giant) when hungry. A few giants of legend were beneficent. The North American lumberjack's tales of the giant Paul Bunyan show him as a kindly soul given to occasional good deeds as well as heroic adventure.

Giants occur prominently in Greek mythology (the Titans, fathers of the gods) and in Norse (Thor had a few encounters with magician-giants). But Celtic myth and legend is especially full of giant lore—and in this case the giants are invariably evil, or at least stupidly malicious. King Arthur and his knights did much battle with the creatures, rescuing damsels from them and so on. As hinted above, many of the Celt giants fed on men (as did the Cyclops in the *Odyssey*); in Cornwall, England, where tales of giants proliferate as nowhere else, a group of giants lived in an immense castle on a hill to which they took captured humans including children and feasted on them. Celtic giants also were believed to have vast hoards of wealth (another reason why so many knights challenged them) obtained from their victims; and Cornish *spriggans* are ghosts of ancient giants who are believed to guard hidden treasure.

The treasure-guarding role is one of the main affinities between giants of legend and the smaller but equally troublesome beings of folklore such as gnomes and trolls. The troll, who hails from Scandinavia, was originally—and sometimes still is—a giant, but especially in Sweden and Denmark he is now usually thought of as a dwarf. His home is in the hills

and caves. Gnomes are always small; they are deformed little
creatures whose element is the earth itself. They are more
dangerous than their cousins the goblins, who in folklore are
more mischievous than malevolent, more of a nuisance than
a danger. Many of the little people of folk tales are, in fact,
friendly creatures: the leprechauns of Ireland, for instance,
are kindly beings unless angered. And, since our focus is on
creatures that inspire fear and horror, there is no question
that the other beings of folklore and fairy tale—the elves,
fairies, etc.—do not belong here (in spite of their supernatural powers).

Perhaps no one area of the Western world has been so in-
fested with strange monstrous creatures as the Ozark mountains in America—according to the folklorist Vance Ran-
dolph, writing in 1951. And perhaps, also, no other collection
of monsters have such fantastic names. The Ozarks claimed
(in 19th-century legends) creature named the gollygog, the
bingbuffer, the moogie, the fillyloo—and the more conventional behemoth. A few seem to be unique creatures—like
the snawfus, an albino deer with supernatural powers. Most
of the others have vague connections with the lizard
family—like the gowrow, a 20-foot, tusked, dragon-like
beast. Here again we have a universally recurring motif—the
giant lizard, which appears in ancient Chinese and Celtic
tales of dragons and in modern "monster" horror films.

It has been claimed that these legends, too, grow from an
ancestral fear-memory of the prehistoric dinosaurs—except
that there is some doubt as to whether man was around in
any form when the great saurians dominated the earth. Still,
there must have been some fairly striking types of lizards
when man finally did appear, for there still are today. Serpent
and dragon lore, of course, deserves an entire book of its own
(and has had several); but it is still worthwhile to allude
briefly to some of its more prominent aspects.

The dragon is a major symbolic figure in Chinese mythology—connected with the creation of the world in some cases,
with leading gods in others. One, the T'ien Lung, supports
and guards the dwelling place of the gods. Some are evil, but
most are beneficent and associated with good fortune.

The Chinese dragon has scales and horns and claws; the
ancient Celtic dragon has these *and* leathery, pterodactyl-like
wings. In Celtic myth the dragon is almost invariably evil,
often a guardian of buried treasure or a servant of malicious

sorcerers, to be killed by noble knights. St. George thus killed his dragon, much as the Greek hero Bellerophon, aided by the winged horse Pegasus, destroyed the three-headed, serpentine monster called the chimera.

No one will need to be reminded that the Devil appears in the form of a serpent in Genesis and a dragon in the Apocalypse—and appears thus in much folklore. Many French legends, for instance, contain diabolical dragons or great serpents—even a flying dragon who was supposed to have devastated the country around the village of Rille, in Vienne, until a heroic soldier fought and killed it. In the same part of France a legend existed of a dragon called the *basilic,* which was driven into the well of Coulaine by the great knight Fretard. It was thought that the basilic surfaced every 10 years for a few moments, and that if a human sighted it first, it would drop back harmlessly; but anyone it looked at without being seen would die within a year.

The dragon/serpent has a cousin that can be generically referred to as the sea serpent—and that can serve to round off this look at the monstrous beings of the supernatural. Sea serpents also are highly ubiquitous, and have been sighted many times by sailors and inhabitants of coastal areas throughout history. It is most often suggested that the creatures seen were whales or overlarge eels or even giant squids. It has similarly been suggested that the mermaid legend grew up because some sailors (who must have been drunk or myopic or both) saw a female seal for the first time. Nonetheless strange reports continue to appear (again much to the delight of newspaper editors everywhere). An extraordinary (but dead) creature was beached in California in 1955, and was described by a Berkeley paper as being about 16 feet long, with a head like a snake and a tail like a fish.

From sea serpents to lake serpents, and the famous Loch Ness monster that has been seen and not seen and searched for and even photographed (usually from a great distance and slightly out of focus) in a Scottish lake. This creature too has relatives elsewhere: in the Okanagan Lake in Canada a serpent called "Ogopogo" was reportedly seen many times in the 1950s. And the Russians have their version, seen in 1962 and again in 1964: According to an American paper (which humorously headlined the story "Lochski Nesski Monsterovich"), a 30-foot, undulating creature was seen (by some prospectors) swimming in a lake in eastern Siberia. Like the Loch

Ness monster, it was serpentine in appearance, with what seemed to be a "fin" along its back; as with the pride of Loch Ness again, it lives in the depths of the lake, surfacing only rarely.

A list of sea or lake serpents, like a list of strange and fabulous monsters in general, could go on interminably, but cannot here. To sum up and conclude, then, we might reiterate one important point that has cropped up continually in our search for possible explanations of these monsters' origins. It is the suggestion that such creatures were first spawned not in the conscious imagination of ancient man (though certainly the tales were elaborated there) but in his inner world, his unconscious—that they grew out of the symbolic monsters that peopled his dreams and fantasies. And they still appear, as potent as ever, in humanity's dreams today.

9 SECTS AND SOCIETIES

In the past all organized groups of people involved in any way with the supernatural seem to have been made up of interested parties—believers, worshipers (like covens of witches or members of Black Mass cults), or practitioners (like priests, magicians, cabbalists). Only comparatively recently have organizations grown up whose involvement is of an investigatory—and professedly detached, scientific—nature. Today, groups like these proliferate, and so we begin with them.

Before the 19th century there were a few sporadic attempts to examine apparently supernatural phenomena objectively—attempts largely centered on Mesmer's "animal magnetism" (see p. 81). In 1784, when Mesmer's theories had become popular and fashionable in Europe, King Louis XVI of France set up two commissions to investigate. They reported that they found strong grounds for skepticism. Throughout the remainder of the 18th century and in the early years of the 19th, other investigators had close looks at mesmerism (which was then, of course, considered highly occult and suspect) and reached rather more favorable conclusions. They became convinced that some of the mesmerized subjects showed "supernormal" abilities—or, as we would say now, telepathic and clairvoyant powers.

In the mid 19th century British investigators such as the physician James Braid and the physicist William Barrett took up the study of mesmerism and of hypnotism, as did the physiologist Charles Richet and the psychologist Pierre Janet in France. But by this time the study of hypnotism was beginning to lead investigators to inquire into more traditionally "occult" matters—telepathy, apparitions, and so on—and (after the Fox sisters gained fame in the 1850s) spiritualism. These then were the boundaries of "psychic investigation" when, in 1851, a few young British students at Cambridge University formed a Ghost Society.

The society grew out of a close if amateur interest in the supernatural; when the classicist Henry Sidgwick joined it in 1859 the interest became closer and less amateur. Then in 1860 Sidgwick formed with Frederic Myers a friendship that owed much to a mutual fascination with psychic matters. The friendship soon included Edmund Gurney, and together the three men began pursuing knowledge of the supernatural.

Throughout the 1860s and 70s other investigators were at work also—among them Sir William Crookes, a distinguished physicist and chemist, who had made extensive studies of mediums—especially of D. D. Home (see p. 84). The London Dialectical Society appointed a committee in 1869 to study spiritualism and other occult phenomena; after 18 months of interviewing mediums, watching them at work, and holding cautious experiments, the committee reported (with several dissenters) that occasionally the phenomena appeared genuine—or at least were worthy of further careful investigation. Oxford also had its Ghost Society, which devoted much time to collecting and sifting accounts of ghosts. All this separate activity led to more frustration than satisfaction: as the field of investigation widened these small amateur societies found it increasingly difficult to keep up with the flow of material for study. It was time for a merger, from the point of view of finance as well as of pooling ideas. So in 1882 the Cambridge group set up a conference of interested parties—and thus the Society for Psychical Research was born.

Sidgwick was its first president; Myers, Gurney, and William Barrett, with Frank Podmore from the Oxford society, were members of the first Council. (Later Myers, Gurney, and Podmore wrote *Phantasms of the Living*—that pioneering and still basic text of apparitions, thought transference, and the like.) The new society (usually called the S.P.R.) defined its terms of reference as the investigation of: mind-to-mind influence; hypnotism; clairvoyance and extra-sensory perception; apparitions, haunts, and poltergeists; and spiritualism. It also undertook to conduct its investigations "without prejudice or prepossession of any kind" and to maintain the spirit of "exact and unimpassioned enquiry. . . ."

One of the earliest tasks to which these principles were applied was the study of thought transference—in experiments with two young girls named Creery. The first set of experiments indicated that the girls seemed to have the ability to guess names and objects thought of by others; in another set, however, Gurney caught the girls cheating (by signaling to each other). But despite the damaging publicity that this case aroused, the society continued to conduct its investigations with other subjects. And it is on the basis of these early—and, to many, extremely controversial—experiments, that Gurney and others came to accept, in principle, with caution and reservation, that telepathy was possible. From this acceptance grew the various "telepathic" theories of apparitions that we dealt with in Chapter 3.

In that chapter we saw some of the techniques used by the S.P.R. in investigating apparitional phenomena, and its emphasis on the need for scientific detachment. This emphasis has remained constant since the early days of the society, when Sidgwick, Myers, and the rest—notwithstanding their impressive scholastic reputations—had to fight against the barriers of prejudice, scorn, and ridicule. The British philosopher F. C. S. Schiller wrote in 1905: "There is at present more social prejudice against researchings into the 'occult' than researchers could remove in a thousand years by purely scientific methods, even were they ten times as numerous and skilful as they are. . . ." For example, Sidgwick's wife delayed joining the society for a few years in order not to bring disrepute on Newnham College, Cambridge, with which she was associated. For another example, the S.P.R. in the beginning made it clear that "Membership of the Society does not imply the acceptance of any particular explanation of the phenomena investigated, nor any belief as to the operation, in the physical world, of forces other than those recognised by Physical Science." It was, perhaps, taking care not to frighten anyone off. (Today the society still protects its flanks by dissociating itself from the opinions of authors expressed in its journal or pamphlets: "The Society does not hold or express corporate views.")

The society's avowed aim of maintaining objectivity in its researches extends to the committees it has appointed to investigate psychical phenomena. An example is the report of three investigators—including Dr. E. J. Dingwall—on the medium known as "Eva C," who gave 40 sittings at the society's headquarters in 1920. "Eva C" was a physical medium who had become celebrated on the continent for her materializations, which included faces appearing near her head. "Discovered" in 1905 in Algiers by Charles Richet, she later moved to Paris where extensive investigations into the phenomena she produced were carried out by a German parapsychologist, Dr. Schrenck-Notzing. He concluded that the phenomena were genuine and published photographs of the materializations (which were later discovered to be newspaper cuttings). The S.P.R., when it made its own investigations of "Eva C," was less impressed. The more striking phenomena observed by Dr. Schrenck-Notzing refused to appear in the presence of the S.P.R. investigators, who finally gave a verdict of "not proven." They added, however, that the research carried out by continental experts could not be discounted.

By this time a similar society was at work in the United States. It had been formed in Boston in 1885, largely through the efforts of the psychologist William James. Four years after its foundation it decided to amalgamate with the "parent" British society but it regained its independence in 1907. The American aims and intentions were and are, of course, much the same as those of the British S.P.R.: to investigate claims of various forms of ESP and of dowsing, spiritualism, apparitions, poltergeists, and so on—"in short, all types of phenomena called parapsychological, mediumistic, psychic, or paranormal." Among the most famous early investigations of the American S.P.R. was a prolonged study by its first president, Richard Hodgson, of the trance medium Mrs. Piper (see p. 88). Hodgson emerged convinced that the phenomena (spirit messages and so on) had a spiritualistic origin. Others were unconvinced, though most commentators agreed with William James that Mrs. Piper displayed "supernatural powers of cognition."

The American society moved to New York in 1906, under the direction of the Columbia philosophy professor J. H. Hyslop. He was succeeded by the British psychologist William McDougall who, while in America, had a major hand in founding the parapsychology laboratory at North Carolina's Duke University that became famous under J. B. Rhine. After his presidency the society came under the control of a group of unscientific enthusiasts led by a medium named Mrs. Margery Crandon. The investigatees had taken over; but eventually they came under suspicion of fraud, and the scientists were restored, as was the society's reputation.

In Europe allied organizations were springing up rapidly. The International Metapsychical Institute was formed in France in 1919 with Charles Richet as its first president. Richet, who was also at one time president of the British S.P.R., had long been deeply involved in the subject. He had made studies of hypnotism when still a student, and was later (in 1922) to produce an important and wide-ranging study of the subject, called (in English) *Thirty Years of Psychical Research.*

Germany, Italy, and Scandinavia soon boasted similar organizations, and the idea continued to spread. Writing in the 1930s, Hereward Carrington offered the following as a list of countries where psychical research societies had been founded (after the countries already mentioned): Austria, Russia, Spain, Portugal, Holland, Belgium, Switzerland, Greece, Poland, Turkey, Iceland, Japan, Mexico, Canada, Ireland, Australia, New Zealand, South Africa, India, China, Argentina; and he added that "informal organizations exist in practically every country in the world."

All this increasingly widespread activity had its fairly regular meeting-point at international psychical-research congresses, the first of which was held in Copenhagen in 1921. A second congress met in Warsaw in 1923, a third in Paris in 1927. (The second conference had sought, among other things, to standardize the terminology in use in psychical research—but failed. Thus the prevalence of many words for the same thing: metapsychics, parapsychology, and so on.) A fourth conference was held in 1930 at Athens, a fifth at Oslo in 1935. At each of these, papers were read, knowledge to a certain extent pooled, and the members (many of them widely known in their own fields—as psychologists, anthropologists, philosophers, physicists, and so on) were able to exchange ideas and hints and theories. The troubled European political situation and the Second World War interrupted these international meetings until 1953 when an International Conference of Parapsychological Studies met at Utrecht.

But private groups continued to be formed to carry on the work of scientific investigation into psychical phenomena—groups like the French Association for Metapsychic Studies, founded in 1941, and the French Group for Parapsychological Studies formed in 1954 under the direction of Robert Amadou, Maurice Colinon, and Dr. Martiny; a Belgian group formed in 1948 with the mouth-filling title The Belgian

Committee for the Scientific Investigation of Phenomena Reputed to be Paranormal; and the Italian Society of Parapsychology founded in 1937. Probably the most prominent of all the newer groups, however (if only because of its solid and sizable financial backing), is the American Parapsychology Foundation, formed in 1951, today operating as a non-profit corporation in New York.

The present president of the Foundation is Mrs. Eileen J. Garrett, who (as *The New Yorker* once put it) "is herself one of the more fascinating psychical phenomena of our times." She is a former trance medium, now retired from the spiritualist scene, who began holding séances in Britain in the 1930s and eventually became interested in her own talents. Invited to America by the A.S.P.R. in 1931, she was carefully studied and investigated by many researchers (including Hereward Carrington), who satisfied themselves that the phenomena—she possessed, like all trance mediums, a "spirit control" who spoke through her—were genuine, in the sense that they were not faked, though some researchers put them down to a split personality. At any rate, Mrs. Garrett eventually tired of the practice of spiritualism, and in 1941 retired as a publicly practicing medium. She occupied herself first with bringing out the magazine *Tomorrow* (with a circulation now of over 10,000) and then, thanks to a few wealthy philanthropists with an interest in psychic matters, to establishing the Foundation.

The Foundation serves as the golden-egg provider for a great many of the research projects going on all over the world, as well as for American work. It makes grants to individual researchers ($3000 a year sometimes), assists other institutions and groups to carry on their work, organizes and sponsors conferences, publishes reports, and directly operates a European center for parapsychology in France.

Aside from being a mainstay to many private research groups around the world, who would otherwise not be able to continue their work, the Foundation gives financial help to various university projects. Universities have in recent years shown some signs of becoming more hospitable to psychical research than they once were—than they were, say, when J. B. Rhine first began his revolutionary investigations of ESP at Duke University.

Rhine, at one time a biologist, began work on parapsychology in the late 1920s with William McDougall in the Duke Psychology Department. In 1935, he organized the Parapsychology Laboratory, conducted experiments in ESP, evaluated them statistically, and published his findings (in the *Journal of Parapsychology*)—to become the most influential and controversial parapsychologist in the world. The battles he fought were those of psychical researchers everywhere—against prejudice, against critics who had never read his published findings, against scientists who feared a breakdown of the status quo and who tried to demolish Rhine's scientific reputation. The controversy over his approach, his methods, and his conclusions is not yet wholly quiet; but the opposition from scientists has been more or less stifled (or at least driven underground) since the president of the American Institute for Mathematical Statistics released an endorsement of Rhine's methods in 1937.

The Duke Laboratory is one of an increasingly large number of university-associated research projects throughout the world. Duke may be the best known, but is certainly not the oldest. Long before McDougall and Rhine began, Stanford University at the beginning of this century possessed a sizable endowment set aside for psychical research, and some instruction in the subject was also being given at Bryn Mawr, Smith, and Minnesota.

In British universities, most psychical research (as we saw in our capsule history of the S.P.R.) was undertaken unofficially by private groups of students. The University of London allowed a series of lectures on parapsychology to be given in 1915. In Europe official recognition came earlier: the French university of Montpellier gave a doctor's degree in 1893 for a thesis on parapsychology. C. G. Jung's thesis for the M.D. degree, delivered in 1902 at Zurich, was entitled "On the Psychology of So-called Occult Phenomena." A pioneer experiment in ESP was carried out at the University of Groningen, Holland, and reported on in 1921.

If this early 20th-century list is sketchy, an account of all the parapsychology study groups attached to various universities is full—too full to be indicated here except in outline. First, then, in America, aside from the universities already mentioned, parapsychological projects (experiments, lectures, or student investigations) are, or have been, carried out in affiliation with 68 colleges and universities. Among the larger institutions included in this number are the universities of California, Minnesota, Denver, and Pittsburgh; Brown and Yale universities; City College of New York; and St. Joseph's College, Philadelphia, Pennsylvania.

Parapsychological work has been done by members of the universities of Innsbruck, Copenhagen, Stockholm, and Rome. In France, aside from Montpellier, many distinguished men at the Sorbonne have worked in the field of parapsychology. In Germany, universities at Bonn, Freiburg, Göttingen, Hamburg, and Munich have seen such activity—as have Amsterdam, Groningen, Leiden, and Utrecht universities in Holland. Parapsychological work is carried out at the University of Rajasthan, India, and there is a Parapsychological Study Group associated with the Hebrew University in Israel. Two institutions in Japan have given time to psychical research.

Increasing interest in the study of parapsychology is also being shown by institutions in the communist world—notably by the Department of Physiology of the University of Leningrad under the chairmanship of Professor L. L. Vasilyev. In South America, university researches are pursued in Argentina, Chile, Uruguay, and the Dominican Republic. Six universities in Canada can be said to allow some sort of parapsychological work—though neither of the big institutions, McGill and Toronto, do so. Five Australian universities, and one in New Zealand, give semi-official encouragement to work on ESP.

Finally, a certain amount of parapsychological work has been done in British universities—including Liverpool, Nottingham, Glasgow, Bristol, and London. Cambridge offers a "studentship" in psychical research, and also boasts a society for research into parapsychology. At Oxford, there is a small Parapsychology Laboratory with an American student as its director, though this laboratory is not university-sponsored (it is privately endowed and uses university facilities when available); and there is a private organization (not connected with the university but having much contact with experts there) in the city of Oxford called the Psycho-physical Research Unit.

This quick outline indicates, if nothing else, that an attitude of openmindedness toward academic psychical research is prevailing. The institutions that frown on such activities are beginning to dwindle practically everywhere. But the outline does not indicate clearly what now must be emphasized: that university interest in psychic matters is almost always restricted to investigations of extra-sensory perception and such allied subjects as precognition and PK. The other preoccupations of private research groups (apparitions, poltergeists, spiritualism) come in for only secondary consideration. Perhaps at some of the more established parapsychology departments or laboratories, investigators will be sent out to look at a reported case of a haunting or a poltergeist (in the way that Duke University parapsychologists studied the occurrences at Seaford, New York in 1958—see page 65); or perhaps occasionally a medium will be invited to perform for a study group. But even then the emphasis is on the "paranormal" effects operating in such incidents, and rarely on the supernatural.

Perhaps part of the reason for the emphasis on ESP is that it lends itself to "quantitative" investigation, with all the paraphernalia of controlled experiments and statistical evaluation, far better than do the spontaneous phenomena of apparitions or the vagaries of magicians. Also, of course, ESP is no longer beyond the pale—thanks to the efforts of men like J. B. Rhine. Just as hypnotism moved from the "occult" to the paranormal, and was then taken up widely by men who were before afraid to soil themselves with superstition, so has ESP followed the same path. (Hypnotism now is of course so normal as to be ultra-respectable, a part of every psychiatrist's armory.) In the same way, the phenomena of possession, stigmata, non-biological disease, etc. were once considered to be either nonsense or devilish. Now, however, readers of psychology-for-the-layman columns in glossy magazines talk knowingly of hysteria and psychosomatic illness.

But still, we have spent some time in earlier chapters trying to indicate possible connections between ESP and theories that might explain ghosts, spiritualist phenomena, and aspects of magic. Perhaps the university investigations into ESP will thus indirectly shed some light on these darker segments of the supernatural. But it is safer to predict that the first light shed, the first links provided, will very probably come from the private organizations—the S.P.R. and others.

Nor should anyone take away the impression that the scientific approach has been monopolized by the academics, leaving the more misty-minded and credulous to operate in the private groups. If anything, the private groups like the S.P.R. or the Metapsychical Institute in France are their own toughest critics, relegating evidential material to the "not conclusive" file if a shadow of a shadow of a doubt can be thrown upon it. It must be remembered that the leading non-university organizations were mostly founded and dominated in their early years by scientifically-inclined men with reputations for clarity and caution, and that this tradition includes statements like the following, from Charles Richet's foreword to his book on psychical research (p. 215):

"Those who hope to find in this book a number of cloudy speculations on human destiny, magic, and theosophy, will be disappointed. I have been concerned with trying to write a work of science, not of dreams. I have therefore confined myself to setting out the facts and discussing their authenticity, not only without offering a theory of my own but without much reference to any theories at all; for those which have so far been formulated in parapsychology seem to me alarmingly fragile. It is possible, even probable, that a useful theory may some day be put forward. But that time has not yet come, since the actual facts on which to build a theory are still in question. It is therefore first of all essential to establish those facts, and to present them in general and in detail, so that their background may be fully understood. This is our first duty; even our sole duty."

As potent a manifesto for psychical research as could be asked for. But sometimes Richet's (and others') warnings can be forgotten, when enthusiasm defeats scientific caution—or ignored, when groups are formed devoted more to propaganda than to critical research. In such ways the whole name of psychical research is tarnished. And there are plenty of the last-mentioned kind of organization around today—the groups of believers and practitioners who band together for spreading "the word." Perhaps this description doesn't entirely apply to, for instance, the British Churches Fellowship for Psychical Study (see p. 96); but its statement of intent leaves it open to some criticisms of this sort. For while it is not an official Church body, it is closely connected through the important (interdenominational) clergymen associated with it; and while it sets about its research with as open a mind as possible, it admits that its way is the middle road. That is, while trying to maintain an "analytical and critical" attitude and claiming little in common with the spiritualists whom it investigates, the Fellowship nevertheless admits to a prior assumption of "survival and, under certain circumstances, communication." Being a Churches' fellowship, of course, it must. But setting out to investigate the truth of something already implicitly accepted by faith is not, one might say, the most objective stance that could be adopted.

And it is closely akin to the stance assumed by the various organizations of spiritualists that flourish today—especially, it seems, in Britain. There is the Spiritualists' Association, which began in 1872 and which serves as a center for believers in and converts to the spiritualist idea of survival after death. They hold public séances and demonstrations, offer facilities for smaller séances, and even instruct budding mediums. There is the Greater World Christian Spiritualist League whose members want to harmonize their spiritualist beliefs with Christianity. And there is the Spiritualists' National Union founded in 1890, which looks on spiritualism as a religion in its own right, and considers that Christ was just a successful medium—one of many.

Then there is the College of Psychic Science—not, as might be thought, devoted to objective psychical research, in the manner of the S.P.R., but dedicated to finding in spiritualism further evidence for survival after death. They profess a certain amount of scientific detachment (seeing spiritualism as a corollary to religion, not a religion itself), but hold public demonstrations of clairvoyance. A similar organization with a misleading title is the British Metaphysical Research Group, which again is not concerned with objective scientific research but with organized study of the subjects it believes in—spiritualism and allied matters. They carry out research on the aura, on astral traveling (p. 78), and so on. They even offer for sale spiritualist equipment like ouija boards, crystal balls, and special goggles through which people's auras can be more readily perceived (and which, according to the advertisement, are also useful for welding). But their "real work" concerns the invention of various kinds of psychic machinery, including equipment to photograph thoughts and spirits.

Similar organizations exist in any country where spiritualism flourishes—which means most countries. In France, for instance, a society called the Group for Spiritualist Studies meets at Nice and offers public lectures on their subject and on allied subjects such as parapsychology. Another French group (centered in Lyons) has a name as apparently misleading as Britain's College of Psychic Science: it calls itself the Society for Psychical Study, and part of its self-professed aim is "to awaken in the public the desire to know human possibilities, para-normal phenomena, and to discover their origins." This group claims to have a detached outlook, but its basic sympathies appear to be largely spiritualistic.

Spiritualism, furthermore, is internationally organized—for instance, in the International Spiritualist Federation, which has fairly regular congresses with the usual public demonstra-

tions of mediumship. At the Congress held in London in
1960 the president of the National Federation of Spirit Healers added his abilities to the demonstrations, and apparently
cured several sufferers from arthritis. To avoid doing too
much injustice to these often highly sincere organizations, we
should add the rider that many, if not most, of them do give
a considerable amount of their time and money to organized
investigation of the subject—that, in other words, not all
their efforts are devoted to converting people through demonstrations (or to defensive letters in the press). Detachment,
after all, is a luxury available only to the uncommitted; and
many times the highly committed spiritualist organizations
have produced material, as evidence, that has proved valuable
to more scientifically oriented groups. Also, if nothing else,
the organizations are one way for the scientists to obtain their
subjects for tests.

From scientific, investigatory societies, through study groups
of convinced believers, we can move now to those groups of
believers who are involved less with study and investigation
of occult phenomena and more with devotion. The distinction
between them is obvious: the S.P.R. and similar organizations set out to examine the supernatural in terms of the objective methods and the language of science. The devotional
groups—that huge wonderworld of sects and more or less occult "systems"—are more concerned with direct and subjective experience than with study and experiment.

The number of occult societies and "fringe" religions in
the world today is remarkably high. Many of these groups in
the Western world seek to incorporate some elements of
Christianity into their doctrines (as does the Christian Spiritualist League, which was mentioned earlier); and so prominent have such groups become that the term "third force" has
been coined to indicate the belief, held by some churchmen
as well as laymen, that they constitute a new manifestation of
Christianity, parallel with Roman Catholicism and Protestant-
ism. Certainly occult groups of all kinds, whether embracing
parts of Christianity or ignoring it altogether, form a definitely powerful segment of modern religious belief. Exactly
how powerful is uncertain, but J. Paul Williams in his book
What Americans Believe and How They Worship (1952)
quotes from different estimates that set the figure at anything
between three and 17 million devotees.

Taken together these occult organizations contain such a

Many experiments into clairvoyance and telepathy involve the use of "free" targets such as drawings and paintings. Above, the target drawing—depicting a belfry tower being struck by lightning—made by the agent in a telepathic test carried out in France in 1930. Right, the sketch made by the percipient of a cross on a pitched roof. *(Revue Métaphysique, Paris.)*

vast spectrum of belief, doctrine, and practice that we can only indicate the scope by sampling. To lead off the sample, we can look at a few of those most resembling the orthodox religions in their breadth and their present influence. Vedanta, for example, has a highly select membership that has included such prominent intellectuals as the late Aldous Huxley, the philosopher Gerald Heard, and the novelist Christopher Isherwood. It also shares with many other established occult groups certain conceptions that seem basic—notably the ideas of reincarnation, of *karma* (the consequences that one must suffer as a result of actions and misdeeds in past incarnations), and of varying levels of consciousness attainable by initiation. It is a system that does not solicit converts, since each person, as he passes through a succession of lives, is thought to have plenty of time and opportunity to find his own individual path to an understanding of the Vedanta philosophy.

The philosophy itself is based on the Vedas, a collection of ancient Indian scriptures and holy writings. As a movement, Vedanta was initially inspired by the ninth-century Indian philosopher Shankara, who formed a system of knowledge out of the Vedic writings. The system became a religious movement through the work of the 19th-century Indian mystic Sri Ramakrishna. His leading disciple, Swami Vivekananda, carried on Ramakrishna's teachings of the "harmony of religions," and met with great success when he spread the teachings into the West by means of lecture tours and so on. In 1894 he founded the first Western Vedanta center in America; today there are 11 centers in the U.S.A., and one each in Britain, France, and Argentina—as well as, of course, many hundreds of centers, sub-centers, hospitals, schools, and other institutions formed by Vedanta in India.

Vedanta teaches that all the great religions can be harmonized, since each in its own way adores one God; and that the aim of man on earth is to discover his own true nature, which is a realization of the divine. This realization can be achieved (in accordance with the individual's particular talents and inclinations) by contemplation, by worship, by yoga, or by work in the service of others. A Vedanta center contains, therefore, a hall for public worship (which combines a lecture, public meditation, and prayer), as well as a meditation room, library, and shrine—in short, the facilities for believers to pursue their spiritual goals in their own ways.

Another system closely associated with Indian mysticism is

Theosophy—a movement that came into prominence during the 19th century. The word itself is formed by the two Greek words *theos,* god, and *sophia,* wisdom. Serge Hutin, writing in the French magazine *Planète* in 1964, refers to Theosophy as "the science of God, and, therefore, the most total knowledge which can be conceived. It starts from the absolute itself, and descends towards the realities which have emanated from this first source through successive planes of manifestation. . . . Theosophy does not present itself as a religion in any way; its aim is to seek beyond all traditions . . . ." In a sense, Theosophy resembles Vedanta in its efforts to harmonize elements from all religions; and, like Vedanta, too, its philosophy incorporates the closely associated concepts of karma and reincarnation.

Many active theosophical organizations exist internationally today, all of which stem from the teachings of the extraordinary Russian occultist Madame Blavatsky, who is said to have codified secret traditional "truths" into two basic textbooks of the occult: *Isis Unveiled* (1877) and *The Secret Doctrine* (1888). Madame Blavatsky established the Theosophical Society in 1875 with a membership of 15. (Today there are about 1500 branches throughout the world, and the adherents must number several hundred thousand.) The founder stated that she had been guided to set up the society by a spirit, and attributed her psychic powers not to herself but to an invisible band of Tibetan "masters of wisdom."

As well as elements of spiritualist belief, the concept of universal brotherhood is also central to the movement. And in 1908, Madame Blavatsky's successor as president of the society, Mrs. Annie Besant, founded the Theosophical Order of Service. Today, with branches in 43 countries, the Order provides theosophists with a focus for their desire to serve others in causes such as race relations, overpopulation problems, and so on. At the same time, the society continues to encourage studies of comparative religion, and to investigate unexplained phenomena such as ESP.

An organization of similar status to Theosophy is Anthroposophy—a name combining the words *anthropos* and *sophia,* and meaning the science of man. Its founder was Rudolph Steiner, the German philosopher and occultist who in 1913 resigned as first president of the German Theosophical Society, because he felt theosophical teaching drew too heavily on Hindu thought. According to Steiner, the role of the anthroposophist (unlike that of the Hindu ascetic who tears himself away from matter) is to scrutinize the mysteries of matter—of the earth and its elements, and of substances and their transformation—and to strive for the regeneration of matter through the spirit imprisoned within it. Steiner maintained that the achievements of modern science were incomplete, and would remain so until the faculties latent in men were developed and used to perceive the "subtler manifestations of nature." Steiner's ideas for developing these faculties seem to have impressed a great number of people including doctors, writers, scientists, artists, educationalists, and even theologians. As a practical expression of his ideas, Steiner introduced a system of education designed to help children develop their potential talents in a natural manner. More than 70 schools existing today in America and England are directly inspired by Steiner's teachings, and it is as an educationalist that Steiner is principally remembered today.

Anthroposophy and Theosophy can be grouped together more or less as fraternal systems for occult research and education. (So for that matter can be the older established societies like the Rosicrucians: the Ancient and Mystical Order of the Rosy Cross goes back, apparently, to the Middle Ages; its mystical and metaphysical philosophy seeks to "awaken the dormant, latent faculties of the individual"—or, as the Encyclopaedia Britannica puts it, the inner consciousness.") Many of these systems may be said to be related to one another in the same way as are parallel scientific disciplines like sociology and anthropology. They have vast numbers of ideas in common, with nevertheless some areas of often violent disagreement. In the same way, too, the occult sciences often resemble differing schools of psychology, which, while crossing the same territory by different routes, reach conclusions that either overlap, or, if conflicting, are eventually reconcilable in the light of some new discovery.

But whatever these occult groups may or may not have in common (which is often a great deal), there is one important feature that they all share. Their contact with the supernatural is always that of direct, personal experience—usually that of their leader or founder. Many of these "prophets" have been men and women of great charismatic force and intellectual capacity, like Madame Blavatsky and Rudolph Steiner, who have built up organizations of reasonable permanence. But the vast majority of the cults that center around the personality and teaching of an individual are more ephemeral. And here we can perhaps draw a distinction between the groups whose teachings have sufficient coherence and meaning to survive the death of their founder and those that owe not only their inception but their continuing existence to the personality of their leader.

Possibly the founder of such a "personality" group has had what he has felt to be a genuinely psychic experience. But then—impelled perhaps by the need to systematize his experience—he goes on to inflate this one incident into some sort of all-embracing philosophy. Sometimes a little of the brilliance of the original experience can be discerned; more often it becomes totally obscured by trivialities.

But whether this encounter with the supernatural seems to be genuine or fake, it is the personality of the founder that acts as the magnet to draw disciples. The popularity of the Four Square Gospellers in America, for example, depended entirely on the dynamism of their prophetess, Aimee Semple McPherson. Aimee arrived penniless in Los Angeles from Canada in 1918, but within seven years had succeeded in gathering together a huge congregation. Attracted by Aimee's message of redemption and her claim to powers of faith healing, crowds flocked to the Angelus Temple, built at a cost of a million and a half dollars. Today the movement still numbers 113,000 followers, 720 churches in America, and 800 mission stations throughout the world, though it has lost its drive. (Aimee died, more or less discredited, in 1944.) Today there is little of the fervor that was shown at Temple services in the 1920s when Aimee, dressed in filmy white robes, declaimed to the accompaniment of "heavenly" (electronic) choirs.

Another revivalist movement that has managed to survive the lifetime of its founder is a Swedish group called the Laestadians. Founded over a century ago in northern Lapland by a preacher called Laestadius (who died in 1861), it combines a rigid adherence to the most puritanical Christian precepts with a strong element of ecstatic mysticism. In 1957 a crowd of more than 6000 gathered in Haparanta, Sweden, for a meeting of the Laestadians. After four days of fiery exhortation, many in the audience were overcome with emotion, and wept, laughed, screamed, and fainted in a frenzy of religious hysteria.

Both Aimee Semple McPherson and Laestadius operated more or less within a Christian framework; but this framework would have to be stretched past breaking point to accommodate some of the more dubious "evangelical" occultist

movements. For example, in Canada a large following was
built up after World War II by William Franklyn Wolsey,
self-styled Archbishop John of Vancouver, who once served
two years in a Milwaukee jail for abandoning his four children. "Ordained" in London as a "Christian minister" by a
former waiter at the Savoy Hotel, Wolsey for 16 years operated the Temple of the More Abundant Way of Life in Vancouver, where he performed marriages, buried the dead, and
ran a school for some 70 pupils. In 1960 *Time* magazine
commented dryly: "For Wolsey, the abundant life has been
worth an estimated $1,500,000. Sources: a tithe on the faith-
ful, and a supply of pretyped wills for the signatures of elderly women."

A recent prophet at the same level was Krishna Venta,
whose real name was Francis Heindswatzer Pencovic. During
the 1950s, he announced to the inhabitants of Los Angeles
that he was Christ returned to earth, and collected a band of
followers—known as the Wisdom, Knowledge, Faith, and
Love Fountain of the World sect—who traded all their
worldly goods in return for the privilege of joining his circle.
Like Wolsey, he had been to prison—for fraud; and while
imposing a regime of sober living on his disciples, himself
lived it up in casinos and night clubs—excursions that he jus-
tified by saying that, although immune from human failing
himself, he needed to understand the temptations of
20th-century man. Pencovic's life (and that of his cult) came
to an abrupt end in 1958 when two ex-disciples, provoked by
his adulterous association with their wives, blew themselves,
their former messiah, and seven other followers sky high with
sticks of dynamite.

A sect of equal dubiety, known as Les Flammes du Cos-
mos, was recently founded in Paris by the Spanish-born
Alfred Belmonte. Described by *Paris-Match* as "a crude mixture of all the religions in the world," its secular activities
seem to have included dancing in as few clothes as possible
by the light of large candles and drinking nothing but water
and eating nothing but fruit, especially oranges. The pay-off
for Belmonte came after one woman had died and another
had lost an immense amount of weight as a result of Belmonte's dietary system. He was arrested by the police on the
charge of "neglect of a person in danger."

(Incidentally, Paris seems to be particularly rife with occult societies of one kind or another. One of these, described
in an article in *Réalités* written in 1960 by Albert Gilou, has

a distinctly satanic flavor. This is the society of "Le Très Haut Lunaire," the very high lunary. Participants in the ceremonies—which are presided over by a "black pope"—prostrate themselves before a horned figure of Satan, called Baphomet, with goat's ears, a woman's breasts, and hairy legs crossed over a skull. The "energies" supposedly induced by these rituals are then used by the "pope" to work either good or harmful magic through images.)

But even here in this bottom layer of the fringe movements one cannot be sure that the "prophets" were total fakes—that is, that they may not have had a fleeting encounter with some sort of mystical experience. Pencovic's feeling that he was the incarnation of Christ for example, might, in more propitious circumstances, have marked the starting-point of a slow and painful road to self-knowledge. But in his case, as in that of many others, the "moment of truth" was greeted in an extravagant and ill-judged manner: it was distorted out of recognition, and distorted, at that, by a dangerous and unbalanced personality.

If we can accept this reasoning, then we can understand why dedicated occult groups have always insisted on proper training for their initiates; undisciplined communion with the occult has often proved to be a dangerous business. (Serious occultists would say that the powers they were in touch with were of a far higher level than those contacted by these dubious "prophets.") The danger of unscrupulously exploiting mystical ideas is luridly illustrated by recent reports of a Mexican cult, whose rituals (which regularly included the drinking of a powerful brew of marijuana leaves) were climaxed by human sacrifice in a cave temple. The lid was taken off these activities when a young brother and sister confessed to the police of their six-year association with the cult and admitted that they had represented themselves respectively as reincarnations of St. Francis of Assissi and of an early American woman faith healer called Mrs. Elaine Fidenzio. Equally vile was the case of the unsolved murder in Liverpool, England, in 1962, which appeared from the evidence to be a ritual "full-moon" sacrifice connected with a cult of the Polynesian god of fertility Tiki.

On these more questionable borders of cultism many sects of course turn away from the Christian or religious approach, and find their own often startling avenues to (as they might say it) spiritual and material health. At the risk of mixing up some wheat with some chaff, a great many of the groups and cults that can be found in such cult-magnets as Southern California base their doctrines on theories of bodily health. These would include various forms of nudism as well as dietary-rule groups. Many others focus their gaze on a kind of scientism—of the kind that was central to the organization called "I Am," which flourished in America in the 1930s.

"I Am" began (not surprisingly) in Los Angeles when a man named Guy W. Ballard proclaimed his vision of the "Ascended Master Saint Germain." The saint, he said had given him "electronic essence" to drink and "concentrated energy" to eat, and had shown him the treasures of the earth. Wealth, luxury, and power were key elements of the pseudophilosophy Ballard erected; the sale of various books and discourses, loaded with esoteric language and peppered with vague allusions to super-science (divine energy, atomic accelerator), plus the sale of various objects—devices, icons, rings, records, and even cold cream brought Ballard quite a sizable amount of real treasure. When investigated for using the mails to defraud, an audit of the books revealed that the "I Am" group had collected over $3,000,000. But the fraud charges and the death of Ballard in 1939 pricked the balloon: "I Am" fell faster than it rose.

The state of California is still today the home of many small "back-street" sects, with membership in the hundreds, drawn from local residents. One such is the Free Union for Creative Karma, of Los Angeles, which holds as a basic tenet the "enabling" quality of sensuality freed from outer restraint but disciplined from within—a quality that can apparently release man from the karmic wheel of action/reaction. (More extravagant still were the recent pronouncements made by Johnny Wisdom, another Los Angeles cultmaker. Wisdom managed to collect an enthusiastic following by announcing the secret he had learned from spending seven years, seven months, and seven days inside an extinct volcano in Eucuador: how to live without eating. Needless to say, the popularity of the cult was short-lived.)

Not surprisingly the holders of such manifestly absurd beliefs find themselves the focus of a great deal of scorn and ridicule. There is of course no denying that many such groups, like the evangelists satirized in Sinclair Lewis's *Elmer Gantry*, are in fact conscious or semi-conscious frauds, and no doubt deserve to be dismissed with scorn. But others are frequently lumped together indiscriminately with the bogus sects—and perhaps undeservedly, for whatever their beliefs they at least hold them devotedly and sincerely.

Among such groups would be included the Aetherius Society, which, describing itself as an international spiritual order, was founded in England in 1956 by George King. The main aim of the society is to spread the teaching of the Master Aetherius (the great Cosmic Master who is thought to inhabit the planet Venus and with whom George King is said to have established "telepathic rapport"), Christ, and other Cosmic Masters. The group relies more on scientific equipment such as tape recorders and telescopes than on orthodox religious paraphernalia. It also believes that "space intelligences" are watching with concern the earth at this critical point in its history—beings whose aid is sought with prayer to avert the catastrophic events that are thought to threaten us.

Another recently founded English occult society is that of the Atlanteans, which receives (through mediums) messages from a transcendental being known as Helio-Arcanophus (a title meaning Solar High Priest of the Occult). The group performs no rituals, believing that true occult power lies in the mind, and one of its main concerns is the promotion of mental healing by means of this power.

And finally, to conclude this scrapbook of sects, cults, and organizations, we can offer an example of cults at their most completely preposterous—the eccentric group in Lausanne, Switzerland, that dresses its devotees in red, white, and blue uniforms and worships Queen Elizabeth II of England as empress saint of the universe.

So, from the reputable groups of various occultists (whose teachings may be as coherent and complex as those of the great orthodox religions) we have descended to the merely absurd—to cults of such naïve belief and nonsensical ritual that the credulity of their followers itself defies credulity. But all these organizations—wherever we place them on our personal scale of creditability—are united in one fundamental conviction. It is that the supernatural can be brought within our understanding, not by objective scientific methods but by exposing ourselves—and making ourselves receptive—to occult experiences. In other words, it is not by logic that we shall learn the truth, but rather by reaching down into the depths of our unconscious—or perhaps beyond it, to the hidden layers of human knowledge. We must learn to accept before we can learn to understand.

This pathway through belief into the hidden world of the occult is one that runs alongside a track opened to us by the modern pharmacologist with his discovery of hallucinogenic drugs such as LSD 25. As we have already mentioned in Chapter 4, it has been reported that people under the influence of LSD seem to be more sensitive to telepathy than in their normal states: LSD has also promoted states of heightened awareness similar to those described by mystics, occultists, and magicians. Some groups, in fact, use hallucinogenic drugs in their rituals to help them produce visions and other mystical experiences. For example, peyote—an hallucinogenic derived from the same cactus plant as in mescalin—is regularly taken during the rituals of the 5000 members of the Native American Church, which flourishes among 46 Indian tribes in the West of America and Canada.

So drugs, like the drumming, the entrancement, and the speaking in tongues to be found in the rituals of many mystical and ecstatic groups, may be part of a process that can propel us toward a new understanding. Perhaps all cults— from the most ridiculous to the most reputable—are attempting to achieve the same thing: an escape from the conventional manner of knowing things into another way of knowing. Like alchemists, magicians, witchdoctors, voodoo worshipers, spiritualists, and other practitioners of the supernatural, they are seeking an understanding of the powers within man and outside him—powers that they believe to exist but that remain unexplained and often unrecognized in terms of the accepted laws of the physical universe. This is a territory that has already been eroded by scientific discovery—as astrology was by the discoveries of the astronomers. Perhaps more territory still will, in the future, be mapped and annexed to the "normal." Meanwhile many questions, many mysteries remain. And possibly the most important and most fundamental of them all is whether the inner adventures of the occultists are always merely fantasy, or whether, sometimes at least, they are experiences that do relate to an external reality. Perhaps as psychology, parapsychology, and the physical sciences move closer together, they may together provide some new—and perhaps startling—answers to these questions.

Index

233